BOOKS IN THE BRANCHES TIMELINES

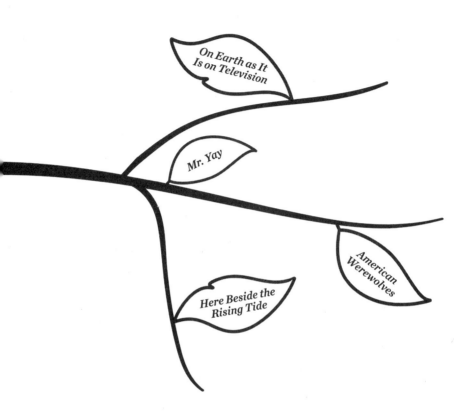

AMERICAN WEREWOLVES

A NOVEL

EMILY JANE

HYPERION AVENUE
LOS ANGELES   NEW YORK

First Edition, September 2025
10 9 8 7 6 5 4 3 2 1
FAC-025438-25184
Printed in the United States of America

Designed by Amy C. King
Moon illustrations inspired by Taylor Hughes
Tree and dog art © Adobe Stock

Library of Congress Control Number: 2025931492
ISBN 978-1-368-11603-9

The authorized representative in the EU for product safety and compliance is Disney Trading B.V., Asterweg 15S, 1031 HL, Amsterdam, The Netherlands
email: DCP.DL-EU.bookscontact@disney.com

www.HyperionAvenueBooks.com

SUSTAINABLE FORESTRY INITIATIVE

Certified Sourcing

www.forests.org
SFI-01681

Logo Applies to Text Stock Only

For Ella Jane

HOW GREAT IT WAS

San Francisco—One Month Ago

"GO ON THEN, Marie," her mama had said, as they'd hugged good-bye. "My girl. Go to America."

The country's vastness astounded Marie Babineaux.

She boarded a Greyhound in Newark (*because I have to see it for myself*) and by Chicago she regretted not having taken the five-hour flight, to bypass all this vastness. By St. Louis she decided she would die if she had to consume another Slim Jim, another prepackaged egg salad sandwich on white bread, another frozen bean burrito made chewable by a gas station microwave. From Kansas City to Denver she sat next to a cowboy whose hand crept beneath the armrest, across her seat, toward her thigh.

Monsieur, your hand! She swatted it away, but it came back, unfazed.

From Grand Junction to Reno she sat next to an older lady dressed in a teal tracksuit with rhinestones. The lady wore a rosary around her neck. She crossed herself. She said a prayer. She prayed at intermittent mile markers on the vast flat highway, through the vast flat desert, where nothing existed but rocks and sand and sky and the glittered lights of a gas-station-slash-casino-slash-gun-shop, a lone oasis in all the vastness.

Marie brushed her teeth in a gas station bathroom. Outside, she heard the *ching-ching-ching-ching-ching* of a triple cherry, a waterfall of quarters. Someone pounded on the bathroom door.

"Hurry up! I gotta pee like a mofo!"

Marie spit a mouthful of blue foam into the stained sink bowl. She looked at herself in the mirror. She crossed herself and said a prayer, the way her seatmate did: *Lord, please let it be better than this.*

She returned to the bus. The bus chugged away, into darkness. Her seatmate said yet another prayer.

"What do you pray for?" Marie asked.

The woman shook her head and laughed. *Wasn't it obvious?* "I pray I'll win big at the slots."

From Reno the land piled up, mountains upon mountains, and then the mountains tumbled down through gold country, wine country, desert-turned-farmland, and when Marie Babineaux stepped off the bus at the Mission Street station, where the sky-scraper spires of San Francisco rose around her, taller, it seemed, than the snow-crested Sierras, when she smelled salty sea air, when she watched the fog roll in over the city, she thought, *Finally*. She thought, *Here, I can make it.*

She had enrolled in a study abroad program. She would study in the US, and then China. She would practice international law. She would buy a flat in Paris, and marry a writer. He would write in the evenings and stay home with their children while she worked. He would carry babies in a sling on his chest and teach them piano. They would vacation in the South of France every August. Their apartment balcony would overlook the Mediterranean Sea. She would rub sunscreen over her children's freckled cheeks and watch them build castles out of sand, watch them catch waves and gather shells, wrap them in towels and hold them in her arms and tell them stories of her travels. Her adventure to America. How great, how big, it was.

Her apartment in San Francisco overlooked the bay, if you climbed onto the roof. Marie's roommate bought bottles of Two-Buck Chuck, skunky weed that made her head spin. She bought concert tickets for American artists she'd never see in France through apps connected to devices connected to the swirling ether of the universe. How great, how big, it was! They drank cheap wine from mugs on the roof, their faces illuminated by the screen-glow of everything.

She wrote to her mother: *Mama, I love it here!*

A photo: Marie Babineaux in a breezy blouse, baggy jeans, standing on the rooftop at dusk, her mug raised, the city gleaming behind her. The photo is still out there. You can find it, if you go looking.

Marie worked as a hostess at the country club near school.

"Bonjour, Monsieur James! Table for six?"

"Bonjour, Madame Barrington. Shall I seat you at your usual table?"

"Bonsoir, bonsoir! Thank you for dining with us at the Olympic Club! We will see you back very soon!"

The members liked that she used French words. In America, French meant fancy. It meant *I'm too good for tap water*. It meant filet mignon, haricots verts, petit fours, chardonnay, all of which they served at the Olympic Club. Members could feel sophisticated in their proximity to something so French as Marie Babineaux, and yet remain comfortable in their inherent superiority.

They were Americans, after all.

Marie folded white napkins. She sprayed the hostess stand with lemony cleaner. She turned the lights out. She put on her sweater and stepped out into a night ripe with possibility. She had a text from her roommate, Natasha. What did she want to do? There was a DJ spinning eighties mash-ups at a Mission dive bar, some midnight movie trivia at a pub on Polk, a house party in the Sunset, a full moon in a cloudless sky. The buses ran infrequently late at night. She walked north, past Lake Merced, past Sloat, Taraval, Noriega. She checked the address for the party on her phone. She found the house. She listened at the door. She heard silence.

Then something else.

More a feeling than a noise; the feeling that something swift and terrifying roamed the streets, unseen; the feeling of vastness unchecked.

She turned, but there was nothing. Just empty sidewalk, parked cars, the dark windows of sleeping houses. She shivered. She checked her phone again for the party address. She had the address right. But there was no party at this house. She decided to catch the N line back toward the city's throbbing center. She walked toward Judah Street. She felt something behind her. She turned again, but again she saw nothing.

"Hello? Who is there?"

She pulled her sweater tight around her waist, her soft underbelly. She felt exposed. She walked swiftly, almost running. She heard the groan of an approaching train. She ran toward the stop at the corner.

"Arrêtez! Stop! Stop!"

She waved her arms. But she was too far. The driver didn't see her. The train sped away. Thirty minutes till the next one, if it came on time. She turned onto Judah Street. The streetlights flickered. The air stirred. She felt a prickle on the back of her neck.

She spun around. Something was watching her. She felt certain now.

"Hello? Hello!"

She glanced at the window of a dry cleaning shop. She saw her reflection in the darkened glass, her eyes wide with fear. Then she saw its eyes, big and yellow as the moon.

Marie ran. She ran up Judah Street. It, whatever it was, chased after her. She could feel its hot breath on her back. She could hear the grit of its teeth, close enough to tear her apart. But it didn't. It growled, and growled, and as Marie fled through the wide, empty streets, its growls turned to laughter.

She bolted ahead, and the laughter receded behind her. Then she felt a rank wind at her back, as the thing pressed forward, its mouth open, snapping and cackling. Its teeth grazed her leg. Then, again, it slowed its gait, letting her run ahead.

It's toying with you, Marie: the truth, spoken in her mother's voice. She was its plaything. She was its fun night out on the town. She was a scream, a pretty face seized by terror, flesh in the shape of a woman.

She ran. Her lungs burned. Her legs ached. The air felt suddenly cool behind her. The awful laughter stopped, and she could feel only the brisk air blowing in from the Pacific. How vast, how empty, it felt. She let herself believe the lie, that she had outrun it, that she had gotten free. That she would go home. That she would tell her mama: *Oh, Mama—the things I saw in America!*

It appeared in front of her.

It looked like a wolf, except larger, misshapen in parts, a child's nightmare drawing of a wolf come to life. It had yellow eyes, claws like raptor talons, huge and crooked, juices dripping from its jowls. Marie screamed. She turned. She ran across the street, north, toward the park. She turned again, onto Lincoln Street. She saw the headlights of an approaching car. She waved. *Stop! S'il vous plaît!* The car breezed past. She ran toward the intersection ahead. She heard the wolf laughing, and its laughter ripped a chasm of nothingness behind her, which seemed able to swallow her up. She ran and her life zipped past her. She saw her mother at the kitchen table with a glass of warm milk, a library book, her arms scooping the child Marie onto her lap; she saw the old woman in the teal tracksuit, kissing her rosary, praying for a big win; she saw her own daughter ride a bike, unsteady the first time, her hair in braids, her eyes smiling. *I can do it, Mama! I can make it here!* But the wolf cut her off at the intersection. It leapt. She dodged left, into the street. It leapt again. She ran in the only direction she could. She ran into Golden Gate Park.

She sprinted into the trees. She sprinted as far and as fast as she could. *I can do it, Mama! I can make it!* Then her foot caught on a vine. She flew forward. She plunged face-first into the soft earth. The wolf snapped at her ankle. Its teeth ripped her tendon. She pushed herself up. She tried to run. Sharp pain bolted from her ankle up through her leg. She felt a stab in her shoulder blade. The wolf's claw. It dug in deeper. It twisted. Marie howled.

"No, please! No!"

The wolf knocked her down. It rolled her over, onto her back. It climbed on top of her, holding her down with its massive paw. It grinned, and inside its mouth she saw a glut of teeth: thick brown canines; rows of smaller teeth, thin and razored like a shark's; sickening lumps of tiny needle teeth. She tried to scream, but the wolf held its paw over her mouth. Then it made her watch, as it finished her off.

FROM WOMAN TO GHOST

San Francisco—Now

"ALL THINGS COME in cycles" was what Natasha Porter's mother had told her, two weeks earlier, the last time they spoke. What her mother meant was that the time had come for Natasha to cycle back home, to the Midwest, to find a man, get married, pop out a few kids. You know, accomplish something. Natasha had accomplished nothing by calling home. She had meant to ask for a loan. Instead, she asked for nothing and hung up mad.

She felt especially mad because her mother was right. All things came in cycles: peaks, valleys, booms, busts, seasons, births, deaths. Natasha had cycled from nowhere special to somewhere cool; from unknown to popular to despised; from decently flush to broke; from comfortable in her apartment, drinking wine on the roof with her lovely French roommate, Marie Babineaux, to sleeping on a bench in Embarcadero Plaza.

Her roommate had cycled from alive to dead.

Broke, hated, homeless—these were all better than dead.

She had, at least, this partially eaten blueberry muffin, which was more than could be said for her roommate Marie. The muffin had, earlier in its cycle, a sugary crumbly top. But someone had eaten the top off of the muffin and left the remains on top of Natasha while she slept, as if she were a human trash can, which was about how she felt. She had crumbs stuck in her unwashed hair. A flock of pigeons circled around her. They eyed her muffin with their greedy black eyes. She watched them and wondered whether the muffin's former owner had viewed the half pastry as a benevolent gift. She wondered how she had appeared, through the honeyed lens of the muffin-rich.

She sniffed the muffin. She was famished. She took a bite, and then she felt appalled, by herself for eating stale street food, and by her own desire to eat more of it. She spit the bite out. She tossed the muffin remains to the pigeons. They swarmed.

Natasha stood up and strapped on her backpack, which had made a lousy pillow. She rubbed her eyes. The sky looked 7:30-ish: pale yellow light, scattered starlings. Downtown had already turned into a zoo: Elephantine buses idled in the gridlocked street. Business-suited goats spilled up from the BART train entrance. Banking lions with roller briefcases and sandaled tech-sloths crowded the sidewalks. A pair of old bears in leather chaps sat on a bench in Embarcadero Plaza and sipped espresso and looked out at the sapphire-and-diamond bay. At their backs, the lost city clamored on.

Natasha walked along Market Street. She walked because

she couldn't just stay on the bench in the plaza. The Nozees were everywhere. Someone might recognize her face. She couldn't dig up the plaza bricks and bury herself beneath them. She couldn't run out to the pier and throw herself into the bay. Or maybe she could. Maybe she needed to demarcate this cycle as done.

She had spent exactly one night sleeping on the street. Plenty of people had lived on the street for weeks, months, whole years on some cold curb, huddled under a tarp, swaddled in the damp fog of the merciless city—which had cycled from working-class town to groovy peace-love dreamville to dot-com capital to dystopian model for the failures of late-stage capitalism—and did it *really* make her a failure that she did not have two grand to pay her share of the monthly rent on the one-bedroom apartment she had shared with Marie?

Twenty-seven nights had passed since Marie got murdered in the park. Twenty-six since Natasha had noticed that her roommate didn't make it home, and started to worry. Twenty-five since the police showed up at the door and asked questions: Did Marie have a boyfriend? Did she date? Had she gotten entangled with any of those rich country club fellows, perhaps a married man? As if those things mattered.

Two nights had passed since Natasha had tried and failed to sleep in her car, her car being too crammed with her stuff. The ninety-degree angle of the driver's seat, forced upright by the overflow of boxes and garbage bags, made her back ache. She had considered sleeping on the top of the car, sprawled out over the hood, but it was too cold, too exposed. Her car could have been sold to pay the rent, if she had a job and money to fix it. Her car could be driven in a Midwesternly direction, if she wanted to admit defeat. She decided instead to stay up and out all night. She could sleep in the day, every day until . . . she didn't know. She didn't think things through.

So the next day she'd packed a backpack and wandered through the early evening, stopping at one café and then another, lingering over empty cups of coffee. She had pretended to browse boutiques, checking the price tags on blouses, holding them up in the mirror to see if their color would complement her eyes, or transform her into a different Natasha. She had almost gone into a favorite dive bar on Polk Street, propelled there by the habits of her body. Then she saw Synergy-Nate and River the Cosmonaut Cosmetologist standing in the doorway, smoking a joint. They were both fanatical Nozees. River had a Nova Z'Rhae tattoo on her calf. Natasha tried to turn around and leave, but the process of turning lasted centuries, long enough for Synergy-Nate to look up and see her, for his head to shake in disgust, for his mouth to form the word: *bitch*.

She pulled her beanie down low over her bangs. She walked with her head down, fixing her eyes on the embedded spots of gum on the sidewalk, the smears of guacamole and dog shit, the dry patches of dirt that surrounded the windblown trees. How they could grow here eluded her. She walked on, and the wind blew and the sky turned nighttime orange. She took shelter in her sweater. She shivered in her sweater. She remembered the time she had drunk shots of absinthe with River the Cosmonaut Cosmetologist at R Bar, and River had slung a loose arm around Natasha's shoulder and suggested that someday they ought to make out, because River liked to taste new mouths. River also had a tattoo of a river on her arm, a polluted river laden with toxic waste and dead fish.

Natasha remembered licking the banks of that river, the salt taste of the woman's skin.

Natasha had walked until her legs ached and her hands felt shivery and bloodless. She saw the spire of a church. She walked to it. She tried the door, but the door was locked. NO SOLICITATION. She read the sign on the door. NO BATHROOMS. NO SLEEPING. Her body remembered its old habit, sleep. It nagged at her. Her body offered untenable suggestions, like *Marriott* and *Hilton* and *Holiday Inn*. Her mind stood vigilant guard to the dregs of her bank account. Her body employed a new strategy: *Homeless shelter!* Her mind replied: *What the fuck! No!* Her body pleaded/whimpered/yelled:

Homeless shelter?

Home-less shel-ter

HOMELESS

SHELTER!!!

It commandeered her feet and marched them toward the doors of St. Vincent de Paul. She stood outside and stared at the building, crammed full of sleeping people. She stared at the shopping carts parked outside. She smelled urine. She couldn't bring herself to open the door. Silver-penned Natasha Porter who had studied comparative literature at Reed College and hashtagged her way to a book deal and, just last month, drank twenty-dollar rosemary pinecone cocktails with B-film darling Mauve Booker and *NYT* bestselling agitator Tyranamo Getmo. She could not slather herself with this dirty word, this unshowered urine-soaked tarp-and-cart word. *Homeless.*

It was safer, in the shelter. She would not get murdered in the shelter, probably. But sleeping in the shelter would require her to confront the reality of sleeping in the shelter. She wasn't ready for that.

The cold bay winds called.

She lurched downward, toward the Embarcadero shallows. She stopped, just to rest her feet. *Just a rest,* she said to herself, as she stretched her feet out on the bench. Then her eyes hinged shut. Then her eyes opened to a view of partially eaten muffin.

Natasha walked up Market Street, regretting her poor muffin decision-making. Her stomach had transformed, from refined processor of tapas and sashimi and charcuterie and wine-matched cheese boards to burbling acid pit. She passed by a Starbucks, a Philz Coffee, a patisserie, another Starbucks. Her mind conjured the butter croissant, flaked with almonds, the cappuccino with a dash of caramel syrup. She kept walking, until the number 38 bus chugged up behind her.

She rode the bus to almost the end of the line, the other, unfashionable side of the city, where the grid of single-family houses sloped toward the sea and the fog persisted and the wind never ceased. She got off a few blocks from the ocean and walked a few more blocks, to where she had parked her car in a free spot, out of the way, where she hoped no one would find it. Back when it was parked in front of her apartment, someone had assailed it with sharp objects. They had carved messages of revulsion. Someone had broken the passenger's-side window. Natasha had replaced the glass with duct tape and plastic wrap. Someone had spray-painted her side-view mirrors red. It looked like a car that belonged to a homeless person.

She opened the hatch and excavated a bag of clean clothes from beneath the dirty laundry piled on top. She shoved a few clean shirts, underwear, and a pair of jeans into her backpack. She repacked the hatch. She wondered: What next? The battery in her phone was dead. Her laptop was dead. Her teeth were unbrushed. She had packed a toothbrush in her backpack, but she had forgotten the toothpaste in the medicine cabinet of her apartment.

She leaned against the hatch and watched the endless fog. Her mind reeled. She thought about Marie Babineaux, and Marie's mother, who had come to the apartment to pack up her daughter's belongings and carry them back to France. She thought about all the advertisements that had gotten pulled from her blog; the email from her literary agent (. . . *Pinnacle Books withdrew their offer. I think we should pull the submission. At this point, it's probably a lost cause.* . . .); her told-you-so mother; the stream of angry-face emojis and judgment tweets. She thought about Nova Z'Rhae, the Fantabulous Queen of Sequin Pop, shrouded in glitzy light, omnipresent, twinkling.

She thought about all the people who she had met in the big city, and who among them might have room for her to crash until she got back on her feet. Half the people she'd met had moved to Austin, or Denver, or Portland, or Oakland, which felt just as far away. The other half existed in the tech-cult's all-inclusive bubble, where work was its own five-star resort, or they had sixteen thousand roommates, some of whom would steal quarters from Natasha's purse or would didgeridoo all-night renditions of Billy-Idol-Headlines-Burning-Man while some shoeless kid named Smokes took a post-acid doze on the wood floor. She sorted through all these people and made a list of one, an apolitical and naturally diazepamed fellow named Lee Curtis.

Natasha remembered a house in the Outer Sunset. Thirty-Second or Thirty-Fourth. Judah or Lawton. Two stories, painted grayish-blue to complement the fog, with an iron front gate and a scooped bay window. She remembered visiting the house in its near-empty state, when the FOR SALE sign still hung outside and Lee Curtis didn't know anyone else in the city, other than his old college acquaintance and one-time hookup, Natasha Porter. They had made out once, at a sophomore keg party. Neither of them enjoyed it, but they had stayed friends.

Natasha drove circles through the Sunset blocks until she spotted a house that matched her memory. She parked outside and rang the buzzer. She waited. She rang the buzzer again. The intercom crackled. She heard a shushing noise. A moment later, Lee Curtis appeared at the gate, with a baby strapped to his chest.

"Natasha," he whispered. "What are you doing here?"

"I didn't know where else to go."

"Are you . . . you look . . ."

"Terrible, I know."

"I was going to say tired."

"Can I come in?"

Lee looked down at the baby.

"It's not a good time," he whispered. "It's nap time."

"It's like eight thirty in the morning."

"Yeah, well, try telling that to the peanut." He nodded at said peanut dozing on his chest. "She woke up at three."

"Ouch."

"So maybe another time would be better."

"Like, in a few hours, or—"

"Well . . ."

"This afternoon?"

"I don't know . . ."

"Or never."

"Natasha, it's . . ."

"It's okay. It's okay, I get it."

"It's just that—"

"You don't have to explain," Natasha said. "She's beautiful, by the way."

At that, Lee smiled. "Yeah. I'm smitten."

"What's her name?"

"Penelope."

"The peanut. I'm glad I got to see her." Natasha turned to leave. "You take care, Lee."

"Natasha, wait—"

"What?"

"It's not . . ." Lee Curtis gazed down at the small sleeping girl. A dream danced across her eyelids. "I . . . Why don't you come on in."

"Are you sure? Because I don't want to impose. If you're busy—"

"I'm not busy. And Laurie won't be home till late. But . . . you might not want to stick around until then. My wife, well, she kind of hates you. Just a little bit."

"Oh."

He nodded his head a few times by way of explanation. "She loves Nova Z'Rhae."

"Everyone loves Nova Z'Rhae."

"We saw her in concert."

"Was she fantabulous?"

"I didn't want to admit it. But yeah."

Natasha followed Lee Curtis inside. His house was a stucco pocket universe of domesticity. Coloring book scribbles and construction paper, glue, and googly-eye cutouts covered the refrigerator. Rows of bottle parts and breast pump parts air-dried on the counter. Stuffed animals occupied the kitchen chairs and drank tea from tiny cups on the kitchen table. A small girl, Lee's older daughter, sat with them. She held a plush rabbit in one hand and a yellow plastic trapezoid in the other.

"It probably doesn't look how you remember it," Lee said.

"Didn't you used to have a glass table?"

"Our glass table days are over." He gestured toward the counter. "Do you want a cup of coffee? Are you hungry?"

"I'm starving."

"We've got, um, cereal, toaster waffles—"

"Whatever's easy. I'll eat anything."

"*Not* my Elmo waffles," Lee Curtis's older daughter declared.

"Now, Veronica, we talked about sharing—"

"Who's *that*?" Veronica pointed her yellow tangram at Natasha.

"This is my old friend, Natasha."

"I never saw her before."

"You did, but you were much smaller."

"Is she a ghost?"

"Yep," Natasha affirmed.

"Vee, I told you there is no such thing as—"

"Is she a *scary* ghost?"

"Nope. I'm mostly friendly."

"Okay," Veronica said. "But she can only have one waffle."

Natasha sat down on a counter stool. She accepted a four-square of miniature waffles studded with blueberries. She listened to Lee Curtis chatter about Veronica's mastery of the alphabet and her tap dance lessons and how she had glued googly eyes onto the crayon animal heads she drew on his dresser while he dared to shower; and about the peanut and her cooing noises and her gurgling noises and how often she threw up and where; and about how lonely he felt, in the perpetual fog of the western city, where nothing exciting had happened since the night he and Laurie went to see Nova Z'Rhae in concert.

"Over a year ago," he said. "She's playing again this weekend, but, you know . . ."

Natasha nodded. She was a ghost with nothing to add. She had already said too much.

"And since then, this has been pretty much it." He held up an empty bottle, the physical manifestation of pretty-much-it.

"That's . . . I'm glad you're doing well."

"What about you? I mean, other than the Nova Z'Rhae thing."

"I . . . well, everything I own is in my car."

"Wait, are you not living out in Bernal Heights still?"

"I'm not really living anywhere. I couldn't pay the rent. And my roommate was mur—" Natasha glanced at the girl who sat on the stool beside her with a stack of blank paper and a box of markers. "Um, M-U-R-D-E-R-E-D."

"What? Oh my God. What happened?"

"Well, you remember, about a month ago, they found that woman's—um—B-O-D-Y? In the park?"

18

Veronica dumped the markers all over the floor, in apparent protest of spelling.

"Hey, Veronica, not on the floor," Lee said, as he picked the markers up. Veronica scowled. "Yeah, I remember," he went on.

"That was my roommate."

"Holy crap. I can't imagine."

"And they still haven't caught the creep who did it. The guy's still out there, roaming around the city."

"Yeah . . ."

"What?"

"It's nothing," Lee said as he picked up the last of the markers.

"No, you have this look, like you were thinking something."

"Yeah, it's just, it's silly."

"So?" Natasha said. "Tell me."

Lee sighed. "You're gonna hound me if I don't."

"Probably."

"Okay, so, I get bored sometimes. And I . . . sometimes I read articles on this site called RVK—"

"Lee! No! That's, like, crazy conspiracy theory stuff!"

"Yeah, okay, and I don't believe it! I swear! It's just, it's entertaining. Except, well, so there was an RVK article about the woman—your roommate—and it said that what got her wasn't human. That it was some sort of animal."

"Was it a elephant?" Veronica asked. She popped the cap off the red marker.

"No, honey."

"Was it a stegosaurus?"

"No, those are extinct. You obviously see why its better to spell. She's always listening."

"A duck?"

"What? No." Lee laughed.

"Maybe a duck with big sharp teeth," said Natasha.

Veronica began to draw something duck-shaped. "Can we get a duck, Dad?"

"Veronica—"

"Please?"

"I don't think—"

"Please please please please please pleeeease?"

"Maybe. Maybe if you finish your tangrams."

"You're going to regret that later, aren't you," Natasha said.

"Probably."

"So what animal did they say it was?"

"They didn't speculate," Lee said. "Which is not what you'd expect from RVK, right? But they did say there were B-I-T-E marks, and that the marks didn't belong to any known animal. And *definitely* not to a human."

"Wouldn't the police know this? I mean, I assume they'd swab for DNA."

"Apparently they did, but it was inconclusive."

"Huh. You think maybe it was a dog?"

"Too small."

"What else would have even been in the city? A coyote? Maybe it got her after she was already, you know."

"I've never heard of there being a coyote in the city before. And anyway, there's something else."

"What?" Natasha asked.

"What?" Veronica asked. She drew a row of sharp teeth on her duck.

"The night it happened," Lee said, "I had gone outside for a walk. It was really late. Eleven maybe. Sometimes when the peanut gets fussy I'll strap her into her carrier and go outside and walk around. Sometimes it's the only way she'll sleep. So that's what I was doing, walking around in the middle of the night. We were maybe ten or so blocks from here. And then I had the oddest feeling, like I was being watched. And we kept walking, and I kept feeling like something was watching me. It totally creeped me out."

"Did you see anything?"

"No, nothing. There was no one around. Until we were about halfway home—I was practically running at this point—and a bus pulled up and a couple got off. And then when the bus drove away, the feeling was gone."

"Well, did you say anything? Like, to the police?"

"What was I supposed to say? 'Officer, I was out wandering around in the middle of the night and I got creeped out'? I didn't *see* anything."

"You think maybe you've been spending too much time on the conspiracy blogs?" Natasha teased.

"Well, yeah, maybe. And I know it was probably nothing. But still, ever since then, if it's really late and the peanut gets fussy, I don't take her outside. I just take her downstairs, and I pace back and forth in the garage until she falls asleep."

Natasha fell asleep on Lee Curtis's couch with a picture of a sharp-toothed duck taped to her back. She dreamed she had fallen asleep in her old room, her on the bottom bunk, Marie tucked in safe on the top bunk. Natasha breathed relief, but only for a moment. Then fear crept over her. She felt watched.

"Ghost?"

She opened her eyes to Veronica Curtis sitting atop her.

"Were you getting a dream?"

"Was I . . . um, yeah. But can you climb off? This is not comfortable."

"Ghostes can't be uncomferble. They have no bodies."

"Well, maybe I'm a different kind of ghost."

Veronica frowned but she scooted down the couch. "And they don't have brains. So how does ghostses dream?"

"I don't know. Maybe you should ask your dad."

"Ask me what?" Lee Curtis emerged from the kitchen. He wore yellow rubber dish gloves, baby still strapped to his chest. "Veronica, remember what I said about personal space?"

"But she's not a *person*, Dad. She's a ghost."

"It's okay, really," said Natasha. "I like being sat on."

"She's supposed to be practicing with her counting beads," said Lee.

"And the ghost should probably head out," Natasha said.

"You don't have to," said Lee. "I mean, I'm sure Laurie wouldn't *really* mind—"

"I really don't want to impose on your family time," Natasha said. "I'm just glad to have gotten some rest."

Veronica nudged forward for a close-up inspection of Natasha's face. She stuck her index finger into Natasha's mouth and peeled back Natasha's lip.

"*Vee,*" her father barked, "personal space!"

"Not sharp," Veronica concluded. "She doesn't look like a scary ghost."

"Thanks," Natasha said, as she got up. "For letting me crash on your couch today."

"It's no problem," Lee Curtis replied. His dish gloves dripped soap suds onto the floor.

"Well, I guess I'll see you."

"Yeah ... um ... look, do you, I mean, if you don't have anywhere else to go, do you maybe want to come back?"

"Like, to hang out?"

"It's just ... it can get kind of boring out here, you know, washing dishes, doing laundry ..."

"Yeah," Natasha said. "I'd like that."

"Laurie usually leaves around seven thirty, so any time after then ..."

"Yeah. Thanks. I'll ... I'll come back again tomorrow."

Natasha bundled into her jacket and strapped on her backpack. She headed for the door.

"Bye, Veronica," she said as she left, to the kid counting beads as she shoved them into the slats of the heating vent.

"Later, Ghost!" Veronica called back.

Lee Curtis's front gate slammed shut behind her. She had slept through the day, and now the dusky sky was sunless, moonless, heavy with fog. She walked to her car, wondering where she would pass the night. In the distance, Natasha could see the forested skyline of Golden Gate Park, shrouded by low clouds. The sight of it sent a shiver down her spine. She hurried to her car, trying not to look at the park beyond. She climbed into the driver's seat and locked the door. Her heart raced. *It's just a park*, she told herself. *There's nothing out there.* And yet, her mind raced too, back to a brighter point, before she had lost her apartment, before she had opened her dumb mouth about Nova Z'Rhae. Before Marie had been killed.

Before, she would have gone to Kyoto Sushi for one-dollar draft, and sake Jell-O shots. She would have parked herself ironically at a North Beach booty pub and watched the parade of drunken bridal parties, with their rhinestone crowns and feather boas and penis straws. She would have wandered down Polk Street, or taken a bus to the Mission, and wandered into one of dozens of places where she would find people she knew playing darts or shooting pool, or she would go to a house party, where one host-roommate was zealous for her blog and another had listened to her give a podcast interview and another knew her from Café Royale last Tuesday, when they had stood together smoking cigarettes outside and discussing the American aristocracy, and how and when democracy had died, and what it all meant. She was infinitely popular.

Before, she might have just stayed home with Marie and ordered vegetable chow fun and egg drop soup for delivery and sat out on the roof with a bottle or two of cheap wine, and all those city lights, glittering all around them.

Natasha drove through the outer rim of the Sunset until she spotted an entirely unfashionable pub, the sort of place that would never serve craft cocktails, that had a disco-era jukebox and a hard-of-hearing bartender who refused to wear hearing aids and gave a Blue Lagoon lager when you'd asked for a glass of water.

"Um, thanks," Natasha said, as the bartender opened the bottle and poured the beer into a chipped San Francisco Giants pint glass, "but could I also get a glass of water?"

"Big night, eh?" the bartender said, producing a second bottle of beer.

"Yeah, you could say that. What time do you close?"

"Last call's one thirty."

Natasha carried her two beers to a table in the back. She checked the time: 8:17 p.m. She counted the hours ahead. Five or so hours in the bar, drinking beer she hadn't ordered and couldn't really afford. Six more hours after that until she could return to Lee Curtis's house, six hours to spend sitting in her car or wandering around outside or riding the bus to the end of the line and back.

The looming hours filled her with dread.

"Couldn't you just go home?" Lee Curtis had asked.

"Like, to my parents' house?"

Wichita, Kansas, filled Natasha with dread. Her parents' house filled her with dread. They had traded the house she grew up in for a condominium with a faux-wood deck and a prohibition on every kind of grill. Their new place exemplified everything Natasha found wrong with American culture in its current perversion. Her mother and father had themselves transitioned, from fleshy Midwestern humanoids to Symbols of Wrongness. Her mother's Wrongness took the shape of pleated chinos, of hamburger salad and pot roast simmered in Fizz Wizard Cola, of the wry accusation that if Natasha could only *tone it down* she might still have time left to find a husband who would take care of her and help her make babies. Her father's Wrongness was personified by golf games *with the guys,* poker nights *with the guys,* sportsball tailgates where *the guys* would guzzle beer and then go watch other guys score goals and get super grunty and mildly belligerent to *other* guys, games that had seemed like great fun to the child Natasha until she asked if she could come along because her younger cousin Frank got to come and her dad said, *No, honey, it's just for guys* and *Why don't you go shopping with your mother instead?*

She had lived with dread through all the hours between her eighth birthday—when she had asked for Pokémon trading cards and received instead a Pretty Lil Miss Princess-Sparkle makeup kit and matching brush and blow-dryer—and the August after her senior year of high school, when she packed her college bags and boarded a plane to Oregon. Then she grew up. And for nearly a decade the hours sped by, and she loved every dashing minute.

She sipped her beer. It was warm and flat. She checked the time again. 8:22. She watched the time tick to 8:23. 8:24. 8:39. She needed a job. She needed enough money to keep the drinks coming all night, to make the hours blur by. She needed somewhere to be between dusk and dawn other than a sad bar out in the foggy Sunset.

She needed to return to the internet.

She powered on her laptop. She would just search for jobs, she told herself, but her fingers unwittingly opened her blog. She had 217 new messages, and they probably all said the same thing: *Dear BITCH. Who do you think you are? How DARE you spew hate about our Nova. You are a tasteless, talentless, ass-faced clump of burning turds.*

She ignored them. She skimmed through her own posts, from her bygone days as an essayist, a successful film and music culture blogger, a writer on the cusp of selling her first book about the feminist underpinnings of the modern indie-glam movement. Her blog had gone from hobby to full-time-job to shit-post site.

Dear BITCH . . .

She finished her first beer. She closed the browser window. She imagined the long drive home, the knock on her parents' condo door, her mother's assessment: *I never understood what you were doing with that silly blog, writing about gender role issues. What does that even have to do with the entertainment industry? I mean, it's not like things are still unequal now. Just look at that girl—what's her name, with the red hair, from high school—that girl is a doctor!*

No. She could not go back there. She needed to focus. She needed work.

She needed to search for job postings, but she had no idea where to look. Jobs she might have applied for back in the infinitely popular era of her life seemed unattainable now. She did not have *at least five years of management experience* or *an aptitude for web design* or *a demonstrated commitment to synergistic relationship-building strategies.* She had a blog smothered by vitriol, a half-written book that would never be published, a name that when mentioned would unleash an avalanche of internet hate. Could she change her name? She consulted the internet. *She could file a petition! She could wait three months!* She calculated the number of hours residing in a span of three months (2,160). She sipped her second unwanted beer. She loathed every one of those 2,160 hours. She loathed herself for getting stuck in this temporal tar pit. She wanted to revel in self-loathing, but loathing herself only made her loathe herself more, because, as she once had written, "female self-loathing originated as a construct of the patriarchy, fabricated to keep a woman docile, insecure, hungry."

The job searching did not go very far.

The job searching stirred up unpleasant feelings: guilt, despair, hopelessness, injustice, all rooted and tangled up in her feelings about Marie. If that *monster*, whoever he was, had not killed her roommate, Natasha might not have been distracted. She might have thought about her words more carefully. She might not have gotten herself canceled. But mostly, if that *monster* had not killed her roommate, there would still be Marie.

Natasha had avoided the newspaper articles about Marie's death before, but her procrastination and indignation led her to them now. The *San Francisco Chronicle* described the uncertainty surrounding the death of Marie Babineaux, age twenty-three, an exchange student from Marseille, France. The *Oakland Times* reported that Marie Babineaux's French father and Nigerian mother had requested an inquiry into their daughter's death as a potential hate crime. Marie Babineaux was the fourteenth immigrant brutally killed in the US that year, a year that had another six months to go. The *Bay Area Tribune* reported that there were bite marks on Marie Babineaux's torso, possibly from a dog or coyote.

An article in the *Examiner* made extraneous claims about Marie Babineaux's personal life. She had, according to the article, two or possibly three boyfriends, none of whom knew about the others (false). She had been known to binge drink (true) and, on occasion, to ingest Molly (false). Her profile picture, posted with every article, showed a vivacious woman dressed in a short skirt and a tight, low-cut blouse. She had worn a blouse like that the night she got torn to shreds.

Natasha read the reputable news articles, but they didn't tell her anything she didn't know already. The fringe websites were more intriguing. She understood why Lee Curtis, alone in his fogbound house with its abundance of boring chores and lack of adult conversation, might click and read a post by RVK.

Natasha clicked on a post by the *Courier Weekly*: "San Francisco Woman Killed and Eaten by Hungry Werewolves!" The tabloid ran an article on the werewolves of California, which appeared on the front page right above the articles "Ghost-Mom Births Live Baby" and "Beach Tourist Claims to Have Found Time-Traveling Squid" and "Inter-dimensional Traveler Visits Alternate Apocalyptic World, Claims Everyone There Killed by Detached Hand." According to the *Courier Weekly*'s account, at least a dozen werewolves lived and worked in the Golden State. Most of them worked in Hollywood, where they lured young aspiring actresses from Oklahoma or Tennessee to full-moon "casting calls," where the *Hollywolves* ate the actresses' aspiring hearts. Eating hearts made the wolves powerful. What the wolves did with the rest of the body was unclear, though some sources suggested blood orgies were involved.

The idea of werewolves was absurd, and the *Courier Weekly* ran only the most implausible fictional stories: "Devil Twins Shoot Fireballs from Their Eyes." "George Soros Plots Destruction of Corn Crops with Alien Warlords from Planet Blastonia." "Sex-Crazed Kitten McInnus Arrested for Imprisoning Celebrity Sex Slaves—LA Lakers, Zack Radigger among Those Rescued."

And yet . . . werewolves would leave bite marks that would not be identified as belonging to any known animal. Werewolves would emerge beneath a full moon and tear a woman to shreds. So when had the moon grown full?

She asked the internet.

Tonight, the internet told her.

Twenty-seven nights ago, it also said.

The night Marie Babineaux died.

Natasha shivered. She closed her laptop browser. She looked around the sad bar. An old, potbellied man drank alone at the window table. The bartender stared at the television, where the stocks kept tumbling and the job market kept missing the mark. *Lovely*, she thought. The minutes clawed at her. She reopened her browser.

She wandered haphazardly through the internet, from service-sector job postings to videos of cats clobbering toddlers, informational pages on succeeding fantastically in chenille loungewear pyramid schemes, horoscopes, quizzes that would reveal her nerd quotient, her most likely manner of death based on dessert preferences, her animal spirit.

Her animal spirit, the internet quiz concluded, was the wolf.

Her internet wanderings kept circling back to the wolf, or its more vicious changeling version. The mythology of werewolves traced back through ancient Europe. Iron Age warriors transformed from men to wolves. They torched villages and devoured farmers. In the 1590s, werewolves terrorized a town in the South of France, killing sixty-two people and several dozen sheep over a five-year period. In 1630, werewolves killed thirteen people beneath a single blood moon. Werewolf murders continued to occur in Europe throughout the seventeenth through nineteenth centuries, but no instances of lycanthropy were reported outside of Europe until 1822, in New York, when a mother and five of her children were found, killed by what the authorities concluded to be a rabid dog but which the sixth child, maimed by the creature but alive, claimed was a boy who could transform into a wolf.

Natasha tracked the internet wolves across conspiracy blogs, tabloids, pseudoscientific journals, right to an interview posted on the online magazine *FreaKountry*, given by, of all people, the Fantabulous Queen of Sequin Pop, Nova Z'Rhae:

Interviewer: I'm not going to ask you all the usual questions.

Z'Rhae: Like the collaboration I've got going with Mr. Yay? Or my upcoming album? It's going to be fabulous, darling.

Interviewer: I cannot wait.

Z'Rhae: Or about how I get my eyes to look this gorgeous and sparkly?

Interviewer: Yes, like those questions. Except, how *do* you get your eyes to look like that? They're, like, cosmic.

Z'Rhae: I'll never tell.

Interviewer: Is it magic?

Z'Rhae: There is some magic to it, darling.

Interviewer: Because, you know, I've heard rumors that you have some, shall we say, unusual—

Z'Rhae: Unusual is delicious.

Interviewer: Okay, unusual beliefs. That you're into some weird shit.

Z'Rhae: Ha, ha, wonderful.

Interviewer: So first, do you believe in magic?

Z'Rhae: Absolutely. But I'm not particularly adept at the practice of magic.

Interviewer: What about aliens?

Z'Rhae: Honey, look up into that great big sky and tell me there aren't aliens up there. But sadly I've never had the pleasure of meeting one.

Interviewer: What would you do if you met one?

Z'Rhae: Fondue. Cheese fondue. Chocolate fondue. I would cook up big vats of fondue, and we would sit around and eat and get drunk and fat. Because is there a more marvelous way to welcome an alien to our little planet? And if the aliens are, you know, one of those planet-conquering types, well, maybe a little fondue will change their mind.

Interviewer: Or they'll conquer the planet and keep all the fondue for themselves.

Z'Rhae: Doubtful. Fondue is meant to be shared.

Interviewer: So what about ghosts? Do you believe in ghosts?

Z'Rhae: Not in the physical sense.

Interviewer: I heard that you used to hold séances at your parties.

Z'Rhae: Where my eyes would roll back in my head and I would communicate with the dead?

Interviewer: Yes, and you would speak in tongues.

Z'Rhae: Honey, I never spoke in tongues.

Interviewer: But the séances?

Z'Rhae: Parlor trick. Except for once. I spoke with this remarkable girl. What was her name, now? Phoenix? Nixie. That was it. But she wasn't dead, I don't think. She was from another dimension or something fantastic like that.

Interviewer: So do you believe in other dimensions?

Z'Rhae: Fervently. My favorite cosmetics all get shipped in from other dimensions.

Interviewer: What about vampires? Do you believe in vampires?

Z'Rhae: I'm not going to name any names, if that's what you're looking for.

Interviewer: What about witches?

Z'Rhae: The real ones all got killed in the seventeenth century. If there are any left, they're in hiding.

Interviewer: What about zombies?

Z'Rhae: Only the corn-syrup kind you see in the movies.

Interviewer: Voodoo?

Z'Rhae: Voodoo is a magnet for con artists and hucksters. But that doesn't mean it's not real.

Interviewer: Werewolves?

Z'Rhae: Oh yes. Werewolves.

Interviewer: You believe in werewolves?

Z'Rhae: Oh, absolutely, darling. Werewolves are absolutely real.

Interviewer: Seriously?

Z'Rhae: It happens that I've met them.

Interviewer: Like, you've met an actual werewolf? Like, a man that turns into a wolf when the moon is full?

Z'Rhae: That's not exactly how it works. And anyhow, darling, what makes you think that the werewolf is a man?

SHANE LaSALLE GETS THE DEAL DONE

San Francisco—Now

SHANE LaSALLE

Senior Associate with Barrington Equity LLC

Profile picture: Headshot. Debonair Shane LaSalle in an Armani suit, no tie, top button undone. His privileged eyes stare straight into the camera. His eyes are the color of trust, flecked with ambition. His lips are supple and unyielding. Their sheen results from a veneer of Fleishman's ManBalm in Malibu Beige, though the magic of Photoshop has erased any trace of artificiality. He has no stray eyebrow hair. He has not a hint of nose hair. His teeth are Hollywood white.

Cover picture: Landscape. Blue sky, cloudless. Blue water, solid, whitecapped. A glint of sun. Shane LaSalle suspended between sky and water, hitched to a parasail. The parasail is black and gold. Shane is gold and tan. The picture shows him in the distance, and yet he seems to occupy the foreground. The coastline exists as an extension of Shane LaSalle, parasailor, an outfit that, like his smile (head back, mouth agape), he wears to convey the adjectives he would like you to use to describe him: *adventurous, fearless, fun.*

About me: Duke University grad (go Blue Devils!). "Rising Star" on *Venture Capitalist Monthly*'s annual list. Loves Korean BBQ, windsurfing, sailing, staying up for the sunrise.

Shane LaSalle did not stay up until sunrise. He fell asleep at his desk, at the bewitched hour of 3:33 a.m.

He startled awake twenty minutes later, with a crook in his neck, a slather of drool along the side of his embarrassingly unshaven face, and the sense that someone was watching him. He got up. He poked his head outside his office door. Light spilled into the hallway from every third office. The conference room window glowed yellow. Dick Barrington's corner office, at the opposite end of the hallway from Shane LaSalle, was lit. Shane heard the warble of a coffee maker in the break room. He heard laughter.

Shane crept back to his desk. He listened for the murmur of leather shoes on the hallway carpet. He heard more laughter, rancorous laughter. The laughter sounded as if it was right behind him, but when he swiveled around, there was nobody there. He rubbed his eyes. He pushed his chair out, angling the seat toward the door to give the impression that he had just stepped away. Then he climbed beneath his desk, curled himself into a Shane-shaped ball, and closed his eyes.

Just for a moment, he told himself. *A quick refresher, then back to work!*

Laughter followed across his dreams.

His eyes snapped open. Gray dawn flooded his office. Shane jerked upright, smacking his head on the bottom of his desk.

"Ow!"

"Shane?"

"Shit," Shane said, under his breath.

"Are you okay, buddy?" Shane recognized the voice of his fellow senior associate, Duane Beckman.

"Yeah, I just . . . dropped my pen."

"You all finished with your market report?"

Panic swept through Shane's body. From far away, at the opposite end of the thirty-second floor, he heard laughter.

"I'm just . . . about to print it out." Shane crawled out from under his desk. The report was still open on his computer, unedited, just as he had left it. He had meant to read through it at least once more, but instead, like an idiot, he had slept.

"Great, that's great. Everyone's waiting on it. Buxby was looking for you, and so was Carver."

"I'm printing it now." Shane hit Print.

"And Carver wants an email copy."

"Right, I'm on it." Shane moved his mouse around and hit Send.

"He said he came by your office, but you weren't here."

"He must have just missed me." Shane's printer spit out pages of his report.

"That's what I said. I said, 'Carver, you must have just missed him.' "

"Right, yeah. I must have been in the bathroom."

"Because LaSalle knows how important this deal is, right?"

"Right."

"And I was thinking we should do something to celebrate when we're all done. So . . ."

"So?"

"I bought us tickets to the Nova Z'Rhae concert this weekend. First-row seats!"

"What? That's awesome! That is so awesome!"

"It's going to be amazing. But keep it on the DL, right?"

"Right, right, of course."

"Oh, and you got something a little bit, uh, crusty there, buddy." Duane patted the corner of his mouth.

"Oh." Shane touched the corner of his own mouth, where the drool had hardened to a crust. "It's just, uh—"

"Toothpaste, probably," Duane supplied. He handed Shane his handkerchief.

"Yes, that's it. I was so focused on the report, I didn't notice that—"

"It's okay, we've all been there." Duane smiled. Something about his smile made Shane feel uneasy.

"Thanks," Shane said. He wiped the drool crust away.

"You're all done, Shane."

"Huh?"

"Your report. It's all done printing. I'll walk with you down to Carver's office, and then we can go grab some espressos before the meeting. Whaddya say?"

"Sounds great," Shane said.

Duane picked the still-warm pages of Shane's report off the printer and handed them to Shane. He clapped his hand on Shane's shoulder. The hand stayed on his shoulder for too long. It felt too hot, too weighty. It made Shane want to crawl back under his desk. Shane should have felt thrilled. It was six a.m. on a banner day for Barrington Equity LLC, a dealmaking day, a day that would flood the company coffers with absurd amounts of cash, 0.2 percent of which would trickle down to Shane in the form of a six-figure bonus check. It was a transformative day that, if all went as planned, would elevate senior associates Shane LaSalle and Duane Beckman to junior partner status. Duane had already begun his Great Condo Hunt. Shane had begun to contemplate his promotion post and envision the stream of likes and loves and comments that would follow:

So proud, Shane!

OMG partner!!! Already promoted and you're not even 40!

LaSalle, you're a BEAST!

Way to go, LaSalle! You sure show 'em how the deal gets done!

Shane should have felt the elated thrill of anticipated success. But instead, the sensation of Duane Beckman's hand on his shoulder made the uneasiness that had dogged Shane all night blossom into inexplicable, full-boil terror.

"Sounds great," Shane repeated himself.

"It will be," Duane said, ushering Shane out the door.

The earliest commuters arrived downtown. The office tower lights flickered on. The gray sky was heavy with fog, and Shane felt heavy beneath it. He walked through vacant Embarcadero Plaza, sipping his triple Americano, waiting for the amphetamine flutter of caffeine and Ritalin to liven him, wishing he had remembered the leftover Ritalin in his desk the night before, and that he had kept his prescription up to date. Duane walked beside him. He sipped a Venti coffee with a shot of espresso. He chattered about condos.

"The place in Nob Hill was pretty spectacular." Duane had a blueberry muffin. He tore a strip of crumbly muffin off with his teeth. "But I'm not sure about the neighborhood. It's too gritty, right? I mean, it's not gritty. But people might see it that way."

Shane nodded. He watched Duane's teeth scrape the sugared top from his muffin. There was something appalling about Duane's teeth. They had the wrong shape. They grew out of the wrong spot in Duane's mouth. They reminded Shane of an alien freak he'd seen in a movie that opened its mouth, a gross mouth full of sharp teeth, and then another nasty little razor-toothed alien head popped out of its throat.

"Maybe Russian Hill instead," Duane said, through a mouthful. Shane nodded. *Yes, Russian Hill, of course.* "That, or Pac Heights. Though it might be worth considering one of those new high-rises down in SoMa, especially if I can find a unit with a bay view. We could be neighbors!"

Shane gazed out past the Ferry Building, at a metallic strip of cold bay. He thought about his own bay view in his own SoMa high-rise, the crested sparkle of blue water by day, the challis of nighttime black cradled by city lights. A new high-rise had begun to rise up in front of Shane's building. It stood at half height now, a Tinkertoy spire of cranes and steel beams sunk into the soft mud and sand. In a few months, it would stand higher than Shane's own dot-com tower, and Shane would have a sparkling view of luxury two-bedroom condos.

"It's too bad, though . . ." Duane said. His weird teeth nibbled the sugared edge of his muffin. Shane's stomach churned. Duane also had a weird mole on the corner of his jaw, a black mole shaped like half a Cheerio, with a single spiky hair growing out of it. Duane had photoshopped the mole out of his Barrington Equity LLC headshot, and yet he let it linger on his face. On late nights, late Ritalin-gobbling nights when the senior associates gathered in the conference room to prove who could work the hardest and who could pawn the most work onto the junior associates, Shane had considered pinching that weird mole between his fingernails and plucking it off.

"That's the problem with this city," Duane went on. "All the trash."

"Yep."

"I'd go for the Nob Hill place, if it weren't for all the trash."

"I don't know, maybe you should hold out for SoMa. You'd think they could pay someone to clean all the trash up."

"They do. But they don't pay them enough to live here, right?" Duane finished stripping the sugar-crumb crust from his blueberry muffin. "Like this," he said. He pointed at a woman who lay asleep on a bench. The woman's head rested on a backpack. Her face was hidden beneath a spill of hair. Obviously unwashed hair, Shane concluded. Dirty, trashy hair, probably infested with lice.

"I know, I wish we didn't have to see it."

"I bet this lady here has a college degree," Duane began. "I bet you she's just like any one of the girls we knew in college. But for whatever reason, here she is, sleeping on a park bench."

"At least they shouldn't be allowed to sleep downtown," Shane said, "where we have to see them."

"Do you think she'd want the rest of this muffin? Wait, do you want it?"

"You ate the good part."

"I can't eat much this early in the morning. And I feel bad, just throwing it out. You know, I'm going to give it to her, just in case." Duane set the remains of his muffin on top of the sleeping woman with some care.

"I don't think she'll eat it. I mean, gross. Who would eat someone's leftover muffin?"

"Shane, you're right," Duane said. "Maybe I should go back and buy a fresh muffin for her."

"No, just leave it. We've got to get back to work."

The six partners of Barrington Equity LLC convened in the conference room through the early morning. They kept the door closed, but their muffled voices echoed in the halls. Sometimes it was a single, yelling voice. Other times, all the voices seemed to speak at once. Occasionally, the door would open. A senior associate, his timidity disguised beneath the feigned esteem of a five-figure suit, would venture in, take orders, and emerge with a list of urgent tasks that no human being could complete in the allotted time. The door would open, and carts would wheel in, carts of fresh-brewed coffee, carts of petit fours and frosted cookies and pastel macarons, silver platter carts bearing catfish and rosemary fingerling potatoes and burgundy beef, carts pushed by seamless girls in push-up bras and three-inch heels.

Barrington Equity had very particular employment standards.

The senior associates scurried. They typed relentlessly. They typed like their fingers had caught fire and only the speed of the keyboard could put the fire out. They insulted the junior associates, whose fingers couldn't go as fast, whose ambition snapped at their feet.

In the mid-morning, senior partner Ron Carver emerged from the conference room red-cheeked and grinning. He walked through the hall, knocking on doors, ordering everyone to assemble. Shane LaSalle followed a trickle of associates into the conference room. He elbowed his way inside, taking a spot at the table next to Duane Beckman and two other partner-hopefuls who had slogged through the Barrington Equity swamp for a decade. More junior associates crammed in, taking spots along the wall. The partners chattered and laughed. Stanley Rollins popped the cork off a bottle of champagne. Darren Buxby ordered the drinks girl to bring another bottle, and glasses for everyone at the table. Don Morgan and Clifton James talked excitedly. *Resort in Switzerland,* Shane heard one of them say. *Sixty-foot yacht,* said the other. Dick Barrington sat at the head of the table. He lit a cigar. He watched the room. He waited for the last associate to shove his way in. He smiled to himself, a sly, wolfish smile.

"Gentlemen," Dick Barrington said. He rapped his fist on the mahogany table. "Gentleman, today is a very good day."

Don Morgan clapped loudly. The other partners clapped harder. Shane looked down at his own sweaty palms as they smacked against each other. He felt suspended, somewhere outside of his own clapping hands, as if time had begun to unravel and everything had slowed to half speed. He looked around him. Everyone clapped and smiled. Everyone stared at Dick Barrington. Dick Barrington glanced around the room. His gaze stopped on Shane LaSalle. A smile flickered across his eyes.

"Today is a very good day," Dick Barrington repeated. The room fell silent. "Barrington Equity"—he paused, drawing out the suspense—"has acquired a new company. You may have heard of our new acquisition. It makes cars."

"Not for long!" someone remarked.

"Creighton Automotive," Dick Barrington said, smiling at the joke.

The conference room buzzed. The buzzing excitement bubbled over. The partners smacked each other on the back. They guzzled champagne. Chattering excitement seized the associates. They had suspected. But no one had known, for certain, other than the partners, and the partners had compartmentalized assignments and redacted every mention of Creighton Automotive from the associate-accessible files. The news, had it gotten out, could have sunk stock prices or served as a trumpet call to the white knights of the business world. Barrington Equity had to keep its involvement top secret if it wanted to suck every penny out of the world's largest automobile manufacturer.

Laughter echoed through the conference room—an ecstatic laughter, except that Shane heard the same scraping laugh he had heard coming from nowhere and everywhere in the middle of the night. His stomach lurched. He could taste the six-figure bonus. He had eaten nothing but Ritalin and coffee since dawn. His heart beat too fast. He looked around, at the faces of the partners, at Duane Beckman, at Duane Beckman's teeth, so obvious, so piercingly obvious in his smiling mouth. Shane looked up at Dick Barrington. Barrington looked back at him, again with that subtle flicker in his eyes.

"I think you know what this means," Dick Barrington said. Dick's fingers manifested a fresh cigar. A glass of champagne appeared in his hand. "Time to celebrate."

Shane LaSalle left the party before it got too terrible. The Barrington Equity associates drank shots of Johnnie Walker Blue. They raided the kitchen cabinets for more champagne. They ordered salads and steaks from Boulevard. They ordered a string quartet, an eighties music DJ, a topless juggler named Busty Pins. She dipped knives in petroleum jelly, lit them on fire, and juggled them on top of the conference room table—until a junior associate reached up and poked his ambitious finger through the mesh of her fishnet stockings and she lost her rhythm and a flaming knife fell point-first into the polished wood table. And there the knife stayed, burning, as the associate struggled to pull his finger free. He had gotten it stuck in the fishnet.

"You creep." Busty Pins kicked at him with her stiletto heel. "You want, I can bite it off."

The associates whooped and hollered.

"Yeah, let 'er bite you!"

"Open your mouth, Tits!"

Shane LaSalle gazed into the future of the party and saw its continued descent. Someone behind him suggested ordering real strippers. Someone else threw up in the wastebasket. Shane looked around for the watchful eyes of the partners. There was only one partner left. Darren Buxby stood in the corner, watching the spectacle, an amused look on his face. Shane tossed back the remains of his champagne. His stomach groaned. He headed toward the door. Duane had already left, he noticed on his way out. Duane and most of the partners. Shane's mind unfurled a jealous fantasy: Duane invited out to dinner by the partners, by Dick Barrington himself. Duane seated in the partners' private Olympic Club room, drinking oak barrel–aged wine. *Give us your most expensive bottle.* Duane laughing with his mouth open, his horrible teeth sticking out. Ron Carver patting Duane on the back. Stanley Rollins raising his glass, to toast. *You're one of us now, Duane.*

Shane shuddered. Duane Beckman was his best work friend, which practically made Duane Beckman his actual best friend, even though he didn't know what books Duane Beckman liked or what movies Duane Beckman liked to rewatch or whether Duane Beckman believed in God or fate or monsters. Shane LaSalle's nonwork best friends, the friends he had rowed with in college, the boys he had known since grade school, all existed in the pseudo-reality of cyberspace and the Thanksgiving–Christmas holiday season. He saw posted photos of their ski vacations to Aspen, their engagement parties, their chubby-legged babies dressed in baby fedoras and bow ties. He saw them in festive holiday sweaters, for twenty minutes, at his mother's best friend's Christmas Eve open house. He shook hands with and then forgot the names of their girlfriends. He crammed a year's worth of job / marriage / birth / grad school / trip to Thailand / grandma has cancer / article published in the *New Yorker* / moving forever to the South of France stories in between the bites of two pieces of pie, pumpkin and pecan, the same two pies his mother ordered every year from a bakery in Charleston, South Carolina, and had shipped overnight to her Bloomfield Hills, Michigan, house.

Duane Beckman's mother baked her own pies, with canned pumpkin and sweetened condensed milk. Shane knew that much about him. He knew that Duane Beckman ran track at Ohio State, that Duane Beckman hated onions, and that Duane Beckman started at Barrington Equity exactly one month before him, which gave Duane Beckman seniority that Duane Beckman would not let him forget. He knew that he hated Duane Beckman.

Shane rode the elevator down to the lobby. He walked outside, into the shock of daylight, its brightness entirely incongruous with the topless juggling and drunken groping of Barrington Equity's thirty-second-floor conference room. Had they drawn the blinds in the conference room, to feign cover of darkness? Shane squinted. The sun hung high over the bay. The water shone blue and silver, all glints and winks. *Hey there, Shane, baby,* Shane imagined he could hear it calling. *Come and ride me.* Shane walked to the corner. West, beyond the cranes and crowded blocks of downtown, beyond the brown hills and the artisanal twelve dollar–coffee galleries and the billion-dollar rows of painted ladies, over the ocean, the fog had already begun to build. Shane could feel the wind behind it. He buttoned his jacket. Despite the sun, he felt cold. He felt *watched.*

That's the Ritalin talking, Duane had said, years earlier, in their junior days. For two years, their first two at Barrington Equity, Duane Beckman and Shane LaSalle had existed between the four windowless walls of a shared office. The office was the size of a closet. The office had, in fact, been a closet, used as storage for envelopes and Dictaphone tapes and the spare fax machine. It barely fit two desks. For twelve, sixteen, sometimes twenty hours a day, Duane Beckman and Shane LaSalle bumped elbows when they typed and inhaled each other's farts and tried to out-excel one another in their capacity to absorb thankless assignments. They snorted Ritalin to keep them awake through the night. They washed the Ritalin down with energy drinks, espresso, and Adderall. Sometimes, late in the night, when only the juniorest of junior associates toiled, Shane heard noises. He heard scratching noises in the bathroom. He heard guttural, growling noises in the hall, but when he stuck his head out of his office to look, there was nothing there.

It sounded like an animal, Shane remembered saying. *It's probably just the Ritalin*, Duane responded. *This stuff makes you paranoid. Jumpy.*

Shane felt jumpy. He crept through the nighttime hallways. He startled at the reflection of himself in the window glass. He had the sensation—despite the apparent emptiness of the office, of the building, of all of the financial district shrouded in fog, streets vacant except for a lone Muni bus and a homeless man sprawled beneath a cardboard tent—despite the emptiness of this all, he had the recurring sensation that it wasn't as empty as it seemed, that something else was out there, stalking them all.

He never told Duane. He mentioned strange noises, sensor lights weirdly illuminated, sandwiches stolen from the office refrigerator on a Sunday night when only Shane and Duane had come to work. But he never told Duane about the time he had felt hot breath on the back of his neck, had panicked and run through the hall, to the dead end, where he turned, shivering with fear, to face it, whatever it was, and saw that it had been nothing. He never told

Duane about the laughter he heard sometimes, laughter that could make your skin crawl like a coat of worms. He never told Duane how it felt, this sensation of being tracked, observed. Being prey. Feelings like that, should they become publicly known, would get Shane demoted, from promising associate at a prestigious equity firm to minimum-wage barista; from "Rising Star" Shane LaSalle to falling star Shane LaSalle.

So treacherous were these paranoid feelings that Shane kept them private from even himself. He attributed them to his meds, his sleep deprivation, his boredom (which, in turn, he also ignored). After eighteen hours in the Excel spreadsheet trenches, Shane's starved imagination had to do something to make real life seem more like the video games and action movies of his youth. And so, as Shane turned down Howard Street on his way home, feeling quite distinctly as if he was being *watched*, he felt equally *un-watched*.

Until he felt a hand slap down on his shoulder.

"LaSalle!"

Shane startled.

He turned and saw that the hand belonged to Clifton James, one of the partners.

"Did I startle you? Sorry about that! Leaving the party early?"

"It was a long night," Shane admitted. "I was ready to go home."

Clifton James had always made him feel at ease. When Shane and Duane worked through the night, Clifton James had midnight pizza delivered to the office. Clifton James invited them to white tablecloth luncheons and cocktail parties, and he took them around and introduced them to all the people he knew, the senators and the start-up CEOs and the hedge fund managers and the ladies who looked as if they had been cut straight from the pages of a dream.

Clifton James had recommended them for promotion, from junior to senior associate. Because of Clifton James, when half their crop of junior associates got fired, Shane and Duane got offices with windows and fifty-thousand-dollar bonus checks.

"I feel ya," Clifton James said. "Some of those fellas were getting a bit carried away. They're a bunch of brutes, if you ask me."

"Yeah."

"They've got no respect. No manners. A man's got to maintain a sense of decorum, don't you think?"

"Absolutely."

"That's what I like about you, LaSalle. You understand the importance of appearances." Clifton James smiled warmly. He patted Shane on the back. "You've got what it takes, I think."

"Thanks, Cliff."

"No need to thank me. I mean it. You grew up right. You're built the right way. You know how to work hard. You can mingle at a party without making an ass of yourself. I've been watching you, you know?"

"You have?" Shane might have felt alarmed, if he hadn't trunked every ounce of paranoia the moment he saw Clifton James's tanned, amiable face. Instead, he felt honored. He was important enough to warrant *watching*.

"I've been watching your career. I think you're ready for the next step."

"I would be . . . I'm—"

"Do you have any plans tonight?"

"No." Shane's heart pounded. "Not yet."

"The other partners and I are going out to celebrate. Why don't you join us?"

"That would be great!"

"Good. Good boy. I'll send a car to pick you up in an hour."

An hour later, Shane LaSalle climbed into the back seat of a Lincoln Town Car. The car traveled south through the city, past the condo towers and three-story Victorian flats, the juiceries, the option-free restaurants that served unpronounceable soufflés and twenty-dollar breadless sandwiches, past the dirty sidewalks and the graffitied public buses and the gleaming white commuter buses, chariots of the South Bay. The driver did not speak, but he honked and swerved and ignored stop signs and drove in the carpool lane. He delivered Shane LaSalle to the airport, where the partners awaited him on board Barrington Equity's private jet.

"LaSalle!" Clifton James announced as Shane ducked into the cabin. "Look, fellas! LaSalle is here."

The partners sat around a table, like the one in the Barrington Equity conference room, except bolted to the floor. They sipped Cognac from monogrammed tumblers. They ate cubes of cheese and fresh figs and Marcona almonds and meats sliced as thin as paper and folded into origami meat swans. They wore suits, but their silk ties had come untied, the top buttons of their shirts undone, the restrained demeanor of business cast aside. There was a palpable giddiness in the cabin air. Shane could almost taste it.

"Have a seat, Shane," Dick Barrington said. Dick Barrington sat at the head of the table, as he did in the conference room. He spoke in an inviting tone, but the brutal glimmer in his eyes made Shane's heart thrum like the ticker of a rabbit caught in an open field while hawks circled above. For a moment, against all reason, he wanted to turn and run, off the jet, down the tarmac, into the bay. "Right there next to Carver. We saved the seat just for you."

Shane sat. His body sunk into the supple leather. Carver sneered.

"LaSalle," Carver said, as if Shane's name was a bit of gristle that he needed to spit out.

"We're so pleased to have you with us," Clifton James said. "Aren't we, gentlemen?"

"Yes," Dick Barrington said, staring at Shane with his vicious eyes.

"Welcome aboard, LaSalle," said Don Morgan. Stanley Rollins nodded, his mouth stuffed full of salmon canapé.

"Someone get LaSalle a drink," Darren Buxby said. "Darla! Get over here and pour LaSalle a drink!"

A coiffed slender girl with blue saucer eyes emerged from nowhere. She teetered across the cabin with a tray of drinks. She set the tray down in front of Shane. Did he want bourbon? Scotch? Cognac? Would he like a line of cocaine? He pointed to a bottle older than himself. She leaned over the tray as she poured his drink. The cut of her blouse slipped lower on her chest, revealing lace and cleavage.

"Darla!"

The girl flinched at the sound of Darren Buxby's voice.

"I'll have another. And a cigar. Go and get us some cigars!"

Darla snapped to. Buxby followed her with his eyes. Stanley Rollins shoved a pastrami swan into his mouth. Dick Barrington whispered something to Don Morgan. He sipped his Cognac. He looked at Shane and smiled.

"How's the bourbon, Mr. LaSalle?" Dick Barrington asked. "Is it acceptable?"

"It's . . ." Shane took a sip. It tasted otherworldly. "Extraordinary."

"It was from my father's personal collection."

"Your father—thank you for sharing. I mean, I feel honored."

"My father was an asshole," Dick Barrington said. Carver chuckled. "But he had good taste in bourbons. He kept a cellar full of the best bourbons you ever tasted. I take them out on special occasions. And tonight—tonight is a very special occasion."

"I'll drink to that," Stanley Rollins remarked. He washed down the swan with a tumbler full of Cognac.

Carver's last chuckle rolled into his next one. Shane might have wondered what he'd missed, but none of the other partners were laughing. Darren Buxby watched drink-girl Darla dig through the buffet drawers in search of matches. Don Morgan cut lines of cocaine.

"What's the occasion?" Shane felt instantly stupid for asking. His REM-starved Ritalin brain should have ordered his mouth to keep shut.

"This is a fucking riot," Carver said, disdainfully. "I can't believe the rest of you agreed to this bullshit." He got up, stomped over to the buffet, and poured himself a drink, even though Darla had just poured one for him.

"Don't mind him," said Clifton James. "He's just bitter because his wife is coming along for the trip."

"His wife?" Shane repeated cluelessly.

Ronald Carver had two modes as far as Shane could tell: contemptibly amused mode and psychotic rage mode. Sometimes the modes overlapped. Once, when a violent stomach flu had caused Shane to miss a deadline, Carver threw Shane's computer monitor across Shane's office and then pissed all over the busted pieces, then stood and watched while Shane cleaned up the pissy mess with his bare hands; the whole time, Carver laughed and laughed like an enraged hyena. It had never occurred to Shane that a man like Ronald Carver would ever have a wife.

"The wives all wanted to come along," Clifton James said.

"Where—"

"For the shopping," Clifton said. "They're all in the back cabin."

"Doing whatever it is they do," Stanley Rollins said.

"All mine does is spend my money," Don Morgan said, as he sniffed up a line of coke.

"You're lucky you're single, LaSalle," Darren Buxby said, his eyes still fixed on Darla.

"Buxby's wife's expecting," said Clifton James.

"Oh, congratulations," Shane said. "Is it a boy or a girl?"

"Hopefully one of the two," Stanley Rollins remarked. Carver snorted a laugh.

"She wanted to wait until it was born to find out," said Buxby.

"A mistake, if you ask me," said Don Morgan. "It's better not to gamble. Cleaner."

"There he is!" Clifton James announced. "Our final passenger!"

Shane LaSalle heard footsteps on the Jetway. The final passenger stepped into the cabin. Dick Barrington stood up to greet him.

"Welcome aboard, Mr. Beckman."

Barrington Equity's private jet flew southeast, over the Sierra range, the formless desert, the empty highways and dusty graze lands of cattle, to the green southland, the land of muddy rivers and vines and weeping forests, cotton fields, colonial estates, and slanted-porch shacks, where the drone of nighttime cicadas hid other, darker noises.

Shane LaSalle detected a (nebulous and thus easy to ignore) malice as the falling sun tempted the horizon and the jet began its descent toward the affluent resort town of Lake Orange. He had, up to that moment, enjoyed himself immensely. He had quickly overcome his annoyance at Duane Beckman, for having the gall to be the final passenger on Barrington's private jet. He hated Duane Beckman, but he also liked Duane Beckman, and Duane Beckman deserved to become a partner just as much as Shane LaSalle. Shane had gone to Duke on his parents' dime—had, while there, squandered hundreds of thousands of his parents' dimes on six-packs, twelve-packs, 90 proofs, eight balls, and five-track ice luges, where he and his buddies would wait with open mouths for ice-cold double shots of Jägermeister. Duane had gone to Ohio State on partial scholarship and spent his evenings and weekends valet parking cars and caddying golf bags. Duane had worked through as many torturous nights at Barrington Equity as Shane, alongside Shane, making stupid jokes, sex jokes, fart jokes, random animal noises, just to make the torture more bearable for them both. Duane Beckman, despite his weird mole and his objectionable teeth, deserved a partnership.

After the takeoff jitters, Shane had found himself feeling more and more relaxed. He drank several tumblers of Dick Barrington's asshole father's bourbon. He smoked a cigar. He conversed with

Duane Beckman about SoMa condos and SoMa bars and restaurants they could go to (for working cocktails and working dinners consumed for only work-related reasons) if they were neighbors. He conversed with Clifton James about rowing and parasailing and college football. He conversed with Don Morgan about Bitcoin and with Stanley Rollins about which San Francisco restaurants served the best foods, and he listened and nodded along to Darren Buxby's exposition on which San Francisco restaurants had the most bangable waitresses. Ron Carver sat in his leather lounge seat, smirking and glaring and laughing meanly at inappropriate times. Shane tuned him out. He listened to Dick Barrington tell stories about conquests, companies that Barrington Equity had acquired, trips the Barrington Equity partners had taken. They had gone on safari in Africa. They had mastered the alpine slopes of Zermatt and St. Moritz. They had dominated the blackjack tables of Monte Carlo. They had hunted a lion and a bear. Shane nibbled origami meats as he listened. He sampled thousand-day cheeses and cheese-stuffed olives. The partners ate, voraciously, until Don Morgan passed around the cocaine. Shane LaSalle might have exercised caution and restraint, but after all the partners, including Dick Barrington (who was older and more buttoned-down than Shane's own father), sniffed up thick lines of cocaine through a rolled-up hundred-dollar bill, Shane sniffed one up too.

He felt invincibly ecstatic when the plane touched down on a private airfield just outside of Lake Orange. Two limousines waited on the tarmac, one for the Barrington Equity partners and soon-to-be partners and one for the partners' wives, who had stayed tucked away in the back cabin for the duration of the flight. Shane had not seen or heard them once.

The limousine delivered the men to the Century Boathouse, a five-star restaurant and event venue perched on the edge of picturesque Lake Orange. Forest surrounded the venue on three sides. The back of the three-story boathouse overlooked the lake, with views from its windows and multiple decks. They arrived during full-swing happy hour.

"It's always happy hour at the Century Boathouse," the hostess told Shane, in a less than happy voice, as she hung up his coat. She flashed an ingratiating smile, but it looked forced.

Shane and Duane followed the partners to the bar. They ordered martinis. Shane didn't like martinis, but all the partners had ordered them. A live Sinatra tribute band crooned in the background. Retired couples swirled around the dance floor. Suited, tan men and Botoxed women in strapless gowns ordered steaks and swordfish and bottles of wine. Fresh-from-the-golf-course gentlemen gathered at the window tables. They drank cocktails and ate handfuls of peanuts. They talked about golf and boats and taxes. They reminded Shane of his own father, and his father's friends, the dentists and doctors and investment bankers with whom his father golfed and drank. Shane felt at ease around these sorts of men. He had gone to their houses for parties. He had played soccer and baseball with their sons.

"This is a great party," Shane heard himself say.

"Yeah, it's nice," Duane said. Duane looked uncomfortable. His skin looked pale and clammy. He had probably drunk too much Cognac on the plane, Shane surmised. "I'm gonna step outside for a minute and get some air."

"Okay, bro."

Shane stayed inside and chatted with the partners. The partners downed martinis like water. The bartender couldn't mix them fast enough.

"Just gimme the bottle of gin," Shane overheard Stanley Rollins say. Shane gingerly sipped his own martini, wary of its introduction to Mr. Cognac and Mr. Cocaine. Dick Barrington ordered round three. Darren Buxby tried to buy one for the hostess. Clifton James chugged a beer between rounds. None of the partners seemed at all inebriated. Shane would need to build his tolerance if he wanted to keep pace. He would need to add a splash of vodka to his regimen of iron-pumping and eyebrow-waxing.

"Say, what happened to Beckman?" Clifton James asked. He slung an arm around Shane's shoulder.

"He just went outside for some air," Shane said.

"You better go find him," Clifton James instructed. "Keep him company."

"Oh, I'm sure he's—"

"Go on, then." Clifton James squeezed Shane's shoulder, and then pushed him toward the door. "Go find him. Good boy."

Shane walked toward the back door, his hate for Duane Beckman rekindled. Stupid lightweight Beckman who couldn't hold his liquor. When he reached the back door, he found it locked. A small golden placard directed him to a different door, accessible through a hallway on the side of the building. Shane proceeded through the hallway to the other door. He pushed it open. He noted the door's incongruity with the boathouse elegance. The door had the weight of an industrial prison door. Shane stepped outside onto a back deck, one floor above the ground.

"Duane?" The door shut behind him. He turned and tried the handle. It was locked. His Duane-hatred flared. "Shit. Duane!"

"Up here!"

Shane looked up and saw Duane, standing on a third-floor balcony, a yellow halo of waning sunlight behind him. "Come up!" the other associate said.

"How'd you get up there?"

"Stairs. On the other side."

Shane walked across the patio, to the stairs on the opposite side. He climbed up onto the balcony. Duane stood at the railing. Shane looked out across the lake, at the white-sailed boats, the steel and shadow crests of the sunset water, the red-orange fury on the horizon, the smear of clouds illuminated by the sun's descent. He thought, *I could sail one of those boats.* Duane at the railing lit a cigarette. His face reflected twilight. His eyes glimmered. Smoke seeped out between his two awful teeth.

"There was a fire," he said. "If you look, you can see where the forest burned."

Shane looked out at the dimming forest, the black spires of burnt trees. "Still," he said. "Still . . ."

"I know, right?"

"This is the life."

The last gasp of sunlight cast an orange glaze across the water. *I could swim in that water,* Shane thought. His brain conjured the epic post of his future water-sporting exploits: Shane LaSalle parasailing the idyllic waters of Lake Orange; Shane LaSalle water-skiing behind the back of his new motorboat; Shane LaSalle drinking champagne cocktails on the deck, while Duane Beckman assembled a cheese plate, and—

"What do you think you'll do?" Duane asked. "When you make partner?"

Duane had asked this question before, during midnight coffee breaks, working lunches at the Slanted Door, over Friday night cocktails at the Starlite after the endless weeks of work had imbibed the last swill of strength from their minds and bodies and all that remained was booze and dreams. The question had existed, in prior incarnations, as an *If*, or in drunker moments, an optimistic *If and When*. But the *When*, in Shane's mind, had at last materialized into a certainty, an identifiable date upon which official paperwork would require his signature and the nameplate on his office door would require updating and everyone would gather in the conference room and eat a cake with his name on it. *Congratulations to Our Newest Partner, Shane LaSalle!* And all the associates would feel rather jealous and insecure about themselves.

"I don't know," Shane said. "Maybe I'll buy a boat."

"Totally, dude." Duane nodded. "A boat. A boat would be awesome."

Shane stared out at the lake. Shane of the future stared back, from the deck of his boat. The sunlit clouds darkened to a ripe plum-red.

"What about you?" Shane asked.

"I've been thinking . . ." Duane inhaled the fumes of his cigarette. "I've been thinking maybe I won't buy a condo in the city. At least . . . maybe not right away. I think first, maybe, I'll buy a house for my mom."

"That's good. That's a good thing to do."

"And maybe pay off the rest of her debt. She still owes some money from when she got her appendix taken out last year. She said she didn't want me to help, but, you know. The interest is ridiculous. It's such a vicious cycle. I've got to help her get out of it."

"Yeah."

"She worked so hard when I was growing up. She had to raise me all by herself. I just think . . . she deserves a break, you know?"

"Yeah," Shane agreed.

He thought about Duane's mom, who rinsed and reused plastic sandwich bags, who gifted practicalities. She sent Duane birthday sneakers, Merry Christmas socks, Tupperware filled with home-made peanut butter bars. Shane had met her once, on an Easter Sunday, for a brunch of deviled eggs and honeyed ham. *Duane is so lucky to have a great friend like you,* she had said, shaking Shane's hand with frantic parental vigor. He thought about Duane's mom, and then his thoughts veered starboard, toward boating dreamland, and what kind of boat he might buy to sail him there.

Duane finished his cigarette. He flicked it into the lake. The last gash of purple faded from the sky. The moon began to rise over the lake. Shane heard an odd sound, echoing through the burnt remains of the forest.

"We better go inside," he said.

"I suppose, yeah," Duane agreed. He turned and looked at Shane. "It's nice out here though. With just us."

Shane shivered. "Yeah, but . . . the partners are probably all wondering where we are."

"Yeah, yeah, you're right."

Shane turned and headed back down the stairs. Duane followed. They reached the door through which Shane had come. Shane knew it was locked, but he tried to open it anyway.

"It's locked." He jiggled the handle.

"Let me try," Duane said. Shane stepped aside. Duane tried the handle. He knocked on the door. "What the hell . . ."

"Is there another door?"

The lower balcony had no other visible door, and no stairs. Shane looked up at the third-floor balcony where they had just been. He saw a row of darkened windows, but no door.

"This is so weird." Duane pounded on the lower balcony door. Shane pressed his ear against the door and listened to the silence on the other side.

"I'll go see if someone will let us in," Shane said.

He walked across the balcony, to the windows. He could see the golfers, sitting around their tables, drinking their martinis, eating their cheese balls and Chex Mix. He knocked on the glass. One of the golfers looked up. He gave a friendly wave. Shane pointed toward the locked door. The golfer smiled. *It's locked*, Shane mouthed. The golfer gave a thumbs-up. *It's locked*, Shane tried again. The golfer shrugged and resumed his drinking. Shane rapped on the window.

"Hey!" he yelled. "Hey! Could someone open the door?"

Either the golfers couldn't hear, or they had decided to ignore him.

"Let's just go around to the front," said Duane.

"What, the front entrance? But—"

"It's not that far down to the ground. We can jump." Duane climbed over the balcony railing. He crouched, grabbed hold of the bottom rail, and lowered himself down. He hung for a moment, suspended six feet over the earth, and then he let himself drop. "See? It's fine," he called up to Shane.

Shane peered over the balcony ledge, at the dark ground. From somewhere in the burnt forest, he heard a screech. *An owl*, he thought, except that the screech sounded less avian and more human. The balmy lakeside air felt suddenly cold. He shivered.

"Do you need some help getting down? I could—"

"No, I got it."

"Come on then!" Duane said. Duane was two window-glass eyes and a white face, disembodied, hovering over the ashen earth. Duane had leapt first, had acted without hesitation, and Shane hated his initiative. He hated Duane. He wished he had beat Duane at the over-the-balcony game, that his own feet had touched down while Duane's feet dangled in uncertain descent. He wished that they could stand together, and grow old and rich together, two peas in the partner pod. Not in a gay sort of way. Shane squirmed inside his own skin. He hated Duane for making him like Duane enough that he would ever find it necessary to fly a definitely-not-gay flag when confronted by his own (definitely-not-gay!) feelings for Duane.

"Damn it, Duane," Shane muttered to himself, as he swung a leg over the railing. He lowered and dropped. He landed with a crunch. Something had crunched beneath him. Twigs. It had to be twigs. But he couldn't see what it was. He took a step and heard another crunch. Then, in the distance, he heard a scream. *No—a screech*, he told himself.

"This place gives me the creeps," said Duane.

"It's just the forest," Shane said. "All those dead trees. They look creepy in the dark. But there's nothing to be afraid of."

"Yeah, right."

"Besides, you saw it during the day. It's gorgeous here. The lake. All those boats." Shane had twirly boats in his eyes. But had it looked gorgeous? Had he gotten taken in by a trick of light? The sun's shell game played well against the country club backdrop of illustrious Lake Orange. If Shane had considered his feelings, instead of immediately recoiling against any feelings he might have in common with Duane, he would have found the creeps, coiling around his heart, raising a panic.

"Come on," Duane said, "let's get back inside."

They walked along the back of the Century Boathouse. The ground squished beneath Shane's feet. Black, stagnant water lapped at the muddy shore of the lake. They turned the corner, around the side of the building.

"Stop," Duane said. He stopped. He reached his arm into Shane's path, stopping Shane as well.

"What?"

"Did you hear that?"

Shane listened. He heard a twig snap. He heard a distant humming, like the machinery of a thousand churning bees.

"No, I don't hear anything."

"I could swear—"

"Come on," Shane said. "It's probably nothing."

Then he looked up and saw it, standing in their path.

It looked like a wolf, but larger, meatier. It wore an Arctic coat, thick and gray. Its eyes shone yellow. It had scythe-like claws, paws like a lion, a vicious smile on its sharp, hungry mouth. Its teeth gleamed with the light of the full moon.

"Shit," Duane murmured.

"Shit," Shane said at the same time. He took a step back. He looked at the wolf. Their eyes locked. He felt a surge of fear, fear like an earthquake tearing through his core. He felt as if he had known, all along, that it would come to this.

He took another step back.

The wolf growled.

Shane turned and ran. Behind him, he heard Duane yell, "Run!"

Shane didn't look back. He ran. He ran as fast as he could run in his party shoes, across the charred floor of the forest, through patches of shadow, cragged spots of moonlight. He could feel the wolf behind him. He could feel its paws, deft and powerful. He could feel the heat of its breath. His own breath felt jagged and wheezy. His heart galloped. His veins moaned, protesting the alcohol and amphetamines that surged through them. His feet felt unstable. He glanced back over his shoulder. Shane did not see the wolf. But he knew it was still there.

He kept running. His arms scraped against the skeletal limbs of scorched trees. His lungs burned. He kept running. He ran until his feet tangled. He toppled forward, into a bed of vines. His own dull teeth clipped his tongue on the way down. He tasted blood. He tried to push himself up. The vines ensnared him. *Duane!* he tried to call out, but his throat trapped the sound. *Duane!* He pulled himself free. He stood up. He looked around. He saw trees in all directions, black and brittle and leafless. He saw yellow bits of moon rising between them. He saw no Duane. No wolf. No boathouse lights. No shimmer of silver lake. Clouds fled across the sky.

"Duane?"

He spun in a circle. His eyes scanned the lifeless forest for Duane. For the wolf. He broke a branch off a tree, a crooked sword of wood. It felt precarious in his clammy palm. It felt like a child's toy, a plywood dagger sanded smooth. It felt like nothing that could pierce the hide of a wolf.

"Duane . . . Duane . . . Duane . . ." he whispered to the dark. "Where are you?"

In the distance, Shane heard a screech.

But it wasn't a screech.

"Where are you, Duane?"

If only Duane had waited on the balcony. If only Duane had stayed put. Shane's heart was mangled with fear. He looked at the creeping moon. He tried to position it. His mind's eye saw the boathouse in a blur, the lake in a dream of lakes, himself standing at the bow of his partnership boat, sipping Dick Barrington's asshole father's fifty-year bourbon.

He pretended he knew the way back. *Forward*, he told himself. *Forward toward the moon.*

He marched toward it like a wingless moth, drawn by the promise of light. He listened to the silence of the forest. This forest housed no orchestra of bugs. It seemed devoid of loping rabbits, turkeys, deer. Mouthless worms burrowed beneath the fast decay of torched trees. Soundless bats slid across the sky. Shane heard a distant, disconcerting buzz. He heard the shuffle of his feet. He heard, and yet did not hear, the terror in his heart.

"Damn it, Duane," he cursed. He could find it in himself to blame Duane, for the forest and the wolf. He could pin his lost-in-the-forest predicament squarely on Duane. *Run*, Duane had said, without saying which way. And where was Duane now, when he needed to get back?

Shane guessed the direction of the boathouse and marched toward it. He clutched his sorry sword. His heart resumed a normal cocaine tempo. He began to wonder whether he had even seen a wolf. Maybe Duane had made the wolf up. Maybe Duane had contrived the illusion of a wolf, to scare off Shane, so he could seize the partnership victory for himself. He wondered how he would explain the wolf to the partners. *I thought I saw a big bad wolf, so I tucked my tail between my legs and ran?* The partners would laugh him all the way back to a windowless office. Shane brainstormed the wolf's rebranding. *I saw a wolf, but Duane got scared and ran, and I ran after to . . .* No, no. He rejected the narrative, for obvious reasons. *I saw a wolf, and I chased it into the forest, but . . .* Better, but what then? Would he appear weak if he couldn't outrun the wolf? he wondered. Then he heard a snap.

A branch breaking.

A deep, guttural growl.

He spun around. It watched him. It hid in the forest and watched his panic swell. He could feel it. He turned. His eyes scanned the tree shapes for its eyes. He thrust his broken-branch sword at the empty air. He turned. He couldn't see it. He couldn't see it.

Then he saw it. He saw its yellow eyes flash. He saw its broad smile, its stabbing teeth. It pounced, and for a moment Shane saw it suspended in the air, two hundred pounds of killer wolf, and then he saw more eyes, more flashes of yellow, more smiles descending.

The wolf landed on him. It knocked him to the ground. It swiped at his chest. Its claws ripped through his flesh. He screamed. The wolf swiped again. Its claws punctured his eye and tore a stripe across his cheek.

"No!" Shane screamed. "Please no!"

The wolf retracted and then extended its claws. Blood gushed out of Shane's chest. Blood seeped from his eye, down his cheek. The wolf placed a single claw on Shane's mouth and then, with a fast, brutal, and seemingly deliberate motion, ripped Shane's lip in half.

"Ahhhhhhhh!" Shane screamed. His mouth filled with blood. A searing pain devoured his face. His chest was a minefield of pain. The wolf opened its mouth. Shane stared up at the mountain range of teeth, the hungry glisten of saliva. Then he saw another mouth. Another wolf. A vast landscape of teeth. He screamed, but his throat was full of blood.

One eye went dark. The other blurred.

The last thing Shane LaSalle saw was teeth, right before they ripped into his neck.

Whether the werewolf still exists in the United States, or has ever existed, is unsettled. There is, perhaps because of the creature's changeling nature, little concrete scientific evidence of lycanthropy. Reports of werewolves are sparse and uncorroborated. There are some reports that suggest that werewolves are more beast than man, and that they have retreated to the deepest forests to reside among the actual wolves. And yet, others suggest that these monsters walk in our midst, undetected—that werewolves are among this country's most powerful figures, occupying prominent positions in business, government, and the arts.

While the status of werewolves in the modern era is uncertain, and even their existence is disputed by many, the origin of American lycanthropy is commonly traced to New York, in 1822. . . .

Marcus Flick, <u>American Myths and Monsters: The Werewolf</u>, 2nd ed. (Denver: Birdhouse Press, 2022), 3

WHEREIN A SMALL LAD DISCOVERS THAT THE LOCK IS BROKEN

New York–Circa 1822

BENEATH THE SLIVER moon, he was timid Bit, feeble Bit, faint of heart.

"Sick with consumption, when you was just a babe," Brigid would say, as Bit's wee hands spilt the lye. "Should've let it have ya. Waste of a boy, you is."

Bit carried the water. He filled the washtub. He scrubbed the soaked cloth against his washing bat until his fingers pruned and his arms ached. He sloshed water onto the floor.

"Such a foozler." Brigid shook her head. She folded her meaty arms across her chest. "That'll be your wash water on the floor, then. Good water don't fall from the sky."

Bit whimpered, silently, inside the small frame of himself. He wrung the clothes, beat the clothes, strung them up. He hung Brigid's first, her ship-sail apron, her bedsheet dress, an immensity of fabric. Then came the children's—Dugan, Molly, Patrick, Bree, Cormac, Kean—the quality of fabric and proximity to sunlight diminishing by order of birth, like the cleanliness of wash water. Bit came last. By the time he'd washed his own patched britches, the water was nearly black.

At night, meek Bit stole glances at the moon, a white shard, a coiled caterpillar rising between the spires of smoke, over the roofs. *Grow*, he willed it. *Go on, then, get big.* The bigger children snorted at Bit on the floor, Bit cowering in his own dainty patch of moonlight. *Like a frog on a lily pad. A frog who thinks he's a prince!*

Inside, Bit was not a frog. He was not a prince.

The bigger children slept together on a bed, Dugan Molly Patrick Bree Cormac Kean, lanky snorers, all of them. Brigid, alone on the other bed, spoke in her sleep. She spoke to her husband, Dugan Molly Patrick Bree Cormac Kean's pa. *But not you*, he had told Bit. *Don't know what made a thing like you, but sure as Sunday it warn't me.*

Dugan Molly Patrick Bree Cormac Kean's pa dreamt up the New World, when Dugan was knee-high and croupy and Molly was still at the teat. He dreamt marvelous details—the soil black and rich as Eden's; the hens that laid twice, three times each day, eggs bigger than a man's palm; the flock of sheep they gave you when you disembarked; the temperate sun, the rain soft as a baby's cheek; the smell of warm baked bread ever present on the tender breeze. His New World ship landed in a gale, the October rain coming sideways in hard pellets, and he waited in line for the plague check with Brigid, Dugan, Molly, and a screaming Patrick, red-faced, already hating the cold new world. There were no sheep. The earth was red and sticky with mud. He set foot, scarcely, and then found work at sea, returning only once or twice each year to make sure Brigid stayed busy.

When the moon's smile blossomed, he was middling Bit, wistful Bit, his mind bent on dreams.

"Now look at what y've done," Brigid would say, when Bit let the broth boil over. "Not payin' proper attention. It's just like you, lettin' your mind wander off, as if it had somewhere important to go. *Ha!*"

Bit chopped onions. He stirred the bone broth. He smelled the marrow, and his heart beat faster. He thought of other things to eat, things he had never tasted, words he had heard at the market, to his ears as plump and foreign as a nectarine. *Linguine. Peanut. Tangerine. Trout.* He picked the worms out of the cabbages. He tucked the worms into his pocket and saved them for night, when hunger was a steam engine in his belly. He ladled soup into bowls, first a big clay bowl for Brigid, and then Dugan Molly Patrick Bree Cormac Kean, the volume of each bowl decreasing with the size of the child. Brigid took seconds. Bit scooped last, a cup of pale broth, a fray of cabbage, a slippery curl of onion.

"Ah, poor Bit," Dugan Molly Patrick Bree Cormac Kean would laugh. "If yer still hungry, there's a piece of bone."

"Why don't ya go on, give it a gnaw?"

"Just like a dog!"

Dugan Molly Patrick Bree Cormac Kean plucked the bone from the empty bottom of the pot and delivered it to a licked bowl. They set the bowl on the floor, for Bit.

"There ya go, Bit!"

"Give it a gnaw!"

"That's right, give it a gnaw, dog boy!"

Bit gripped the bone between his lips. He licked across it, tasting for marrow, but all the sweet life had seeped out.

At night, when Dugan Molly Patrick Bree Cormac Kean lay asleep in their bed, Bit ate his worms. He ate them one at a time. He let them linger on his tongue. He let his mind transform them into meals of liver, mutton, crispy pork. He stared up at the smiling moon.

Show your teeth, he told it. *Let them be sharp.*

But the genial half-moon would shed no blood. Its smile was faulty. There would be no biting yet.

When the moon swelled into a luminous egg, he was quick Bit, cunning Bit, and his will-o'-the-wisp eyes shone in the dark, bright and devious.

"Where'd my spool of thread disappear to now," Brigid would say. "Do you know, Bit? Do you know where it went off to, ya wee devil?"

"No'm," Bit would say, shaking his head, as he clutched the stolen thread beneath his toes. "I've no idea."

"Did you take it, boy?"

"No'm. I swear."

"Well, ya best be findin' it, 'therwise you'll be findin' yerself with a whippin'."

Bit crouched on the floor. He skimmed his hand along the splintered boards. He unmade the beds and searched beneath the quilts, careful to rub against them with his blackened feet. He had stolen a needle, too, and he left it in the bed, pointed up, for Dugan Molly Patrick Bree Cormac Kean to uncover. When Brigid turned her fat back, he crept up behind her and dropped the missing spool into the folds of her apron.

"Would you look at that!" Brigid said, finding it. "It was right here all along."

"I'm glad you found it."

"Hmm. Well, I suppose you can do the shoppin' this mornin' after all. My back's all aches anyhow, so you'd be savin' me the trip."

Brigid counted precious coins. She made Bit recite the shopping list. He was weak-minded and apt to forget.

"And don't you let yourself get swindled, boy," Brigid would say. "Don't you count wrong neither. I know how much all this ought to cost. If you come back one penny short, you'll be payin' it back outta your dinner, you will!"

Bit dashed down the stairs. He ran to the market. The coins jangled in his pocket. Timid Bit had gone, but cunning Bit knew how to conjure him. *Please, sir, how much for the apples?* He spoke in a downy voice. He paid for a lone apple as he snatched four more. *Excuse me, miss, but I'd like to buy a loaf of bread.* The baker counted Bit's coins while Bit counted fresh-baked buns: one in the right sleeve, two and three in the left, four five six into his basket, concealed by the bounty of apples. Bit took the long way home. He wandered down to the port. He sat at the end of the dock. He watched the waves slosh. He ate a bun, an apple, a hunk of stolen cheese. The leather-limbed sailors whistled and spat. *To be free*, Bit thought. To whistle and spit. To feel the salt sea air, the careless sun. To ride the waves beneath a tumid moon. His small heart ached.

He plodded back, taking too long.

"Oh? The little prince, home at last," Brigid said, as always, no matter how long he took. "Did you get yerself lost on the way home?"

"No'm." Bit handed over the basket.

"It'd be just like you. Slow in the mind, slow in the feet. We ought've bundled you up and tossed you in the river, like we did those kittens. Don't know why we keep you around."

"So I can help out." Bit lied, "Please. All's I want is to help."

"I suppose everything's here, then?" Brigid sifted through the basket. Her eyes hunted for mistakes.

"Yes'm." Bit nodded. "And the change." He plunked a coin down on the table.

"Change? Well, I guess you're not as stupid as you look."

Bit was smart enough to save two coins for himself. Bit was smart enough to hide his coins. He hid them behind a piss-drenched board in the privy, where Bit emptied the chamber pot, where Dugan Molly Patrick Bree Cormac Kean would never look.

"Got another pot for ya, piss boy!"

Dugan Molly Patrick Bree Cormac Kean filled the pot all the way to the top so it would slop over and soak Bit's sleeves as he carried it down to the privy.

"Aw, didja wet yerself, Bit?"

"Is that . . . why, is that a bit o' night soil on your arm there, Bit?"

Dugan Molly Patrick Bree Cormac Kean each took a turn in

the pot, and then they climbed into bed and fell asleep. Bit crept across the room. He gathered prizes: Dugan's shoe, Molly's mitten, Patrick's comb, Bree's doll, Cormac's knife, Kean's carved horse. One by one, he dunked each prize in the pot. His work done, he sat by the window and stared out at the lustrous moon.

Hello, Bit, the moon said.

Hello, Moon, Bit replied. *I'm lonely and sad. When will you come for me?*

Soon... the moon said.

The moon swelled. Bit could feel it in his blood. He could smell the core of an apple browning on the street below. He could smell the acrid copper of his coins, buried in the privy. He could smell the fresh-baked buns at the market, the salted fish the sailors carted off their boats, the sun and the sea.

"Into the closet, boy!" Brigid would say.

"But it's too soon! I'm fine, see! I'm fine!"

Brigid would wrap her hands around Bit's neck. She would squeeze until Bit gasped for breath. She would let go, and Bit would fall to the floor.

"Kick him!" Dugan Molly Patrick Bree Cormac Kean would yell.

"I should've kicked you dead," Brigid would say. "An abomination like you."

"You should do it!"

"Yeah, Ma, kick 'im dead!"

"I would, oh you know I would. But death is for the Lord to decide, not me. Now, get you into the closet, boy!"

Bit stepped inside the closet. He held out his wrists. Brigid tied them together with a length of rope.

"You'll be sorry," Bit whispered.

"What did you just say, boy?" Brigid pulled the rope taut. Bit looked up at her. He stared into her chalky eyes. He smiled. He felt the weight of the moon inside him. He felt his own power.

"I said, you'll be sorry. One day I'll break loose, and then you'll be sorry!"

"You freak!" Brigid hissed. She kicked him. He let his legs buckle. He let himself fall back.

"You'll be sorry—" Bit howled.

"Freak!" Dugan Molly Patrick Bree Cormac Kean jeered.

"—all of you—"

"You're the devil!" yelled Brigid.

"The devil!" echoed Dugan Molly Patrick Bree Cormac Kean.

"—but not for long." Bit laughed. "Because then you'll be dead."

Brigid kicked him again. Then she stood back so that Dugan Molly Patrick Bree Cormac Kean could have their turn. Bit went limp. He lay on the closet floor, a dirty rag of a boy. His brothers and sisters kicked him until he bled. But he didn't cry.

The closet door slammed shut. The lock clicked. Bit licked his bloody hand. He lay on the floor and listened. He listened to the scrape of Brigid's ladle along the side of the cooking pot, the flames flapping beneath it, the wheeze of the floorboards beneath her heavy feet. He could hear her heartbeat. He could hear the tepid hearts of Dugan Molly Patrick Bree Cormac Kean. He could hear his own growling belly. He could hear hooves on the street, rats in the basement. He could hear the sailors, whistling. He could hear the sun slinking down behind the city, the lanterns flickering on.

The moon called to him, and he heard her, in his ears, in his heart. It felt as if his heart exploded. A scream burbled up. Bit swallowed it down. *Quiet, you,* he told himself. *Quiet quiet quiet.* The explosion billowed out through his chest. It surged through his bones. He felt them bending, wrenching, reforging. He thrashed against the closet wall. He rolled over, opened his mouth, vomited hot acidy bile. The moon conveyed the pain of the banished sun, devouring him eternal. The pain seared his eyes shut. He wanted to scream. *Quiet quiet quiet.* He had to be strong.

He felt a sharp sprouting in his mouth, a hardening in his muscles, a bristling across his skin.

His fingers twisted into claws.

He opened his eyes.

He saw a stripe of silver moonlight beneath the door. He saw his hands, monstrous, dark with fur. The rope that bound them was a silly parlor trick. Bit held it to his mouth, his teeth sawing through it. He felt the hunger of all his new moon days, his crescent days, his gibbous days, his belly empty and aching, his belly churning with a scrap of onion, a plundered worm.

The rope fell away. He felt enormously hungry.

But no meat for you, boy, his mother had told him. *No meat for a freak like you.*

Bit bared his teeth. His paw reached for the door. The door was locked. He could hear Brigid's flabby snores. He could hear Dugan Molly Patrick Bree Cormac Kean, wheezing, snuffling. Their hearts were wide-eyed fawns in a bed-land meadow. He growled, quietly.

Quiet quiet quiet.

He pressed against the door. He leaned his weight against the door, but there wasn't much of him. Bit was still Bit, except now his forty pounds had claws and teeth. He dug his claw between the door and the frame, feeling for the groove of the lock. His claw stuck. He pulled it out. He tried again. His claw tapped against the metal lock. He scraped it. *Quiet quiet.* He scraped again. He felt it loosen. He scraped again. He felt it snap.

The broken lock clunked onto the floor. Brigid snorted in her sleep. Bit pushed the closet door open. He padded across the room. He thought about the kittens that Brigid had tied in a sack and thrown in the river to drown. *Freaks like you.* He climbed up onto Brigid's bed. The ravenous moon dangled in the window, drenching the room in silvery light. He crept over Brigid's legs, up along the whole length of her torso. He placed his paw atop her chest. She mumbled. He extended a claw. Her skin split. A bead of blood leaked out, round and red as an apple. Brigid opened her eyes. Bit smiled with all his teeth. She started to scream, but he was quick Bit, vicious Bit, Bit the unquenchable. He tore the scream from her throat. Blood spewed from the hole in her neck, rivers of it. Brigid's jaw flapped. Her heart poured blood. Bit tore the throat from beneath her head. Her life leaked out. Bit lapped it up.

Bit walked across his mother's drained torso. He jumped down onto the floor. He landed softly, in a square of moonlight.

Hello, Moon, Bit said, silently.

Hello, Bit, my beautiful boy, my fierce cunning boy, the moon replied.

Bit licked the blood from his paws. He imagined the moonlight at sea, rippling across the waves. He imagined the moonlight over mountains, endless dark forests where a wolf could stalk, unseen by any but the moon. He listened to Dugan Molly Patrick Bree

Cormac Kean, snoring, dreaming. (*Kick him! Kick him dead!*) He
hopped up onto the foot of their bed. (*Another pot for you, piss
boy!*) He slunk up, through the center of them. Patrick batted at
him with a sleeping hand. Cormac moaned. Bit readied his claws.
A spurt of blood from a cut jugular woke the first one. A slash
across the face woke the second. Bit swiped. He clawed. He bit.
Dugan Molly Patrick Bree Cormac Kean screamed and thrashed
and bled. He tore them apart.

All except one.

Bit paced across the pulp of Dugan Molly Patrick Bree Cormac,
his senses overloaded with the scent of blood, the taste of moon.
He heard a whimper. He leapt off the bed. He followed the sound,
to Kean. Kean, the next youngest, cowered in the closet from which
Bit had broken free. He cupped his palm over his ruined eye.

"No," Kean cried. "Please, no."

Bit stared at his brother. He sniffed. He could smell Kean's fear.

"Please, no," Kean begged. "Please, God, no."

But there's no God here, Bit would have said, if he'd had the
words. *There's only me. Only me and Moon.*

"I don't want to die. Please, I don't—"

Bit snapped his teeth. Kean shut his mouth. A trail of blood
seeped from Kean's eye, down his cheek. Bit opened his mouth.
Kean's small body shook, riddled with fear. Bit stepped closer to
his brother. He stuck out his tongue and licked the blood from his
brother's cheek.

"Please," Kean sobbed. "Please, dog—"

Bit was not a dog.

He snapped his teeth down over Kean's hand. It tore off at the wrist. Bit swallowed a finger and then tossed the rest aside. Kean howled. Bit's brother didn't want to die. Well, what happened to him next was for the Lord to decide.

Bit pushed the closet door shut with his snout. He ran to the window. Brigid had left it open. The night was warm and full of promise. Bit climbed out, onto the fire escape. He walked down two stories, and then he jumped. He landed on his four strong feet. He took off running. He ran at first in the shadows, but no one paid him any mind. He was just a dog, a stray dog, a vicious-looking one. *Best to stay away* was what anyone who saw him would think. The few people out at that late hour stayed away, or averted their gaze. They saw Bit come running, and they turned and went in the other direction, and after a time, Bit shed the shadows and ran right down the middle of the road, soaked in moonlight.

He ran down to the port. He ran out onto a dock. He reached the end, where the dock met the sea, and he leapt. He plunged into the cool water. He found that he could swim, and he swam until he had washed away his mother's blood, until he had washed away every last splatter of Dugan Molly Patrick Bree Cormac Kean.

When he was clean, Bit swam to shore. He shook off. He ran back, through the empty streets, to the building where he had lived. His neighbors had heard screams, and awoken. People gathered outside the building. They pointed and conjectured. A pair of constables stood by the door. No one noticed the small stray dog prance past the building and let itself into the privy.

Bit pried open the piss-soaked board with his claws. He fished out his sack of coins. Crafty Bit had tied the coins in cloth, wrapped them twice with loops of string that a claw could easily catch. He held the sack of coins in his teeth and took off running. No one saw him go. He ran as fast and as far as he could, until his paws grew weary and the moon faded in a blueing sky. He found a tree, thick with leaves. He curled up beneath it.

When he awoke, the sun hovered at the height of the sky, and Bit was just a boy.

DARLA

LUCKY RABBIT

Lake Orange—Now

SHE WAITED ON the Barrington Equity jet, gorgeous Darla, drop-dead Darla.

"Stay put," Mr. Buxby had told her.

He had a voice like ice cracking, cold and sudden. She polished martini glasses. She filled glass bowls with peanuts and crackers. She traced her finger across the polished wood, the leather seat backs. All smooth, inside the cocoon of the private jet. All uneventful. She felt like a caged rabbit, except the cage cost twenty million and everyone said she was lucky to have gotten penned inside it.

She stared out the window. The sun set over the tarmac. Tiny planes came and went. Out there, life happened!

She wrote a letter in her head:

Dear Mom, my new job is great. They pay me well, and there are real opportunities for advancement. I get to travel a lot. Right now, I'm visiting Lake Orange. You always wanted to go there, didn't you?

Moving away from that asshole Ted was the best thing I ever did. You should try it! Not that you ever will. I kind of miss you, I guess, but not any more than I did those last years when I still lived with you. BTW, please tell Ted that he can go fuck himself.

She went into the back cabin, where the partners' wives rode. The partners' wives made her uneasy. Mostly she moved past them unseen. But when they saw her, their eyes glittered with contempt, or pity. Doe-faced Darla, sexy Darla. (*Was that why we stopped talking, Mom? You couldn't stand the way your dearest Ted leered, when I cleared the table, when I vacuumed your shitty carpets, when I wore yoga pants and Ted had to remark about my ass. The wolf.*)

The wives wore perfume and carried handbags worth more than everything Darla owned. One of them had left her handbag on a seat. Because she was rich—Darla decided—and when you were rich, everything paid for itself. Darla opened the bag and rifled through: two tubes of lipstick, a car key, another car key, a cell phone in a Swarovski crystal case, tampons, safety pins, hair ties, eye drops, sunglasses, a miniature wine-stain-remover kit, a silver pocketknife, a plump wallet with a bevy of black cards, gold cards, memberships. Shannon S. James belonged to the City Athletic Club, the Olympic Club, the Napa Valley Wine Connoisseur Association, to museums, foundations, and private dining establishments, so many of them that Darla had the creeping notion that the whole of Shannon S. James's wallet was phony, that the woman herself was no more than a fabricated assortment of elite-level memberships. Darla removed the various membership cards from Shannon S. James's wallet and lined them up on the table. Then, from outside, she heard voices. She hastily shoved the cards back into the wallet. She threw the wallet back into the handbag. She ran for the front cabin, expecting the door to open, expecting Mr. Buxby to step through. *I thought I told you to stay put.*

But he didn't. Darla looked out the window. She saw two airport workers walking away across the tarmac. Their voices receded into the hot night.

The worst part was not knowing when to expect him. Her jaw could not unclench. Beautiful Darla, grinding her beautiful teeth.

You'll never make it, Ted had told her, the first time she threatened to leave. *Girl like you. Nothin' but fluff inside that pretty little head of yours.* But then it had all seemed so easy. The bus ticket to the big city, the apartment she rented on the other side of the bay, the job she landed as a server at a steak house downtown, and then the offer for a better job from one of the regulars, a salaried job in a gleaming high-rise, with a wardrobe stipend and a signing bonus. *Girl like you, nothin' but fluff.* She paid her signing bonus over to the state college, tuition deposit for classes next semester. She bought the requisite wardrobe items for her new professional life.

The last Darla didn't make it, the receptionist told her, a few weeks in. Moved back home to live with her parents. The Darla before that didn't make it either. How many Darlas had there been? She thought about Ted's prognostication: *You'll never make it.* She thought about it the first time Darren Buxby grabbed her in the hallway and pulled her into his office. She thought about it when she kneeled over him. Her jaw ached. The next cycle of bills came due. The tuition bill, the water bill, the electric bill, the dentist bill, the rent. She dreamed a recurring dream where her teeth all fell out and she ran home to her mother's house and Ted pushed her head down and said, *Good, bitch, now you can't bite.* She couldn't not make it, couldn't couldn't couldn't.

She fell asleep. She awoke to the sound of the cabin door opening. The sound of his feet. The icy grating of his voice.

"Darla!"

She jumped up. She smoothed back her hair. She tried to look pleased to see him. She had a stack of bills on her table at home. She couldn't afford not to look pleased. She poured him a drink, his favorite scotch. Darren Buxby tossed it back. He pushed her face down onto the table. She could see the reflection of her pretty face on the glossy table surface. She thought about all the Darlas before her, and all the Darlas after.

WHEREIN SHANE LaSALLE FINDS HIMSELF A CHANGED MAN

Lake Orange—Now

SHANE LaSALLE OPENED his eyes. (*You Da Man, LaSalle!!!*) (*Sun emoji; tree emoji; surprised-face emoji.*) He saw blue sky, white tufted clouds. He saw black spider limbs of bare trees. (*Status update: Took my first trip in a private jet! Slept out under the stars!*) Had he slept? Something had happened. It didn't feel like sleep. It felt hollow and hungry. His eyes swiveled in their myopic sockets, scanning the limited frame of sky and trees. The trees reminded him of *Beetlejuice*, which made him feel odd and uncomfortable. The trees had a disturbing resemblance to kindling. He distrusted their leaflessness. They made him feel leafless.

He *was* leafless.

A calm breeze batted his leafless parts. He lifted his head, just enough to confirm his suspicion. (*Status update: What the hell happened to my pants?!*) His head plopped back onto the vine-strewn earth. The dizzy sky stared down at him. The white clouds shifted into shapes: The shape of a lamb. The shape of a wolf. *Which shape are you, LaSalle?* the wolf cloud taunted. *Are you a pretty boy? Are you a laaaaamb chop?* The last thing he recalled, before awaking naked in the sunshine, was the anticipation of getting eaten alive, and how normal it seemed. How perfectly natural it seemed that his life's achievements would culminate with wolves chowing down on his intestines, his thigh meat, and his soft neck parts while his beating heart pumped fresh blood down their throats. He recalled the yellow infinity of the wolf's eye. The glint of moonlight reflected in the stark whiteness of the wolf's teeth.

The teeth.

He thought of Duane's teeth, those vampiric hustlers, refusing to stick to the shadows of Duane's mouth. He shuddered at the thought of those teeth. What if—

No, the idea was too absurd to even consider.

But what if—

His brain produced the image of Duane the vampire bat: bat-sized body, oversized cartoon Duane-head, red *Twilight Zone* eyes. The vampire bat reconstituted into Duane the vampire, death-pale and grinning, the white darlings of his mouth dripping with blood. He wore a long, black velvet cloak with a trim of red silk, and he pulled the cloak back over his muscular shoulders and beneath it his chest was bare and—

No. Too absurd to consider.

But let's be realistic here, Shaney-boy. You were the prime rib on

Wolvesey's menu, and now you're fully stocked in ribs and missing your shoes and pants. Shane's eye spotted a distant bare toe. He wriggled the one toe, and then the rest, testing them out. He had a brief, frightening vision of his toes getting torn off and then reattached. Except that they did not hurt. His legs (also bare, but hairy) didn't hurt. His dick felt rather nice. His gut—the part he had expected to find partially eaten, with entrails slopping out over the sides—felt sour and acidy, but it did not hurt in the just-eaten-by-wolves sense. His head felt limp-noodled and achy, but it had felt worse after ice-luge night in college.

His eyes felt like different eyes.

He could see the breeze and heat in the air. He could see the burn patterns on the charred tree bark. A bird flapped high over the sad remains of the forest, and he saw that it was a hawk. He saw the gloss of feathers on its wings. He saw the reflection of a rabbit exposed on the ground below. He saw hunger.

Shane lifted his head again and looked down at his chest. It was smattered with dried blood. He saw his undershirt, bloody and weirdly stretched but still intact. His abs groaned as he hoisted his torso into a nearly upright position. His arms and shoulders felt oddly disjointed and capable of freak-show contortions. Part of him, the leafless part, had already risen to an entirely vertical position.

He had the sensation, which had long trailed him, that he was being watched. He heard a rustle of vines. He heard a twig snap. He looked up and saw a deer, standing in a spot of sunlight between two blackened trees. The deer looked at him curiously. It seemed to smile.

"What?" he said hoarsely.

He pushed himself further, onto his feet. The deer's eyes

mocked him. He felt terribly, painfully embarrassed that the deer would see him like this, confused, partially naked. It was worse, somehow, that it had found him naked from the waist down, instead of completely nude. He pulled his tattered undershirt up and over his head. He stepped through the armholes and tucked the rest of the bloody shirt around his hips, folding it into a makeshift man-diaper. The deer rolled its black eyes and then galloped away.

Shane walked through the forest. The sun hovered at its highest point, some indiscernible midday hour. Days might have passed. Weeks might have passed. The loss of his pants would seem more plausible, over the course of weeks.

At first, he walked gingerly, cautious of the sharp, splintery objects that could pierce the tender soles of his feet, cautious of rusty nails because his mother had instilled in him—along with a refined taste for artisanal cheeses and a delusionally optimistic belief in the cause-and-effect relation between Shane LaSalle's hard work (which itself exemplified his self-worth and moral stature) and Shane LaSalle's inevitable procurement of a Gold Coast vacation home with views of Lake Michigan—an unreasonable fear of *tetanus*. Every garage or shed or creaky old stairway was a minefield of rusty nails just waiting to puncture his heel or scrape open the exposed skin of his arm. He never walked barefoot, not even in his own apartment, where he wore hard-soled house slippers. He wore water socks at the beach. The ocean teemed with millions of salt-rusted nails from garbage dumps and shipwrecks, and some of those nails would invariably travel to shore and give people tetanus. Shane's mother had told him a story of a girl who got tetanus and her jaw locked up and the doctors had to *cut her jaw off*. At least, that was how Shane remembered the story. He remembered the picture his mind had formed, of the girl with no bottom jaw, whose face stopped right below her top teeth. He would look at his own face in the mirror, his own well-defined jaw, and imagine a gaping fleshy hole straddling the space between his top teeth and his neck. Genetics had blessed him with a gorgeous jawline, but tetanus could snatch that jawline away. So could a wolf, he had thought, when the wolf's jagged mouth had opened over his neck. He had thought: *Oh no, not my chin!*

After just a few steps, Shane realized that his feet felt different. His feet felt sensitive and attuned to even the slightest variation of the forest floor, but concurrently not sensitive, and lacking their usual tenderness. He stepped on a serrated branch, and he felt the stab of sharp wood, but the pain was muted. He stopped and examined the bottom of the accosted foot. The branch looked like just the sort of thing that would send him to the hospital for stitches, or infect him with tetanus if (and this was absolutely plausible, something told him) sharp branches could carry tetanus acquired from some ancient encounter with a rusty nail. And yet the branch had barely broken his skin. He saw no blood, only a minor indentation in what appeared, strangely, to be a callus.

He took a few more steps, faster, less cautious steps. He picked up speed. He found that he could run. He sped through the forest, running, leaping over decaying logs and burnt fallen branches, pounding over rocks and twigs. The ground felt delightful beneath his new feet. He wanted to sprint. He wanted to jump up and twirl! Then he stopped, derailed by the sudden self-conscious image of a dirty man in a blood-smeared loincloth pirouetting through a scorched forest. (#LunaticInALoincloth; #BurnedForestBallet). What if someone found him dancing through the forest, be-diapered and bloody? What if the partners found him? What if someone took video footage, and the video went viral, and he became an unwitting KlipSwatch sensation, the Raving Tarzan of Lake Orange? How would he ever dock his yacht in Lake Orange if any of them knew?

Shane, ol' buddy, ol' pal, you seriously believe your yacht belongs in that lake? That's not even a yacht. That's just a couple of sticks held together to make them look like a boat.

Shane looked down at his hands and saw that they held a couple of sticks, arranged in a vaguely boatlike shape. He dropped the sticks, alarmed by their implication, and by their ability to appear in his hands without his conscious invitation. Had anyone seen how they got there? His eyes scanned the trees for the hidden lens of a video camera, for a recording drone disguised as a forest bird. What if they already knew? What if the partners had known all along that he was—

Shane, ol' buddy, ol' pal, shouldn't you be trying to find your pants?

He started walking again, this time at a balanced pace that, if recorded, would merit the caption: *Bare-Chested Man Enjoys a Nature Walk before Returning to His Pants.* His eyes searched the ground for slacks in charcoal gray, a pair of polished Italian loafers, a set of blue-and-purple argyle socks, a starched white J.Crew button-up shirt, an almost antique Rolex Yacht-Master watch—his dad's first Rolex, presented as a gift for Shane's college graduation. He saw, instead, a plump brown rabbit, and a pang of hunger burrowed through his gut. He imagined the rabbit simmering in sauces, rabbit stew with sea salt and golden Yukon potatoes and a dash of balsamic reduction, which gave the stew a sweet tang and colored it reddish brown. Except as the image, and his hunger, intensified,

Shane saw that his mind had not seasoned the stew with balsamic reduction, that the reddish-brown color was blood, and the rabbit wasn't simmering. It was raw.

He stopped, leaned over, and puked acidy bile into the vines. His vomit was streaked with blood. Agonizing hunger filled the void in his gut. He wiped his mouth with the back of his dirty arm. He saw a metallic glint on the ground. His watch! He picked it up and inspected it. It appeared functional, and unscratched, except for a tooth mark left on the band.

He strapped on his watch and continued the hunt for his clothes. He found his shirt next. The shirt looked like a costume from a slasher movie. The entire front of the shirt was shredded and soaked in blood, so much blood that it was still damp. Shane held the shirt to his nose and sniffed. He detected a trace of Armani Code Eau de Parfum, the dreamy fragrance of Duane's Gauloises, Dick Barrington's Cuban cigar, the salty nectar of blood he recognized as his own. He knew the smell of his own blood instinctually, and did not question why. And yet, a shirt-drenching volume of blood could not possibly have drained out of him. He did not have even a scratch on his chest.

Shane tossed the unwearable shirt into the vines. He started to walk away, but then he changed his mind. He ran back and grabbed the garment. He couldn't leave a bloody shirt just sitting out in the open, where someone would find it and wonder what atrocities the shirt had committed. He tied a knot with its sleeves so it formed a ball. He tucked the bloody package under his armpit. He noticed the smell of his armpits, which smelled exactly like them and not like them at all. He felt as if he might be going insane. *What's this "going"? Looks to me like you've already gone.* His brain conjured posts for the socials:

Beautiful hike in a magical forest!

Unwinding with some quality nature time.

I am just crazy about Lake Orange!

The wildlife here is epic. Last night I came face-to-face with two wolves!

Or had it been one wolf?

He remembered the one wolf at the boathouse, and then the wolf standing on top of him, opening its maw, shining its rows of teeth down upon him. In Shane's mind, the wolf had several rows of teeth—big sharp front ones, middling razors, and tiny needles lining the roof of its mouth, highlighting the dimensional disconnect between the normal-sized exterior of the wolf's mouth and the monstrous expanse of its inside. It was horrific. But had Shane seen one mouth, or had he seen more than one wolf with more than one awful mouth? The wolf he encountered near the boathouse had, in Shane's memory, a smooth gray coat and a black sheen around its eyes. The wolf that had stood on Shane's chest, whose mouth defied the laws of physics, had seemed smaller, despite its proximity, and browner. And when that physics-defying mouth had opened, Shane had sensed other wolves, at least one but maybe more. Maybe terror had many mouths. Shane shuddered at the thought of all those teeth.

Shane walked for a while longer, until he came across his shoes and his socks, all four of them together, out on a double date in the magical burnt forest of Lake Orange, and remarkably free of bloodstains. He slid feet into socks, and socks into shoes, and he felt very accomplished. But as he started walking, his feet revolted. They didn't want the shoes.

"No!" Shane yelled, thinking about tetanus. "We're wearing shoes!"

He walked for a while in the shoes, and they felt as lovely as the $600 he had spent on them ($595, but Shane rounded up), but they also felt unnatural. The more he walked, the more he loathed the restrictive fibers of his socks, the soulless soles of these shoes that, he recognized now in the lucidity of the present, were absurdly overpriced. He wanted dirt between his toes.

"No, LaSalle," he told himself. "You don't. You don't want dirt."

He wanted dirt. He wanted rocks and leaves, textures hard and slippery to inform the momentum of his gait. He tried to scare himself sensible by envisioning a rusty nail stabbing through the bottom of his foot and coming out the top, the invasive tetanus in his veins, his gorgeous jaw locked up and then sliced off by some tetanus-inflicted instrument, like a rusty saw. Shane screamed.

His scream echoed across the forest. It bounced back into his ears. He heard the full volume of his burgeoning insanity.

He gave himself a pep talk. "Get with it, LaSalle! You gotta get with it. Find your pants. Get yourself home. Stop talking to yourself like some kind of lunatic."

But you are a LUNA-tic, aren't you, LaSalle?

"No. You are Shane LaSalle. You are Shane LaSalle, senior associate—no, soon to be partner—with Barrington Equity LLC. You are thirty-three years old. You are a *Venture Capitalist Monthly* rising star. You were voted most likely to succeed in the field of finance in your Bloomfield Hills senior class yearbook. You graduated top of your class at Duke. You love parasailing. You're going to buy a boat someday. No, not someday. Soon. You will buy a boat. You will buy a boat. You absolutely will."

His brain flashed a gratuitous image of Duane Beckman, shirtless, staring out over the waters of Lake Orange. The image zoomed in on Duane Beckman's sharp, offending teeth.

The thing was, Shane LaSalle hated needles. He feared needles as much as he feared tetanus, which explained why tetanus was such a threat. He had not gotten his tetanus shot. And there was something profoundly needling about Duane Beckman's teeth.

He forced himself to succumb to the tyranny of shoes. He continued the quest for his pants. He walked in circles, around and around the same burnt tree husks, the same proliferations of kudzu and pickleweeds, the same squirrels and rodents, the sight of which ignited in him a vicious hunger. He saw a snake, thick and meaty, slither into the hollowed-out trunk of a fallen tree. He imagined catching the snake, holding its meat in his hands, eating it raw.

"No, you do not eat snakes. You do not eat snakes. Snakes are gross."

He imagined the clandestine video footage of Shane LaSalle eating a raw snake, and all the people who would see it, and their cruel laughter, their judgment, condemning him to internet infamy as Tarzan Shane, the snake-eater.

The high sun relaxed into the pillowed clouds along the horizon. Tarzan Shane smelled butter. He smelled focaccia with rosemary, pan-fried shrimp, olives bathed in vodka, tri-tip soaked in garlic Worcestershire marinade. He smelled meat searing on the grill. *Burning*, he thought. *They're burning it.* He followed the burning smell, until he saw the Century Boathouse in the distance. He could smell the timber bones of the boathouse building, the newness of its paint, the fresh shellac of its wood floors. He could smell Dick Barrington, Ronald Carver, Duane Beckman, but the scent of them seemed far away. The scent belonged to ghosts.

He walked straight toward the boathouse, and almost out into the parking lot, until he saw the tuxedoed valet standing in front of the building, which made him think of Duane and also made him remember that he still hadn't found his pants.

Shane took cover behind a tree. He stood and watched for a while as cars drove up to the boathouse entrance and people got out and tossed their keys to the valet and went inside. Those were his people. He was one of them. And yet, here he was, outside, hating his shoes, hating every pomade-haired golfer, every Audi driver, every string of pearls, every sports coat, every man with a twinkling resemblance to Duane. A Lamborghini pulled up at the entrance and a snow-haired fellow stepped out of the driver's seat, and at first Shane thought that the Lamborghini and the snowy hair belonged to Dick Barrington. But the man, whoever he was, did not smell like Dick Barrington. He had a swampy, earthy smell, like the smell of an algal bloom, layered with coconut tanning oil and sparkling water with a squirt of fresh lime. Shane could smell the lime on the man's breath, dozens of yards away.

"You are not smelling lime," Shane whispered to himself. "You are not."

(*Status update: olfactory dysfunction, pantslessness, and other indicia of traumatic brain swelling. Just kidding! Having a fabulous vacation weekend in Lake Orange! Sun emoji—golf-cart emoji— sailboat emoji!!!*)

The lime smell made him hungrier. He considered his options: Tarzan Shane marches up to the host stand and demands a table.

Tarzan Shane storms the Century Boathouse and snatches steak kebabs and shrimp cocktails off the tables, guzzles people's gin and tonics, pours whole bowls of Chex Mix into his bottomless mouth-pit. Tarzan Shane swings in through the kitchen window and steals raw slabs of veal, devouring some and hiding others in his loincloth. Hungry, hungry Shane chases a lime-dressed live meal out of the boathouse, into the forest, and rips the meat from his bones and drinks his coconut-scented blood.

"No, no, no!" Shane sprang back, physically repelled by the thought of coconut-scented blood and tangy Lamborghini-driving meat, and repelled, in particular, by how delicious it sounded. His mouth watered. His tongue twitched. He could smell the man even now, inside the boathouse, ordering a glass of pinot gris, to complement his flavors.

"No!" Shane shouted.

The valet turned toward the sound of Shane's voice, but the valet had faulty human eyes and a weak human nose. The valet could neither see nor smell him. Still, Shane turned and ran. He ran back into the forest. He ran until he could no longer smell the boathouse, until he could no longer smell the boathouse's steak and gin and fingerling potatoes and mouthwatering clientele, with their warm blood and their hint of lime, until his lungs ought to have burned but felt cool instead, refreshed by the surge of air and speed, by the sensation of near flight. He had never run so fast in his life.

He stopped to remove his shoes and socks. He shoved the socks into his shoes, and he tucked the shoes beneath his armpit, in case he needed the detestable things later. Unfettered by footwear, he took off. He ran hard, erasing from his mind everything but the sensation of running. The sun descended and the sky turned dark, and Shane felt strong and sharp. He could see the myriad shapes of the forest. He saw at once the broad sweeps of land and sky, and the tiniest details, the charred texture of tree bark, the fiddle legs of a crooning cricket, the pistil of a wildflower blooming in a sea of vines. He could smell the forest life, surprising in its abundance. Life reasserted itself. Life bled on. He could smell the blood of rabbits, chipmunks, wild turkeys, raccoons. He could smell his own blood, oddly pungent, saltier than he would have imagined. He could smell the moon as it ascended in the sky, bright, bright, bright. He ran until life was a dream of running. His calloused feet blistered. He saw a squirrel in his hands. He saw a black eternity in its eyes as he broke its neck and ripped off its head. He imagined he had dreamed the squirrel, even as he tasted its blood in his mouth. He ran. He ran.

He awoke, and again it was daylight. He looked up at the slate sky. He blinked away the brightness. He saw a streak of dark gray, like a flag draped over the limb of a tree. His pants! He stood up. He felt well rested, and abnormally normal. He approached his pants. He pulled them down from the tree. He removed his undershirt loincloth and stepped into his pants. He felt the heavy lump of his wallet in his back pocket. He checked his front pockets. He found his keys, but his phone was gone. He put his shoes back on. Then he noticed, hanging from the branch of another tree, a strip of white fabric.

He picked it up. It was a Lake Orange souvenir T-shirt, the

cheap gas-station variety, stiff cotton with the words ORANGE I GLAD I VISITED LAKE ORANGE printed on the chest.

He sniffed it. It smelled like ethanol and plastic. It still had a tag attached, displaying its $10.99 price. He ripped off the tag and pulled the T-shirt over his head. He started walking back toward the boathouse, led by the scent of frying bacon, over-easy eggs drenched in hollandaise sauce, biscuits and toast, hotcakes on the griddle. He stopped beside the lake and crouched down over the water, uncertain of what he would see reflected in its placid sheen. He half expected a monster, a fanged tangle of hair and teeth and matted blood. Instead, he saw his own face, his clear symmetrical eyes, his sculpted jaw, his lips curled into a faint smile. He splashed his face with water. He combed his hair with wet hands. He rinsed away the dirt and dried blood.

Sufficiently cleaned, he continued on, up to the front door of the boathouse. He shoved the bloodied ball of his old shirt into the trash. He invited himself in. The hostess smiled when she saw him. She did not look alarmed.

"Good morning, sir. One for breakfast?"

"Yes," Shane said. "Table for one."

"Are you just visiting?"

"I'm just . . . I was just—"

"Because your shirt—"

Shane looked down at his shirt.

"Oh, right, of course. Yes. Just visiting. Just glad to be visiting Lake Orange."

"Right, well . . ." The hostess leaned in toward Shane and said, quietly, "If I was you, I'd stay out of the forest."

NATASHA

SEQUINED OUTRAGE

San Francisco—Now

NOVA Z'RHAE WAS omnipresent. Her gold-brown eyes glittered on magazine covers, in record store windows, on the sides of Muni buses plastered with ads for her upcoming tour.

She enchanted the television. She gave late-night interviews adorned in sequined jumpsuits and feather headdresses. She did commercials for AIDS relief, for St. Jude's, for the Natural Resources Defense Council. She appeared as Lady Z'Rhae in a fruit hat, bare shouldered, red lips gleaming, to dance with Muppets and teach preschoolers how to count, and how to be open-minded and accepting of people of all sorts, the beige and the brown and the blue, the *hes* and the *shes* and the *thems*. She glorified "The Alphabet Song" and sang the spider up the spout, but this time, *this time*, the spider, that enterprising gal, made it all the way to the top and stayed up there, dancing in the rain. Nova Z'Rhae danced in a rain of confetti. She danced across the airwaves. She pulsed from the dance club speakers, from bars and boutiques, from passing cars. Her voice flew from the windows and caught in the air, and she rang across the city, a calling, an anthem, a dazzling mantra of hope with a sick bass beat.

Natasha Porter could not escape her.

Nova Z'Rhae watched from her lighted billboard, her eyes luminous, her hair sculpted into a peacock fan, her skin the texture of liquid bronze, flecked with stardust. Her expression seemed to change, as if behind the billboard sheen neurons fired and synapses ignited and whole other universes came and went. Sometimes Natasha saw sympathy in the glossed curve of Nova Z'Rhae's lips, compassion in her jeweled eyes, forgiveness. Then the light shifted, and Nova Z'Rhae gazed down at Natasha with the condemnation of her fans, and her compassion turned to outrage.

Natasha walked under the billboard, past Sunset, Stonestown, Parkmerced, toward her new job, at the Olympic Club. Marie had worked as a hostess at the Olympic Club. Natasha, on a whim, filled out an application for the vacant hostess position. She did not actually want to work there, but she needed a job, and they were hiring. And maybe someone there had seen something that could lead to her roommate's killer.

Natasha clocked in. She took her spot at the hostess stand. She counted the hours ahead. She counted the hours she had clocked acquiring her degree, the hours passed writing essays and taking quizzes and practicing for the SAT, the hours devoted to collecting extracurriculars and polishing her résumé and all the hours of work since, real adult important work that had made her feel as if she had gotten somewhere, as if she had become a person of significance, all of it leading to this: the hostess stand.

She hated herself for thinking that she was too good for it.

"Right this way, ma'am, sir."

She directed late-middle-aged socialites to white-cloth tables.

She brought baskets of warm bread.

"Does this bread have gluten?"

Butter came carved in the shape of stars.

"We prefer the oil and vinegar with the bread," said a woman with a silk blouse and a diamond tennis bracelet. "But just a dash of vinegar. Four-fifths oil, one-fifth vinegar. With a sprig of rosemary. That's how we like it. The last hostess, she always got it just right."

"The last hostess?" Natasha shivered. "You knew her?"

"Yes, it's such a—"

"Barb, let's not," the husband interrupted, with a voice practiced in orders and interruptions.

"Fine, fine," the woman said. "Just a dash of vinegar. You'll learn."

Guests swished her away with their hands. She was *just the hostess*. She was *excuse me, miss* to the well-mannered, *hey, you* to the impatient and maligned. She was a motionless breeze; an inaudible whisper; a ghost.

She poured ice waters and swept crumbs. She watched and listened. She watched the men. Certain men raised her hackles. Their voices intoned privilege. They said, *There'll be six of us tonight* or *We'd like to sit outside*, but their tone said: *I'll take what I want.* They swaggered. They stared, sizing her up. She didn't amount to much, but sometimes *I'll take what I want* meant *I'll take what I can get*, like it had one summer during college, when Natasha served hors d'oeuvres and bused plates of half-eaten opera cream wedding cake for minimum wage, and somebody's salt-and-pepper uncle grabbed her around the waist and pulled her onto his lap, *like a child*, she remembered thinking, compelled to have a little sit on Uncle Creepy's knee. She called him out. She called him Uncle Creepy, to his face, and it didn't matter that it was true—Natasha's boss made her apologize, and then he suggested that she find a different job. She didn't have the right skills to succeed in the catering industry.

Some men sized her up, but she sized them up, too. She gauged the authenticity of their smiles, the warmth of their eyes. Was this the sort of man, she would ask herself, to tear the guts from a twenty-three-year-old exchange student from Marseille? The sort who would make no effort to clean his mess, who would leave Marie Babineaux's mutilated body in the park?

Marie Babineax had played Nova Z'Rhae's latest album on repeat. She dusted her own eyelids with glitter, like Nova. She bought a sequin top to wear out dancing, but she never wore it. Marie had loved Nova Z'Rhae.

She is brilliant, Marie had said. *Her songs, her style, her, eh, je ne sais quoi! She is magical. I see her and think, that is what I love about America.*

Natasha had never bought a Nova Z'Rhae album, though she knew the popular singles well enough to sing along when she heard them on the radio. She had never thought much about Nova Z'Rhae, or her music, or her journey to becoming the Fantabulous Queen of Sequin Pop. But Nova Z'Rhae was on her mind the day after her roommate had disappeared.

The evening before, Natasha had texted Marie about meeting

up. Marie didn't text back, and Natasha didn't think much of it. Marie didn't always respond to texts. But in the morning, the top bunk was empty. Marie had not come home.

Natasha worried all day. She tried to work, but her apartment felt unnervingly empty. Her mind kept circling back to Marie. Marie had a picture of Nova Z'Rhae taped to the bedroom mirror. *I see her and think, that is what I love about America.* She had a collection of glitter eyeshadows and tiaras and sequin tops like all the Nozees wore. Early the next morning, the police showed up at her door and asked when she had last seen her roommate. They'd found a body in the park, unidentified, but they thought it might belong to Marie.

Natasha's entire career crashed and burned that day.

She should have canceled the interview. But she'd already rescheduled the Bertrand Mailer interview twice. Bertrand Mailer had a huge following. The interview might tilt the book-deal scales in her favor and bring traffic to her blog. She needed to do it. *You can do it,* she convinced herself. *You are strong.*

But she'd felt anxious as she rode the bus across town. She nearly missed her stop. She was sweaty, late, frazzled when she rang the buzzer to Bertrand Mailer's studio. She marched up three flights of stairs. She felt like she shouldn't be there, that she should be at home texting and calling everyone in San Francisco who had ever met Marie to ask if they had seen her, that she should be out searching all of Marie's favorite spots.

You are strong, she coached herself, with each step up the three flights of stairs. *You're strong. You're strong. You're strong.*

She convinced her brain that the body found by the cops was not Marie's. But in her heart, she knew.

Bertrand Mailer recorded his podcast live. He invited special guests. He met her at the door. He shook her hand. He poured cups of tea. They had tea and biscuits. He talked about women in media. He talked about the feminist underpinnings of the indie-glam movement, which had been subsumed by the larger genre of sequin pop, with its glitter-crown icons—most notably, Nova Z'Rhae.

A ladies' a cappella group sang before the interview portion. They sang "Cherry Bomb." The singers had the myriad bodies of real women, plum and pear, plump and washboard. None of them wore heels. They had the voices of angels, but not the sweet kind. Angels of fire and might. Natasha's anxious heart calmed. For a moment, she forgot about Marie.

Then the interview began. Bertrand Mailer asked Natasha about her blog, her book deal, her Wichita upbringing. She bantered. She relaxed. She was good at this.

"So, in addition to all that work," Bertrand said, "I understand you've also been nominated to serve as one of ten spokeswomen for the Orion Foundation's Glass Ceiling Initiative."

"I was."

"And you'll be serving alongside the fantabulous Nova Z'Rhae."

"Yeah, yeah I guess I heard that."

"You don't sound all that enthused."

An image of Marie flashed through Natasha's mind. First Marie. Then Marie's empty bunk. Then the cops standing at her door.

"No, no," Natasha said. "It's not that. I'm excited to be there."

"But you're not a fan of Nova Z'Rhae?"

"It's not that I'm not a fan. It's just that, you know, the Orion Foundation is—they're doing serious, important work. And Nova Z'Rhae is . . ."

Marie Babineaux had been playing Nova Z'Rhae the last time Natasha had seen her, dancing in the bathroom, brushing her teeth, braiding her hair for work. Natasha's heart pounded. Her head felt swimmy.

"Is what?"

"I mean, she's just kind of, like, an empty vessel."

Things might not have turned out so bad if the interview had ended there. But Bertrand Mailer smiled and asked for more.

"Oh? Do you mean her, personally? Or her music? Or both?"

"I've never met her. But her stage personality is just, well, vacuous. It's all about sequins and glitter and confetti cannons. And, like, is that what we need right now? She has a huge platform. She could use it to speak up about important issues. But instead, it's all just silly sequin pop. Whatever sells best to the lowest common denominator."

Even then, Natasha hardly noticed the problem. Her mind was still back at home, with Marie, putting glitter on her eyelids while Nova Z'Rhae's latest played in the background. Natasha didn't realize what she had said wrong until later, when she stepped out into the internet, where the icy troll-storm of collective outrage had already descended.

BIT

WHEREIN A BOY TAKETH

Pennsylvania—1822

BIT HAD HEARD of the vastness of the earth; of the endless land that spilt, an eternity away, into an endless sea. He had heard of mountains that lorded over the clouds, of lakes that fancied themselves oceans, of impassable rivers of thunder and mud. He could not conceive, in the least, what this meant, this sprawling continent. He had traveled further than he had imagined possible, and had not yet come to the land's end.

He had traveled all the way to Pennsylvania!

The boy Bit had once dreamed of a sailing ship, of the wind cradled by white sails, the waves emblazoned with gold, the taste of salt spray in a boy's mouth, salt and fish, sun and rain. But Bit, in his wolf form, knew how it felt to be chained and trapped. He feared the exposure of the open sea, the lilting enclosure of the ship, the inevitable night when the moon would rise high and bright and his crewmates would see what he was—a beast, an affront to the laws of man and God—and throw him overboard.

Bit the beast steered the boy west, into the trees. They traveled by night, as one, the beast's instincts balanced in the boy's body, strong beneath the plump moon. At dawn, Bit settled in a hammock of branches, a bed of leaves. He slept like a prince beneath the blue and milky skies. He woke in the early evening, when the gibbous moon tugged on the horizon. He walked and thought and thought. How big could the world be? Once, his world had started at Brigid and ended with Kean, and in between he had Dugan Molly Patrick Bree and Cormac to call him *dog. Devil. Freak.* He thought about Brigid's fat throat in his mouth, and the taste of her blood, tinged with lye. He thought about Kean, whose life he had spared, whose eye and hand he had not. Kean's finger caused him indigestion. Kean's finger taught him an important lesson: It taught him not to swallow the bone.

The world widened. The land unfurled, from Parsippany to Bridgewater to Allentown, and all along the way Bit found treasures to steal. He snatched sleeping hens from their coops. He gathered all the eggs he could carry in his arms. He drank them raw, golden and soupy in their brown shells. He stole the apples from trees, bushels of carrots and potatoes from root cellars, loaves of bread and jars of jam from unguarded kitchens. At sunrise, he crouched in the shadows of a barn and waited for the farmer to finish the morning milking, and when the farmer squeezed the last drops from the cow's teats, he yowled like a goat and huffed like a lion and neighed and whinnied and sometimes cried, the false tears of a small, hungry, clever boy, until the farmer stepped outside to see: What strange animal could produce such cries? Stealthy Bit, who slunk past and guzzled warm milk from the pail. Stealthy Bit, who took the pail with him as he ran away laughing, and the farmer shook his empty fists and yelled his empty curses at the cockcrow. Bit started out naked. He liked running naked. He liked the soft dirt beneath his feet, the sunlight on his back as he dozed, the glaze of moonlight on his chest. Brigid had dressed him in clothes previously worn by Dugan, Patrick, Cormac, and finally Kean. They came to him threadbare. The trousers had holes in the knees and scratchy waistbands. The shirts had stains down their fronts, stew drips and grease smears from sloppy Patrick, splotches of dirt pies and mud castles added by filthy Kean. Even after Kean split the seams and cast the clothes aside, they did not belong to Bit. The rags belonged to Brigid, as she made sure to remind him.

Bit might have stayed naked, if nakedness had made it easier to steal pie. He smelled the pie a mile away. He followed the apple-butter breeze to a big house. He stuck his head through the open window. Seeing no one, he invited himself inside. Hand pies cooled on a kitchen table. Bit tore a length of crust. He ate it. He peeled the top crust back and inhaled the apple steam. Then he looked up and saw a woman standing in the doorway, her eyes wide.

"He's naked!" the woman shrieked.

Bit had not detected the smell of her, beneath the overpowering surge of pie, but he could smell her now. She had a blood smell, iron and salt. She had a purplish black swell beneath her eye, and a plump eyelid swollen shut.

"He's naked!" she shrieked again, and Bit could smell her fear, not of him, but of something else. She wrapped her arms tight across her chest. Her hands shook. Bit heard heavy feet pound across a wood floor. He smelled metal, oil, whiskey. He grabbed a glob of apple, shoved it into his mouth, and leapt out of the window. He ran from the house. He heard a hard fist sound. He heard a woman's cry. He swallowed the apple in his mouth. He scorned the naked skin of his human form. So obvious, so conspicuous he was, in this coat of skin. So shiny and pale and pink. So pocketless.

If he'd had pockets, he could have stuffed them full with pie.

He stole himself a fine set of clothes. He stole a rich boy's britches, sewn with silky pockets in the front and the back. He stole an ivory shirt embroidered with tiny crosses. It was God's will, Bit told himself, that he should have this excellent shirt. The Lord giveth and the Lord taketh away, and when the Lord taketh, a boy needed to taketh back for himself. He carried his saved coins in the front right pocket of his new pants. *Why giveth the coins,* Bit thought, *when people leave loaves cooling on their windowsills and clothes sun-drying outside, right there for a boy to take?*

Bit transformed in fine clothes. He became a nice young Christian lad, a trustworthy little fellow. He stole a Bible from a church pew in Palmyra and carried it through the streets of Harrisburg, cradled like the Christ child in his arms, and the good people of Harrisburg nodded and smiled when they saw him, and one shopkeep even asked Bit if he would like a stick of candy.

"Where's your ma and pa, young sir?" the shopkeep asked. He took the lid off the candy jar. The peppermint sugar smell gusted out. Bit's head spun. He felt dizzy with hunger.

"They're . . . I don't know," Bit fumbled to say. "Can I have the candy now?"

"You're awful small to be out wandering, 'thout knowing where your parents be. Maybe we oughts to take you down to the constable and sees if we can find them."

Bit's inner eye saw his mother as she choked on the gush of her own blood, her fat limbs flopping, her jellied eyes wide and terrified by the truth of her smallest boy. Bit's inner voice said *run*. He growled, an involuntary primal growl that gathered in his wolf's belly and pounced from his boy's mouth. He threw the Bible at the shopkeep's head. The Lord giveth. The boy taketh away. Bit took away a handful of candy sticks. He sprinted away with a candy stick in his mouth, the rest in his pocket. He could hear the shopkeep behind him, yelling. He could smell the man, a smell of oats and salted pork and confusion that a man could be good and God-fearing and generous, that a man could offer aid to a boy in need and be repaid in turn by thievery. The Lord giveth and the Lord taketh away, and the Lord's justice was mysterious, if any justice existed at all.

In the next town, Bit sniffed his way to candy. He followed the smell to a store full of smells: flour, barley, molasses, flax and rye, cotton and cake. Jars of candy sticks in different colors sat on a shelf, just beyond a boy's reach, and a man with a polished mustache stood behind a counter in front of them. At the counter, Bit saw another boy, not much older than himself.

"My ma's taken ill," Bit heard the boy say. "She sent me to get some laudanum tonic." The boy traded a coin for a bottle of tonic and a candy stick. Bit stole the boy's story, and a pot of butter on his way out.

He tried the story out in the next town. His nose found a tavern with a good cook. He climbed up onto a counter seat and ordered a potpie.

"My ma's taken ill." Bit blinked back tears from his deceptive sad eyes. He embellished his stolen story. "She can't get out of bed." That part was true. Bit's ma would never get herself out of bed again. "So my pa sent me to go fetch my uncle in Newburg. But I've been walking all day, I'm awful tired." He let a calculated tear leak out. "And I'm scared I'll never see my ma again."

"Oh, you poor lad!"

Bit got his potpie for free, and a slab of buttered corn bread for the road. He traveled on, in the opposite direction of Newburg, feeling pleased with himself, with his fine clothes and his full belly and his pocket full of coins. He felt free and strong, so free and strong that he felt as if his strength might just burst out of him.

And it did.

The moon rounded to its biggest, brightest self. Bit's skin tingled from the growth of fur. His fingers arced into claws. His eyes yellowed and his teeth grew and sharpened. His pants split at the seams. The buttons shot off his lovely, embroidered shirt.

He had not counted the days. He did not know his counting past ten. He had felt, in the halcyon month of roaming, the merging of boy and beast, as if the beast in its prior revolutions had emerged only because the boy had lived as a captive scrubber of laundry and bearer of piss pots, himself the figurative pot for Dugan Molly Patrick Bree Cormac Kean to piss their hatreds, for Brigid to expel the miseries of her life. He had not thought the unfettered beast would return, now that Brigid was gone and the pissing days of Dugan Molly Patrick Bree Cormac and possibly Kean had ended, now that he could feel his beast self in him always.

And yet it did.

The moon grew full, and the boy became the wolf.

He tore off the remains of his tattered clothes with his claws and teeth. He lamented the loss of such fine clothes, and yet he felt glad to be free of them. He gathered his sack of coins, holding it gently in his jaw, like a mother cat carrying her kitten by the scruff of its neck. He ran through the forest, swift on his strong legs. The moon filled the sky, and Bit's mind filled with the thoughts of a wolf, less thought than sensation. He became his paws bounding across the earth. He became the dirt, the rocks, the decaying leaves, the lichen and moss. He became the web of trees, the spider's glistening thread spun between them. He became the spark of a firefly, the swoop of a bat, the flap of an owl's feathered wings. The night hunters emerged, and Bit the Wolf was among them.

He could smell the humans, and the scent of their blood made him hungry. And yet, he recalled Brigid's blood, how her blood had tasted of soap, of milk gone sour, of curdled rot from the infected tooth in the back of her mouth, of all her lonely nights, and the non-lonely nights when Bit's pa rolled atop her and she squeezed her legs tight shut and begged *not another please I can't take another* and *how will I feed it* until Bit's pa pried her open and shoved himself inside and she lay limp and prayed to the Lord, sinfully, that he not give her another child.

The Lord granted her prayers. The Lord giveth, the Lord taketh away.

The taste of humans was complicated. Less so with the smaller ones, but still. Bit had tasted petty hatreds and little wretched jealousies when he lapped the blood of Dugan Molly Patrick Bree Cormac Kean. He had tasted the extra gristle Patrick had spooned from Cormac's stew, the curses Dugan spit at the dark-skinned girls he passed on his way to school, the opprobrium heaped by Molly on her sister's frizzy hair and bony stature because she knew that Bree was the fairer of the two. Bit the Wolf wanted the spurt of clean blood, human blood, without the complicating sorrows and vulgarities. Bit the Boy had misgivings about dining on the purely innocent. He doubted he could find them, for one, and if he did, he imagined himself transfixed, staring at the rarefied innocent flower as it ran from the safety of his slack jaws.

Instead, Bit the Wolf hunted rabbits and fawns. He crept up on them and pounced unseen, so that their fluttering small hearts would not taint their unpolluted blood with the flavor of fear. He hunted more than he could eat and ate until his belly felt sick with warm blood. He ran and hunted and killed and ate until the moon set and the sun snuck up on the horizon and his wolf body reverted into its less lustrous boy form.

Bit the Boy was covered in dried blood and dirt, and completely naked. He had only his sack of coins and his painfully full belly. The wolf had a larger belly, and Bit's smaller one could not fit all the meat the wolf had devoured. Up it came, the chunks of rabbit and spotted deer, hot flesh with the matted fur still attached.

Bit the Boy had a lot to learn about werewolves.

He started to cry. He lay down on the forest floor and coiled himself into a small seed. In that moment, the full-bellied wolf slept in the den of Bit's deepest self, and Bit was just a small boy, five or six or seven, though he didn't know how many, and he had not ever celebrated his birthday. Brigid counted Bit's trips around the moon, not his trips around the sun. *'Tain't nothin' to celebrate, the birth of you,* she had said. Had he been born this way? Had he come into the world with claws? Had his mother offered her milky teat, only for him to snap down with his sharp teeth? He had been Bit for every day that he could remember, Bit the Boy, Bit the Wolf.

He lay and cried through the morning. Then he got up and

wiped the tears from his blood-smeared cheeks. His skin felt stiff, his mouth dry. He walked until he came across a creek. He bathed himself. He watched the red wash away, until the cold water ran clear, and he could see himself in its reflection: his blazing eyes, his sturdy jaw, his lips curled into a faint smile.

He began again.

He walked through the forest by day. When he felt sleepy, he stopped to doze. He didn't need to stop for long. He could feel the weighty moon, bright and big, the golden coin of the sky. Even in the daylight, it made him strong. He wandered through the towns by night. He scoped the largest houses, the ones built of brick and stone, with broad front porches and glass windows, and oil lamps that burned late into the night. It was summer, and the humans slept with their windows open, allowing entry of the cool night air and the small crafty boy. Bit found himself a new set of clothes even nicer than the first. He found stores of dried salted meats, bowls of gathered wild strawberries, butter cookies and crumbly biscuits and jars of raspberry preserves. He grew bolder, stealthier. He crept into carpeted bedrooms where humans slumbered in posted beds. He could hear their hearts beat. He could detect the quiet of their blood, which would quicken if rousted by the sound of the wood floor creaking beneath a boy's foot or the squeak of a dresser drawer. Sometimes they woke, and Bit crouched low, still and silent as a rock, until they fell back to sleep. Bit searched their pockets and wardrobes. He found coins and trinkets, rings made of real gold, a ticking watch on a silver chain, a pendant set with glittering jewels, sapphires and rubies. Bit stole away with the treasures. He played the role of pirate, of king and captain, of fire-snorting dragon, hoarder of gold and gems.

He stole a piece of cloth, cut and sewn into the shape of a wolf, its legs and belly and snout stuffed full with cotton. He stole the stuffed wolf from the bed of a sleeping boy, a boy the same size as Bit. "This should be mine," he whispered to the slumbering boy, as he threaded the wolf between the boy's arms. "Mine. I'm the wolf." He held the stuffed wolf in his own arms. He stared into its black embroidered eyes. He saw through the wolf's eyes: the racing forest, the gleaming moon, the stalk and the hunt. His greatest treasure. He hugged the stuffed wolf to his chest. The sleeping boy stirred. Bit slunk away, but then he felt bad. The boy smelled as innocent as a boy could smell, and how could any boy not love a soft wolf like this? Bit would not give the wolf back. Instead, he slid a golden ring set with a trio of diamonds onto the boy's finger, and then he climbed out the boy's window and ran away.

After his nighttime raids, Bit returned to the forest. He ran through creek beds and shallow rivers, to mask his scent. He ran until he had gone far enough that he couldn't smell the pale humans any longer, to where the trees grew thick and the land treacherous, where the pale humans would not think to look for a boy dressed up like a tiny lord. *The Lord giveth*, Bit thought, as he climbed high up in the tree branches and took his treasures out of his pocket. *The Lord giveth* and Bit did the taking part himself. What else could a boy do, alone in the cruel world? *The Lord giveth*, Bit thought, as he examined his treasures, as he turned the coins over between his ringed fingers, as he held his toy wolf tight against his chest.

He taught himself to count: He counted by ten, once, twice, and almost a third time. At dusk, when he felt the moon coming for him, he stripped himself bare and hid his clothes and his treasures high up in a tree. And when he changed, this time, he hunted himself a fat doe and ate only the best parts of her.

Summer turned to fall, and Bit continued roaming and plundering. He found himself a pair of shoes, which he hated because he liked to feel the dirt between his toes, but the boy's toes turned cold and stiff on brisk nights. He found himself a coat, which he hated because he liked to feel the breeze on his skin, but the boy's skin grew goose bumps from the damp chill. Even in his coat and shoes, the boy shivered, because he was just a bit of a boy, a small slip who should have died of consumption as a babe. On dismal days, Bit wandered along the mud streets of provincial towns and stared at the pillars of chimney smoke that twisted skyward, merging into the expanse of gray, and he wondered at the lives of the boys who lived inside, who warmed their fingers and toes by the fire and ate hot food cooked just for them. Boys who did not roam and plunder, because they were fed and loved. *The Lord giveth.* Bit could take and take, but some things could only be given.

SHANE LaSALLE

WHEREIN SHANE LaSALLE RETURNS TO WORK

San Francisco—Now

SHANE LaSALLE CIRCLED the building. He stopped near the entrance. He peered through the glass doors into the lobby. The lobby looked like he remembered, but an odd smell emanated through the glass, an ozone smell, like the scent of rain just over the horizon.

"Hey, dude, could you like—"

"What?" Shane startled.

"Move. You're blocking the door. Some of us have to get to work."

"Oh, sorry," Shane mumbled. He stepped aside.

Mr. Had To Get To Work pushed past him, and when he opened the door, the odd smell gusted out. The ozone had an undertone of pine, eucalyptus, salty blood. Shane's mind flashed back, to the charred forest of Lake Orange, to the panic he had felt when the wolf mounted him, the taste of his own hot blood in his throat, and then the frenzy of the day after, when he had run barefoot through the forest, his senses overwhelmed, his nose inflamed by the scent of a rabbit, a raccoon, a deer, his eyes hawkish, the moon pulsing above him, the sky swirling with stars. For a moment, he was there again, his raw feet gripping the earth, his heart pounding. He smelled bacon. He smelled blood. He smelled Duane. Then he flashed back. He felt his hands shake, but when he looked down at them, they held steady. From the tips of his fingers, he could almost see a phantom curl of claws.

Shane LaSalle had to get to work. He loved work, and he dreaded it. He wanted to rip it apart with his teeth, to swallow it whole. He wanted to stalk away, to hide in the cold cave of middle America where the venture capitalists would never find him. What would the partners say when they saw him? They had flown him across the country and abandoned him there. They had not called the cops or reported him missing. They had not left concerned voicemails. He had returned to San Francisco, to a dark apartment, had stood at his panoramic window, and stared out at all the little lights, at the skeleton of the skyscraper that rose up like a zombie from the dead to consume his view, and felt acutely the emptiness below and around him. He had turned on his computer, checked his accounts, confirmed the absence of concern, from the partners or from anyone (other than his Stone Age mother, who sent him *Dear Shane* letters by *email* and *emailed* to admonish him for not pen-paling her back). He set aside his mother's email and posted a quick status update: *Just took a fabulous weekend trip to Lake Orange. Great food, beautiful scenery, top spot for water sports. Home now, taking a few much deserved days of R&R.* He ordered a large pizza with extra sausage and pepperoni. He ate the whole of it in one sitting. His stomach wrenched, demanding more. He ordered a second pizza, from an inferior pizza parlor, so that none of his preferred pizza parlor's employees would know what a pig he had been. He fretted over his gluttony, and the swell of his physique. Photoshop could only do so much.

His stomach revolted, and he found himself standing in the open fridge spooning globs of peanut butter into his mouth. The smell of the peanut butter made his head spin. He finished the jar of peanut butter. He checked his accounts. His mother had sent another email: *Dear Shane, I'm glad you are getting some rest and relaxation. I wish, though, that you had told me you were going to Lake Orange! I would have had you . . .* He couldn't finish reading. He could smell his mother from more than two thousand miles away: her lilac perfume imported from a boutique on the Champs-Élysées, the steel-cut oatmeal she ate for breakfast, the chemical musk of her dry-cleaned cashmere sweaters, the mild sweet scent of cranberry almond salad from her lunch out with the friend whose daughter she claimed would be perfect, just perfect, for Shane. He felt sick and alone. He had to get back to work.

For two days after he'd returned to the city, Shane LaSalle hid in his apartment and ate enough takeout to feed an army of Shane LaSalles. He did not call the office of Barrington Equity, and the office did not call him. He ate a box of donuts and suffered no heartburn. He ate a dozen egg rolls. In a matter of minutes, he felt hungry again. He examined himself in the mirror. He took a photo of himself topless, and carefully compared it to the nonaugmented topless photo he had taken of himself the month before. If anything, he looked slimmer.

Then, on his third day back, his appetite waned. He felt less sick, less alone, more Shane LaSalle-ish. He ordered himself a new phone. He shaved his face and waxed his chest. The hair on both seemed thicker, more tenacious than he remembered it. He wrote to his mother. He called his office.

"You've reached the offices of Barrington Equity." A sultry woman's voice, the voice of a twilight phone-sex operator. "How may I direct your call?"

"Um, yeah, this is, um, Shane LaSalle—"

"Oh, Mr. LaSalle, my apologies, I should have recognized your voice. How was your trip?"

"Uh . . . it was . . . fine."

"Good. The other partners said you were taking a few days off, but that you'd return to work tomorrow. Unless you weren't feeling up to it. Can we expect you in tomorrow, Mr. LaSalle?"

"Yes," Shane heard himself say, in a voice that sounded far more confident than he felt.

"Great. The other partners said to tell you they'd have all the paperwork ready. Congratulations, Mr. LaSalle."

His brain seized the *congratulations* and frolicked through the speculative meadow of professional success. The ticker on his imagined post ticked out *likes* and *loves* into the hundreds. His mother bragged to all her friends, until the news of his spectacular success resounded through the whole of Bloomfield Hills.

My son Shane just made partner!

My son Shane just bought a new boat!

Oh, our trip to Paris was fantastic. Shane sent us there as an anniversary gift!

Then Shane imagined the look on Duane Beckman's face. *We did it, buddy!* Duane floated over a sea of soft grass and wildflowers. He was the heart of the meadow. He was gilded in sunlight, his hair luminous, his lips upturned into a smile, his twee canines poking out, his eyes glistening with tears of elation. *We did it, buddy! We made it!* Except that Shane had an awful feeling that Duane hadn't made it. Elated Duane morphed into Decaying Duane. His thick hair fell out. His lips shriveled. His eyes looked cold and dead. A worm wriggled out of his tear duct, down his face, across his gray snaggletooth, and Duane's black tongue slugged out and licked the worm up.

All that night, Shane dreamed feverish Duane dreams. Duane slipped in between the dead and the living. His skin sloughed away to reveal an under-skin of rot. Shane slipped in between sleep and restless twitchy tossing. He sweated through his sheets. His alarm sounded at six a.m. He ran five miles on the treadmill in the building gym. He ran with his eyes closed. He tried to conjure the forest, the feeling of earth beneath his feet, the smell of pine and charred wood and sky, the vision of Duane standing on the boathouse deck at twilight, gazing out over the lake, his features like velvet in the near-dark. But then Shane's hawk eyes saw the sallow paste of dead skin, the nose half rotted off, the fingers turned to bones. He smelled decomposing flesh, dried blood. He smelled Windex and rubber. He opened his eyes and looked at himself in the mirror, handsome running Shane with his rugged, photographable jawline.

What happened to Duane? he asked his mirror-self. His mirror-self smiled wickedly back.

He kept thinking about Duane as he ate an entire box of frosted shredded wheat, as he guzzled down a pot of coffee, as he brushed his gorgeous and professionally bleached teeth, as he peeled the protective plastic from his dry-cleaned suit and shirt, and dressed, and rode a cab downtown because the thought of riding the bus made his stomach sick. All those smells. He felt insane, in the back seat of the cab, with all those smells outside, creeping in through the window. He felt hungry. He imagined plunging forward into the front seat and taking a big, meaty bite of cabdriver arm. He felt sickened by the thought, sickened by the unwashed smell of the cabdriver's shirt, sickened by the ambiguity of Duane. *We did it, buddy!* He caught a whiff of Duane-smell as the cab pulled up in front of his office building. He paced outside the building. He gathered strength to go inside. He feared that he wouldn't find Duane inside. He feared that he would.

The lobby door opened again. A buttery, flaky smell wafted out. Shane breathed deeply as he stepped in.

"Good morning, Mr. LaSalle," the security guard at the front desk greeted him.

"Good morning," Shane replied.

How did the guard know his name? He did not recall any security guard ever greeting him by name before. He pressed the elevator call button. He rode the elevator up. The doors opened at the thirty-second floor. The buttery, flaky smell enveloped him, but underneath it, Shane detected the odd ozone smell he had noticed before, stronger now, balanced by another smell, a primal smell, a smell that reminded him of the forest along the edge of Lake Orange.

"Good morning, Mr. LaSalle," the receptionist said. She smiled broadly, but Shane noticed a slight quiver to her jaw.

"Good morning," Shane said. His voice echoed against the stark marble surfaces of the Barrington Equity reception area. The voice belonged to him, and yet it sounded like it had come from somewhere else.

"Your breakfast just arrived, Mr. LaSalle."

"My breakfast?" Shane recalled the box of cereal he had just consumed.

"I had it brought straight to your office."

"Okay."

"Unless, if you prefer I send it somewhere else, or if you like to carry it in yourself, I—"

"No, no that's fine. Thanks."

"Thank you, Mr. LaSalle."

"Okay."

"If you need anything else at all, Mr. LaSalle, anything, you can let me know."

"Okay."

"Here, let me get that door for you." The receptionist trotted over to the door in her three-inch pointy heels. She pulled the door open for Shane. She averted her eyes as he walked past. Shane glanced down at her hands. They were shaking.

Shane headed toward his office. He passed Duane Beckman's office on his way. Duane's door was shut. He went into his own office, where he found a tray of breakfast waiting on his desk: a carafe of coffee with a warmed mug, a plate of assorted pastries, bacon, sausage, and ham, and pulpy orange juice squeezed fresh. He sat down at his desk. He ate a flaky, buttery croissant with a slab of chocolate in its center. He ate a second croissant, flecked with almond shards and cinnamon icing. He ate the bacon. He started on the sausage, and then he heard the sound of leather shoes on plush carpet.

"LaSalle!" Clifton James appeared in the doorway. "You're back!"

"I'm back," Shane repeated, through a mouthful of sausage.

"I knew you'd make it. I've had my eye on you, LaSalle."

"Hey, is that LaSalle?" Stanley Rollins called from the hallway.

"It is indeed," said Clifton James.

"Great. That's fantastic. How's the sausage, LaSalle?" Stanley Rollins poked his fat head through the door.

"It's great."

"Too well-done, if you ask me, but we can't really order it raw, now can we? Ha, ha, no! I took the liberty of having my secretary order breakfast for you. I hope it's enough!"

"Enough?" Clifton James shook his head. "It's a good thing Rollins isn't your mentor, LaSalle. All he'd teach you is how to eat like a horse."

"Or how to eat a horse," Rollins added.

"Disgusting."

"Hey, the world is my buffet." Rollins winked. "I'll have my secretary stop by once you're all settled in, LaSalle. She'll get your meal plan all set up."

"So, if you're finished gorging—" James said, derisively, after Rollins had gone.

"I'm done." Shane eyed the slabs of ham.

"Good. You won't last, LaSalle, if you can't exercise some self-control. Come on, then. Dick's got all the paperwork waiting in his office."

They walked together to Dick Barrington's corner office.

"Shane LaSalle," Dick Barrington said, as he stood up to greet them. "Welcome."

He smiled warmly. He reached for Shane's hand, and as he shook it, Shane felt as if Dick Barrington, managing partner, had just invited him to join the most exclusive of clubs. He also felt something sharp, something clawlike, digging into his wrist.

"Thank you, sir."

"Call me Dick. You're one of us now."

"Thank you. It's an honor."

"Yes, well . . ." Dick Barrington released Shane's hand. "You surprised us all, LaSalle. Except Clifton here."

"What did I say?" Clifton James exclaimed. "I said, 'That LaSalle, he's got real potential.'"

"You did. Clifton here was behind you all the way. But you've still got to show us that we bet on the right wolf, so to speak."

Dick Barrington smiled. Shane felt a welling fear in the pit of his stomach. He felt his hackles rise. For a moment, he was back in Lake Orange, lying on the forest floor, staring up at the swollen moon as the jaws of a wolf closed around him.

"You'll do fine, Shane," Clifton James said, reassuringly. "It's just a matter of pulling your weight. Finding the right investments. Getting the deals done."

"Of course," Dick Barrington said, in a voice that sounded almost like a growl.

"You did," Shane said, retreating from his fear. "You made the right bet. I'll make sure of it."

"Good. Good boy. Now, I've got the paperwork ready right here." Dick Barrington produced a leather folder from his desk drawer. He handed the folder, heavy with the weight of the partnership paperwork, to Shane. "All ready for you to sign.... Unless you'd like your lawyer to take a look. Though, naturally, that would delay everything, but if you'd prefer—"

"No," Shane said, fearful of the delay that would cause Dick Barrington to change his mind. "I think I can manage."

"It's fairly standard," Clifton James said, as Shane skimmed through the pages. "Just sign right there, at the end."

Dick Barrington produced a pen. Shane signed his name to the last page. From somewhere across the office, he heard a rattling, wicked laughter.

"There we are," Barrington said, as he took the pen and the paperwork from Shane's hands. "Barrington Equity's newest partner. Welcome aboard, Shane."

So what, then, is the werewolf? There are no conclusory scientific findings regarding the causes and effects of lycanthropy. This is due, in part, to a dearth of physical evidence. There are scant reports of modern werewolves attacking humans. They are thought, generally, to hunt animals, principally deer, bison, rabbits, and other smaller mammals. There is no database of werewolf DNA. Werewolf bites are generally attributed to common wolves, coyotes, or other "unidentified animals." Investigators, presuming no human involvement, do not scrutinize the scene of a werewolf crime for evidence. Even if more evidence were available, the study of lycanthropy is typically viewed as pseudoscience, in the same camp as telepathy and astrology. Thus, the field lacks both serious scientists and research funding.

Historically, as we will explore in the following chapters, the werewolf was viewed as a mystical creature, its powers resulting from magic, witchcraft, or demonic possession. As the intrepid monster hunter George Corcoran McCloud wrote, in his article describing monsters of the mid-Atlantic region:

> The Were-Wolf is a devilish form, occurring when, after carnal relations with an unchaste woman, a Man's body becomes possessed. Such an impure coupling is the principal cause of many disorders and ailments, lycanthropy

being the most devious among them. The possessing demon, in the case of the Were-Wolf, is the Mephistophelian moon spirit. The woman, as descendent of Eve, is inherently corrupt and beholden to the moon's cycles. Thus, the woman's flesh often serves as a repository for demons known to inflict lycanthropy. (George Corcoran McCloud, "The Were-Wolf Curse," The American Scientician [1873]: 18–19)

Such outdated misogynistic theories have been widely rejected by modern scholars of lycanthropy, although they remain pervasive among certain fringe sectors, as discussed in chapter 14. The prevailing view is that lycanthropy is pathogenic, resulting from a microbe that is transmitted through blood.

Marcus Flick, American Myths and Monsters: The Werewolf, 2nd ed. (Denver: Birdhouse Press, 2022), 7

SOME HISTORY OF THE FAMILY BUSINESS

Kernville, Ohio–Now

SHANE LaSALLE POSTED a selfie of Shane LaSalle against the backdrop of the company jet.

He typed: *Barrington Equity knows how to travel in style.*

Then he deleted it and wrote: *Check out my new ride!*

He deleted that, too. The picture spoke for itself. Shane LaSalle had ascended to the lofty realm of projected nonchalance about travel on the company's private jet, although, admittedly, he felt like a child who woke up early on Easter morning and gobbled a pound of jelly beans and a solid milk chocolate bunny before any parent could stop him. He felt giddy, but also guilty that Duane Beckman would not relax in the leather flight chair and enjoy a cruising-altitude glass of Pinot with cheese plate and caviar . . . because where had Duane Beckman gone off to?

"Duane? He said he'd decided to take a few weeks of vacation," Clifton James assured Shane. He sipped Perrier. He reclined in his chair. He looked unconcerned. The petty world unfolded beneath him at six hundred miles per hour.

"Did he say where he was going?" Shane asked.

"Gosh, I don't recall."

"Well, did he—"

"You know, LaSalle, sometimes it's best not to ask about a person's private business. I mean, I haven't asked you why you wandered away from the party at the boathouse. We went out looking for you, you know?"

The senior partner grinned. He had the endearing grin of an earnest lad who just wanted to make an honest dollar mowing your lawn or washing your car. He had a grin that made you trust him.

"You did?"

"We absolutely did, after I called your phone and you didn't answer. We all went out looking for you. Even Duane. But then Duane said you'd been tired, so we just figured that you had gone and gotten yourself a nice hotel room and gone to bed. And isn't that just what happened?"

"Yes," Shane lied. He recalled waking the next morning, on the ground in the forest, uncertain as to whether he had slept, uncertain whether he had dreamed the crushing paw of the wolf on his chest, its needled mouth opening around him. He recalled Duane's parting word: *Run!*

"So did Duane . . . or will he, I mean, make partner?"

"LaSalle, I hate to break it to you"—Clifton James sighed—"because I know he's your buddy and you were rooting for him to succeed. That's admirable, LaSalle. Admirable. Especially in the cutthroat world of finance. But Duane Beckman just isn't partnership material."

"He's not? But what about, on the way to Lake Orange, Dick said . . . Didn't he say . . ."

"That's what I like about you, LaSalle. You're so enthusiastic. Always able to see the best of things. That's why I wanted you to train with me. But no. Dick didn't say anything about Duane making partner. We only invited him along in the first place because he had worked so dang hard, and every now and then we like to reward an associate's labor with a bit of celebration. But, the truth is, Duane Beckman doesn't have it in him to make the cut. Not like you, LaSalle."

The Barrington Equity private jet landed in an airfield just outside the smallish town of Kernville, Ohio. A black town car waited on the tarmac.

"I told my secretary not to arrange a car," Clifton James said to Shane. "I always tell her not to arrange the car. But Dick always tells her to send one anyway. Because, he says, why would I ride in a public taxi like some sort of plebeian? You ride in a cab and you come away smelling like pleb, he says." Clifton James strode up to the driver. "Excuse me, sir, but would you mind calling a taxi for us?"

"Uh—"

"You'll be paid, don't worry. Plus here's a little extra for the trouble." Clifton palmed a fifty to the driver.

"Sure, whatever."

"Wait, why are we not taking the car?" Shane asked. "It's right here."

"Ah, LaSalle, LaSalle. You've got so much to learn. What do you think when you see a car like that?" Clifton James extended his arm toward the town car dramatically.

"I think, um . . ."

"You think, 'Look at that rich fellow. That fellow who thinks he's more important than the rest of us, getting driven around in his fancy car.' Well, maybe you don't, but another sort of man would think just that."

"Right."

"So you see, the car creates a problem of perception. It's bad enough with the private jet, not that any of us could stand to fly commercial. But the jet doesn't go rolling through the streets for everyone to see. Perception matters, especially in a town like this in Ohio. We show up in a taxi, and what do we look like? Just a couple of regular guys."

Shane understood better what Clifton James meant, as they rode in the back seat of the cab through blue-collar Kernville, big-box-store country, home to the Kernville Cougars, state varsity football champions two years running, land of the Double Chick'n Bac'n Cheese on a French Fry Tower. The cab drove down Main Street, past the Cash Advance Advantage, the storefront Baptist church, the county police station, the greasy diner where you could order anything on the menu drenched in gravy. Shane could smell the gravy from inside the cab, with the windows up. He could smell the residual pleb, embedded in the fibers of the cab's back seat.

Clifton James made small talk with the driver.

"This town is lovely," he said, several times. "So quaint." He pointed at landmarks through the window. "Well, I'll say, has that bakery really been there since 1942? I bet they make a *killer* slice of apple pie!"

The cab pulled up in front of a three-story brick building with a hand-painted sign out front: ALVIN'S SPORTS AND SUPPLIES, EST. 1950.

The late Alvin's granddaughter met them at the entrance.

"Jeanie Glass," she said, introducing herself.

Jeanie Glass was petite, plainly dressed in black slacks and an ivory blouse, her brown hair pulled back in a loose ponytail. She reminded Shane of his mother's friends' daughters: Women who baked cookies for the annual holiday exchange in between conference calls. Women who knit sweaters and fostered dogs and juggled three cell phones. Women whose mothers conspired with Shane's mother to set up dinner dates whenever Shane visited home, dates that never seemed to work out. *But she's so nice,* Shane's mother would always say, and Shane would just nod and shrug, because, yes, she was so nice. And yet, the dates fizzled out.

"Ms. Glass," Clifton said. He shook her hand. "I'm Clifton James, and this is my partner, Shane LaSalle."

The *P*-word sent an electric spark up Shane's spine. *Partner partner partner.* His brain panted like an eager puppy. He should have felt elated. He had flown the private jet through the land of partnerdom. But an indeterminate fear tempered his elation. He could not pinpoint the source of his fear. Dick Barrington. Ron Carver. Duane Beckman. Tetanus. Needles. The awful laughter he heard in the office late at night. The sense that he was a fraud; that he would be found out; that his whole existence was confined to selfies, status updates, shares, likes; that behind the Photoshop magic of his headshot, the immaculate white of his teeth, the enviable windswept hair, the carefully cultivated repertoire of windsurfing, sailing, venture-capitalizing, there was nothing. Nothing adventurous. Nothing fearless. Nothing fun. Nothing but poseable Ken-doll Shane, flying the fake skies in his plastic plane toy, package-perfect with his Armani ascot, his hairless pecs, his painted smile concealing an even greater fear.

Wolves.

"Please, call me Jeanie."

"Nice to meet you," Shane said.

"It's a real pleasure," said Clifton James. "We're just honored you're willing to give us this opportunity."

"Well, you'd be the ones doing us a favor," Jeanie Glass said. "We're so pleased that you're willing to come all this way."

"This is the only way to do business," Clifton said. "We'll be making an investment in you if we decide to work together. But you'll be making an investment in us, too. You need to know for yourself that it's the right decision."

"Why don't you come on inside and I'll give you a tour," Jeanie said. She led them into a wood-paneled lobby, where framed photos of Alvin Sports and Supplies employees hung on the walls, beneath mounted hockey sticks and baseball bats and other vintage sporting paraphernalia.

"Just look at this place!" Clifton James exclaimed. He looked genuinely excited. "Look at all this history."

"My granddad, Alvin Glass, he hung a photo up here of every employee who worked for us for at least a year, which was most of them. He wanted this company to be a place where the employees would stick around, and most of them do, even now. We eventually ran out of room, when the company got bigger, so you'll see the more recent photos in the hallway to your left there."

"Is that him, in that photo right there?" Clifton James pointed to a black-and-white photo, larger than the rest, of a young man standing in front of a wood-framed shack, holding a hand-painted wood sign that read ALVIN'S SPORTS GRAND OPENING.

"That's him. He was twenty-seven, I think, when he first opened up shop. He bought a little piece of land down on Morris Avenue and built that building himself. My granddad, he was a sports fanatic. He loved all kinds of sports. Baseball, football, tennis, hockey. And back then, you could buy some of the basic supplies at Woolworth's, but there were a lot of sporting goods that you'd have to travel all the way to Columbus or Cleveland to pick up."

"What a fantastic story," Clifton James crooned. "From that little shack all the way to a major national chain with stores in, what is it, thirty states?"

"Thirty-two."

"I'm truly impressed, Jeanie," said Clifton.

"It was my dad, actually, who really helped the company grow. He took over in the eighties. We had several stores across the state by then, but my dad had a bigger vision. I wish he could have been here to meet you."

"We were sorry to hear that he's taken ill. How is he doing?"

"He's in good spirits, considering."

"Is his health—"

"He's officially retired, if that's what you're concerned about."

"Oh no, I was just wondering whether he was still involved

with running the company," Clifton James said. "Or whether he'd handed the reins over to you."

"Yes, although the board will need to approve any major decision...."

"I'm sorry, this must be so hard for you," Clifton James said.

Shane nodded. He had sensed her distrust, of the two California financiers in their fine suits, flying all the way to small-town Ohio to see firsthand the company her grandfather had built out of a small shack. He had smelled it, the scent of distrust, faintly metallic. But as Clifton James spoke, tailoring the cadence of his words to the Kernville ear, offering earnest praise of the generational accomplishments of which Alvin Glass's granddaughter would feel proud, Jeanie Glass relaxed, and Shane smelled it happen. He smelled cedar and honey and feather pillows. He glanced over at Clifton James, and Clifton James smiled and winked. *See how it's done*, his wink said, and Shane smiled back, because Clifton James had opened the door and invited him in. *Partner partner partner partner*. And if Clifton James had invited him in, it meant that he was a good boy, a real boy, a presence behind the gloss of his profile picture.

"It's fine," Jeanie Glass said. "He's had a good life, you know. And I understand, you have to ask all the hard questions."

"But since you mentioned it," Clifton James said, "how is your standing with the board?"

"Half of them have known me since I was a little girl," Jeanie said. "So ..."

Clifton James smiled wide, with a reassuring shrug. "Of course."

"I used to come here with my dad in the summer, as a kid. I'd set up a lemonade stand right out front." She motioned toward the entrance.

"And I'll bet everyone bought your lemonade."

Jeanie laughed. "Boss's daughter. So yeah. Some of the board members, I think sometimes they still see me as the little girl who sold them lemonade and Girl Scout cookies."

"See, that's why we're interested, Jeanie," Clifton James said. "Because of what type of company Alvin Sports and Supplies is. Because it's a family company. You know, ours is a family company too."

"Oh?"

"It is, in fact. Our managing partner, Dick Barrington, his grandfather established Barrington Equity in 1922. But even before that, Dick's great-great-granddad, I believe—but who can really keep track of all the *greats*—he was a fellow named Bartholomew Barrington, and he founded one of the first banks on the West Coast. I remember, years back, when I first met Dick Barrington, I remember asking him, 'Dick, how'd you get into this business?' And he said, 'Clifton, this business is in my blood.'"

"That's remarkable. So the Barringtons have been in the business since—"

"1842."

"1842." Jeanie nodded. "Wow."

"And maybe that's part of it, Jeanie," Clifton said. "But I've got a good feeling about this investment. I mean, we'll still need to see all the financials, but just being here ... it just feels, well ... Shane?"

"Oh yes," Shane agreed, as he pictured himself wearing the

same jaunty sweater and trapper hat that Alvin Glass wore in his grand opening photo. "This place is great."

"I'll need to run it past the other partners, of course—"

"Of course," Jeanie said.

"But I think," Clifton James said, "that Barrington Equity will be able to provide all the equity your company needs."

THE KERNVILLE STANDARD

Kernville, Ohio–Now

JEANIE GLASS BROUGHT the Kernville Standard breakfast platter to her dad in the hospital: three eggs scrambled, biscuits, bacon, and a short stack of cornmeal pancakes, plus a side of financial statements he'd asked to peruse.

"You shouldn't work," she told him. "You should rest."

He looked skinnier than before, there on the hospital bed, as if he had sprung a leak in the night, and the life had seeped out.

"Hand me that sweater."

"Here, let me—"

"No, I can put on my own damn sweater." Bill Glass pulled the sweater over his hospital gown. His hands shook. His arms got lost in the sleeves.

"Here—" She reached in and found his hand.

"It's these sleeves, the way they make them these days—"

"I know. They're all made in China."

"By *children*, Jeanie. Factories full of children, not much older than you—"

"Dad, I'm not a kid anymore."

Bill Glass looked at his daughter. His milky eyes came into focus. Jeanie could still see the spark behind them. "Yes," he said. "Yes. You're all grown-up, I know.... It's these drugs they've got me on, Jeanie. They got my brain all scrambled up."

"Speaking of scrambled, I brought you breakfast."

"The Kernville Standard?"

"What else?"

He smiled. He patted Jeanie's shoulder with his bony hand. "I can't eat the food in this place."

"It doesn't look appetizing."

"It's like the hospital has this special process for turning any food into rubber. The eggs are rubbery. The bacon is rubbery. They even rubberize the toast! Don't ask me how! But that"—he pointed at the plate she'd brought, still hot, the same breakfast he had ordered every Sunday for thirty years—"*that's* a breakfast."

Jeanie fed him three bites of egg, a slice of bacon, a sliver of biscuit.

"That's ... that's enough," he said.

"Just a few more bites."

"I'm full."

"You hardly ate."

"I'm full.... It's these drugs they've got me on. I'm all ... I'm all scrambled up."

Jeanie paused at hearing the phrase again. "I know, Dad. But you'll feel better soon."

"I won't."

"You will, and then—"

"You've got to look after the company, Jeanie. You're... you're... You've got the right mind for it. You've got all the training. And the right instincts. And you know a lot more than I did, when I took over for your granddad."

"Well... thanks." She smiled, but worry creased her brow.

"What is it, Jeanie?" her dad asked.

"Nothing. It's nothing."

"I know that look, Jeanie. What's on your mind?"

"It's just... the board wants us to bring on investors. They've got us talking with this private equity firm. Barrington Equity. And there are plenty of reasons why it's a good idea, you know..."

"But?"

"But I don't trust them." She bit her lip. "I tried to explain to the board. I've read some things about this firm that make me wary. But when I brought it up at the meeting, they just didn't seem receptive. They want us to make the deal. And Dale Prichard—"

"Dale Prichard is a chipmunk. Those fat cheeks. That squeaky voice."

"Well, yes, but he's also—"

"Do you want me to make some calls? I can call up Jack and Bernard. We've been golfing together since—"

"Dad, you can't call up everyone on the board. Because then what am I supposed to do when... when... when you're gone?"

Bill Glass nodded. "I see. You're right. But, at least let me call Dale Prichard and tell him where he can shove his acorns."

Jeanie Glass walked into a room full of men, plus one oversized chipmunk. The men all wore business suits. They all had skin in shades of pale, hair in stages of gray. They kept talking as Jeanie took her seat at the head of the table. They talked in the language of sports. Jeanie's dad had tried to teach her, but she never felt fluent. *How about them Reds?* Her non-sportsball accent was obvious.

"Gentlemen—"

"Oh, hiya, Jeanie."

"Got any Girl Scout cookies for us today?"

The men snickered.

"Let's get started," Jeanie said. "We need to discuss—"

"The Barrington Equity offer. I think we need to jump on this one, fellas. We need capital. It's exactly what we've been waiting for."

"I think we need to be cautious about this," Jeanie said. "I'm skeptical that—"

One of the men raised a finger and interrupted. "If we don't jump on it soon, they might find somewhere else to invest their money."

"I was skeptical at first, too," another man said. "You know, those big-city types. But they seemed really down-to-earth. I vote we go for it."

"I second that. Their terms seem quite generous," another agreed.

"Yes, at first glance," Jeanie said, "but we would be prudent to—"

"Now, Jeanie . . ."

And so forth. Until the meeting ended, with the gentlemen of the board believing they themselves had thought up the idea of prudence and caution, and would at least get to know the big city investors better before agreeing to terms. *Aren't you glad we're here to make sure you don't do anything hasty with your dad's company?* Jeanie left. She felt defeated, as if she had sprung a leak. All the confidence seeped out. Then she overheard them in the hallway, Mark Jack Bernard Daryl it didn't matter.

"—only there because of her dad."

"Well, soon enough . . ."

"She'll never last."

"It's too bad she's not better looking."

"Yeah, her face isn't half bad. But her tits—"

"What tits?"

"Ha, ha, ha."

"About the same as what she had back when she was a Girl Scout."

SHANE LaSALLE

MOONSICKNESS

San Francisco—Now

SHANE LaSALLE SLEPT through his alarm. He crawled from bed. He stared out the window at blue sky, radiant glass, a skyline of cranes. His mind felt fogged in. He stumbled into the bathroom. He examined his face in the mirror. He had shaved the night before, but already the stubble had returned. He took a hot, groggy shower. He shaved again. He nicked his chin with the razor. The smell of blood sent a shiver down his spine. He noticed a new grove of hairs on his back. He plucked them with his tweezers. He felt ashamed and exhausted. How could he go on, suffering this indignity of back hair?

He slumped into the kitchen. He pawed through the refrigerator, searching for foods requiring minimal effort: cold pizza, cartons of leftover noodles, cheese, peanut butter. He had devoured them all, over the past few days. He had come home beat from work, crashed on the couch, stared at the TV, gorged until he'd nearly cleared the fridge and stripped the cupboards. He found a half a carton of eggs. He cracked all six into a frying pan. He fried them in butter. The smell made him hungry and sick at the same time. He ate at the table, a slab of glass perched on an irregular stack of gold squares, placed beneath an industrial chandelier repurposed from the remains of a shuttered manufacturing plant, for which he had paid an exorbitant amount, an amount large enough that his mind had blotted out the digits. *It'll look stunning in the photos*, the interior designer had advised. She had picked the table, too, and the minimalist olive sofa with its minimalist airport terminal comfort, and the abstract paint-splotch canvases on the walls, the soup spill–patterned rug, the furry throw that felt initially soft but got itchier with increasing use. Everything in the room looked stunning in the photos. Shane looked stunning in the photos, posed at the table, adjacent to an untouched cheese plate, with the blur of city dusk behind him, arms outstretched, legs crossed, on the couch with a glass of wine in his hand, the gleam of orchestrated light caught perfectly by his eyes. The interior designer had pointed out the most photographable angles of Shane's new apartment, and she had given him a complimentary bottle of Fleishman's ManBalm in Malibu Beige. He had paid her an undisclosed sum and invested a weekend in taking, altering, and captioning photos of Shane LaSalle's Stunning Life in Shane LaSalle's Stunning Apartment and only now, as he sat at his hideously lovely table gulping buttery fried eggs dipped in maple syrup, did he realize he hated it all.

He shamefully licked the syrup from his plate. Then he drank the dregs of syrup from the bottle. He felt hungry and sick. He lumbered back into his bedroom. He caught a glimpse of himself in the mirror on the way. He looked terrible, despite his interior designer's assessment that no one could ever look terrible in such an apartment. His cheeks looked sunken. His eyelids drooped. The shadow of his beard had grown back over breakfast. He hurled himself into bed and burritoed himself in covers.

His telephone rang with the urgent chime of work.

"Hello?" Even his voice sounded sick.

"LaSalle," Clifton James said, "where are you?" Shane was too immersed in his own infirmity to notice the frail tenor of Clifton James's voice.

"At home. In bed. I'm sorry, I'll get ready right now and—"

"No need. You're not feeling well?"

"I feel awful."

"It'll pass in a day or two."

"I hope so, because—"

"It will. Don't worry, LaSalle. You'll feel better. And you'll get used to it."

"What do you—"

"All things come in cycles. You just stay in bed and rest it off."

"I, uh—"

"Get some sleep. Go easy on the carbs. Too many carbs'll just make it worse. Best to stick to meats, things of that sort. Rollins is calling in an order as we speak. You take care now. We'll see you soon."

Clifton James hung up. Shane nestled deeper beneath his covers. He felt wholly disoriented. Never in his tenure with Barrington Equity had he ever heard anyone suggest a course of staying in bed and resting it off, not even when Duane Beckman had the stomach flu. Duane Beckman had worked right through the worst of it, dashing off to the restroom every few minutes, sometimes not making it and retching into a garbage can, filling their shared office with the rank odor of his stomach acid. Shane had helped tie up the offending garbage bag and ferried it out to the dumpster. He had brought back a stack of paper towels soaked in cold water. He pressed one against Duane's burning forehead, and smoothed the sweat-soaked curls that framed Duane's anguished face, and then Ron Carver appeared in the doorway. His nostrils flared and his black eyes flickered with disdain as he growled, "This isn't a social hour. We don't pay you for this. We pay you to work."

Duane and Shane didn't speak for nearly a week after. They just sat at their desks and worked and worked, until the sour vomit smell had faded completely and Ron Carver went away on a business trip. They didn't speak until late at night, when there was no one left in the office but them, and Duane turned to Shane and said, "I'm sorry," and Shane gazed back into Duane's eyes and said, "I'm sorry too," and Shane felt something that he had blotted out of his mind, because the price of it was too high.

Shane closed his eyes. He beckoned sleep, but sleep snubbed him. *Maybe it's the back hair.* Shane's mind knit paranoid, unreasonable yarns. Back hair made him itchy and undeserving of rest. He couldn't sleep because of the hideous chandelier in his open-plan dining area. He couldn't sleep because the carb-tacular syrup that smothered his eggs had made *it* worse, and Clifton James knew what *it* was, somehow, because . . . because . . . because . . .

. . . *because of the horrible things he does . . .*

No, those lyrics didn't sound right. Clifton James was a good man. A trustworthy, reliable man. Clifton James had his back (except what if he saw the hair—what then?!). He couldn't let Clifton James down. Clifton James believed in him. Clifton James had been watching out for him, had been watching out for his career. . . .

But he didn't say *watching out*. He said *watching*.

Clifton James had been *watching watching watching* him.

Hadn't Clifton James recommended the interior designer who saddled Shane's apartment with the mandate of photographability? What if she had installed hidden cameras in the hateful furniture, to send a live feed of spectacular photos straight to Clifton James?

He had sensed observing eyes in the office. He had heard brutal laughter. He could hear it now, like the tinkle of a distant ice-cream truck roaming the back alleys of his mind, because, because, *because . . .*

He heard a knock on the door.

It's Duane!

Shane leapt from bed. He tripped over his own feet. He crashed on the hardwood floor. Pain spiked through his hands, up his arms. *No, you absolutely do not want carpets. Carpet will look terrible in your photos.* His teeth chomped down on his upper lip. He had a vision of Duane's darling snaggleteeth, caught mid-smile. He tasted blood.

Knock knock knock.

"Delivery for Shane LaSalle!"

Shane got up. He stumbled to the door. He peered through the peephole. His heart hoped for Duane Beckman, but his hope was more absurd than hidden cameras in a five-figure chandelier cobbled out of ten bucks' worth of scrap metal. He saw a nose-ringed, ear-gauged man with two paper bags from Harris' steak house.

Shane opened the door.

The delivery man produced a slip of paper and a pen. "Sign here."

Shane signed his name as directed. He felt as if he ought to read the fine print, but his hand still tingled from the pain of his fall, and who read the fine print anyhow?

The delivery man handed Shane the bags. The delivery man gave him a look. The look said, *Shit, you look terrible, even against the backdrop of your stunning apartment.* The look said, *Who the hell orders eight steak dinners hold the mashed potatoes at nine in the morning?*

The look said, *They're watching you.*

Shane shuddered. The delivery man was gone. Shane was left holding the bags. He stuck one in his fridge. He opened the other. He took out a disposable platter. Inside, he found a steak, cooked rare. He slit the steak with a knife. The inside looked pink, nearly raw, bloody. The sight made him sick, but the smell made him ravenous. He ripped into it. He felt the animal's juices in his throat, the animal's muscles in his stomach, the muffled cry of the animal's death in his bones. He finished the first steak and started another. His heart pounded. Tears tumbled from his eyes, down his face, and he didn't understand why. All he could think of was the taste of flesh, and the sensation of the earth beneath his feet as he ran through the charred forest of Lake Orange, and the way Duane Beckman's eyes glimmered in the moonlight.

Because because because something was horrifying and wrong. Ever since the wolf. Ever since he had seen the wolf and run into the forest and then . . . *But you knew, buddy,* Duane's voice said, inside Shane's head. *You* knew. *I was gonna buy a house for my mom.* Duane had such sharp teeth, such wolfish teeth. *Getting colder, buddy. You really think I'd bite you? Well, maybe if you'd asked.*

Shane spit out his last bite of steak. He was still hungry, but his stomach couldn't fit any more. He went into his bedroom, where he had left his phone. He called Duane. The phone went straight to voicemail. *You've reached the voicemail of Duane Beckman, senior associate with Barrington—* Shane hung up. He opened his browser and searched for Duane on the internet. He found nothing but a bland professional profile. He threw his phone on the floor. He climbed beneath the covers and hid his head, and in the darkness an idea blossomed.

Shane slumped onto the floor. He crawled to his phone, where his darling internet waited. He searched *Lake Orange newspaper.* He found a site for the *Lake Orange Gazette.*

There, on the front page, he found the article:

Hikers Find Body in First Bank of Lake Orange Forest
by Emma Barrett

Hikers Michael Bockus and Danz Landry, brother of Lake Orange resident Chaz Landry, stumbled on something unexpected yesterday during a twenty-mile hike around the First Bank of Lake Orange Forest. They found a dead body. Unlike the others that have been found in the area—all victims of the hostile swarms of killer bees that invaded the forest two years ago—the deceased did not appear to have suffered any stings. Rather, it appears he was bitten by some sort of large, vicious creature. Police estimate that the attack took place between ten and fifteen days earlier, based on the state of decomposition. The victim was a male, thought to be in his twenties or thirties. The victim's face and hands had been disfigured, and police have been unable to identify him. After the killer bee outbreak, local residents are concerned that this might be the beginning of another onslaught of wildlife attacks.

BIT

WHEREIN BIT FINDS A HOME

Pennsylvania—1822

ON A FROSTY morning in late October, when the pale sliver moon clung to the edge of the sky, Bit—feeling weak and dizzy, with three days since his last plunder, all the windows he tried shut and locked to keep out the chill—happened upon a log cabin. The cabin sat on the edge of a clearing, against a forest backdrop of waning fall. A spire of smoke rose from its chimney. Bit crouched in the brown grass. He tried to smell inside the cabin, but the cold made his nose drip and he could scarcely smell beyond the smoke and dying leaves. The cabin door opened and a woman stepped outside. She carried an axe. She walked around to the side of the house, where a pile of logs was stacked beside a tree stump. She set a log atop the stump and chopped it in half with her axe. She quartered the halves, then carried the cut logs back and forth to the small front porch of her cabin.

Bit stayed hidden in the grass. He crawled forward, as close as he could get without being seen. Close enough to smell her. He could smell the warm pulse of her blood. He could smell cloves and venison, woodsmoke, tea. He could smell her feather bed and the stack of letters she kept beside it and her loneliness. He wanted to crawl closer, right up beneath her, to press his small snout into the crook of her neck and breathe in the sweet intensity of her smells, but instead he lay and watched, the stealthy wolf in the grass.

He watched her arms as they chopped wood, her strong back, her frosted breath in the air. He watched her finish and go inside, and then he stayed and watched the smoke rise out of her chimney, and he thought and thought. His mind felt as weak as the fingernail moon. His thoughts trickled slowly and got lost in the cold. Then he saw a streak of motion in the grass, and he smelled the beating of an avian heart.

He came to her door with a wild turkey in his arms. Its body was still warm, but its head hung limp. He had broken its neck.

"Excuse me, ma'am," Bit recited, in his best devout voice. "My ma's taken ill. She can't get out of bed. So my pa sent me to go fetch my uncle in Newburg. He said to stick to the road and the Lord would see me there safe, but I've been walking all day, and I'm awful tired and cold and hungry." Bit squeezed a tear out of his eye. "Please, ma'am, can I come inside?"

The woman stared down at him. She looked neither disbelieving nor moved. Her heart beat steady.

"Newburg, you say?"

"Yes, ma'am."

"Newburg's fifty miles from here." The woman looked Bit in the eye, and then she looked down at the pendant that hung around his neck, a golden cross inlaid with tiny emeralds. "And your pa sent you all that way on foot?"

"My pa said . . . my pa said the Lord would see me there safe."

"Did he now? That's what they always say." She reached down and took the turkey from Bit's hands. "Well, come on inside, then. You can help pluck the feathers out."

The woman's name was Mary, like the virgin mother. Bit wanted to prove himself as a good boy, a boy beloved by God, whose goodness would see him safely to Newburg on foot. He pointed out what he knew of the Mother Mary, which was not much. Mary of the Log Cabin shook her head.

"Is that the story they're telling now?"

In the morning, Bit followed Mary of the Log Cabin through the invocation of chores. He gathered kindling. He swept the porch with a pine-needle broom. He tilled fallen leaves into the garden soil. His fingers remembered how to wring the wash water out of clothes and string them on the line to dry, how to scrub the black eyes from the face of a potato. He scrubbed and wrung and gazed up at Mary, searching for her blessing.

Mary nodded, simply, and said nothing.

She said, "Put the kindling by the hearth."

She said, "You can have some bread. There's butter in the cupboard."

She stared out the window, where the tree limbs bent in the breeze and the clouds scrolled their endless orison to the sky. She pressed her hand to her belly and Bit listened to her heart break and break again.

In the afternoon, Bit wandered through the forest. He gathered nuts and small sour berries. He shimmied up trees and swung from branches. He hunted small creatures, bits of creatures that he could catch in his hands and thrash until their hummingbird hearts thumped out. He ran on his bare feet and felt inside them the sturdy paws of the wolf.

He returned at dusk, bearing a rabbit, a goose, a squirrel, a trout he had speared with a sharpened tree branch, his hand slippery with blood and scales.

"Slit it," Mary said, handing him a knife.

"Pluck out its feathers," she said.

"Cut off its skin."

Bit cut the skin off with a knife and wondered about his own skin. If he peeled it off, would the wolf climb out?

He held the skinned animal to his mouth, remembering the raw taste of it, the way its juices leaked out. He saw Mary watch him, and he felt ashamed. He felt as hungry as a stray dog for the weight of her hand as it patted his head. *What a good boy*, he wanted her to proclaim.

She said nothing.

She said nothing of the rings Bit wore on his thumbs, a man's wide wedding band, a lady's circlet of silver and pearl, each big enough to straddle two fingers on Bit's small hands. She said nothing of Bit's watch and chain, of the coins that jingled in his pocket, of the emeralds on his brooch. She said nothing of his coat, which he rolled up at the sleeves, which had the initials *J. C. M.* embroidered onto the hidden inside pocket, where Bit stored his pyrite treasure. She saw Bit's toy wolf and said simply, "He needs a wash and a mend."

She stitched the wolf's leg, where the stuffing had begun to come out. She soaked and washed him gently, rubbing away his dirt with the tips of her fingers, and set him by the fire to dry. Then she said, "All right, what's his name then?"

And Bit felt magic bubble up inside, as the toy wolf became real.

Bit stared into the fire and thought. He ate rabbit stew, chunks of carrots and potatoes and meat simmered soft, and thought about who the wolf might be.

Not a Dugan. Not a Patrick Cormac Kean.

Not a Bit.

He curled by the fire and his eyes fluttered shut. He slept by the fire. He woke by the fire. The fire danced across his dreams, which were streaked with moon and forest and blood. Except now he felt a warmth behind him; arms that would catch him if he fell into the darkness; eyes that watched him but declined to judge.

He felt himself grow stronger.

The moon opened its bright eye and fixed it upon him.

He counted two hands plus five fingers. Six fingers. Seven. He sat by the fire and looked out through the window. The night was clear and cold.

"I'm going," he said to Mary.

"Well then," Mary said back.

He ran outside. He pinched his hand over his nose, so as not to smell her. He ran into the forest. His small body shook. He was just a boy. Just a boy with a toy wolf in his pocket, a real wolf in his soul. He ran until he lost all scent of her. He paced. He waited. He waited. He remembered: eight fingers, not seven. But he could not go back that night. He could not wake her, could not have her see inside him.

Bit shivered through the night, and in the morning the leafy earth was glazed with frost. He huddled in a spot of sun. He turned his pyrite over and over between his fingers. He smelled Mary of the Log Cabin in the cloth of his stuffed wolf. He shivered and waited for the sun to sink. He stripped off his clothes and stashed them up high in a tree, tied in a knot with his treasures.

The full moon ascended, and Bit became Wolf.

Wolf hunted and howled. Wolf gorged. Wolf smelled his Mother Mary from far, far away, and he ran toward her scent. He prowled the perimeter of her cabin. Inside him, the boy Bit shivered and prayed she would not come out.

The lights in the cabin turned off, and Wolf grew restless and returned to his hunting. He stole the life of a deer. He stole the life of a fox. He licked his bloody chops and howled to his Lord, the moon.

Then the night ended, and Wolf slunk away and the boy returned: vigorous, full, refreshed. He dressed himself in his fine clothes. He walked back toward the log cabin, catching himself a plump rabbit along the way.

Woodsmoke coiled from her chimney. He knocked on the door. She opened it. She smelled like molasses and hotcakes.

"I'm back," he said to Mary, offering the rabbit.

"Well then," Mary said back.

ALL THE PRETTY WIVES

San Francisco—Now

THE BOMB HAD obliterated Natasha before she even realized it
had hit:

*NOZEES did you hear this interview? BERTRAND MAILER
WTF??!!!!*

OMG who does this bitch think she is??????

You all realize she called us the lowest common denominator???

Natasha Porter is a jealous tasteless bitch

Just called Orion to complain. Everyone call! #NOZEES Unite!!!

No one insults our Nova! #NOZEES let's take this bitch down!!!

#NOZEES if you want to find this hateful bitch click link here. Let's all give her what she deserves. #NovaLove #SequinPop #NovaForGod

Natasha Porter WE ARE COMING FOR YOU

Six weeks had passed since Marie's death, and since the explosion of Nozee outrage. It had spread too far too fast for Natasha to hope to control the damage. The Nozees were relentless in their devotion to Nova Z'Rhae and their efforts to defend her. The sprawling hate-fire obliterated Natasha's blog, her book deal, her online life. The only blessing of her homeless state was that doxing didn't mean as much—she had no address that the Nozee horde could stake out, SWAT, or whatever people did nowadays—though at least a dozen hateful letters had been mailed to her parents' house.

Natasha tried to ignore the outrage in the weeks that followed. She thought about Marie, and Marie's mom, and the rent she could no longer afford. She thought about how she would fit everything she owned into her car and where she would park it each night. She toggled between Lee Curtis's house and her boring job. She poured sparkling water and champagne. She carried platters of oysters, smoked salmon canapés, goat-cheese-stuffed figs, truffle-oil olives. She served petite quiche and opera cream tortes with frosting storks to women with five-figure handbags.

A pack of women had reserved a private room for their baby shower luncheon, and Natasha volunteered for the extra shift. The women pecked and nibbled. They had straight backs and preternaturally white teeth. They had pearls and diamonds, manicured nails, designer dresses and heels. Most of them were glossy and slim, especially the pregnant one, whose moon belly rose over her slender legs like a balloon on a string, and Natasha wondered when she might drift up into the sky and float away.

The pregnant woman ate an olive, an almond, and two figs with the goat cheese squeezed out.

"I am just stuffed," she said. "I've been eating like a horse."

"Well, you look fabulous," said a middle-aged lady with kind brown eyes. She looked rich like the others, in her silk blouse and blazer, but otherwise normal.

"I just hope Darren thinks so." The pregnant woman rubbed her belly.

"Don't you worry."

"The more you worry, the more Botox you'll need later," said a lady whose taut skin and bony frame betrayed a regimen of diet pills and Botox.

"Botox. Jesus. I think there are more pressing concerns."

"Like the baby," said the eldest, a refined lady with cold, calculating eyes.

"Ooh, the baby!"

"Besides, you're too young for Botox."

Natasha made the appetizer plate disappear. She swept crumbs from the white tablecloth. She was a ghost, practiced in the art of passing unseen.

"Maybe she should worry just a bit," whispered an older lady with an arsenal of diamonds after the pregnant one had waddled off to the restroom.

"Clara—"

"Well, you remember what happened to Darren's last wife—"

"I know, but—"

"The last one was a crazy bitch."

"Obviously."

"And the one before that?"

"Darren definitely has a type, doesn't he?"

"I liked his first wife better."

"I don't know how any of his wives can stand it. He reeks of pussy."

"Poor girl."

"Not anymore. I mean, let's be honest—"

"Well," the Botoxed lady began, "all I'm saying is that maybe she should be careful. If she didn't let herself go—"

"She's pregnant," said the lady with the kind eyes.

"She can't starve herself," a stout older woman agreed.

"Easy for you to say, Nora," the Botoxed lady sneered. "Your husband likes them on the plump side."

"Stanley likes me the way I am. As opposed to your husband, who's—"

"Ron is—"

"Ladies, please—"

"I was just saying, she can't starve herself. That poor baby—"

"The baby will be fine."

"Do you think . . ."

"What?"

"Do you think Misti knows?"

"What? About Darren's, um—"

"Yeah."

The women looked at each other, wide-eyed and blinking,

except for the cold-eyed eldest, who ate a spoonful of soup. Natasha did not like the sound of this Darren fellow. He sounded like a creep.

"Darren didn't tell the last one."

"Until after she saw him. So—"

"Shh—" The eldest of the six women shushed the rest.

Pregnant Misti toddled back to the table.

"We were just saying, Misti, how lucky you are."

"Me?"

"Oh yes." The eldest lady flashed a devious smile. "Because of the penthouse."

"What penthouse?"

"The one in New York, of course."

"New York..."

"Oh my. Darren didn't tell you?"

"He didn't...."

"Gosh, I feel terrible," the cold-eyed eldest said. "He must have meant it as a surprise. But since I've ruined it ... Darren's bought a penthouse in New York, so you and the baby will have a nice place to stay when he has to travel back there for business."

"Oh, wow! That's just ... that's ..."

"It's *marvelous*." The eldest lady grinned. Her face was both disarming and wicked, and her bright eyes crackled blue with fire. "You just need to make sure to thank him properly. You must let him know how grateful you are. And that means that you must do whatever it takes to keep yourself svelte and lovely."

Natasha served salads with dressing on the side, platters of grilled salmon, roasted asparagus. The ladies picked and nibbled. Natasha cleared away plates of uneaten food. She thought about what it would feel like: to be a rich woman; to order expensive food and not eat it; to do whatever it took to stay svelte and lovely; to be married to a creep named Darren who bought a penthouse in New York without even telling you.

"I went with the yellow-and-white color scheme," the Botoxed one said after lunch as Misti unwrapped a box of silky newborn pajamas. "Ducklings. Nice and neutral."

"I still think you ought to find out the sex," said the stout lady.

"I want it to be a surprise."

"Don't you think Darren would rather you find out?"

"I don't know. He said—"

"Maybe it's better not to know," said the one with the kind eyes. "So you don't get too attached."

"To the *idea*. That's what Shannon means. So you don't get too attached to the idea."

"Well, hopefully for you," the eldest lady said, "it'll be a boy."

The lady glanced up at Natasha. Her simmering blue eyes narrowed. A false smile spread across her thin lips. Natasha saw, in a flash, a sordid lifetime of painful footwear, Botox, personal Pilates sessions, slices of pie dumped in the garbage.

Of course, Natasha thought, and she wondered whether she could get away with spitting in these women's drinks. *Of course. A boy.*

BEST FOR BABY

San Francisco—Now

SHE TEETERED THROUGH her apartment building hallway to the elevator in three-inch heels, emerald-green. She wore a short skirt and pantyhose. She had perfect legs. Except they had stopped looking perfect, around month four, when a hideous lacework of varicose veins spread up her calves and across her thighs.

She'd consulted her dermatologist: *Can't you take them out? Isn't there a cream, or . . .*

The doctor laughed at her silly question, her airhead, rich-girl question. *You have to put the baby first,* he said. As if she should have consulted the baby to determine its leg cream preferences. *Besides, maybe they'll go away on their own, after the baby comes. That happens sometimes.*

Other things also happened sometimes: Like, sometimes your husband came home with panties in his pocket, black lace thong panties that did not look like your particular black lace thong panties, which you couldn't wear anymore because of the h-e-m-o-r-r ... Did the rest need to be spelled out? Because it was embarrassing, even more so than varicose veins. The veins you could at least keep covered up with foundation and hosiery.

"Here, let me," said a man looming in the elevator. "What floor?"

"Lobby."

"Right, lobby. Well, look at you ... how far along?"

"Seven and a half months."

"Seven and a half! I would have guessed any day now. You look like you're about to pop!"

"Yes, well ..."

"Is it twins?"

"Just one."

"Boy or girl?"

"It'll be a surprise."

"Well, here we are." The elevator dinged. The doors opened to an apartment lobby of marble and glass. "You take care now! Good luck making it another month and a half!"

"Thanks," Misti said.

She didn't feel thankful. *My God, this lobby! Would you look at this lobby!* She had felt thankful, when Darren Buxby asked if he could buy her a drink after her shift ended, when Darren Buxby fastened a diamond tennis bracelet around her wrist, when he gave her the key to his penthouse apartment, when they said their vows beneath a rose-covered archway overlooking Big Sur while a full symphony orchestra played "Canon in D," when she took the pee test and the plus sign appeared and she could not believe, could *not not not* believe how lucky she had gotten. Well. She was right not to believe it.

She walked two blocks. She went into a coffee shop. She ordered a small-sized nonfat decaf latte.

"Are you sure you want this?" the barista asked.

"I, um—"

"Because you know there are trace amounts of caffeine, even though it's decaf. . . ."

"Gosh, trace amounts of caffeine! Do you think it'll kill the baby?"

The barista blinked. "Probably not."

"Then yes, I'm sure."

"Well, it's your choice."

Jerk, she thought.

Misti paid. She did not want to tip. She could not resist the programming that compelled her to tip anyway. Four years waiting tables. Two years taking drink orders at a Starbucks. A year before that, asking if you'd like fries with that, wearing a paper hat, coming home each day smelling like grease, tasting grease, feeling with each breath the smothering film of grease in her lungs. She could *not not not* go back there, she had told herself, attempting to justify her current situation.

She drank her latte outside. She pretended to be engrossed in her phone, to discourage conversation. Everyone had ideas about breastfeeding, swaddling, cloth-diapering, room-sharing, round-the-clock baby-mother skin contact, Japanese language yoga cooking ukulele programs for the under-one set, and everyone wanted to stuff their ideas down your throat, and Misti had stuffed enough down her throat already that morning: a cup of yogurt, half a banana, two egg whites scrambled with sprouts. She threw out the rest of her latte. She hailed a cab.

"San Francisco General."

"Are you—" the cabbie asked skeptically through an open window.

"Just a checkup."

"Okay. Good. . . ." He nodded for her to get in. "As long as you don't go into labor in the back seat."

Misti got into the cab, choosing to ignore the man's discomfort. She had felt unbelievably, ridiculously thankful right up until the night, two months earlier, that Darren took her out to dinner at Jardinière and a woman had stomped up to Darren and hocked a big wad of spit right onto his slice of buttered bread. The woman had Misti's same straight blond hair, Misti's same doe eyes, Misti's same slender physique, except her face looked pinched around the mouth. *Now, Cindi,* Darren chastised, *did you really have to . . .* Misti's older, meaner doppelganger said, *Yes, she really did have to.* Then she turned and looked at Misti and said: *Has he started logging late nights at the office? Won't be home for dinner. Business trip over the weekend.* Misti looked at Darren, who swirled his finger around his ear in a gesture of *would you look at this crazy bitch.* But, *Yes,* Misti thought. Last weekend and the weekend before and every night he seemed to get home later. The doppelgänger shook her head. *He never changes. Except, you know, for his monthly cycle.* She laughed and turned to leave. Then, as she walked away, she looked over her shoulder at Misti and said: *You better hope it's a boy.*

Cindi the doppelgänger was Darren's ex-wife. His crazy ex-wife, who came a-spitting at his food; spouting paranoid accusations; insinuating that Darren menstruated, like a woman. Misti nodded and purred. She picked the avocado out of her salad and slid it to the edge of her plate. She dipped the tip of her fork in the side of dressing, just the tip. That was enough. She thought: *Oh my God I'm so lucky I'm so lucky out for dinner at Jardinière with this . . .*

. . . man . . .

And yet the spell had been broken.

When she had run into Darren's partner at the gym, she inquired about their recent trip to Los Angeles, only to be met with *What trip?* And then a *Oh, LA. Right. Right. It was gravy.*

And yet . . .

As the days went on, he stopped even trying to hide it.

The lipstick on his collar, so cliché.

The panties she found in his pocket.

The cum stain on his brand-new shirt.

She tried to deduce which of Darren's partners' wives would know the most, and which would share it. Then Shannon James invited her over for coffee. In her resplendent house, a sleek homage to the golden mid-century, the woman poured a cup for Misti, with cream and sugar. *It's regular. A little caffeine won't hurt.*

Shannon James listened and nodded and she had this look, practiced, like she'd done this all before.

"Yes," she said, when Misti finished. "Darren is a slut. But there's more. There's a lot more."

The cab dropped Misti off outside the hospital. She went in. She filled out the paperwork.

"How much?"

"We'll just bill your insurance."

"No, no," Misti said. "I need to pay in cash."

She handed over a stack of twenties. She waited for the nurse. The nurse made her stand on the scale. Misti closed her eyes. She covered her ears with her hands so she wouldn't hear the fateful number. Every extra pound was one pound closer to her fate. The nurse took her back to a room, told her to lie on her back, squirted her navel with clear jelly.

"There," the nurse said. She pressed the wand into Misti's belly. "Right there, you see?"

"No..."

"You're having a girl.... And look, there are her little arms, her fingers, and..."

"What?"

"Um..."

"What? What is it?"

"Oh, it's nothing. I thought I saw something unusual about her spinal column, but no. She looks just fine. Must have just been a trick of the light."

BIT

WHEREIN BIT LEARNS OF CYCLES

Pennsylvania—1822–1824

IN THE SMALL cabin between forest and meadow, Bit grew bigger. He fell asleep every night with his belly full. In the winter, he slept on the floor of the cabin, curled by the fire. His dreams crackled as the fire burned to embers. In the summer, he slept in the branches of an oak tree behind the cabin. He rested his head on the rough bark, until Mary laid out a quilt. Mary stitched ties to the quilt, and the quilt became a hammock. Bit's dreams whirled with stars.

Mary taught Bit his letters. She taught him to count past ten, to eleven, twelve, past twenty-eight. Bit counted the days as they rolled through the hundreds. He counted the scars on Mary's arms. She had six. She kept them covered. Bit did not ask what had made them.

Mary taught Bit how to gut a fish. She taught him how to turn sour berries into sweet jam. She taught him how to turn butter into pie, wood into kindling, the skins of rabbits into a hat for when the world turned cold, as it would every year.

All things came in cycles, she taught him.

"Even me?" Bit asked.

"You especially."

Bit turned tired and cranky. Then the moon grew fat, and Bit grew vibrant and charming. He told stories his mind had conjured all on its own, stories about human boys whose bodies grew wings or antlers or fur; boys who turned into sparrows, owls, bucks; boys who slayed the wicked; boys who found their real mothers, hidden away in the land between the forest and the meadow; boys who stole away in the holds of great ships and sailed across the sea, to the Lord's kingdom on Earth. Brigid had said that the Lord lived *up there*, and she waved a fat hand at the dingy sky. But the Lord, Bit thought, needed a place to plant his feet. The sky was so vast, so riddled with stars.

Mary sang songs in words Bit had never heard. Her voice sounded like the place where a stream became a river, where the soft dance of water became a flood. Bit sang songs cobbled from the notes of birds. They twittered what they knew, as he ran through the forest. *Bit-to-Wolf,* he heard them chirp. *Bit-to-Wolf, Bit-to-Wolf, Bit-to-Wolf.* They kept silent when he changed, reverent of the transformation, Bit to Wolf beneath the full bright moon.

On those nights, Bit left.

"I'm going," he said to Mary.

"Well then," Mary said back.

He packed his treasures and ran for the woods. He ran wild

through the night. He returned in the morning, bearing his kills, lifeless and bloodied by his triumph, so that she would say "Well then" and he would know what she meant:

Good Bit.

Good Wolf.

Good boy, that one I love.

He counted days into hundreds and the land again grew green and lush, and life blossomed across it. The moon peaked, and Bit ran for the woods, but eventually he left his rings and brooches and other treasures behind.

"I'm going," he said to Mary.

"Well then," Mary said back.

"I'll come home tomorrow."

"Home," Mary said. From beneath her impassive face, there rose a smile. "Well then."

He ran wild through the night, and in the morning Mary opened the cabin door and found Bit's kills—birds, rabbits, deer—laid out on the front porch, and Bit there, grinning broadly.

Look at what I brought for you, the boy said with his eyes.

Well then, Mary said back, her eyes shining their approval.

Bit counted more days, and the greens turned to yellows, golds, to reds and browns. Rain's light paws padded across the cabin roof. The sky churned with southing birds.

"See?" Mary said, as the moon rose on a clear night and she covered the garden with sheets, to shield the tender limbs from frost. *All things come in cycles*, she meant.

Inside, by the building warmth of the fire, she gathered the boy Bit in her arms.

"I'll always go," Bit told her. He spoke in his small voice, because the moon was a slender wisp in the great big sky. "But I'll always come back."

The next day, Bit fell ill.

"Just a cough," he said.

Outside, the wind blew and the branches whipped. The boy watched the flurry of leaves and considered the tightness in his chest. He felt (though he could not heed his feeling at the time) the end of this cycle coming.

The next day, Bit coughed worse.

"Just a cough," he said. Mary pressed her hand against his forehead. Her hand felt like cool cloth. He was clammy, hot.

"Mayhap," Mary said. "Still . . ." She ordered Bit into the big bed and tucked him in tight, and he smiled because he could smell her in the covers, all around him.

She cooked stew. She brought a steaming cup to the boy in bed. The stew had a rabbit in it, one that Bit had caught, in his last cycle as Wolf. The rabbit had started small, nothing but bones and ears, and then it grew fat enough to eat. Bit had started hungry, and now he was not. All things came in cycles.

Over the next days, Bit coughed even worse. The moon began to grow stronger, but Bit did not.

"Just a cough," he whispered, through parched lips.

"Well then," Mary said. She blinked, and for a second Bit saw the worry in her eyes. But then she tucked the worry away and peered down at little Bit with the eyes of a mother. "I suppose you'll be all better soon."

"Any day now, you'll be better," Mary said, the next day, when Bit could barely sit up. She held a cool rag against his forehead to quell the burning.

"Just a cough," Bit wheezed. The cough disagreed. It rattled his chest. It hoarded his breath.

"Any day now, you'll be better," Mary said, in the early morning, when the hefty moon slumped down in the winter sky. Bit's chest ached. His left eye had swollen, then crusted shut. He could not sit up to swallow, so Mary squeezed the water into his mouth in drops, and the drops burned his throat, and he thought: *All things come in cycles.* He thought: *Where will I go when I die?* He thought about whether he could take his treasures with him when he went, his sack of coins, his fine clothes, his gold rings, his pendant set with dragon jewels, his cloth-sewn wolf. *Yes,* he decided, with the logic of a small feverish boy. He could take all his treasures along, every one of them. Except for Mary.

"Any day now," Mary said, the next morning, when the snow fell outside and the ice etched crystals on the windowpanes. "Any day now."

Bit gasped his breaths. He chased thoughts through the inferno in his little brain. He saw rabbits on the mantel, crows in the rafter, a black-eyed buck at the window, freezing the glass with its dead breath. He saw other beds, where other children slept. He saw Dugan Molly Patrick Bree Cormac Kean, the hot mess of them, tangled in the mutilated bedsheets. He saw Kean floating on a bed that was a boat, his severed hand replaced by a pirate's hook, his dreams laden with mutiny and revenge. He saw the boy from whom he had stolen the stuffed wolf, except it wasn't stealing, really; the wolf belonged with Bit. He saw Brigid, her bloodied face in shadow, her thick arms reaching for the neck of his real mother. Mary kissed Bit's forehead.

"Any day now."

She laid his treasures out around him. His fine clothes hung on the bedpost. His pendant, his rings, his jewels set on the pillow where he could see. His stuffed wolf tucked in the crook of his arm.

"Any day now."

She kissed his hot, damp forehead.

"You've forgotten."

She sang to him, and his memory trickled back.

"You've forgotten, Little Bit."

She sang, and the trickle became a stream. The stream became a river.

"You've forgotten to count the days," Bit heard her say, but he knew when he heard that, that the voice had spoken from inside his head.

The river rushed through him. *You've forgotten to count the days.* It would carry him away. He looked out the window, toward the pale sky. The night would come. *Which night, which night?* But Bit knew. He could feel the moon in his bones.

He tried to sit up, but his body would not go. His chest convulsed with coughing.

"Now," Mary said. She pressed the covers tight around him. "You rest now."

But Wolf did not feel restful.

Bit tried, again, to sit. Failing, he rolled to the side. He inched toward the distant edge of the bed. He coughed, and then coughed coughed coughed and could not do anything but cough, and all he hoped was for the cough to propel him off the bed, out the door, away, away, to where Mary could not find him. Because Wolf was vicious. Wolf was wild. Because sickness had zapped what strength Bit had to control the wolf inside him when the moon called it out.

"Any day now," Mary said, as Bit tried to move, but could not. "You'll be all better." Her mouth quivered. A tear formed in the corner of her eye. She blinked it away. "You'll be all better. You'll grow up big and strong. You'll grow into a fine young man, you will. And you'll have many adventures. I know it. Out West, Bit, there are great big mountains and wide blue rivers and rich earth, far as the eye can see. And all of it, my Bit, it's all just there for the taking. Someday you'll see, Bit. Someday. You'll travel all the way to the edge of the land, I bet, and maybe then you'll even sail across the sea.

"But first," Mary said, as she squeezed Bit's small, sweaty hand, "first you rest."

Bit felt Wolf stir. He tried to pull his paw away. He opened his mouth. Terror squeaked out.

"It's all right, Bit."

Mary held his hand tight. Bit felt Wolf clawing at his chest. He coughed.

"You just rest now. There'll be time to grow big and strong soon enough."

Bit closed his eyes. He sang a song inside his head. He tried to sing Wolf to sleep.

"All things in cycles, my boy. My Bit."

Wolf awoke. It happened fast, too fast. Bit's back arched. His ears grew sharp. His face contorted, beautifully, elongating into a snout. Fur rippled across his skin. His hands bulbed into paws, and his claws shot out and pierced through Mary's palm. She screamed with pain. She tried to pull her hand away, but Wolf's claws stuck inside it.

I'm sorry! Bit tried to yell, but his voice had gone. Wolf growled.

"Well then," Mary said, as she stared into the yellow eyes of her fate.

I tried! Bit said, silently. *I tried but—*

The fever-voice of his forsaken mother interrupted. *Should've let it have ya,* Bit heard Brigid say. *Waste of a boy, you is.*

Wolf snarled. Wolf was no mere boy.

No! Bit called. His weak body grappled for the reins. For a moment, he felt himself grab hold of the beast. He stared into Mary's eyes. Mary stared back.

I love you, my Bit. My boy, her eyes said.

Then Wolf ripped free.

No no NO NO! Bit screamed with all his soul. But Wolf would not listen. Wolf was vicious. Wolf was wild. Wolf opened its jaw and tore out Mary's throat.

Well then.

Wolf made him stronger, but the boy felt sick inside.

No, Wolf growled, from deep in the gullet. *Aren't no mothers could keep a thing like you.* Wolf spoke in feelings, and the boy translated to words. *You ain't no boy.*

He sat in Mary's bed in Mary's blood and pawed at his treasures: his sack of coins, his gold rings, his cloth-sewn wolf. He sat for days and nights in his weak boy's body. Wolf howled, anxious of the walls, the ceiling, the cold bedsheets stained brown.

Bit's fever cooled. His cough turned dry. He coughed the last of it away. He thought about how he might have died.

Should've let it have ya, Bit said, to Wolf. *Waste of a boy, you is.*

No . . . Wolf growled. *Ain't no boy left here.*

Bit thought if he had died there would be Mary, to dig a grave in the cold earth, to lay Wolf to rest. Mary to sing. Mary to stack the kindling just so. Mary to skin the rabbits and boil them to stew. Mary to watch through the window: the drift of snow, the scatter of starlings, the moonrise.

Mary lay on the floor, stiff and foul. Wolf recoiled from the stench. *Smell,* the boy ordered, and he clung tight to the mattress and forced his eyes to watch her, Mary the Unmoving. *You did that. You.* Wolf the Unmoved. *You're the devil,* Brigid had said, before Wolf killed her, before Wolf killed Dugan Molly Patrick Bree Cormac and severed the hand of little Kean. Mayhap, Bit thought, she had been right.

Mary grew stiffer and fouler. The moon faded, then grew fuller. Wolf grew restless.

You stay, Bit commanded. *You look at her. Smell her. You did that.*

Wolf leapt over the corpse. He swept the dishes from the table. He tore at Mary's linens with his small paws, his dull teeth. He bashed the window with Mary's hammer. Cold damp swept through the splintered glass. Wolf screamed through Bit's mouth.

We're HUNGRY! Wolf roared. Wolf's demands stalked Lost Bit across the wilderness of the boy's mind. Wolf thought blood-thoughts: teeth sunk into a buck's neck; the salt bleed of a limp rabbit; the scream and spurt of a kid when his hand got tore off. Wolf's mouth watered.

You. You. You're the devil.

Wolf had him cornered.

Mayhap. Wolf grinned. *Mayhap so. Mayhap I just take what I want.*

The devil was strong, at least. Bit grew stronger, and he made Bit-and-Wolf stay and watch. *Smell her.* He made them crouch over her. He made them stare into the smoke of her dead eyes. He made them stare at the scuttlers, the small worms, the flies that found in Mary, just as he had, their new home. He ate the stores that Mary had saved for winter, the canned beans, the pickles, the potatoes and preserves. Wolf was ravenous. Wolf ate a week's lot of food in an afternoon. Wolf licked the last jar clean. He dressed in his fine clothes.

You may look like a boy . . . Wolf said to Bit.

But I'm not, Bit agreed.

He wore his rabbit fur hat, the one Mary had helped him make. He wore Mary's fur coat. It hung down to his ankles. He could smell her in it. *Smell*, Bit told Wolf. *You took that away.* Wolf could smell her exactly as she had been, could smell the curvature of neck, the heartbeat in her cobalt vein, the flutter of her eyelids when she slept.

Well then. Wolf laughed, with a devious glint to his grin. He tucked his treasures into the pockets of Mary's fur coat. He grabbed Mary by the ankles. He pulled. A cloud of flies swirled up from her body. He dragged her across the house, out onto the porch. He left her there, in the spot where he had piled his kills to make her proud. The earth had frozen too hard to shovel. His breath steamed. His cheeks burned from the cold. He bent down over her body. He placed his cloth-sewn wolf in her hand, the last of the boy for the last of Mary to hold. He turned away, toward the forest.

Away, away he went.

SHANE LaSALLE

A WEREWOLF DINNER PARTY

San Francisco—Now

FOR TWO DAYS, Shane lazed in bed. He scrolled obsessively through internet photos of college classmates, of men from his Duke rowing team, of the stellar progeny of his parents' friends, of the former junior associates of Barrington Equity who never made the senior status cut. Everyone worked in law or finance, or had gotten elected governor of a Caribbean Bitcoin island nation, or had married the Brazilian yoga-instructor-slash-model-slash-bestselling-keto-cookbook-author they'd met on a stint in Taipei teaching English to business travelers, or had just sold their tech start-up and moved into a yacht docked in Santorini.

Shane LaSalle wanted a yacht. He wanted a fleet of yachts, and he felt sick with envy that he owned exactly none. And every time he thought of yachts, or sailboats, motorboats, cruise ships, or any vessel capable of navigating scenic waters and possessing onboard cocktail-making capacities, he felt sick. Sick to his meat-filled stomach. A person more practiced in self-reflection than Shane LaSalle might have noted that when Shane LaSalle envisioned these luxury vessels, he envisioned them afloat in the mildly chemical-scented waters of Lake Orange, and that when Shane LaSalle thought about Lake Orange, he thought about the article he had read in the *Lake Orange Gazette*, and about Duane Beckman, and about the wolf—that strange needle-toothed apparition—that had, in Shane's twisted recollection, stood atop his chest and ripped open his neck. Shane LaSalle blamed the sick feeling on the combination of hamburgers and Korean barbecue ribs. Stanley Rollins's secretary had sent over three rib dinners, cooked rare. Shane had ordered hamburgers all on his own. He had tossed the buns and eaten only the insides, salted lightly. He felt lightheaded and sweaty in a way that could only result from excess meats, and yet he could not stop excessively eating meats.

For two days, Shane's mind trolled him with embarrassing posts:

Status update: Drowning my yachtless shame at a rate of two burgers an hour.

I've eaten so much meat, I can feel it coming out of my nose!

Back hair update: the hairs are back! And they're longer!

Busy internet-stalking everyone I know and comparing their accomplishments to my own, because my current social network rank (i.e., number of likes, number of impressive "friends," number of yachts) determines my value as a person, and because the neurotic assessment of the success (or lack thereof) of my "friends" diverts my mind from thoughts of Duane Beckman.

Shane drifted toward sleep on a life raft of neurotic comparison, his only refuge in a sea of Duane Beckman. He dreamed of Duane Beckman grilling hamburgers on the deck of a forty-foot yacht, of Duane Beckman boarding the Lake Orange–bound Barrington Equity jet, of Duane Beckman riding bareback atop a massive wolf, Duane Beckman with his odd mole and his offensively untamed teeth, his un-photographable teeth, teeth that would clash painfully against the picturesque backdrop of Shane's designer apartment, teeth that Shane, should he ever embark on a self-reflective journey, would find that he actually considered quite cute.

Shane's journey, at this juncture, had not yet taken a self-reflective turn. He ate five plain pink-centered hamburger patties in a row, and did not reflect on why they tasted so delicious even though he had previously preferred his meats cooked medium well and smothered in sauces.

An unwillingness to engage in self-reflection often stems from fear as to what the reflection might reveal: For example, that a person does not actually enjoy parasailing and windsurfing as he might profess, that such activities in fact make his hands sweat and his heart race anxiously, and always mess up his hair unless he slathers it with sticky gel, and he would prefer to stand firmly on the deck with a drink in his hand. Or, for example, that a person has created a fictitious persona more "interesting" and "adventurous" than his actual self, and has encouraged that persona to subsume the actual self, such that the self, in any real sense, has ceased to exist. The fiction became the reality. Yet even if Shane were to reflect on the fictionalization of himself, his rational mind would only take reflection so far, certainly not so far as the narrative—the implausible, preposterous narrative—that he had become an actual werewolf.

Then, after two days, Shane awoke from his meat coma feeling sluggish but otherwise normal. He showered. He quickly waxed his back and plucked his stray eyebrow hairs. He ate a normal amount of eggs and sausage for breakfast and scrolled through the morning feed of status updates and posts in a normal, nonobsessive fashion. He put on his suit. He called for a Lincoln Town Car to ferry him to work.

I'm saving up—he recalled Duane Beckman saying the first time, at a midnight bus stop—*so I can buy my own place in the city.*

Back when Duane and Shane had shared a windowless office, Duane had carried a bus pass and packed his own lunch every day. He wore department store suits. He shined his own shoes. He kept a jar of black polish in his desk drawer.

Shane stopped for a coffee on his way in. He walked past the shopping-cart encampments of Embarcadero Plaza.

That's the problem with this city, he recalled Duane Beckman saying. *All the trash* . . .

Shane shoved the memory aside. He went in to work.

"Good morning, Mr. LaSalle!"

"What a pleasure to see you, Mr. LaSalle!"

"We've missed you, Mr. LaSalle! Are you feeling well rested?"

"Breakfast is waiting in your office, Mr. LaSalle!"

The associates nodded reverently as he passed them in the halls. He found Clifton James was waiting in his office, sitting casually in his chair. "LaSalle! Welcome back! You're looking better."

"Thanks," Shane replied.

"That new moon, she's a bitch." James stood up.

"Yes," Shane said, pretending that he understood.

"Especially the first cycle. All things come in cycles, don't they, buddy!"

Shane nodded agreeably. "Yes."

"But it'll get easier. Are you up for a trip?"

"Of course."

"We've got to take a little trip back to Kernville. The Glass lady is having doubts."

"She is?"

"Someone has planted some dangerous ideas in her little head, and we need to pluck them out before they start to grow." Clifton James made a plucking motion with his hand. Shane shuddered, reminded of his back hairs.

"What kind of ideas?"

"Ha, ha, ha!" Clifton James patted Shane on the back. "That's what I like about you, LaSalle. You're so earnest. You're absolutely believable!"

In the days that followed, Shane LaSalle and Clifton James enjoyed an extended trip to Kernville, Ohio. Clifton James woke early and took a crew of Alvin Sports and Supplies employees out for a round of golf. He aimed for sand bunkers and water traps on the last few holes so the employees who thought they'd been bested would win in the end. He treated them to lunch at the golf club, a round of drinks for his new best friends. He compared Kernville Country Club favorably to Pebble Beach: less ostentatious and just as scenic. Clifton James was absolutely believable.

"Take her out to lunch." Clifton James offered Shane advice

on Jeanie Glass, as they shopped for casual, Midwestern clothes at the local Value Valley. "Nothing pretentious. You're sick of pretentiousness."

"I am?"

"Say 'I am!'"

"I am!"

"You're tired of California, and how pretentious it all is." Clifton James handed Shane a stiff cotton T-shirt.

"Okay."

"You want to go someplace . . . someplace simple. Homey. A greasy spoon joint. A burger joint. Someplace like that."

"A burger joint?" Shane had eaten a lifetime of hamburgers over two moon-sick days. He wondered if the burger smell would sicken him or, worse, prompt him to wolf down a plate stacked high with barely cooked bun-less burger patties.

"Hmm, I see," Clifton said, seeming to read Shane's mind. "So go for breakfast. Order grits, because you miss grits and there's no good place to get grits in California."

"Grits. Okay."

Shane LaSalle had never eaten grits. The thought of a *greasy spoon joint* made Shane want a hot shower to preemptively loofah away the grease. His choice restaurants served infused vodka cocktails, aperitifs, roulades, escarole and fennel, radicchio and pickled sea vegetables, pâtés, ponzus, chocolate dulce de leche, prickly pear and vanilla bean panna cotta adorned with hand-seared chili hazelnuts.

"Perfect. That's the look you want to have." Clifton James tossed a stack of discount jeans in the shopping cart. "You complain about how pretentious California is, and how *fake* everyone is. You almost left Barrington Equity because you missed the Midwest. That's what you tell her. But then, you couldn't leave . . ."

"I couldn't leave."

"Because there isn't another company like Barrington Equity. A company always willing to invest in the underdog. A company that puts family first. Barrington Equity is your home now. That's what you tell her."

Shane LaSalle had never considered leaving Barrington Equity. There were a dozen other companies like it, though none quite so prestigious. And once Shane had begun his scramble up the slippery partnership slope, he did not want to slide back down and begin the climb anew elsewhere. And Barrington Equity did put family first, albeit mainly the families of Barrington Equity partners, what with their designer-handbag wives and the children they shipped off to boarding school in Switzerland and never spoke of. Yet, when Clifton James described Barrington Equity as a "family first" company always "willing to invest in the underdog," he said it with such conviction that Shane ignored his own mind and believed him, in a way.

"We put family first," Shane repeated. "Barrington Equity is my home now. I could never leave."

He nodded fervently, confident in his company's ability to balance altruism and profits. He felt almost giddy. And yet, a small, dark splotch had begun to form in the corner of his vision. He had a vague and unarticulated notion that "could never leave" meant that the firm was *his home now*, whether he wanted it or not.

Still, Shane LaSalle invited Jeanie Glass out for breakfast. They went to the Kernville Fry Shack. Shane ordered grits. He dunked his biscuits in gravy. He told her about his one family, outside of

Detroit (say "outside of Detroit," Clifton James had instructed, because it fit better with the bootstraps narrative than Shane's affluent hometown), and the barbeques his dad liked to host, and the dog he had growing up. His dad, like Jeanie's dad, had pursued the family business, law, until Shane went into finance. His dad, like Jeanie's dad, had a favorite breakfast spot frequented every Sunday. Shane spoke of his other family—his work family—which had seen his potential and rewarded him for all his devotion and hard labor.

He took a meet-and-greet tour. He shook hands with second-generation Alvin Sports and Supplies employees, with septuagenarian supervisors who had started working for the company as high school sophomores, with machinists and factory workers and sales reps. He listened to their recommendations on which diner cooked the best bacon cheeseburger in town, where to get the best pancakes, the best goetta, the best chicken and biscuits. He asked Jeanie Glass to come along. He asked her where to go and what to do in Kernville. She took him paddleboating. They paddled across a lake in a plastic boat molded into the shape of giant swan. It wasn't the boat he wanted, but it would suffice for an afternoon. He waited in the hospital lobby while Jeanie Glass and her father—the man who had transformed a regional sporting goods store into a national chain—watched Kevin Costner transform his cornfield into a baseball diamond for long-dead ballplayers; afterward, when her father had dozed off and Jeanie Glass had reappeared in the lobby, Shane LaSalle hugged her and took her out for a slice of pie.

"I appreciate you being here," Jeanie Glass said, after they ordered two cups of coffee and two slices of apple pie. "I really do."

"It's . . . I like it here. Everyone's so down-to-earth. It's been fun, you know, hanging out with you. . . ."

"Eating lots of pie . . ."

"Yeah. It beats staying in the office all day. Especially since . . ."

Duane.

He almost let it slip. Then his mind flashed a memory-warning of Clifton James. *Someone has planted some dangerous ideas in her little head, and we need to pluck them out before they start to grow.* Duane was a dangerous idea. Shane took a bite of pie.

"Since what?"

"Oh, just since I became a partner. There's so much more responsibility, you know?"

"Yeah. Yeah, I know what that's like. My dad . . ."

"You're really close," Shane said.

"We've always been close."

"It must be hard to see him go through this."

"Yes, yes of course. . . . And he hates not being able to work. The company means so much to him."

"Understandably."

"It's his life's work, you know? And there's nothing he wants more than to see it succeed. And without the funding, we just won't be able to stay competitive. But . . ."

"But what?" Shane said.

He looked at Jeanie. *You can trust me,* he said, with his eyes. *You can trust us.*

"He said something, about Creighton Automotive?"

"Yes," Shane said. His mind flashed back to the celebration following Barrington Equity's acquisition of Creighton Automotive, the champagne corks popping, the cigars, the shots, the topless juggler, the flight to Lake Orange in the Barrington private jet. "What about it?"

"He said they were in trouble."

"Well, they *were* in trouble. That's why they reached out to us. They were . . ."

On the verge of bankruptcy, Clifton James had said. *If she asks about Creighton Automotive, that's what you tell her.*

But Shane knew how his company made its millions. Creighton Automotive had not been anywhere close to bankruptcy until Barrington Equity took a controlling interest and began to pile on the debt. But Creighton Automotive had, from Shane's perspective, existed only on paper. And as Shane recalled what Clifton James advised he say and how to say it, and as Shane thought about the factory workers and sales reps whose hands he had shaken, about the whole lifetimes devoted to Alvin Sports and Supplies, about Jeanie Glass and her cancer-addled father and the family legacy she wanted Barrington to help protect, the dark splotch in the corner of Shane's vision grew.

"They were what?"

"Well, I probably shouldn't discuss this, so . . . if I tell you, can you keep this to yourself?"

"Yes, of course."

Shane leaned in. "Creighton Automotive was in a different spot. They weren't trying to fund an expansion like you are. They were on the verge of bankruptcy. That's why they reached out to us."

"I see."

"And we're still working to turn things around. But it's precarious, so—"

"I won't say a word."

"Good."

Shane smiled. He felt excellent. Clifton James had judged him correctly, he decided. He was earnest. He instilled trust in others. He was top-notch partnership material.

As the days passed, his depraved episode as an internet-obsessed meat glutton seemed further and further behind him. Duane Beckman seemed further and further behind him. The past grew fuzzy in its remoteness, so fuzzy that he could practically blur it out altogether. He felt more and more excellent; stronger; fiercer; indomitable.

"Time to go home," Clifton James said one morning.

"What? Why? All I need is a few more days," Shane said. "Just a few more days and we'll be able to close."

"We're not the closers," Clifton James said, which puzzled Shane. "Besides, Barrington is throwing a dinner party."

Back in the city, Shane felt spectacular. A limousine picked him up outside his apartment and delivered him to the Olympic Club. He wore his best suit. His eyes sparkled. His supple lips bore the undetectable perfecting sheen of Fleishman's ManBalm in Malibu Beige. He took several selfies: (1) Shane illuminated by the glow of his stylish chandelier; (2) Shane in front of the limo; (3) Shane in the back seat with a tumbler of scotch on the rocks; (4) Shane against the golf course backdrop. He would post them later, captioned with well-devised epithets of his obvious success. His debonair appearance required no caption. He thought, briefly, of Duane Beckman, exiled from illustrious partnershipland. But Duane Beckman had shrunk down, mosquito-sized, compared to Shane's outsized élan. *Fuck Duane Beckman*, Shane thought. Duane Beckman was just another associate flunky. Duane Beckman could eat gruel and freeze his tight ass off at base camp while Shane scaled the Big Rock Candy Mountain. Shane LaSalle, and not Duane, got to taste the sweet riches of the Barrington Equity partnership. The scent of private jet had lingered on his skin long after he disembarked. Shane LaSalle, not Duane, got invited to the partners' dinner party, and the red carpet rolled out for him when he exited his limo, and everyone fucking clapped and cheered.

"Mr. LaSalle, good evening." A lowly hostess with a name tag that read NATASHA held open the front door. "The rest of your party has already arrived. Right this way." She ushered him past the main dining room, which was empty and dark.

"Is it—"

"Closed for the evening. The entire club was rented out for your party."

"Yes." Shane chuckled. He flashed the hostess a suave grin.

"Which is kind of bizarre, if you ask me," she said, under her breath.

"I didn't." Shane's hearing had improved alongside his sense of well-being. The more excellent he felt, the more it seemed he could hear the inaudible.

"This way, sir," she said, turning down a dark corridor. Shane heard her pulse quicken. She stopped, halfway down, and pointed to a door at the end. "Right in there."

Beyond the door, the other partners waited.

"LaSalle!" Clifton James said congenially when Shane entered the room.

"Have a seat, LaSalle," Barrington said. "Right down here next to me."

"Someone pour LaSalle some champagne!"

The partners had all brought their wives along. One of the wives, a curvy middle-aged woman who Shane guessed was married to Stanley Rollins, stood up. She poured a glass of champagne and handed it to him.

"Aren't you cute," she said. "Better be careful, though. Stanley was cute once too, before all those years of eating like a—"

"Like a wolf," said the cruel-eyed Ron Carver.

"Like a wolf!" fat Stanley chuckled.

"He goes through a pint of ice cream every night!"

"A pint?"

"I have a weakness for ice cream."

"And that's after dessert."

"Oh, LaSalle wouldn't let that happen," said Clifton James. "He's got to keep up his good looks. You should have seen our mark, Stan. She was *smitten*."

"I'll bet. Look at those eyes."

"And his lips!"

"So handsome!"

"Well, thanks," Shane said. He took a gulp of champagne. He felt heroic. Also, he felt like a slab of meat. Stanley Rollins, Ron Carver, Clifton James, and their three wives all looked at Shane. They all smiled approvingly. Shane took another sip of champagne.

"Drink up, Mr. LaSalle," Dick Barrington growled. "You'll be glad for it when the moon rises."

It was a weird thing for a human to say, but Dick Barrington was not quite human, said Shane's subconscious—though conscious Shane felt too elated to notice minor eccentricities. He swallowed down his first glass of champagne and accepted another, poured by Dick Barrington's wife. Don Morgan's wife passed baskets of bread and plates of antipasti around the table. Clifton James's wife uncorked bottles of wine and filled the glasses. Ron Carver's wife slapped Darren Buxby's wife's hand away when she reached for a second piece of bread. Shane thought perhaps he ought to invest in a wife, a pretty, glossy wife who would photograph nicely at the partners' dinner parties. He glanced around the table for wife-department ideas. Ron Carver's wife had a magazine-model beauty: heavy makeup, visible ribs, waifish enough to pass for a teenager, debatably under sixteen, unless you looked closely and saw the crow's-feet around her eyes. Darren Buxby's wife looked hugely pregnant and miserable. Stanley Rollins's wife was buxom and beautiful, but her curvy hips and full breasts would not look right in Shane's sleek, modernist apartment. Don Morgan's and Dick Barrington's elegant wives reminded Shane of the bourbon he drank to celebrate his first trip on the Barrington private jet. Their age refined them. They wore gowns and silk gloves. The tip of a scar arced from the top of Don Morgan's wife's glove. Another scar, a moon shape the width of a claw, adorned her bare shoulder. Clifton James's wife saw Shane looking at the scar. Their eyes locked.

She's lovely looking, Shane thought, academically. *Just the right style of wife.*

She moved her mouth, but no words came out.

What? Shane mouthed.

She shook her head. Her lips moved. *Get out*, it looked like.

Shane felt the hackles rise along his back, though his rapidly growing back hairs hardly counted as hackles. Clifton James's wife glanced at the door, then turned back to Shane.

Get. Out, her lips said, soundlessly. *Now.*

"Shannon, grab us another plate of antipasti," Clifton James proclaimed.

"Of course, dear," his wife said. She flashed a saccharine smile. She stood up. She fetched another plate of antipasti from the cart near the door. Shane felt too elated to wonder why the partners' wives fetched food, cleared plates, and poured drinks, or why the food and drinks came on a cart instead of delivered by waiters directly to the table, or why, in the corner of the room, there was a large cage full of rabbits. Shane could smell the rabbits, and the smell made him very hungry, but it seemed a perfectly natural sort of hunger. The whole dinner party seemed perfectly natural to Shane in that the ultrarich could afford to act bizarre, and so naturally they would.

Shane finished his champagne and accepted a glass of wine. He nibbled antipasti and avoided making eye contact with Clifton James's wife. Ron Carver's wife wheeled away the appetizer cart and returned with a salad cart. Steak and salmon followed the salad. Don Morgan's wife opened a bottle of wine that smelled like a year's salary. Shane felt giddy and slightly drunk. Darren Buxby's wife cleared away his dinner plate.

"Did you ask first if he was done, Misti?" Darren Buxby said sternly.

"I just assumed that, because his steak is all gone, and—"

"I'm all done," Shane reassured her.

"Okay, take it," Buxby ordered. His wife teetered away with Shane's empty plate. "She's not got much in the brain department," Buxby said to Shane. "But she's easy on the eyes. Or at least, she was a few months ago."

"Who would like a slice of cake?" Dick Barrington's wife asked. "It's chocolate—"

"Mary," Dick Barrington said. "The time—"

"Darling, it'll be fine. We have time to cut the cake and serve you at least."

"Well, make it quick."

"Yes, of course. Ladies?"

The other wives stood up. They quickly cleared the table and ferried plates of chocolate cake to their husbands, and to Shane. Then they grabbed their five-figure handbags and headed toward the door.

"Have fun tonight, gentleman," Mary Barrington said. "Especially you, Mr. LaSalle."

Shane shoveled cake into his mouth. It did not taste like any chocolate cake he had eaten before. It was saltier.

When he looked up, the wives were gone, but he had missed their departure.

"You like the cake?" Stanley Rollins asked, as he helped himself to another slice.

"It's amazing."

"It's the blood."

"The . . ." Shane felt suddenly dizzy.

"It's an old family recipe," Dick Barrington said. "Mary substitutes the milk and oil with blood."

Fat Stanley Rollins stabbed a chunk of cake with his fork. His fat tongue licked it off the fork. The cake had a red tint, Shane noticed, and he must have made a grimace.

"Oh, don't look so shocked, LaSalle! It's not like it's human blood." Rollins chuckled.

Ron Carver laughed.

Shane felt his throat constrict. His tongue felt too large, and he wondered whether it would slop out of his mouth and lick the blood cake from his plate.

Ron Carver laughed again, and something clicked in Shane's mind. He had heard that laugh before, in the office late at night. He had heard that wicked laugh echo through the empty halls, and the terror of it sent his heart into a tailspin. He could have fled. A better, younger Shane—a Shane not entrapped by status updates, selfies, internet-worthy photographs, the perception that he adored aquatics and had come by his tan naturally, the expectation that his mother would introduce him at holiday parties as *my son the investment banker* and he would say *actually, I work in venture capital* and his mother would exclaim *he just made partner!* and all the middle-aged ladies with moderately less successful offspring would smile and congratulate him and feel secretly jealous—*that* Shane might have fled Barrington Equity the first time he had heard Ron Carver's horrible laugh, before he had grown used to helping Barrington Equity gobble up companies, leverage them, strip their assets, pay out glorious dividends, and leave their debt-ridden husks nearly dead on the side of the road that led to riches. But after subsisting on an internet diet for years, even before his first associate day at Barrington Equity, appearances mattered more to Shane than reality.

And then, of course, there was Duane Beckman.

Duane Beckman swirled through Shane's mind: Duane Beckman who shared his leftover food with the homeless; Duane Beckman who wanted to buy a house for his mother but left instead without saying goodbye; Duane Beckman, who might have been the body those hikers found, left to rot on the shores of Lake Orange, or who might have broken Shane LaSalle's heart.

Shane gulped.

The chocolate cake tasted like sick death. He wanted to cry. He opened his mouth.

Duane, he tried to say, but his throat felt as if it was getting clawed apart from the inside, and the words got stuck. *Duane!* he tried to cry. *What happened to Duane?!*

But the words came out as yelps. Shane's mouth burned. A painful, buzzing sensation spread across his face. He could smell everything at once, all the food they had eaten, the wives' perfumes, the trace of detergent left on the tablecloth, the last drops of wine drying in an empty bottle, the hostess standing behind the closed door, with her ear pressed against it. He tried again to yell *What happened to Duane!* and *Get out*, at the same time, but his voice garbled. His tongue did not feel like his tongue anymore. It brushed against something sharp in his mouth—*oh fuck, I have needles in my mouth,* he thought, and he tried to spit them out. A glob of yellow foam, flecked with blood-chocolate crumbs, landed on the tablecloth.

Ron Carver laughed villainously. Shane looked up. Ron Carver stared at him, grinning. All the partners still sat at the table, casual, as if this was a perfectly normal dinner party. They all stared at him.

"LaSalle, have some manners," Clifton James teased as he lit a cigar.

"Look at his face!" Stanley Rollins guffawed, spitting crumbles of blood cake.

"His teeth!"

"He's hideous!"

"Someone take his picture!"

No, Shane tried to say. *Please no no no!* But again his throat mangled the words and they came out as feral yips.

"He's early," Darren Buxby remarked, accepting a cigar from Clifton James.

"The body takes a few cycles to adjust," said Dick Barrington. "The first one is always the worst."

"Good God, look at him!"

Ron Carver laughed harder.

Shane stood up. He took a step back from the table. His legs felt rubbery and unsteady. He tried to take another step, but his back bent involuntarily forward.

"LaSalle, you should take off your suit so you don't ruin it," Clifton James said.

"Too late." Don Morgan laughed.

Shane felt a splitting sensation along his back. His suit, he thought, at first. He had eaten too much and split his suit. But the sensation burrowed down, deep into his spine, and it felt as if his whole back had split open. His skin tingled. He screamed, and his scream was a howl. All the partners stared at him and laughed, all except Dick Barrington, who sipped his Cognac and watched with an amused smile. Darren Buxby recorded a video. Ron Carver laughed so hard and so loud that Shane felt as if his ears might explode. Stanley Rollins's fat face turned red from his unstoppable laughter. Shane could smell the remnants of a cornucopia on Rollins's breath, the booze, the salmon and steak, bread, eggs with hollandaise sauce, shrimp cocktail, tater tots dipped in mayonnaise, chocolate raspberry chip ice cream. Blood. Raw hamburger meat. Uncooked chicken. Goldfish straight from the tank.

He's going to eat me, Shane thought. His irrational mind told his arm to reach for a fork and knife, to protect himself, but when he lifted his arm, he watched thick fur bristle across it. He watched his fingers shrink, his hand thicken into a paw. He watched the claws grow out of it.

Shane scrambled back from the table. His body contorted. His front paws fell forward onto the floor. *What's happening what's happening what's happening?!*

He howled in pain, in panic.

But he knew.

He had seen it happen: the wolf on his chest, tearing out his throat; the insatiable hunger; the moon-sickness. And Duane Beckman, the body in the woods, the wounds inflicted by something vicious, by something that should not exist. And yet, here he was. He howled, and the partners howled with laughter. They pointed at him. They stared, with their rancorous black eyes, and Shane knew it was too late. He could not *get out*. The partners had seen behind his glossy profile pictures, behind his plucked eyebrows and his Fleishman's ManBalm and the Instagram femmes he occasionally dated and cast aside after capitalizing on their photogenic brilliance because, despite their luster, they couldn't stir him. The partners had peeled away the veneer of Windsurfing Shane, Shane the Rising Star in the venture capitalist skyline, and had seen the hideous beast underneath.

Shane's mind spun from *what's happening* to *there goes my partnership* to *now they'll slit my throat* to *blood cake blood cake blood cake.* He could still taste it on the wolf's tongue. Not human blood, Rollins had said, but what blood, whose blood? Duane Beckman stuck in his mind, and all his thoughts spun out around Duane, and he wondered whether he had *tasted* Duane Beckman at last or maybe he had *tasted Duane* before on the blood-orange shores of the lake on the night of the wolf, if maybe he had tasted Duane Beckman with his *teeth*, if maybe he had ripped him apart because he wanted him so badly.

Shane howled, and the man inside the wolf shook and sobbed, but the wolf stood steady and listened to his partners ridicule him. Mr. Handsome was *grotesque. A freak. All things in cycles.* Ron Carver snickered. The partners' laughter rang louder, meaner. Their laughter clawed at Shane's ears and cleaved at his meager heart. He could never be one of them. He saw this now, through his wolf eyes. He could wear the partner suit and ride the partner jet and crew the company-gobbling private equity yacht but he would always be pretending. He would always be the kid on deck, dressed up in his fancy playclothes, waving his tiny arms. *Look at me, guys! I can parasail! I'm a partner now! A partner!* And look! They had given him a lollipop! They handed him partnership paperwork and told him where to sign, and he scribbled his name, Shane LaSalle, in green crayon. He hadn't even read it. Even if he had, he would never be one of them. He would never possess a designer-handbag wife, or any wife. He would never be *bloodthirsty* enough. He didn't want Barrington Equity to buy Jeanie Glass's family business and load its stores with lead debt and watch it sink. Shane LaSalle the pretend parasailor was not a Barrington Equity pirate. His partners would declare mutiny and toss him overboard. He was nothing but a sorry beast: a slobbering, coarse-furred, misshapen wolf with crooked fangs and foul breath and a yellow heart.

The partners' cruel laughter filled the room, but it did not sound like laughter anymore. It sounded feral. The light of the rising moon shone through the window.

Hello, Moon.

Dick Barrington turned his face toward the light, but it did not look like his face anymore. His nose elongated into a snout. Fur rippled across his skin. He smiled at Shane, revealing his razor teeth.

Shane watched in terror as the other partners transformed. Their faces extended. Their necks stretched and thickened. Their skins sprouted fur. Their bodies contorted, replacing arms with forelegs, hands with paws, dull white teeth with jagged incisors, monstrous canines, jutting horribly out between the rows of tiny gray knives in their foaming mouths. They laughed as they changed, reveling in the transformation from man to gruesome beast, and in Shane's terror, his disgust, his shame. *Blood cake blood cake blood cake.* Shane stared at Dick Barrington's awful mouth. He had seen that mouth before, had seen it close around his throat. And what had it done to Duane Beckman? He shuddered. Dick Barrington the wolf laughed. He tore his shredded clothes off with his teeth. He leapt up onto the table. Plates of half-eaten cake fell to the floor. *Blood cake blood cake blood cake.* The alpha wolf howled for the moon. The other partners howled for the moon. The moon howled back.

GREED AND GLUTTONS

At the Olympic Club–Earlier

NATASHA DROVE TO work. She parked sufficiently far from the Olympic Club entrance so that none of the club members would suffer the indignity of seeing her rusty car packed full with the garbage-bagged contents of her life. She seated guests for late lunches and post-golf snacks, with the caveat that they would have to finish up and leave by five p.m.

"The club will be closed for a private party," she told them.

"But what if I want to stay for another round?"

"I'm sorry, sir." Natasha tried to feign sympathy.

"This is just ridiculous! I'm a paying member! I should get to stay if I want to stay!"

"I'm sorry, sir, but the club will be closed. Do you still want to be seated?"

"I want a word with your manager, is what I want."

Natasha soon found that whoever had rented out the club had

paid enough for management to offer steak house gift cards and spa treatments to disgruntled guests. The club staff got sent home for a paid night off, with only a skeleton crew of cooks, a dishwasher, and Natasha left to service the private party.

"'The server is not to enter the banquet room,'" the event manager read from the private party's list of demands.

"Well, how am I supposed to serve them?"

The manager sighed. He pushed up the glasses that kept slipping down his thin nose. "You load the food onto the cart, then wheel the cart into the hallway and leave it by the door."

"That's really weird. Don't you think that's weird?"

"They're not paying me to think. They're paying me to read you this list and then go home and watch television all night."

"So who rented the club, anyway?"

"Some company," the manager said. "Wolfsbane or Wolfsmane or something like that."

Something sleazy, Natasha thought.

"So is it, like, a business meeting, or—"

"I don't know, but let me finish with the instructions so I can get the hell out of here, okay?"

"Fine."

"Okay. It says, 'The server understands that if he enters the banquet room at any time, he will be subject to immediate dismissal from employment.'"

"Are you serious? If I enter the banquet room, I'm going to get fired? This whole thing is ridiculous."

"Yeah, well, if you pay enough money, I guess you can be as ridiculous as you want," the manager said.

"Can I ask you a question?" Natasha said. The question had

twittered around Natasha's brain for several weeks, while she observed the staff and pondered who might be worth asking.

"You can ask." He glanced at his watch.

"Did you know the woman who worked here, the one who got killed?"

"Marie?"

"Yeah. Marie Babineaux. You know, she was my roommate."

"No shit," he said, seeming, for the first time, not entirely bored. "And you came to work here? That's not exactly, like, a psychologically healthy career move."

Natasha loaded shrimp cocktails and salmon croquettes and charcuterie boards onto the cart. She wheeled the cart down the hallway. She left it by the door. She did not go into the banquet room. She walked back to the kitchen. She waited. She heard the door open, heard the cart be retrieved. She loaded more carts with rib-eye-steak crostini, glazed pork skewers, prosciutto-and-Gruyère croissants, bacon-stuffed mushrooms wrapped in bacon, olives and nuts and salads, focaccia and French bread baskets with extra butter. She left the carts at the door. She could hear the party on the other side. There were about twelve or fifteen of them, Natasha surmised. Not so many to warrant this excessive volume of food. Their appetizers alone would cost more than she made in a month at the Olympic Club. Their wastefulness irked her. She despised the hungry sound of their voices. She felt incensed by their gratuitous wealth and consumption, their ridiculous rules, the entitlement inherent in the instruction that she be fired for stepping foot into their rented room. That was the sort of entitlement and privilege that made a man think he had the right to kill a girl and dump her body in the park.

A thought struck Natasha just then: Their stupid rules never said anything about listening at the door of the banquet room.

After the last appetizer cart had been retrieved, Natasha crept back to the door. She pressed her ear against it. She heard men, loud bantering, clinking glasses, orders barked. *Pour us another round! Not that one, Misti. The bottle of red. She's not got much in the brain department, but* . . . She heard women, subdued voices, high heels on a wood floor, plates cleared. She heard the *click-clack* of painful footwear moving in her direction.

Natasha ran back down the hall, around the corner. Two women pushed through the staff entrance to deposit carts stacked with dirty dishes. The carts rattled down the hall, nearly to the end, where Natasha stood and listened.

"I can't do this," one of the women whispered to the other.

"Shhhh. You can. You can do it."

"But what if they—"

"You have to try. You have to, for your baby girl."

"I'm so scared."

"I know. I know, honey. I'll do everything I can, okay?"

"There was another one last night. Some office girl named Darla."

"He told you?"

"He didn't used to. But now that I'm pregnant and huge . . . he brags about it when he drinks."

"Oh, honey."

"I can't believe I thought Darren was nice. Before we got married..."

"He was nice. They all seem that way at first. And then they change. Chin up, okay? No tears. You can do this. Keep up the dumb act. He's buying it. You ready?"

"Okay. Okay, I'm ready."

Natasha tried to get a glimpse of the women as they retreated, but the hallway was dark.

She retrieved the carts. She had expected plates of uneaten food, but all the plates were nearly clean. She wheeled them back to the kitchen. Her mind reeled, and each thought felt like a cringe. *Darla... He brags about it when he drinks... Keep up the dumb act... Baby girl...*

She wondered whether one of the women had been the special guest at the baby shower held in the same room a few weeks back, showered with couture babywear and advice on how close a gal could get to anorexia while pregnant without making it official.

She loaded the next cart with steaks and scalloped potatoes. Then came swordfish, salmon, pork chops, meat loaf. She delivered the carts to the door and left them there. Ladies retrieved them. Ladies served. The carts came back out stacked with empty plates.

Natasha loaded a new cart with dessert plates, coffee and tea, bottles of limoncello and port wine and bourbon, and a cake. The cake looked like a chocolate cake, with a red velvet tint. It had an odd, salty odor, like dead fish. Natasha held her breath as she pushed it into the hall.

She waited near the kitchen while the ladies came to retrieve it. She could not understand how the party had consumed so much.

She wandered back to the staff entrance door to the banquet room. She pressed her ear against it. She listened. The ladies sliced and served the cake. Then she heard them pack up their purses and say their goodbyes. Their designer heels marched across the wood floor, out through the main banquet room door.

Only the men were left.

"You like the cake?" Natasha heard a man ask.

"It's amazing."

"It's the blood."

A sudden, sweltering terror filled Natasha's chest.

It's the blood.

She felt terror pulse outward through her veins. Her face flushed. Her limbs felt hot and useless.

It's the blood.

She wanted to move, but her limbs stuck. Her ear stayed pressed to the door. She heard forks scraping, glasses refilled, men helping themselves to seconds of blood cake. Then she heard an awful yelping, like the cries of a drowning puppy.

"LaSalle, have some manners."

She heard more yelping, then laughter.

"Look at his face!"

"His teeth!"

"He's hideous!"

The yelping became desperate, fearful.

"Someone take his picture!"

The laughter grew louder, more vicious.

"He's early."

"The body takes a few cycles to adjust . . ."

The laughter changed pitch. It had an unsettling, animalistic quality. Natasha covered her ears with her hands, but the laughter slashed through. She heard a terrible howling, a tearing sound, escalating laughter that made her want to stab knives into her eardrums, to cut them out so she would never have to hear it again. She heard rustles, thumps, claws on the table. She caught the scent of damp fur. The men on the other side of the door cackled on, but their laughter had shed the last vestige of man-sound. It burbled up from the throats of beasts.

For a moment, the laughter subsided. Natasha exhaled relief. She could hear her own heart thudding at the silence. Then a new terror struck her: *They know I'm here,* she thought.

She crept back from the door. She knocked against a cart loaded with extra dishware and booze. The sound of clinking glass echoed through the hallway. She turned and ran. She ran down the hallway, past the kitchen. The cooks had already left for the night. The lights were out. She kept running, past the dining room, through the front entrance, out into the parking lot. The full moon filled the dimming sky with hungry light.

Natasha ran through the parking lot, out to the road. She walked halfway to her car before she realized she had left her purse behind at the Olympic Club. She stopped. She took a deep breath. She was overreacting, she told herself. What had she actually heard? Thumps, cackles, vicious laughter. She had no reason to think that any of those absurdly rich, gluttonous men knew or cared that she had heard them laughing and goading each other. And she needed her purse. Her purse contained her car keys, and her car might get towed if someone found it parked near the golf club in the morning. Her purse contained the can of pepper spray she had carried ever since Marie had gotten killed. Marie, who had been torn up . . .

She would be safer with her purse.

She turned back.

She hurried through the parking lot. Her eyes scanned for vicious men signs. But there was no one out there, nothing except a lone rabbit darting across the golf course green.

She went inside. She crept back through the dining room, into the staff lounge, where she had stashed her coat and purse. She stood for a moment and listened. She did not hear any laughter, or talking, or anything other than her own heart, her breath, the soft hum of the HVAC. She took her coat and purse from the locker. She walked back into the dining room.

Then she felt a prickle along the back of her neck, the sensation that someone—something—was watching her. She glanced at the window. She saw the navy sky, the golf course frosted with velvet moonlight. No men. No one out there but that rabbit, its black eyes wide with fear. It scurried across the green, around the side of the building. She heard the screech of animal laughter.

Her heart thumped with dread. She felt like the rabbit, caught in the gaze of something vicious. She fled the dining room. She sprinted toward the main entrance. She pushed through the door, into the parking lot. But she wasn't fast enough.

The wolf intercepted.

The wolf stood in her path.

The wolf was larger, uglier, more vicious than anything she had ever seen up close. It had enormous claws, dripping jowls, rancorous hackles down its hefty back. It stared at her through yellow, bulging eyes.

It opened its mouth, to show her its jagged abundance of teeth, and smiled.

The werewolf, in the words of monster hunter George Corcoran McCloud, is an "insatiable curse wrought upon these American lands by godless savages and heathens," "a brutish, wicked creature," and "the devil himself, molded into flesh" ("Monsters of Pennsylvania," *The American Scientician* [1872]: 18–22).

To the extent this is accurate, as the many accounts of werewolf attacks suggest it may be, can the werewolf then escape his nature? Is the werewolf destined, by virtue of his condition, to transform each full moon into a brutal killing machine? And to what extent does this inevitable monthly transformation predispose the werewolf, in his human form, to wicked and violent behaviors? Or is the werewolf's savage form simply an excuse? That is, does the werewolf, in witnessing his own transformation, permit, encourage, and even revel in the wickedness that his werewolf form allows?

This philosophical inquiry is, of course, of general relevance. Humans too are bedeviled by wrath, greed, violence, and other faults, which, it may be said, are inherent to our nature. But in no creature is this moral struggle between nature and choice more apparent than in the werewolf. . . .

Marcus Flick, American Myths and Monsters: The Werewolf, 2nd ed. (Denver: Birdhouse Press, 2022), 96–97

WHEREIN THE WOLF SHANE LaSALLE GOES ON A HUNT

San Francisco—Now

AFTER HIS PARTNERS completed their transformations, and shredded their clothes and lapped the last of the wine from their glasses indecorously, their fat tongues splattering liquid and staining the tablecloth, and after the Wolf Stanley Rollins stood atop the table and devoured, without bothering to chew, the remains of the blood cake while the other wolves watched and cackled, their awful hyena laughter driving spikes of terror and disgust into Shane's mutated heart, the Wolf Clifton James padded over to him, and smiled with a mouth full of barbed teeth. He had foul, rust-colored teeth—teeth that had gone unbrushed for a thousand years. Just the sight of those teeth could give a person tetanus. Shane slid his wolf's tongue across the treacherous range in his own mouth. He knew from the jumbled, grimy feel of them that his own teeth looked worse. He imagined the wolf in photographs, the gaping mouth with its heaps of pond-scum teeth, the bloodshot eyes, the slime-drool leaking from the fleshy flaps of jowl. Status update: *I'm a freak! Hashtag: SoUglyYourEyeballsWillExplode!* The Wolf Clifton James nodded, as if to say, *It's okay, LaSalle,* even though it wasn't, or *You're one of us now,* even though Shane did not want to find out what it meant to be *one of us,* and in his beastly heart he knew it could not be true.

And yet, he felt the wolvian pull of his instinct. The wolf that was Clifton James looked at him, and then looked toward the corner of the room where the caged rabbits had cowered watching Barrington Equity's esteemed partners feast on blood cake, their petite hearts aflutter with fear for this unseen thing, the shadow of the wolf that the moonlight revealed to their animal sense. The cages were empty now. The Wolf Clifton James looked back at Shane, and Shane understood what he had meant to say: This was just a dinner party, a little celebration to welcome Shane to the pack. They baked a blood cake in his honor! They brought live rabbits, for a post-dinner hunt! Despite a belly full of rib eye and prosciutto and champagne, live rabbit did sound tasty. A wolf could not be expected to subsist entirely on cooked meats. A wolf deserved to wrap its jaws around thrashing flesh, to feel the spurt of blood in its mouth from a live kill. A wolf could hardly help its nature.

The Wolf Shane LaSalle looked and nodded at his most trusted wolf partner, who turned and trotted toward the back door, which opened out onto a patio overlooking the golf course. The Wolf

Clifton James opened the door with his paws and stepped outside.
The Wolf Shane LaSalle followed. He felt the rest of the pack behind
him. He felt moonlight on his back, moonlight warm as the sun on
a summer's day. Moonlight euphoria filled his wolf body. He felt
strong, gleeful, fabulously ferocious. His senses buzzed. His ears
tilted skyward, to the sound of a circling hawk. His eyes spotted
a white shadow, a rabbit in the sand trap. He could smell the salt
sea, the rich flank of sea lion, the leathery breast of gulls, pigeons,
backyard chickens. *Mine*, his wolvian instinct told him. He could
take what he wanted. He could take all of it.

The Wolf Dick Barrington streaked past. He ran out onto the
golf course. He leapt. Shane heard a crunching sound. He smelled
hot blood. The Wolf Dick Barrington held the dead rabbit in his jaw,
for the rest to see. He took a sip of its blood, then tossed it aside.
The Wolves Stanley Rollins and Don Morgan claimed the remains.
Morgan, the stronger beast, ate from the rabbit's soft belly. The Fat
Wolf Rollins gobbled the head and cleaned the bones, and then he
lifted his leg and pissed on the golf course green. The Wolf Ron
Carver gathered the bones and carried them off. *He's cleaning up*,
the Wolf Clifton James said through a glance. But the Wolf Ron
Carver had wicked eyes, and Shane wondered what he meant to
do with those bones, if *cleaning* meant *collecting*.

Wolf Dick Barrington ran off into the woods abutting the golf
course. The other wolves ran too, and for a while they ran as a
pack, but then one would smell something intriguing and veer
off to investigate, and after a few minutes the Wolf LaSalle found
himself alone. He ran along the edge of the golf course. His eyes
scanned the forest for rabbits, or other creatures. He reveled in
the sensation of his paws on the earth, the effortless flight of his

stride, made buoyant by Moon. He looked up at the moon, the great transforming moon.

Hello, Moon, he said.

Hello, Shane, the moon said back, with a wink.

As a wolf, Shane circled around the golf course. He thought about how maybe he might like this wolf self, this powerful hideous form he now occupied (provided no one took pictures), and how maybe fate (which he did not believe in generally but might blame when convenient) had dovetailed with tireless effort (which he believed in fervently, when it worked for him) to make him a partner wolf. Maybe all partners in venture capitalist firms were werewolves? Making werewolf was the new prerequisite for financial success? Shane didn't like this idea so much, because it made him less exceptional, and he was *exceptional*! His studiousness, his penchant for all-nighters in the office, his fashionable taste in menswear, his hair-removal regime, his cultivated parasailing persona, all of this made him entitled to wolfdom. Maybe he ought to seize it, he thought. He deserved it.

But then, hadn't Duane Beckman deserved it, too?

Shane saw now, clear through his wolf eyes, what must have happened: the wolves that had attacked Duane Beckman as he tried to flee, the wolves that flung Duane Beckman supine, so to ensure he could see the teeth that tore him open. Wolves had attacked them both, that moon-full night in the burnt forests of Lake Orange, but he had made partner and Duane had not. The unfairness of this made him furious. Shane already owned a luxury apartment, and his mother had a lovely house, and Duane's mother did not. Duane had worked no less hard than Shane, had toiled no fewer nights and witnessed no fewer dawns from the thirty-second floor;

moreover, he had a better mind for business than Shane, and his online persona was sparser and less intriguing because it was all real and true, whereas Shane LaSalle existed in the margins of reality, on the internet and outside it. He was faux-real. He was a man in the body of a wolf. A wolf in the body of a man. He was a fraud.

Shane seethed, and mourned, for his lost Duane. His anger foamed from the corners of the Wolf Shane LaSalle's repugnant mouth. His mourning presented as howls.

Why, Moon? He fixed his gaze on the bright demon of the sky. He cried.

You think I've got the answers? The moon laughed. *Silly wolf.*

The Wolf Shane LaSalle circled back to where he had started. He saw a rabbit in the Olympic Club front lawn. He contemplated killing it, snapping its thin neck with his jaws, piercing its artery and drinking it up like a juice box. But it looked so pleasant, sitting there beneath the velvet shadow of the building, sniffing life from the grass.

He thought: *What would Duane Beckman do?*

Silly wolf, his mind answered. *Duane Beckman is dead.*

He would not kill it, he decided. He would let it be. But as he turned away, he saw the Wolf Ron Carver; the beast stalked toward the rabbit. It opened its mouth and howled, but the sound was like deranged laughter.

He's going to kill it, Shane thought.

Then he watched the wolf change course, and he saw that the Wolf Ron Carver had interests bigger than the rabbit.

Shane did not recognize her shadowed face as she emerged from the building, but he knew her smell. He had smelled her hiding behind the door of the banquet room. The Wolf Ron Carver had smelled her, too. The partners had all smelled her. They had all known she was there. She ran into the parking lot and the Wolf Ron Carver leapt into her path.

For a moment, she stood there, staring at the grotesque wolf, her headlight eyes bright with terror. She was immobilized, but the fear in her eyes was tinged by a burgeoning perception; she had contemplated this brand of bloodthirsty horror before.

Then the Wolf Ron Carver growled—a cruel, voracious growl— and he opened his mouth to show her all his pretty teeth.

The woman screamed.

The wolf laughed. His teeth twinkled in the moonlight. He stepped closer to the woman.

He's going to kill her, Shane thought. *Blood cake blood cake blood cake.*

The Wolf Ron Carver pounced. He could have toppled her, but he landed feet away. He wanted her to run. He wanted a chase. He wanted to terrorize.

The woman turned and ran back toward the club entrance. The Wolf Ron Carver plunged past her and blocked the door. She turned and ran for the parking lot, but the beast blocked her again. He leapt and blocked, steering her toward the trees. Shane followed. She sprinted through the woods, the wolves on her heels.

The Wolf Ron Carver sped up, close enough to swipe her with his grizzled paw. Then he pulled back, to let her get ahead, toying with her, making her think she had a chance. The Wolf Shane LaSalle sprinted up alongside the beast. The partner turned his head and looked at Shane with his yellow eyes, and Shane saw what he had always known to be there but refused to see: malice, insatiable hunger, greed at its razored pinnacle. Carver could kill this woman as a wolf—or maybe even not as a wolf, Shane saw—and her death would mean nothing to him. She was a fly to be swatted, a hapless rabbit, a nightcap to wash down the blood cake.

Shane could still taste the blood salt in his mouth. He felt the voracious fury of his wolf-self course through his veins, the brutal beat of his wolf heart, the sadistic lust of his gruesome teeth. He could imagine his teeth tearing this woman apart on the golf course green. Carver and him, blood-moon brothers. Him, and murderous Carver, and their Barrington Equity pack.

But Shane couldn't kill her. His pitiful heart knew it. He couldn't let the Wolf Ron Carver kill her either. So he did the only thing he could think to do. The thing he did best. He faked it.

The Wolf Shane LaSalle looked back at his colleague. He growled. The Wolf Ron Carver laughed. Shane decided to growl again, his most vicious, dangerous growl. *Let me kill her*, he meant to say. He grinned at the other wolf, with his mouth full of horrifying teeth. He snapped his jaws at him. *LET ME KILL HER*, he growled again. The elder wolf laughed, but he fell back. He let this Wolf Shane LaSalle take the lead. *Good boy. You kill that bitch*, he growled. But he followed along on Shane's heels, snapping and growling, breathing his hot, rank breath, close enough that Shane could smell and be appalled, knowing his own breath probably stank worse, and Shane realized the mistake he had made. The Wolf Ron Carver, of course, wanted to watch.

The problem with faking it was that sometimes people expected you to follow through. Hoping to save the woman from the wicked wolf, you volunteered to kill her yourself, and now your partner wanted a show. The Wolf Shane LaSalle wanted to kill her, but Shane, partially muted by wolvian instincts, existed somewhere inside this hideous wolf body. The Man Shane revolted at the spectacle of killing, the wet messiness of it, the bloodstains on his fur coat. The woman herself had a familiar smell, a lavender-and-salt smell that reminded him of his mother's friends' daughters post-Pilates class, the svelte JDs and PhDs and MBAs whom his mother always suggested he might like to date, because weren't they just lovely and sweet? No, he did not want to kill this woman. He did not want the Wolf Carver to watch, because both parts of Carver would take pleasure in it. This was the sick fuck who finished off the half-eaten roll left to grossify on someone else's plate, who slogged it through the gravy blubber polluted with someone else's germs. This was the sick fuck who would revel in the blood splatter. Shane hated Carver, and not in the same way he had hated Duane Beckman.

The Wolf Shane LaSalle tried to draw out the chase. He played the predator's game: Fall back, let her think she had gotten ahead, dash up and snap at her heels, huff his hot nasty breath at the back of her neck, repeat.

She screamed, but there was no human out on the golf course to hear her. Carver had surely gotten away with killing before. Shane knew him well enough to know that much. The Wolf Shane LaSalle leapt forward. He bit down on her shirt and tore a piece of it off. The Wolf Ron Carver laughed: *That bitch.* Shane let her escape. He couldn't keep pretending for much longer. He sensed an itching restlessness in his partner. He growled, for show. He ran after her, uncertain what to do. He couldn't take on his partner. Carver was more comfortable in his wolf body. Carver was merciless. Carver outranked him. Carver would make just as big a mess, if Shane succeeded in killing him. All that blood and mangled fur.

And what if death turned him back into a man? The prospect appalled Shane.

Wolf Shane LaSalle slowed his gait, trying to gather more time to think up a plan.

But when he heard the growl right behind him—*What are you waiting for? Kill her!*—Shane looked up ahead and saw that their victim had stopped running. She had found a good climbing tree.

Go on, kill her! the Wolf Ron Carver growled again as she pulled herself up through the branches.

Could wolves climb trees? Shane had no idea. He ran up to the tree. He reached out his front claws and dug them into the tree trunk.

"You fucker!" she yelled.

Shane looked up at her. He saw something in her hand. *A gun,* he thought. *Silver bullets.* Then the thing in her hand released an aerosol hiss, and he felt a horrible burning sensation in his eyes. He yelped in pain. Everything turned black and blurry. He was blind. His nose burned. He couldn't smell anything but burning pepper. He tried to retract his claws, but they stuck in the tree. He howled. He heard the other wolf's hideous laughter beside him.

Wolves, it turned out, could not climb trees. At least, Carver couldn't, or he didn't care enough to bother. He grunted and ran off, into the woods, and left Shane behind, blinded and stuck.

NATASHA

WEREWOLVES ARE ABSOLUTELY REAL

San Francisco–Now

NATASHA WATCHED THE first wolf stalk away into the forest. Her heart pounded. Her hands shook. She shimmied higher up the tree and found a seat on a high-up branch, her back against the trunk. She peered down at the beast below, its hulking form obscured by shadows. Then the swift clouds that sailed in from the cold Pacific parted to let the moon shine through, dappling the animal in silver light, and Natasha saw how awful and hideous it was.

It was not a wolf.

When, in the parking lot outside the clubhouse, she had seen the first wolf, her brain had labeled it *wolf*. It had a wolfish shape and demeanor, and she had no other plausible label to give it. As for its excessive teeth, its grisly claws, its misshapen proportions, they all accorded with the terror that it struck; it was the most terrifying thing she had ever seen, and so her brain had revised the wolf's appearance to correspond with the intensity of her fear.

Now, gazing down at the moon-streaked creature, Natasha knew that her fear had *not* exaggerated its features. It was truly the most awful thing she had ever seen. Its eyes were bulbous yellow orbs, bloodshot, glazed in a sheen of slime. Crooked, grimy razor teeth sloped out of its mouth. Its jowls dripped gross juices. Patchy coarse fur covered its misshapen body, matted in some spots but growing long and wild in others.

"Holy shit," she gasped.

The wolf, which had been trying to extricate its claws from the tree trunk, stopped and looked up at her. Was this, she wondered, the creature that had killed her roommate? She had presumed that Marie's murderer was human. She had seen the articles about the bite marks on Marie's body, but killer animals in Golden Gate Park did not fit any narrative that Natasha would be predisposed to believe. Killer wolf-creatures were preposterous. And yet here was this lupine beast, its yellow eyes gleaming grotesquely in the full-moon light.

"Wow," she said, as she stared down at the beast. "You are the most hideous thing I have ever seen."

The wolf, which had been staring up at her, tucked its ugly head. It whimpered.

"Yeah, I hope it hurts," she said. "But fuck. Now what?"

She did not want to stay up here all night. Someone needed to come and get this monster and haul it off the golf course before the early-morning tee times. It was stuck now, but it might get unstuck. It might be rabid. Its buddy was definitely rabid. Or something.

Natasha took her phone out of her purse and unlocked it,

wondering who she might call to extract a creature this large and gross. The wolf raised its head. It looked up at Natasha and her phone. Its face contorted. It howled. It thrashed, trying to unhook its claws from the tree. The trunk shook, and Natasha's phone slipped from her hand and fell to the ground.

"Fuck! Damn it!"

She was stuck. The wolf was stuck. It kept thrashing and whimpering. Its whole disgusting body shook. Almost as if it was sobbing. It looked over its shoulder at Natasha's phone. Its hind leg reached back and batted the phone away.

"What did . . . Did you just . . ."

It whimpered and moaned. It was not just a wolf. It was not just a dumb beast. It was hideous and awful, but for whatever reason, it was not as frightening as the creature that had chased Natasha out of the parking lot. It looked almost pitiful.

"Can you understand me?" she asked it. The creature buried its head between its forelegs. It whimpered. Natasha yelled, "Hey! You! Can you understand me?"

Slowly, the creature looked up.

"Well, fuck. So. What are you?"

The creature looked at Natasha. Its eyeballs turned toward the moon. Natasha remembered the interview she had read, in *FreaKountry* magazine. The interviewer had asked Nova Z'Rhae if she believed in werewolves.

Oh, absolutely, darling, Nova Z'Rhae had said. *Werewolves are absolutely real.*

SHANE LaSALLE

THE MOST HIDEOUS CREATURE

San Francisco—Now

"IS THAT WHAT you are?" the woman asked. "A werewolf?"

He did not want to believe it. But it was true. He was the most hideous werewolf anyone had ever seen. He looked up at her. His sight had returned after the pepper spray, but his eyes still burned. He nodded.

"This is unreal," she whispered.

Shane nodded.

"So. My friend. My roommate, Marie." She stared down at Shane, sizing him up. Her fear had subsided, Shane could tell, from the scent of her. "She was killed. Murdered. She had bite marks. . . . They found her body in the park. *Was it you?*"

Shane looked at the figure in the tree. The moonlight caught her eyes, and in them he saw resolve, determination, a hint of vengeance. He thought about Duane, his ruined body found in the woods by a pair of hikers. The Wolf Shane LaSalle shook his head.

"You didn't kill her?"

He shook his head vigorously. Slime drool sprayed from his shaking jowls.

"What about your buddy? Did he kill her?"

It seemed like something Carver would do, but Shane didn't know. He yelped.

"Is that yes or no?"

He yelped three times. *I—don't—know.*

"Is that maybe?"

The Wolf Shane LaSalle nodded.

"Well, your buddy's gone while you're stuck there," Natasha said. "He's a true friend, isn't he?"

The Wolf Shane LaSalle whimpered and thrashed, trying to unhook his claw from the tree.

He's not my friend, Shane would have said. *He's my partner—a work partner—but really, he's an asshole.* And what if he returned, with the other partners, so that they could all have a good laugh? Ugly Shane LaSalle, caught by a tree! What if he didn't return, and the sun rose and Shane transformed back into a man? Naked on the golf course! His once gorgeous hair smeared with the disgusting wolf slime that fountained from his floppy jowls! What if she got her phone back and took pictures and posted them on the internet? Panic trampled his rational mind. He yanked his stuck forefeet back hard. He heard a snap. He felt excruciating pain in his paws as his stuck claws ripped out of them.

"Oh, ouch!" she said, with too much gusto for her sentiment to be sympathy.

Shane fell back onto the ground. He whimpered. He licked the blood from his claw stubs.

"Oh, gross . . . Is that really clean?" she said, pressing his buttons. "I mean, you might not want to lick your open wounds with that mouth. Have you seen it? You could give yourself—"

Tetanus! Shane barked.

He pulled his shameful paw away from his mouth. God, what if he had just given himself tetanus? Wait—could he *give* himself tetanus, if he already had tetanus to give? The burning pepper in his eyes and nose (and mouth, apparently, because now his licked paw had started to feel like fire) distorted his thoughts, and he could feel his jaw beginning to lock up from the tetanus in his bloodstream.

"—some horrible bacterial infection. Or, like, what is that one amoeba called, that turns your brain to slurry? I wouldn't be surprised if you have some of that shit living in your mouth there."

Shane whimpered. His eyes had crusted over. Horrific quantities of sticky drool seeped out of his mouth. Amoebic slurry clogged his synapses. He might as well just lie down and die, right there on the golf course. Except that death would ruin the artifice of life he had so carefully constructed. The nightmare thread of comments responding to the discovery of his naked corpse on the golf course green flashed through Shane's mind. It was too horrible to read.

"That bad, huh?"

Shane moaned. He lay limp on the ground. He could feel her gloating, up there in her tree.

"You look pretty miserable. But maybe it's just an act."

It was all an act. Every facet of Shane's fake existence had serviced the illusion of the Shane LaSalle he envisioned for himself. Until now—in this disgusting body, his head smoldering with despair and pain, his heart broken for his lost Duane—when Shane felt more real than he ever had.

"I'm not coming down, if that's what you're waiting for."

You shouldn't, if you want to stay alive, Shane thought.

He didn't think his wolf self would hurt her, but the golf course was full of wolves tonight. Shane rested his slimy chin on his paws. He curled his torso into a wolf-ball. Minutes passed. Hours passed. The moon drifted through the sky. Shane listened to the howls of his partners, further and further away.

"Well, this is fantastic, isn't it?" she said sarcastically.

He whined in assent.

"So are you, like, totally werewolf right now, or is there still a person in there?"

The Wolf Shane LaSalle licked at his snout.

"Right, obviously you can't talk. Hmm . . . how about, if you've still got your human self inside there, raise your right paw."

Shane raised his right paw.

"I see. So you're, like, conscious of everything that you're doing as a werewolf?"

Shane cringed at the *W*-word, but he raised his right paw.

"So you're not just, like, a mindless killer? Raise your left paw, if you're not a mindless killer."

Shane raised his left paw.

"Good boy." She cocked her head sideways. "Of course, if you were, you'd never admit it."

Shane shook his head.

"No?"

Shane flapped his left paw vigorously.

"You really didn't kill Marie?"

The Wolf Shane LaSalle nodded, yelped, and flapped his paw faster.

"I guess . . . you don't exactly seem like the murdering type. But you have to admit, you really look like a monster."

Shane sunk onto the ground. He moped. She asked more questions, but Shane didn't want to play her pantomime game. *Raise your paw! There's a good boy!* He wasn't a good boy. He was a boy who chased that partnership rabbit out into the woods, who believed that if only he caught it—if only he could post that glory pic, the LaSalle selfie with his partnership catch dangling from his jaw, if only he could surpass all his peers on the digital success-o-meter, and then retain through continued updates his success trajectory, catching rabbit after rabbit after rabbit—then he would achieve good-boy status. But status was elusive, and a good boy would have appreciated what he already had, instead of running off into the woods. A good boy would have loved who he loved. A good boy would not let his love's death go unpunished.

Shane moped through the night, at the base of the tree he couldn't climb. His mind tried to untangle the threads that had knotted up his life: the Duane Beckman thread, the Ron Carver thread, tetanus-wielding teeth, quick-growing back hair, Jeanie Glass, private jets, blood cake. Natasha sat above him. She had given up asking him questions at some point. The hours passed. The moon slunk toward the horizon. Blue tinged the edge of the sky.

The Wolf Shane got up. Any threat his partners posed to the woman had passed. Their howls had traveled west, then south through the night, until finally Shane could no longer hear them. The salt air carried no trace of their smell. Shane needed to get away from the woman before she had the chance to snap embarrassing photographs of him in his man-skin. He needed to get the woman's phone away from the woman.

He walked over to her phone, which still lay on the ground. He opened his mouth and tried to pick the phone up with his teeth.

"Hey!" Natasha yelled. "Hey! What are you doing? Stop it!"

His wolf teeth were unskilled at carrying things. The phone tumbled out of his mouth, covered in drool.

"Ugh, yuck! You got it all gross!"

Shane felt like a jerk, for trying to take the woman's phone, for be-sliming it. He just needed to get away. He turned and limped toward the clubhouse. He mourned his ruined Armani suit. The partners could have told him, at least, not to wear his best suit. They could have told him what would happen. Not that he would have believed them. Werewolves were preposterous. He hoped that enough shreds of suit remained for him to assemble something to wear on the way home. He heard the woman shimmy down the tree. He heard her follow behind him.

He stopped, turned, and growled, *Don't follow me.*

She instinctively quick-drew her can of pepper spray and sprayed him in the eyes.

Shane's eyelids snapped shut. His whole face burned. He howled. He lashed his paw at the woman. *Get away,* he tried to yell. *Just stay away from me!* He swiped at her again, but his front leg felt rubbery and weak. The rubbery feeling spread up into his torso. His head felt pinched. He couldn't see what was happening, but he felt an implosion, as if his body was vacuuming itself up.

"Oh my God!"

What? What's happening? Shane tried to say. His throat

produced a strange guttural sound, some unseemly amalgamation of human and wolf.

"I can't fucking believe it. Werewolves. Fuck. This is ... so ... so ... disgusting...."

No! No no no no! Shane cried. He felt the pores of his skin split open and suck up his fur. He felt the needly rows of tetanus teeth recede into his mouth, as slobber gushed out of it. His body contorted. His arms felt small, like little tyrannosaur arms. A cold breeze swatted at his exposed dick.

"Jesus."

Please don't take a picture please don't please don't—

The gurgled wetness in his throat suddenly dried up, and Shane LaSalle's voice returned. "—take my picture."

"You want me to take your picture?" Natasha asked in a mocking tone.

"No—"

"Because you're, like, naked. And slimy."

"No, no, don't take my picture!" Shane cried. "Please!"

"Are you sure?" She ribbed him further. But he must have seemed so pitiful that instead of reminding him again how hideous he looked, she said, "Well, okay. But only if you cooperate."

"Anything. Just ... please ... I'm ... I don't want to be seen like this!"

"I'm sure. Um ... okay look, here's my sweater. Why don't you, uh, cover yourself up, okay? And then you should probably get yourself cleaned up. And then you're going to tell me everything you know about werewolves."

THE LOVELY ELEANOR

Pennsylvania–Circa 1832

THE BOY BIT roamed the wilds until the boy Bit was gone, and only Wolf was left.

He shed the boy like a skin. The boy's songs and stories sloughed off; his manners; his words. His boy dreams became the dreams of Wolf. He dreamed of the forest at night, the spindled pines, the clawed branches of winter oaks, the dead leaves beneath his paws. He dreamed of the chase, the hunt, the spurt of hot blood when his jaw snapped shut. He dreamed, at first, of the woman Mary, Mary the mother with her arms around him, Mary the corpse with her stiff arms at her sides, her hands stained brown.

But as the days and nights and moons spun their cycles, Mary turned to shadow, to breeze. She became a fleeting warmth. He felt her when he built a fire and warmed his thin hands over it, when he saw the heat of the sun through closed eyelids. Then he opened his eyes and the glare was too bright. Mary had retreated. She slipped from his dreams, until, at last, she came only when the moon was thin and wan, in the nebulous space between dream and waking, as a fragment of a song whose words he had forgotten.

In the winters, he was hungry and lean. He scavenged grubs and ate berries that turned to poison in his gut. *But yer already poison, aren't you, boy?* In his sickness he saw lumberjack Brigid, tall and broad, her eyeless face drawn in shadow. *Aren't you, boy?*

I am not a boy, Bit answered, though his mouth formed no words. *'Sides, poison kills much cleaner than me.*

On dry cold nights, when Bit's breath spilled out in billowed clouds, he built fires of twigs and sticks. *Hello, smoke. Hello, breath.* The frozen stars flickered. The ice moon floated across the sky. *Hello, Moon.* The moon made him strong, then weak. The moon loved him and left him.

You're a changeling, Bit said, as he looked up at its craggy face.

So are you, the moon replied.

Bit wrapped himself snug in Mary's coat. He could smell her. But her smell faded. Her soft coat turned ragged. It frayed. Its threads came loose, as Bit's threads loosened, as the boy unraveled.

In the summers, he plundered and feasted. He swam in the rivers, cooling his toes in the mud. He stole apples from orchards, crookneck squash and string beans from gardens, hens from the henhouse, life from the living. He stole at night so that the humans would not see him. He stayed clear of the towns. He wore the shape of a boy still, on most nights, but he had been too wild too long. The humans would see past his shape, to the vicious heart of him.

Bit grew bigger. He grew swift and harsh. He forwent the coat and wore instead the skins of the creatures he killed, the bucks and badgers, raccoons, rabbits, foxes. He wore strips of fur still matted with blood, tied with twine around his arms and legs, caped across his shoulders, crowned upon his head, empty holes where their animal eyes had been. He wore his treasures in a pouch slung across his chest. He remembered the *clink* of coins in his pocket, on market day, in the great city on the sea. He remembered a cloth-sewn wolf toy plucked from the arm of a sleeping boy. He forgot to count the days. He didn't need to count. He carried the moon in his heart. His ears perked at the sound of passing warblers, pulled southward by the waning daylight. His eyes tracked a formation of geese, a field mouse hoarding winter acorns, a black swarm of newborn ants. *All things come in cycles.* He knew this, but had forgotten why.

Then one day, as Bit strolled along a riverbank, scanning the cold water for the silvery glint of a fish, he heard a girl's unfettered laughter. To his wildling ears it sounded like a clarion chime. The trees tittered with awakening birds. The river frothed with snow-melt. Bit stopped and listened. He dug his toes into the cool mud of the riverbank. He recalled church bells. He recalled steamboats whistling farewell to the squalid land.

Again the girl laughed, a sweet ringing. Bit followed. He had muddy shins. He wore deerskin smocking; a fox-head hat; his finest clothes. He crept back from the river, into the trees, where he could move unseen.

"Bart, don't you—"

Another laugh.

"I will!"

"Bartholomew, don't you dare!"

"Just you watch me!"

"But your trousers! You'll soil them, and then Mrs. Barrington will say—"

"Eleanor, I care not what Mother will say. We shall have fish for our supper, if I have to catch it with my bare hands!"

Bit slunk through the low brush, a tangle of yellow blossoms. He slunk toward the smell of her, soap and cotton and chamomile, vivid against the palette of soil and spring moss, rosebuds, crocuses. He saw her near the riverbank, beneath a grove of early dogwood, their budding branches tipped white. She was pink-cheeked, half-bloomed. She gathered the petals of her dress. She stepped closer, toward the muddy bank, where a young man unlaced his boots.

"I'm quite ready," he said, after he extricated his pale foot from its boot. "Shall I catch us a trout? Or perhaps a shark?"

"Bartholomew!"

"I'm going in!" He stomped into the water, stirring up sediment.

She covered her face gently, as if restraining more laughter. "How is it?"

"Unbearably cold."

"Come out!"

"No, I shall not come out. Not until I have proven myself a worthy fisherman."

This Bartholomew stirred the water with his arms, splashing, scaring away the fish.

Bit cringed. This creature, was this creature a *man*? This gangly, splashing buffoon?

"Come now!" Eleanor called.

"I shan't." The fool whirled his arms. He had long, delicate fingers, harpsichord and silverware fingers. He wore the flush of wealth on his cheeks.

"I do not require a fish," she called. And still he thrashed uselessly at the water. Bit felt ashamed by the soft remnant of himself that bore resemblance to this creature. He felt, also, the hot pulse of his blood toward southward regions. He felt an unfamiliar hunger, clawing at his throat. Even when he fixed his eyes on the detestable man-creature, he could still see, quite clearly, the girl Eleanor perched on the riverbank. He could see the satin gleam of her slippers, her corn-silk hair swept back, her lips poised for laughter. He wanted to touch them, but his fingers were too rough. He wanted to tear the petals from her dress.

"Oh, there!" The man swiped at a shadow in the current. "No, darn it!"

"I really do not require a fish. All I require is ... is ..."

Wolf, Bit thought.

"What if I were to catch a whale?"

"Oh, Bartholomew!"

"Would you love me more?"

"How could I love you more? My heart is full to bursting!"

Bit understood, and yet he did not. He had lost his boy self to the wilds, and what emerged was altogether different. He crouched low, concealed by a thicket of nascent branches. His mind was muddled by the smells of soap and chamomile and cotton, the cascade of Eleanor's dress, the swell of Eleanor's breasts, the chime of her laughter across the blossoming forest. He watched. The man Bartholomew tromped out of the water. He wiped his muddy feet on the grass. His pants were heavy and wet.

The girl pointed. "Oh, your trousers!"

"Perhaps I shall take them off to dry? Perhaps if I hang them in the sun?"

"You rascal!" Eleanor giggled. "What have you got underneath your trousers?"

"I should bet you would like to see."

"If Mrs. Barrington—"

"Yes, I know. She would be quite scandalized." He stripped off his sopping trousers. "But you see, I am wearing underpants beneath."

"Quite scandalous."

"And now that I have shown you mine . . ."

He went over to the girl and whispered words into her ear. Bit could not hear them against the sound of the river, but he could smell them.

The man Bartholomew spread a quilt down over the grass. He and Eleanor sat. They opened a picnic basket. They dined on fresh bread slathered with butter and strawberry preserves, hard cheese, soft cheese, and boiled eggs. They spoke in soft voices. They stared, moony eyed, at each other.

Bit's heart thudded. He felt strong, rapturous, chock-full of hate. The animal inside him paced and prowled.

He had lost track of days.

The smitten couple had lost track of hours. The sky turned milky. The pink tongue of sunset lapped its edges.

"It is late," the girl Eleanor said. "I think we ought to go home."

"I could stay out here all night with you."

"Mrs. Barrington would be scandalized," she said. She stood. She swept the crinkles from her dress.

"Mother will always find something. Stay, Ellie."

"I think not. We do not want to be out in the woods after dark. There are savages out here, you know, and . . . and other things. I heard—"

"Those are just stories, Ellie. And there have not been any savages in this part of Pennsylvania since, well, since—"

"It is not them I fear most. There are other creatures, more savage, more terrifying even than—"

At this Bartholomew stood with fanciful vigor. "I shall protect you!" So weak he looked, Bit thought. So doughy, so pathetic. A decent set of teeth could rip his arms from their soft sockets.

Bit's pulse quickened. He felt something quicken inside him.

"Oh, Bart—"

"I should just like to kiss you, Eleanor."

"Bartholomew Barrington! I should think that—"

"Just once, Eleanor?"

"I think we ought to go."

"I implore you. Just one kiss?"

The man Bartholomew reached his gangling arms toward Eleanor. She allowed his embrace, but even in the gloaming Bit could see disquiet on her face. The man Bartholomew could not, or else he chose to ignore it.

She closed her eyes, offering one last defense: "You may kiss me when we are betrothed, yes, but—"

"I feel that if I do not kiss you now, I shall fall down dead!"

The man tightened his grip on the girl.

Bit's heart sweltered. His capillaries flooded. His veins surged. His lips burned.

He wanted to coil his own arms around this Eleanor, this diminutive lady-flower.

Unwittingly, he stepped forward. A twig snapped beneath his foot.

"What was that?" the girl Eleanor said, managing to push

away slightly from her suitor. "I thought I heard something."

"I reckon you just imagined it," the man said, shaking his head dismissively. "You let your head get filled with all sorts of silly stories, which lead to false imaginings."

"I do not—"

It was his turn to laugh, though there wasn't much mirth present. "I don't mind, Ellie. You can hardly help it, being a girl."

"I am fairly certain I *did* hear something."

"Perhaps it was my heart. Do you know, Eleanor? Do you know what you have done to my heart?"

"I—"

"Here," he said. He took her hand and guided it down his belly. "Feel it, Ellie."

"But your heart, is it not further up, there in your chest?"

"Silly stories, Ellie. Silly girlish stories." He pulled her hand down, beneath his waist.

"Bart—"

He pressed his lips against hers. She struggled to pull herself free.

"Bar—"

His lips smashed her words. His one hand pressed her hand down, against a part of himself that most definitely was not his heart. His other hand tugged at the back of her dress. Bit felt fury in his core. He felt sick with hunger and lust. He stepped forward, out from the brush behind which he had hidden. He walked down toward the riverbank. On the other side, the man Bartholomew pushed Eleanor down onto the quilt. Eleanor tried to break free, but she was pinned. Bit opened his mouth to scream, but no sound came out. His throat constricted. His chest tightened. He felt a familiar bristling of his skin. He looked up, into the darkening sky.

Hello, Moon.

His face contorted into a snout. His ears sharpened. His hands and feet rounded into paws. Fur pushed outward through his skin. Claws erupted from his fingers. Wolf opened his mouth to howl and his howl resounded across the forest. All the animals who heard it turned and ran, the deer, the beavers and groundhogs, the foxes and bears. The hawks and swallows took flight. The rabbits and mice burrowed beneath the ground. There were savage creatures in the forests of western Pennsylvania. Terrifying creatures.

Eleanor's eyes grew wide with terror, but Bartholomew Barrington was heedless, engrossed by the pulsing danger of his own self. He pulled up Eleanor's dress.

"My heart, Ellie . . . My heart needs this. . . ."

Bit howled again. He leapt into the river. He swam across it. He ran up the muddy bank. He pounced. Bartholomew Barrington did not see him coming.

Bit's teeth closed around the man's shoulder. He tore a chunk of soft flesh. Bartholomew Barrington screamed. Bit tried to pull the man back, to reach the girl underneath. Eleanor struggled to free herself, but she was trapped beneath the weight of man and wolf. Bit gnawed at the man until his teeth hit bone. He yanked. He ripped. He pulled the man's arm from its socket and tossed it aside. He opened his jaws and sunk his teeth into the other shoulder. He chewed and shredded the shoulder flesh, and when he reached the bone again, he ripped, tore, and tossed the other mangled arm onto the muddy riverbank. Then with his teeth he dragged Bartholomew Barrington from his beloved Eleanor. He dragged the man down the muddy slope, into the river. He watched the river carry the armless man away.

Bit shook the bloodied water from his fur. He looked to where Eleanor had been, but she had fled. He followed her scent, chamomile and soap now tinged with the metallic smell of Bartholomew Barrington's death blood.

But Bit could smell her blood as well.

His wolf heart pounded. He needed to see her. He needed to touch her skin, to bury his snout in the soft folds of her dress, to press his paws against her and . . . then what? Anchor his claws in her downy arm? Caress her neck with his bloodstained snout?

He sprinted forward, dizzy with the mingled scents of Eleanor and blood. He saw her, silhouetted against the cerulean sky, amid the dark trunks of watchful trees, clutching her arm. He saw the back of her dress, soiled and torn. He heard the fearful thudding of her small, animal heart. He walked beside her, unseen. He listened to her heart. He breathed in her scent. *How could I love you more?* The boy, what little remained of him, felt nearly content.

But Wolf was rapacious.

Wolf ran ahead. He circled around. He stopped in her path. In the dim light, she had nearly reached him before she noticed the moonlight glint on his sharp, smiling teeth. *How could I love you more?*

He professed his adoration with a snarl.

Eleanor screamed.

But Eleanor's mother and father and the rarefied Mr. and Mrs. Barrington and the concerned citizens of Washington, Pennsylvania, would not begin to search the forest for errant young lovers until dawn, and smallpox and muskets had decimated the Shawnee that had once lived in earshot, so Eleanor's screams struck without impact at the brimming darkness.

How could I love you more? Bit asked in his way. He stepped into a patch of moonlight. Eleanor, seeing him clearly now, screamed again. Her face twisted with horror. Her eyes recoiled at the sight of him. How large he had grown! How brutal and grotesque he appeared, with his monstrous rows of jagged teeth, his eyeless fox-head hat atop a wolf's visage, his coarse bloodstained fur! Seeing Eleanor's terror, her revulsion, he wished, for the first time, for the boy's return. He wished for his boy's body, enhanced by the resolve, the tenacity, of Wolf. *I'm a boy,* he tried to tell her. *Just a boy! I shall not hurt you!* His words dripped out in snarls and growls. Eleanor screamed. Tears spilled down her blood-splattered cheeks. She cradled one of her arms in the other.

For the toll had been taken already.

Bit saw the wound along her bicep. In the fury of ripping off Bartholomew Barrington's grabby arms, his teeth had pierced her flesh and torn off a piece of it. Blood seeped out of the gash, though Bit could see it was not deep. Her arm would recover. She would return home to Washington, Pennsylvania, her maidenhood intact, her heart damaged but not broken, for she had seen her darling Bartholomew Barrington for the changeling that he was. She would tell stories of the ferocious wolf that attacked her, the massive hideous wolf that tore the limbs from the young Mr. Barrington, the tender or wicked Mr. Barrington, who fought bravely or died a coward, who will be missed or should best be forgotten. The young Mr. Barrington, unable to interrupt her account, would in death be at her mercy, for her to venerate or condemn as she saw fit. All things came in cycles, and the young Mr. Barrington's cycle had ended. Then, some months later, when Eleanor's heart had recovered in full, a handsome wealthy lad, an earnest, God-fearing lad, of whom even the refined Mrs. Barrington would approve, would present himself to lovely Eleanor and steal the remains of her heart.

Except . . .

Bit smelled something he had not smelled before. Layered beneath the soap and cotton and chamomile scent of Eleanor, beneath the pine and flowering dogwood, the decomposing leaves, the iron splatter of Bartholomew Barrington's final spurts, the salty tender smell that leached from Eleanor's torn arm, Bit smelled something bitter. Something primal. He stepped back from Eleanor, who stood motionless and terrified before him, but the smell intensified. The hackles rose along Bit's neck and back. He sniffed the air. The smell seemed to come from Eleanor. Her face crinkled. She scrunched her nose. She could smell it, too. The odor got stronger, more feral. Eleanor let her injured arm fall to the side. She stared at Bit the Wolf. Her eyes looked different, Bit noticed. Keener. Darker. Her pupils shone with the light of the swollen moon.

Slowly, she lifted her uninjured arm. She held out her hand. She examined it, turning it over. She curled her fingers into a fist. Then her fingers sprang out, and from their tips sharp claws emerged. Eleanor screamed. The claws grew. Her fingers shrunk away. Her body convulsed. Her arms and torso whipped around. The seams of her dress split and the bodice fell away and for a moment Bit stared, in awe, at the soft breast buds of the topless girl bathed in moonlight. Then her chest flattened. Hair rippled across her torso. Her face twisted into a hideous snout.

It was wrong, Bit thought. All wrong. Lovely Eleanor. To see her transformed. To see her mutilated from the inside out. She opened her mouth to scream, but her straight lovely teeth had morphed into crooked blades, and a repugnant howl gurgled from her mouth. Lovely Eleanor. Bit took a step closer. The lady wolf shook her head. Her snout was damp with tears. Bit saw that the wound on her arm had already begun to heal. Bit took another step closer. *A horror*, he thought, as he looked into her yellow eyes, the twin moons that mirrored his own. *A freak. An abomination.* He stepped closer. Eleanor writhed in her new skin, but she did not run. *She is not Eleanor*, Bit thought. Not anymore. The Eleanor smell of soap and chamomile and cotton had gone, and Bit could only smell the hot breath of the lady wolf, rank with hunger and lust.

Bit stepped closer. *All wrong*, he thought. His wolf eyes narrowed with derision. *An abomination.* He stepped closer. Eleanor stood her ground. Perhaps she trusted him. Perhaps she refused to acknowledge that these wolf legs and paws belonged to her. Perhaps she realized that ferocity was a gift, that the likes of Bartholomew Barrington did not stand the faintest chance against Eleanor Wolf.

Bit stepped closer, close enough to kiss. He opened his mouth. He pounced. She was bigger than him, but uncertain. She had not learned how to fight. She did not know what her teeth could do. He tore her apart.

Weeks later, two men traveling south to Washington from Burgettstown brought news of the body of a wolf, a gnarly, grotesque wolf that had quite possibly eaten the young lady Eleanor, before getting killed itself, by some creature even more awful.

NATASHA

THE AFTER-SLIME

San Francisco—Now

THE PRETTY BOY, it turned out, didn't know much about werewolves.

Natasha led him to her car. She rearranged the bags in her front seat and covered it with a towel so he wouldn't slime it.

"Is this a car?" he asked as he climbed in. His hands fumbled, grasping the bags she'd shoved to the side and on the floor. "I can't . . . Where am I supposed to put my feet?"

"Just coil yourself into a ball. You'll fit, technically."

"But the seat belt—"

Natasha laughed. It seemed absurd that a naked man whose sticky frame had just enveloped a werewolf body would fret about seat belts. She shut the door behind him. She climbed into the driver's seat.

"Please don't turn me in," Shane whimpered. "I swear, I didn't kill anyone. I would never . . . I . . . This was only the first time, I mean, since I got turned . . . I didn't even know . . . and I'm so, so hideous . . ."

"So you weren't a werewolf two months ago?"

"No."

"That sounds like the sort of lie a werewolf might tell."

"I swear. I wasn't."

"What's your name, pretty boy?"

"Shane. Shane LaSalle."

"I'm Natasha. And, well, if it makes you feel any better, you're not hideous now."

"Oh. Thanks. But the slime—"

"I'm sure you can wash that off. It better wash off, otherwise you owe me a new sweater." He had the thing wrapped around his hips, covering his front parts. But his butt cheeks were still exposed.

"I need to go home. Oh, God, but I can't go home! I can't just walk into my building like this, and everyone will see—"

"I'll take you home after we go somewhere safe where you can get all cleaned up."

Natasha drove to Lee Curtis's house. Lee's wife had a trial in Seattle and had left town for a week. Natasha trusted Lee to not think that she was insane. And, based on his vigorous reaction when she'd confronted him about Marie, and the fact that he'd stayed beneath the tree all night without once trying to attack her, she trusted the werewolf in her front seat.

They parked outside a two-story stucco house. Shane cowered behind her as she rang the doorbell.

"Thank God you're here," Lee called, on his way down the stairs to let her in. "I'm covered in spit-up. I'm in desperate need

of a shower, and the peanut screams every time I try to put her—
Um . . . who is . . ."

Lee stared at the man standing outside of his door: his eyes
pinched shut, naked except for the sweater tied around his waist,
gorgeous except for the greasy film that coated his skin and clung
to his ears and neck in congealed lumps.

"I caught a werewolf," Natasha said bluntly.

"But there's . . . Are you serious?"

"I caught him with my pepper spray."

"And *that's* the werewolf?"

"One of them. His name is Shane. Can we come in?"

"Yes, but . . . uh, what's that gross stuff all over his skin?"

"Oh, my skin . . ." Shane cried.

"I don't think he knows. He's a new werewolf."

"Right. Okay. Okay . . . But he needs to be hosed off. I don't
want that slimy stuff he's got all over him clogging up the drain."

Natasha led Shane into Lee's small backyard. She sprayed him
off with the hose while he moaned and whimpered—not because
the water was ice-cold but because the neighbors might spot him.
Then she led naked, dripping Shane inside to the bathroom, while
Lee kept Veronica distracted.

"So, can we talk about this?" Lee said to Natasha, while Shane
washed off.

"I know, it's crazy."

"Natasha, there's no such thing as werewolves. They're not
real."

"But, *Dad*," Veronica said, poking her head around the corner,
"ghostes are real."

"Veronica, were you eavesdropping? It's not polite to eavesdrop."

"But my ears got stuck, Dad."

"She's got a point, Lee," said Natasha.

"And Santa Claus is real," Veronica added.

Lee nodded solemnly, dutifully. "Yes, of course he is, darling."

"And fairies, and lepercons, and Spider-Man—"

"Spider-Man?"

"So werewolveses are probly real too."

"They're not."

"Lee, I swear, I saw it with my own eyes. And you saw the slime on him. I mean, that's not, like, natural slime."

"Okay, yeah," Lee said. He looked skeptical, until she reminded him of his own watched-by-a-mysterious-something full moon story. "So, where'd you find this guy anyway?" he asked.

Natasha relayed the story of her evening on the golf course.

"So what," Lee said, frowning, "these werewolves are, like, country club werewolves?"

"Yeah. I mean, wolves are pack animals. So they'd want to belong to a club."

"Right . . . Unless they're a lone wolf?"

"Well, okay." Natasha laughed, nervously, as the conversation veered further into the suspect realm of occult conspiracy. "But maybe a lone wolf would still *want* to belong. Maybe it would prowl the golf course hoping someday it'll get a membership. But there were definitely multiple wolves, so . . ."

It seemed even crazier now, in the sunlight: country club werewolves; werewolves riding around on their golf carts; werewolves playing bridge and sipping martinis at the bar; tuxedoed werewolves giving dinner party champagne toasts. Werewolves were absurdist fiction. Werewolves were not showering the slime off their tanned shoulders and waxed backs in her friend's bathroom. Werewolves only existed in the deluded woods outside Crazy Town—and this was America.

"Look! I drew a picture!" Veronica held up a picture of a big brown scribble with a smaller yellow scribble on top. "That's the werewolf." She pointed to the splotch of brown, and then to the yellow. "And that's its hat. It's wearing a hat."

"That's lovely," her father said.

"It really is," Natasha agreed.

"And that," Veronica said to Natasha, as she pointed at a blank white space above the werewolf scribble, "is you. You're inbisible. Because you're a ghost, and no one can see ghostses, 'cept for me and Dad."

Lee Curtis cooked breakfast. They all sat around the kitchen table and ate the SAHD (stay-at-home dad) special: sausage, toaster waffles, apple slices, strawberry yogurt with saltine crackers.

"Veronica spoons the yogurt up with the crackers," he explained. "It's the only way to get her to eat the yogurt."

"This is great, thank you," Shane said. "I'm starved. I feel like I could eat a horse."

"I mean, *would* you eat a horse?" Natasha asked, but then felt a little bad when the pretty boy looked unnerved.

"I don't . . . I hope I wouldn't . . . I don't know what I might do," Shane said as he ate a whole link of sausage in a single bite.

"But you're still there, right? When you turn into a wolf? I mean, the way you were whimpering . . . Your conscious mind is all still there?"

"Well, yes and no." Shane eyed the sausage on Natasha's plate. "I mean, I still know what I'm doing, but it feels kind of like the wolf is steering, and I'm just in the passenger seat."

"So, last night, if I had come down from the tree, would you have killed me?"

"Oh God, no! No! I just . . . I was trying to protect you, from my partner. And I stayed because I wanted to make sure my partner didn't come back."

"Would he have killed me?" Natasha asked in a voice that suggested she knew the answer.

"I think . . . I think he might have. He's—"

"A *bad* werewolf?" Veronica asked. She popped up from underneath the table. She had a yogurt beard, and a handful of waffle crumbs, which she laid on the table. "I knew it!"

"Veronica, what did I tell you about tearing your waffle apart?"

The little girl gestured at the crumbs. "But, Dad, those parts are the crungy parts." She leaned closer to Shane and sniffed. "Are you a bad werewolf?"

"I . . . I don't think so."

"I think you're a good werewolf," Veronica declared. "Here," she said, brushing the waffle crumbs across the table to him, "these are for you."

"Um, thanks."

"But your partner," Natasha asked as she forked her own sausage and deposited it on Shane's plate, "the other werewolf you were with—what about him?"

"He's . . . well, he's . . . I never liked—"

She held up a flat palm. "You think maybe he killed my friend?"

"Oh God." Shane LaSalle started to cry, and once he started, he couldn't stop. Tears surged from the slits of his inflamed eyes. His chest heaved with the weight of his sobs. His lovely lips trembled.

"Dad," Veronica whispered. "Why's he crying?"

"Duane . . ." Shane cried. Lee Curtis handed him a tissue. Veronica patted his back. "Oh, Duane . . ."

"Who is Duane?" Veronica asked. "Is he a werewolf too?"

"No, he's . . . he was . . . "

Veronica tried to convince him that werewolves weren't supposed to cry, until her dad explained that werewolves could cry when they needed to and it didn't make them any less werewolvesy. Natasha went to the kitchen to make more tea, because it always made her feel uncomfortable to watch other people cry.

After a few minutes, Shane LaSalle collected himself. He wiped his puffy eyes. "Duane . . ." he said, fighting fresh tears. "Duane was my . . . he was my friend. My true friend . . . I loved him."

Shane LaSalle told them what had happened, that night in Lake Orange when the werewolves made him one of them. He told them how the wolves had attacked, how he had roamed the forest, naked and confused, and how he had finally returned, to find that Duane Beckman had not. He told them about the article he had found in the *Lake Orange Gazette*, about the mauled body, which had to have belonged to Duane.

"He wouldn't have just left," Shane explained. "He thought he was about to make partner. And he . . . he wouldn't have left without saying goodbye."

"Do you think they meant to kill him?" Lee Curtis asked. "I

mean, you get turned into a werewolf if you get bit by a werewolf, right? At least, that's what happened to you. Maybe they meant to make him a werewolf too, but it didn't work."

"So maybe it was an accident?" Shane asked.

"Does it matter?" Natasha said. "They didn't ask your permission when they bit you. They just did it. So it was probably the same with your friend. And maybe they were thinking, 'Oh, he totally wants this because this is how he gets to join our secret werewolf cult,' or whatever, but the point is that they didn't ask, and it got your friend killed. And he's not the first one they've killed either."

"Your friend—the woman you said got killed—you really think a werewolf killed her?" Shane asked.

"She worked at the Olympic Club," Natasha said. "The moon was full the night she got killed. She had bite marks on her body that, apparently, don't match any known animal. So I think there's a good chance that one of your partners is responsible. It all makes sense."

"As much as any of this makes sense," Lee said. "But you can't prove it."

"And we can't prove they killed Duane, either," Shane said. "We don't even know which one did it, and even if we did, just look at them. They're rich. They're powerful. They do whatever they want and get away with it. Because that's how it works, if you're rich enough. If you're rich, the rules don't apply. And no one knows they're werewolves. No one even knows werewolves exist!" Fresh tears flowed down Shane's sculpted cheekbones.

"Actually," Natasha said, "I think there might be someone who knows."

Subject: Werewolf in need of help

Dear Ms. Z'Rhae,

I know this is going to sound absolutely crazy. And I know you probably think I'm an asshole. But I didn't know where else to turn. I read an interview you gave about werewolves, and I'm writing to you in hopes that you'll be willing to help a young werewolf out. He got bitten just over a month ago. He's freaked out, and he's gotten involved with some bad werewolf types who we think may have killed his friend on the same night they bit him. We think they might have killed my roommate, too. But this guy—his name is Shane—I think he's a good guy. I met him in his werewolf state, and he could have killed me, but he didn't, and then he stuck around to make sure the other werewolves couldn't hurt me either. If you have any ideas about how to help him, or how we could catch the werewolves who murdered our friends, we'd really appreciate it.

Sincerely,

Natasha Porter

PS: You may recognize my name, and I want to say up front that I'm sorry for what I said about you on the Bertrand Mailer show. It was unfair of me to judge. I hope that any bad feelings you may have for me don't stop you from helping a werewolf in need.

WEREWOLF HANGOVER

San Francisco–Now

FIRST YOU SEE ME. Duane Beckman reclined, his feet on his desk, the top buttons on his shirt undone, revealing a smooth crescent of man-chest. *Now you don't.* In a magic *zap,* Duane Beckman vanished. His clothes lay crumpled where his body had been. Shane picked up Duane's blazer. He held it to his cheek. *Duane Duane Duane . . .* He heard the twinkle chime of magic behind him. He turned. He saw a fog in the shape of Duane. *Duane, is that you? Please let it be you.* Duane appeared from a haze of sparkles. The air cleared. He held his hand to Shane's cheek. *It's always been me,* he said. Duane wore nothing. His skin had changed to shimmering scales. His hair was studded with sequins—his Duaneness diminished, and yet brighter than any Duane that had shone before. *Who are you?* Shane asked him. Duane laughed. *I think the question,* he said, *is who are YOU?*

Shane awoke suddenly, and with a werewolf hangover.

He could still feel Duane's hand on his cheek.

He wanted bacon and sausage.

He wanted a big breakfast platter with nothing but bacon and sausage. Fuck the eggs. Toast was for puny humans. He ripped off his bedsheets savagely. He prowled through his luxury hallway, the hallway designed to *make a statement*. The statement was . . .

. . . was . . .

He turned into the bathroom. He looked at himself in the mirror: Shane LaSalle flanked by gold-flecked marble sink and matching Escher chandelier, Shane LaSalle reflected by disassembled mirror reassembled into tiny mirror pieces, to the annoyance of Shane's housekeeper. Every view in the apartment was a *photortunity*. But what sort of image-obsessed douche used a word like *photortunity*? Shane LaSalle. Shane LaSalle used it on the regular. But who was Shane LaSalle?

Shane looked at himself, at his trust-inducing eyes, his pristine face. Somewhere behind that face existed his real face. His mutant teeth. His gnarled snout. His jowl, with its fountains of slobber-slime.

"Who the hell are you?!" he yelled at his gorgeous reflection. It felt good to yell, so he did it again. *"Who the hell are you, Shane?!"*

That pesky back hair had regrown overnight, and his eyebrows needed waxing. *But fuck it*, he decided. He got into the shower. He jerked himself off, all the while thinking about Duane Beckman painted in shimmering scales. But after he came, he felt disgusted with himself, because Duane Beckman was dead, and what had he done about it?

Shane LaSalle is a coward: his first conclusion, in this long-postponed moment of self-reflection.

Shane LaSalle is gay, or at least gay enough to fall in love with Duane Beckman.

Shane LaSalle is not a parasailor.

Shane LaSalle regrets having cast himself as a devoted aquatics acolyte. He would rather stay on the boat and drink a martini.

Shane LaSalle wants a crystal chandelier, not a polished junkyard piece of modern art with stupid light bulbs attached to it.

Shane LaSalle is a motherfucking werewolf.

This last revelation repelled him, aesthetically, but morally as well. And yet, in that moment Shane was also filled with vicious rage. He wanted to punch through the bubbled glass of his shower door. He wanted to slam his pretty head into the asymmetrical subway-tiled shower walls. He resisted the urge. *Duane Duane Duane . . .* He allowed himself to indulge in a short sob. Then he dried himself off with a towel—which was too short, too thin, selected only for its sleek appearance as an accessory to his bathroom—and got ready to go into the office.

"Good morning, Mr. LaSalle!"

"So nice to see you, Mr. LaSalle!"

"Oh, Mr. LaSalle! Hello! I hope you have a great day!"

Stanley Rollins had taken it upon himself to instruct his sec-retary to have breakfast delivered to Shane's office again. A silver platter–laden cart waited by Shane's desk with a week's worth of breakfast foods. Because maybe Shane had a hankering for blueberry pancakes. Maybe he wanted a crepe. Maybe he wanted goetta topped with bacon. Perhaps he would like a nibble of each item on the cart! It was his right, now that he was a partner!

He recalled something Duane had said once. *Such a waste,* he had said, and Shane remembered wanting to shush him because of his sense that the partners were always behind him, always listening. *All those people right out there who probably don't have enough to eat, and they're throwing out bags of perfectly good food every day.*

Shane pushed the cart aside. He didn't feel like eating. He felt like feeling hungry. He wanted that ache in his gut, the sheer clarity of mind that hunger brought.

Clifton James walked into Shane's office.

"LaSalle! You're looking well. Did you enjoy the dinner party?"

"It was great fun," Shane lied.

"Dick caught a deer."

"How delicious."

"Sorry about your suit."

"Not to worry. It was my least favorite."

"And about Carver, we all appreciate you keeping him in check."

"What do you—"

"The girl, the one he chased after. He might have killed her, if you hadn't intervened and stood guard all night. It's unfortunate, you know, because you didn't get to have as much fun. But Carver . . ." Clifton James popped his head out to scan the hallway, before shutting the door. "Carver goes too far sometimes, in my opinion. We've told him so before. He's not strategic. He makes messes, and then we have to clean them up, which is a pain in the ass. You saved us some trouble by stopping him from making a mess of that girl. It's bad form to do something like that on the golf course."

"Yeah. Right. Yes," Shane agreed.

Clifton James looked at him. "You okay there, buddy?"

"Yeah, totally."

"Look, its . . ." Clifton James put his hand on Shane's shoulder. "I know it's a rough adjustment. But you can handle it. I know you can. And I think you'll find, once you get used to it, that your new werewolf nature is really an attribute. You're more perceptive, stronger, sharper. You're a better version of the Shane LaSalle you always were."

"Thanks." Shane felt stronger, sharper, better. But he also felt the weight of his partner's hand on his shoulder.

"We're not all like Carver. Hell, I'm definitely not. You won't be either, LaSalle."

"If he goes too far," Shane said, "if he's not strategic, like you said, then—"

"Ah, LaSalle. That's what I like about you. I knew the moment I met you. I thought, here's a man who will do what it takes. Yes, what you are thinking could happen if it had to. But Carver has his uses. Barrington wants to keep him around. They go way back. I would just ignore him if I were you. You just make sure you stay on Barrington's good side. You do that, LaSalle, and you're golden."

"Right, golden. I'll do that . . . so, to change the topic to work," Shane said. He felt uncomfortable hearing Clifton James casually discuss the . . . *W* issue. "Alvin's Sports and Supplies."

"What about them?"

"I'd like to go back and talk to Jeanie Glass one more time. To make sure we can get this deal done. I think if we could just fly back there, and I could talk to her more—"

And tell her to keep her family business far, far away from these vicious wolves? Shane hadn't thought through what to tell her, but he knew he needed to say something.

"There's no need," Clifton said. "The board is on board, so to speak. Don and Stan are on their way out there right now."

"Oh. Okay, good."

"And if Jeanie Glass gets in the way," Clifton said with a smile, "then . . . well . . . hopefully it won't come to that. But if it does, we'll just send Carver to take care of it."

Who was Shane LaSalle?

Was he a Carver? Was he a Clifton James? Was he a brutal, bloodthirsty killer? Was he golden?

Was he a good boy?

Shane paced along the dock, phone to his ear. He was blocks away from the office, at the end of a wooden dock beyond the Embarcadero, overlooking the blue waters of San Francisco Bay. He couldn't smell his partners, but he sensed that they might be watching, lying in wait, doused in cologne to conceal their true selves.

The telephone rang.

Pick up pick up pick up pick up, he pleaded.

"Hello?"

"Jeanie?"

"Yes?"

"Jeanie, its Shane LaSalle." Cold wind blew off the bay, and Shane shivered.

"Oh, hi, Shane. How are—"

"Jeanie, I need to make this quick. My partners are on their way out there."

"Yes, I know. They're bringing papers."

"Look, Jeanie, you have to be careful."

"What . . . what do you mean?"

"It's . . . I can't explain . . . I just . . ." Shane looked back at the gleaming city, the billion-dollar skyscrapers, the foggy hills seeded with unfathomable wealth. How many people had his partners killed? "You remember when we went out for pie, and I . . . I gushed about how Barrington Equity is a family business? Just because something is a family business—I mean, the mob is a family business. Jeanie, you can't let your company get involved with my firm. We'll load it up with debt and then we'll bankrupt it and then . . ."

"I know."

"You know?"

"I did my research. Look, you seem like a nice guy, Shane, but your firm has . . . Let's just say they've got some questionable business practices."

"So you're not going to sign the papers?"

"I might not have much of a choice. The board is all for it."

"No . . ."

"What's this about? What's going on, Shane?"

"Look, just . . . can you delay them? Tell them you're still interested but you need to have your lawyers look over the papers again?"

"I could probably delay them for a few weeks."

"A few weeks. Okay. That'll at least give me some time to come up with a plan. But in the meantime you need to get out of town, okay? Take a trip somewhere no one can find you."

"Shane, my dad—"

"Take him with you. The guys in my firm, they're dangerous. If they think you're going to stand in their way . . ."

"So I'll call the police."

"And tell them what? They're not going to make threats first. They'll just . . . you won't even see them coming. Please, trust me. Just, get yourself out of there, okay?"

A curious question is why, in almost all werewolf accounts, the werewolf is reported as male. Assuming lycanthropy to be pathogenic in nature, there is simply no reason why the condition should not be evenly distributed between the sexes. One possible explanation is that there actually are relatively equal numbers of both female and male werewolves, but that the humans who report having encountered one presume the creature to be male. Indeed, the descriptors typically given to werewolves—ferocious, hairy, brutal, vicious, aggressive, grotesque—have historically been associated with masculinity. Attributes stereotypically deemed feminine in nature—modesty, nurturance, tenderness, passivity, to name a few—are, if one subscribes to these stereotypes, antithetical to wolfdom. Such gender conventions are mirrored in fictional accounts of werewolves. Throughout literature, film, and television, nearly all werewolves are male. Female werewolves, where they do appear, are often depicted as inappropriately aggressive, overly sexualized, or weaker than their male counterparts.

The explanation that the gender discrepancy in werewolf reporting simply reflects gender stereotypes, while plausible, is undercut by the factual accounts of the werewolves in their human forms. With only two exceptions (discussed later, in chapter 12, which explores notable werewolf incidents of the twentieth century), all the Americans who reportedly possess the ability (or curse) to transform from human to wolf have been described as men.

The more likely explanation for the dearth of female werewolves, rather, is that werewolves are self-selecting; that is, to the extent that werewolves differentiate between the victims they choose to kill and the victims whom they leave alive for transformation, male werewolves, themselves influenced by gender conventions, simply elect to pass the condition to males.

Marcus Flick, <u>American Myths and Monsters: The Werewolf</u>, 2nd ed. (Denver: Birdhouse Press, 2022), 112-13

BIT

WHEREIN BIT TAKES THE CITY

Cincinnati—1841-42

LOVELY ELEANOR HAD drawn the boy from the wolf. Or at least, her death had.

Bit strayed from the forest, back into the lands of the humans. He ventured first at night. He pressed his face against the dark glass of a farmhouse window and peered inside. He gathered apples and potatoes from a barn while the sheep and horses slept. He squeezed early milk from a dairy cow and laughed from the rafters at the old biddy who arrived at dawn with her milking tin only to find the teats dry. *The old hag.* Bit was gone before she could return with her gun. *I should have a gun*, Bit decided, so he stole one. He had no bullets, but he liked the look of it, tucked into his cape of skins. He ventured farther, in daylight, barefoot over the cobbles of a paved road. The townsfolk stared at Bit's exposed chest, his mottled skins and furs, the fox's head set atop his own. He had painted its eye sockets with rings of blood and pinned his jeweled brooch to its snout, a crown for King Bit. *The devil, he is,* voices whispered as he passed. *The devil needs some clothes,* Bit thought, so he stole clothes. He snatched them off sun-soaked wash lines. He pilfered them from chests of drawers, in sleeping houses, where he crept without causing a single floorboard creak. He stole a golden cross on a golden chain from the bedside of a sleeping woman. He stole her Bible, and he stared at the markings on its pages until he remembered how to read, as Mary had taught him. The Mother Mary. She had loved him, even if he was the devil. Mayhap another would as well.

Lovely Eleanor drew the man out of the boy. He conjured her before sleep. He imagined her fair skin, her hair like silk, her body beneath him instead of his transient bed of branches, the solid flesh of her for him to hold. He saw her as he wanted her to be, supple and smiling, pliant, angelic. She was an angel, all right. *With the Lord, now,* said a voice from Bit's past, a voice that Wolf had tried to bury. He exiled from his mind any trace of Eleanor incongruous with his vision—the lady who fought back, the strong lady wolf, the lady who he killed. *Got 'erself killed,* Bit thought. *Shouldn't have turned into that*

that

that THING.

Should have stayed the good, lovely Eleanor.

"Why, Lord?" Bit asked, tasting the words in his mouth, to see if he liked their flavor.

The Lord responded with silence.

"Why, Moon?" Bit asked, turning his eyes to the great egg in the sky.

The moon glistened.

Why not? Moon replied. *You think any of us have the answers? Don't ask stupid questions, Bit.*

Lovely, dead Eleanor lured the young man west.

It wasn't Eleanor, but Bit pretended until pretense became belief.

"Out West, that's where," Bit overheard another young man say. "A man can make something of himself, out West. More land than you can imagine, and they're just giving it away!"

Bit imagined: vast forested tracks for Wolf to roam; a dark road winding through them, on which a stealthy wolf would attack wealthy travelers and free them of their belongings; a castle for King Bit, with all the lovely Eleanor courtiers he could devour.

Bit was a young man dressed in fine stolen clothes when he saw the city. He saw her smoke from afar, late on a winter's day. He smelled burnt wood, charcoal, kerosene. He smelled barley, pork stew, corn bread and potatoes, the blood of a fresh-slaughtered pig. He walked toward it, carrying the shoes he wore for show, his Bible tucked beneath his arm, his pockets heavy with coins. He smelled soap, chamomile, cotton, and the smell hardened him, made him resolute, and hungry. He would take whatever he could from this city.

He walked down to the river, along the road that snaked its banks. He came into the city at night. He invited himself inside a boarding house.

"How much for the night?" he asked, in his most trustworthy voice.

"How much you got?" the innkeeper replied. Bit passed him a coin. "Humph. Well, that'll do. But supper's done for the night."

He observed the innkeeper plunk the coin into a drawer, intending to steal it back in the morning. The innkeeper handed Bit a chunk of dry bread and a jug of water and showed him to his room. Alone, Bit tested the bed. He stretched out and stared up at the cracks in the ceiling. He tried to sleep, but the smells of the city overwhelmed him, and after a few minutes he was out the window, down on the street, following his nose.

He walked up Vine Street until he came to a tavern. He caught the scent of lovely Eleanor inside. He went in. He sat at the bar. Eleanor's scent emanated from the barmaid: Eleanor, but leaner, sharper.

"What'll it be?" she asked as she turned to face him.

This one cast Eleanor into the shadows. She was all brightness. She had the keen eyes of a fox, though inside of them Bit saw the spark of something wolfish.

"I'll have . . ." Bit looked around.

The moon was a sliver, and he felt meek and uncertain. He had never drunk at a tavern. The only thing he wanted to drink was her.

"Wolf got your tongue?"

He looked back at the woman. "What?"

"Something my ma used to say. Her ma, my grandmamma, was a mute. Had her tongue cut out and fed to the wolves."

"How'd she get her tongue cut out?"

"In the usual way." She looked closer at him. "You ain't been in no tavern before, have ya?"

"I have."

"Sure. You'll be wanting a pint, then. And the meat Wellington. You'll like that."

"Okay."

She filled a tall mug with beer and handed it to Bit. "I won't tell ya what meat it is. Probably best that you don't know."

"Okay. How much?"

"You hand me one of them coins in yer pocket and I'll make change."

Bit sat at the bar and watched the new Eleanor, more luminous than the one he'd killed. He watched her swift hands in the dishwater, soaping off the mugs. He drank the curve of her waist, the swish of her hip as she bustled past with a tray of ale and pickles. He observed the way she bit her lip when she counted, the way she scanned the room. She picked out the drunks and sold them another round. Bit felt hot and giddy. His head swam from the beer. He ate the meat Wellington as slowly as he could, savoring every glimpse of Barmaid. The meat tasted stringy and overcooked.

"So, you want to know what it is?" she asked, after Bit had finished and after the tables had gotten wiped, the chairs stacked, the drunks sent off into the night.

"What what is?"

"The meat in the Wellington. Changes every week, depending on what the cook can get hold of. This week it's cat."

"It wasn't very good cat. I've had better."

She laughed. Bit grinned. Cat tasted better fresh, after a chase, with its hot blood still spurting.

"You're somethin', ain't ya," she said. She stepped right up next to him, close enough that he could hear her steady heartbeat beneath her breast. Her scent flooded his nose. "Time to go now," she whispered. "But I'll be seein' you tomorrow."

Bit nodded.

He left the tavern. As he walked back down Vine toward the boarding house, he noticed that his pockets felt light. She had swift hands, he thought, and smiled to himself.

In daylight, Bit walked the streets downtown. He observed the humans. He studied their mannerisms, their methods. He did not dare steal, in the city, with so many eyes to see him. At least, not until he discerned how to move beneath them unseen.

At night, he returned to the tavern. He drank a pint, or two. He minded his pockets. He ate the meat Wellington, the meat potpie, the brisket surprise. His eyes devoured Barmaid. His hunger for Barmaid pained him. The moon swelled, and Bit fled the city, lest the scent of her tempt him. He raged at the moon, because it kept him away from her.

Hello, Bit, Moon said, as it rose over snow-mottled hillsides.

Go away, Wolf growled.

Not happy to see me, are you?

You keep me from her, Wolf growled.

Do I? Or is that your choice?

Moon knew nothing, Bit decided. A wolf could not wander the peaceful city streets in broad lamplight and not get shot. A wolf could only roam the countryside, and kill, and kill, to try and fill the hole inside itself.

"Missed you last night," the barmaid said when Moon had subsided and Bit returned.

"You did?" Bit asked.

She laughed. "I'm getting to be fond of you."

Sometimes, Bit pretended not to mind his pockets, so that she would reach in and steal a coin. A man would not have felt her hand, so swift she was, but Bit was not exactly a man.

"I've always been fond of you," Bit said.

"You don't know me. You don't know a thing about me."

"I know how beautiful you are."

"Ha! You and every other fellow that comes in here."

"I know that you've been stealing coins from my pocket."

"Well, that's something interesting, now."

"I know you deserve someplace better than this."

"Someplace where they serve cows and chickens, instead of rats and cats?"

"Someplace like that, yes."

"And you're going to give it to me." She leaned on the bar. She stared at him with piercing eyes. "Is that it?"

"Well, I—"

She turned and walked away.

Bit's stomach filled with sour bile. He drank a pint, and then another. She cleaned the tables and washed the dishes. She poured a pint for herself and sat down beside him.

"My grandmamma got her tongue cut out her mouth, but she had it better," the barmaid said. "My ma, she got beat every night. Lost every one of her teeth. Lost what was in 'er head, too. All turned to jelly. So which is the worse to lose? Me, I thought I'd come to the city and take care of myself."

"You seem to be doing fine."

"For a barmaid."

"You don't want to be a barmaid?"

"It doesn't much matter what I want. I don't get to choose." She sipped her beer. Bit watched her. He could smell the coins in her pocket. He could smell her ambition. "What's your name?" she asked.

"I'm B—"

Bit. What sad sort of name was that? None that he had heard anywhere else. *Bit.* She would laugh him out of the tavern. He needed another name. Something respectable. So he stole one.

"Bartholomew. Bartholomew Barrington."

"Pleased to make your acquaintance, Mr. Barrington." She offered her hand, for him to shake. "You can call me Rosalina."

Bartholomew Barrington got himself a job as a teller at the Losantiville Bank. He counted coins and bills. His nose learned the scent of money. He learned which customers possessed the most substantial deposits, and where they lived.

He earned his first real paycheck three weeks in, after a thin man with a thin mustache withdrew $250.

"Here you go, Mr. Avery."

"Thank you, young sir."

"You have a pleasant day, Mr. Avery!"

"And you as well!"

The day did not turn out so pleasant for Mr. Avery. A congenial young bank teller visited his house after hours, pried open the dark window, and invited himself inside. Mr. Avery had strayed from his bed, in pursuit of a midnight glass of sherry to quell his restless mind. He stumbled upon the young bank teller in the foyer, carrying away his tin of cash.

"My tin! How did you—"

The young teller grinned.

"I know you!" Mr. Avery said. "From the bank! You give that back! I'll—"

The young teller punched Mr. Avery in the face. The man was not only thin, but rubbery and weak. He fell back onto the floor. The resourceful teller picked up a coatrack, shook the coats and hats off it, and beat all recognition from Mr. Avery's mind. When he had finished, he poured himself a glass of Mr. Avery's sherry and ate the wheel of cheese he found in Mr. Avery's kitchen. Then he selected a fine fur coat from the floor where they had fallen, one of Mrs. Avery's. The brazen teller walked out the front door with his coat and his cash, into the blustery late winter's night. He felt hungrier than ever.

He presented the fur to Rosalina.

"I brought you a gift."

"It's quite beautiful. I dare say you don't earn enough as a bank teller to afford a coat like this."

"I'm resourceful."

"There's a spot of blood on the collar there."

"Oh, I—"

"Don't worry, I can just cut that bit out. It's hardly noticeable."

Rosalina tried on her new coat. Bit felt fire in his groin. He wanted to rip her out of it.

She twirled across the sticky tavern floor. "You know what would look just perfect with this coat?"

"What?"

"Pearls."

Bit never stole from the bank, but he made regular house calls to its customers. He avoided messes like the one he had made of Mr. Avery. He learned to steal in little bits, small percentages, fees: a single brooch from a box full of jewels, a single coin from a jar of twenty. He never snatched a whole set of silverware. He took one of each utensil, plus an extra silver spoon to tuck in the help's apron.

You can't let them suspect they're being robbed by someone who works at the bank, Rosalina had instructed. At first, Bit had thought: *So what if they suspect? They'll never catch Wolf!* The plump moon made him cocky. But Rosalina was shrewd: *You have to give them someone else to blame.*

For example:

"My lazy cook!"

"That dull gardener."

"The slovenly chimney sweep."

"That maid, I never trusted her. A mistake to let her into our home! And that husband of hers! We tried to be generous to these people, but maybe your mother was right about the lot of them!"

Bartholomew Barrington, on the other hand, appeared conscientious and trustworthy.

"Oh, Mr. Lindner, you dropped your billfold on the ground!"

he would exclaim, after reaching across the counter with a swift hand and plucking the billfold from Mr. Lindner's pocket himself.

"Oh, Mrs. Ludlow, that's a beautiful brooch. Is it new?" he would ask, as he counted out Mrs. Ludlow's weekly allotment.

"You're such a nice, observant young man, aren't you," Mrs. Ludlow would say. "It is new. My old brooch was stolen."

"Gee, I'm sorry to hear that."

"Yes, well, the *housekeeper*. We found it in her quarters, except that she had pried the stone out of it. She refused to tell us what she'd done with it."

"That's terrible," he said sympathetically. The emerald stone looked lovely on Rosalina's finger.

"Well, her thieving days are over. She's set to be hanged on Saturday."

Rosalina accompanied Bartholomew Barrington to the hanging. She wore her best fur coat.

"You should not watch."

"Why not?"

The crowd was raucous, eager, everyone dressed like this was church on Easter Sunday.

"It's gruesome," Bit said, as he tried to stand in front of her. "You're a lady. A lady should not watch these sorts of things."

"But I need to see it." She pushed past him.

"I can describe it to you."

"But I need to see for myself what we've done."

He did not like that his lady's eyes would be despoiled by the sight of a broken neck. But Rosalina was not all his. He offered to shield her eyes with his hands. She stepped forward into the crowd, just beyond his reach. She stroked the emerald on her finger and did not avert her eyes when the housekeeper swung from the gallows.

Summer came angry and hot that year. Rain renounced the Queen City. Fissures formed in the streets. The hooves of horses and pigs stomped clouds of dust from the earth. The river shrunk. Bartholomew Barrington sweated through the finely tailored shirts he wore to the bank. He robbed restlessly, taking more than advisable, as if he could steal his way toward cooler weather.

The city itself grew restless. The wealthy fired their cooks, their housekeepers, their gardeners, their drivers. *Caught stealing,* the story went. *Thought I lost my pendant, and then I found it in her pocket!* The poor stole from each other. They roamed the city in vicious packs, demanding work. The unemployed poor despised the working poor, who either had taken or might take their jobs, and the workers despised the unemployed for lazing in the shade while they toiled in the hot sun.

On the last night of August, Bit watched men brawl in the streets. He watched an Irishman club a young Black boy near to death. He watched the boy's wailing brother stab another pale-faced man in the gut. Bit went to the tavern for a pint of beer.

"People are fighting out there," he told Rosalina.

"'Course they are," she said. "They're mad. I heard there's to be an assembly tomorrow."

"Whereabouts?"

"Over on Fifth Street. I should like to go and watch."

"You should not," Bit said. "It might not be safe, for a woman."

"It will likely not be safe for anyone." Rosalina poured herself a glass of beer. She wiped the sweat from her forehead with her apron sleeve. "When I was a girl, my younger brother fell ill. My dad had gone away to find work, and my ma had no money to pay the doctor, but the doctor came anyway. He came every day for a week, and he made my brother well again. A giver of miracles, I thought he was. I decided that when I grew up, I wanted to be a doctor. And I told my ma, and she laughed, o' course. Ain't no one ever heard of a woman doctor. The best I could do, she said, was to hitch my wagon to the doctor's horse. I didn't know what she meant, at the time. Though later . . . later I found out that the doctor had not treated my brother for free. My ma had been hitching her wagon, so to speak. Anyway, the reason I'm tellin' you this is 'cause, well . . . a wagon don't go nowhere on its own. I can't be no doctor, but maybe you can. I can't work in no bank, or buy myself a nice big house, but you can. You're shrewd, Bartholomew Barrington. You've got somethin' in you, somethin' that can't be stopped."

"Would you like a big house, Rosalina?"

"I would take one."

"Will you stay away from that assembly? I should not want you to get hurt."

"I reckon you wouldn't." She smiled at him knowingly. "If I got hurt, I might have to hitch my wagon to a doctor's horse, 'stead of yours."

The next day, Bartholomew Barrington joined the armed men assembled on Fifth Street. He did not bring a weapon. He did not need one. The men marched toward a neighborhood occupied by the darker-skinned cooks and gardeners and housekeepers in whose pockets and bags Bit had planted stolen earrings, bracelets, silver forks, and crystal goblets. Bit stayed toward the back. When gunfire broke out, the white men withdrew and reassembled a few blocks away.

"Let's wait till nightfall," one said. The others agreed.

Bit looked up at the darkening sky. The moon would rise full, come nightfall.

Bit knew the feeling of its coming. He smelled an empty house and let himself inside. He stripped. He folded his clothes and hid them beneath a bush near the back door. The moon rose, and he laughed at the glory of it as Wolf rippled through him.

He stalked out onto the street, up behind the red-faced mob. He raised his front paw. He swiped. His claw dug into a man's back.

The man screamed.

Wolf pulled his claw out and darted into the shadows.

"My back!" The man screamed again. "I've been stabbed!"

"He's been stabbed!"

"Those savages!"

"Let's get 'em!"

"We'll make 'em pay!"

The mob advanced. Wolf advanced alongside them, his form obscured by the darkness. But if they did see him, who or what would they presume he was? Every chance he got, he slashed a fellow in the back, or clawed a fellow in the leg, or got underfoot, a mean streak of fur, causing commotion. The mob came upon a house. They dragged the occupants out and beat them, even the kids, because otherwise those kids might grow up and steal their jobs. They torched the house and moved on to the next one.

The darker-skinned men came out to defend their neighborhood. They came with guns and knives, with cast-iron pans, boards, and bats. Wolf circled around behind them. He clawed the flesh from their backs.

"I've been stabbed!" they cried. They spun around, looking for the pale assailant behind them, but Wolf had already retreated to shadow.

Wolf attacked again, again, again, he cared not who. Blood was blood. Wolf hungered for it. Men stabbed each other, punched each other, slit each other's throats. Wolf sniffed out the fallen.

"Please," they cried, when they saw him. "Lord, no! I have a wife! A family!"

Wolf cared not. He lapped up their blood. He finished them off.

The men fought while the neighborhood burned, and their brothers died in the streets, and Wolf strayed from the shadows. He did not need to hide himself, amidst all this delicious bloodshed. Pale-skinned men saw Wolf and exclaimed, *God has sent this wolf to fight on our side!* Dark-skinned men saw Wolf and exclaimed, *The Lord has sent this beast to avenge us!*

Wolf had only his own side, his hunger, his thirst for blood.

When the heat subsided, Bartholomew Barrington bought a nice big house on the edge of the Queen City, buffeted by forests for Wolf to roam, overlooking the river. Then he stole the biggest diamond Rosalina had ever seen.

"Will you be my wife?" he asked her.

She gazed into the rock on her finger. "Yes, Bartholomew Barrington. Yes, I will."

They married the next day, at the courthouse. Rosalina Barrington said farewell to her job at the tavern and moved into her husband's nice big house. Bartholomew Barrington said farewell to his job at the Losantiville Bank. He bought a small building on Fourth Street and opened his own bank.

"You came into an inheritance," Rosalina instructed. "That is what you say, if anyone asks."

"I came into an inheritance," Bit told his former employer, who happened to pass by while Bit's workers painted the signage: BARRINGTON BANK AND INVESTMENT COMPANY. "My uncle died. He was very rich."

"Yes, of course." Bit's former employer nodded, never doubting for an instant the demise of a rich uncle to Bartholomew Barrington's benefit.

Barrington Bank and Investment Company had few customers, at first, though its holdings continued to grow. And yet, financial misfortunes continued to befall the clients of Losantiville Bank, and rumors spread of a conspiracy of thieves led by its employees, though no one suspected the venerable Bartholomew Barrington, the former employee who had come into an inheritance. One by one, its clients withdrew their funds and deposited them securely with Barrington Bank and Investment Company.

"You have made me so proud," Rosalina told her husband. "What a fine, successful man you are!"

Except Bartholomew Barrington was not exactly a man, and Rosalina had begun to wonder where he went, one night each month, when he walked off into the woods at dusk and returned just after dawn, filthy and wild-eyed and ravenous.

Bit saw this query in her eyes, and thought to himself, *She must know.* He wanted her esteem, her unfettered affections. He wanted her to love his true, awful self. He wanted her to wash the soil from between his toes, the dried blood from his face.

And if she saw what he was and withdrew her love?

Wolf would kill her.

When dusk glazed the windows, Bartholomew Barrington led his wife to the bedroom. He locked the door.

"You're not going out tonight?" she asked.

"Light the lamp," he told her.

"Yes, dear." Rosalina obeyed.

"You said that I made you proud."

"Yes, dear."

"You said that I was a fine man."

"You are a very fine man."

"Close your eyes," he said.

Rosalina closed her eyes.

His fingers shook as he tied a strip of cloth around her eyes. He could feel Wolf inside, trying to break free of him. "Do not look," he instructed her. "Do not remove this blindfold until you feel something sharp on your hand."

"Bartholomew, what is—"

"You will do what I say. Do not ask questions."

"Yes. Yes, dear."

Bit removed his clothes. He folded them and placed them on the dresser. He examined his wife. Her lip trembled, betraying her fear, a type of fear he had never smelled before. The scent of her fear made his blood flow hot, and he wanted to push her back onto the bed and have her right then. But there was another scent, faint, unfamiliar to him, and as he stood naked before her, trying to identify it, he felt the tug of moonrise, and the tidal wave of Wolf rushed through him.

When his transformation was complete, he reached out his claw and pricked the back of his wife's hand.

"Ouch!" She pulled her hand away. "Bartholomew—"

Bit growled.

"Bartholomew!" she cried, with panic in her voice. She pulled the blindfold from her eyes. "Bartholomew—"

Bit leapt onto the bed. He opened his mouth, for his wife to see. He held out his razor-studded paw. *This is what I am.*

She stared back, terrified.

Bit did not move. He listened to her heartbeat. He smelled her fear waning.

"Bartholomew," she said. He growled softly, in answer. "I see what you are. But I suppose . . . Yes, I suppose I had always seen."

Slowly, she reached her hand toward him. She laid it on the side of his face. She stared into his yellow eyes. Wolf loved her so much. He wanted to rip her apart.

"I shall make you proud, too," she said. She took his paw. She placed it on her belly. "My fine man. I shall make you very proud."

Mr. and Mrs. Barrington did not speak of Wolf. They spoke of riches. They spoke of Bartholomew Barrington's work, his plans, his hopes and schemes. They spoke of the family they would build, an empire of Barringtons. They began to build that empire. They expanded the bank and acquired a second building downtown, on Sycamore Street. They hired a second housekeeper, a handyman, a gardener, a cook, a coachman. They planted gardens. They purchased horses, chickens, goats, and cows. And they hired a young dark-skinned man from New Orleans to look after the animals. The young caretaker of their animals woke before dawn every morning. Every morning, he walked from his ramshackle shed in the woods outside the Barringtons' estate to the Barringtons' barn to milk the Barringtons' cows so that the Lady Rosalina would have fresh milk with her breakfast.

One hot night in early October, the caretaker woke too early. It was still dark outside, but he was awake and restless, and there was work to be done. He left his shed and set off toward the barn. The bright full moon settled over the trees. The leaves crunched under his boots. Then, beneath his feet, he felt something soft and pliant. He stopped. He looked down. He saw a rabbit, dead, its guts torn out. He crouched down and touched it.

"Still warm," he whispered. He held his lantern over its body. It had been bitten in half but left uneaten, as if it had been killed for sport. The caretaker examined the bite marks. He looked up at the full moon.

"I knew it. Oh, I felt it when I saw him, Lord. The devil himself, he takes the body of the wolf," he said to himself, quietly.

But not so quietly that Bit could not hear.

The caretaker stepped back, away from the rabbit. He felt a

sudden chill, though the night was hot. He felt something behind him. The devil, in the body of a wolf.

Bit leapt from the shadows. He knocked the young caretaker onto the ground. He slashed the man's chest with his claws. He tore open his shoulder. The hot blood made Bit dizzy, but he also felt lightheaded with impending dawn. He could still hear the faint beat of the man's heart as he dragged his body through the woods, down to the river. He pulled the former caretaker of his animals into the water, leaving a trail of blood behind them. The man's heart slowed. The river would finish him off.

At least, that was what Bit thought, as he watched the current drag Efram Z'Rhae away.

Subject: Re: Werewolf in need of help

Dear Ms. Porter,

Ms. Z'Rhae would be happy to help your young werewolf friend. She is available to meet you on Friday afternoon at 2:00 p.m. There's a very small town called Pescadero an hour or so south of San Francisco. She can meet you at the coffee shop there. Please confirm that this date and time works for you.

Sincerely,

Amira Upande
Assistant to Nova Z'Rhae

THE FANTABULOUS QUEEN OF SEQUIN POP

The Redwoods—Now

EVEN DRESSED AS a mortal, she still sparkled. Natasha saw her through the window as she approached the coffee shop, Veronica skipping alongside. The Fantabulous Queen of Sequin Pop wore jeans and a T-shirt. Her face was bare, but for a light brush of mascara and a clear gloss on her lips. Her curled hair was pulled back in a ponytail. She sat at a table by the window with a mug of tea and an open paperback book.

Veronica recognized her instantly. She squealed.

"The Glitter Lady! It's her! Dad, it's *her*!"

"Now, Veronica—"

"It's all right," Nova Z'Rhae said, in a voice that was deep and rich and, at the same time, high and airy.

Hearing it, the fear, regret, and embarrassment Natasha had felt receded; the coffee shop and the people in it and everything around them faded, and only Nova Z'Rhae remained, a bright diamond in the coal mine darkness of the world. It seemed that for Nova everything similarly receded as she focused all her sparkling attention on Veronica.

"You know, darling," she told the little girl, in a voice that indicated she took the moment playfully serious, "I think I may have something special for you."

"For me?" Veronica chirped.

"Yes," said Nova Z'Rhae, "if your dad says it's all right."

Lee stepped closer. "Yes, it's fine."

Nova Z'Rhae reached into the pocket of her jeans. She pulled out a vial of glitter. "You know what this is?"

"It's glitter!"

"It's not just any glitter. It's very special magic glitter. And you know what it does?"

"It makes you fly?"

"Ha! That would be spectacular! But not quite, honey. Not quite. This glitter, if you wear it, will make you stronger. It'll make you tougher, and smarter."

"And more beautiful?"

"And more beautiful. Because you know what?"

"What?"

"You're already all of those things. And this glitter here, it's like a magnet. It draws out all the things inside that make you great and brings them right up to the surface, where you can use them. Where everyone can see."

Nova Z'Rhae opened the vial and dabbed glitter onto her finger.

She touched her glittered finger to the tip of Veronica's nose.

"I can feel it!" Veronica flapped her arms. "I'm stronger!"

"And let me tell you a secret about this glitter." Nova leaned down. She whispered. "Even when you can't see it anymore, it's still there."

"Yeeee!" Veronica twirled around. "But . . . but can you also give my sister some? So she can be strong too?"

"If your dad says it's okay."

"Okay," Lee Curtis said. He held the sleepy-eyed peanut glitter distance from Nova Z'Rhae. Nova stood and looked at the rest of her visitors, briefly, before putting a small dot of glitter on the top of the baby's soft head.

"What about you, Ghost?" Veronica asked.

"I'm . . ." *Fine*, Natasha wanted to say. Except that she wasn't. She didn't feel strong or tough or smart or beautiful. She felt broke, homeless, and hated.

"Honey," Nova said, "we all need glitter sometimes. May I?"

Natasha nodded. Nova poured another dab of glitter from her bottle. She brushed it across Natasha's cheeks. A tear slipped out of Natasha's eye.

"I'm sorry," she said. "I'm sorry. I didn't mean . . . what I said about you . . ."

"Ahhhh. Honey," Nova replied, "you're the woman who wrote a letter asking for my help?"

"Yes, that was me."

"But your friend there, that's not the same friend you wrote to me about, is he?"

"Oh him? No, that's Lee. He's just my friend. He drove, because my car is a kind of a mess."

"And we *really* wanted to meet you," Lee gushed suddenly. "We're *huge* fans. Your work is just, it's *great*. And your latest album, *really amazing*. It's such a pleasure."

Nova gave a curtsy. "Thank you, darling. It's always a pleasure for me to meet my fans. You send an email to my assistant after this so she knows how to reach you, and you'll have some backstage passes to the next show."

"Wow, really? That's just . . . *Thank you!*"

Natasha had never seen Lee so exuberant before.

"My pleasure, darling," Nova said. "So where is this other friend of yours—the young wolf?"

"He should be here any minute," Natasha said, glancing over her shoulder at the door. "He's meeting us here. But . . . look, Ms. Z'Rhae, I just wanted to tell you in person, it's really kind of you to meet us, and to help him out. Especially after what I said. I'm so sorry. I really am."

"Honey, your very sincere apology is already accepted. We've all said and done things that we regret. We learn, we grow. We try and do our best, as you clearly are."

"Thank you. It was wrong for me to judge. Especially when I . . . I mean, I'd heard your songs. But . . ." Natasha rocked awkwardly on her heels. Nova Z'Rhae looked down at her. The pop star was impressively tall, imposing, but her eyes shone warmly. "It's not like I've ever sat down and *really* listened."

"Darling, what you said isn't untrue. It *is* all about glitter and sequins and confetti. Because I think that's exactly what we need right now. Glitter to get us through the darkness. You catch more bees with honey, so to speak."

"Yeah, I guess that makes sense."

"I admit," Nova said, "I didn't even know what you were apologizing for when you wrote me. I looked you up, of course. And I'm sorry that the Nozees came after you. They have minds of their own, but I'll try to call them off. My fans are delightful, and I appreciate their loyalty. But they should have tried to convert you instead of condemning you. It's not our place to condemn anyone. I believe in grace, darling. Grace and glitter. And I believe we're all on the same team here. It's us against the wolves."

Just then, a wolf blustered through the coffee shop door.

"Your friend just arrived," Nova said, nodding at the door.

"You can tell?" Natasha asked.

"I've learned to spot them. It's something in the eyes."

Natasha stared at Shane. She squinted. He looked like a regular human, but a finely polished fancy version that only got taken out of the china cabinet on special occasions.

Shane waved. Then blubbered. "Oh my God, it's . . . You're . . . oh my God you're . . . you're . . . are you . . . oh, wow! Natasha! It's . . . this is Nova Z'Rhae!" He pointed at the singer and practically yelled, "*You're* Nova Z'Rhae!"

The barista and the few other customers in the coffee shop didn't react. They must have seen the pop star here before, Natasha assumed.

"I am her, honey," Nova said. "I'm your two o'clock appointment."

"You? We're meeting *you*? Oh my God! Natasha didn't tell me . . . She didn't tell me . . . She just said . . ."

"I know, dear."

"I can't believe it. You're . . . Duane would be . . . My friend Duane was a huge fan . . . He would have—"

Shane gulped. Sadness flooded his starstruck eyes.

"Well, let's go take a ride, shall we? And on the way you can tell me all about Duane."

They drove inland, past the farms of Pescadero, into the forest, where the trees grew tall, and ancient.

"We have the same car," Natasha said. Nova drove a silver Prius, which she said she called the Blend-In-Mobile. "Except mine is full of garbage bags."

"Of course we do. And what did you expect, darling? A limousine? A black SUV with tinted windows?"

"A Pegasus!" Veronica called, from the back seat. She had demanded to come along, because Ghost and Wolf got to go with the Glitter Lady, and she was more glittery than either of them, so why should she have to go home and take a bath? Her dad and the peanut followed behind in Lee's car.

"You're right," Nova agreed. "I would look fantastic on a Pegasus. But as far as I know, all the Pegasuses are extinct, or in hiding."

"Wait, what? Were there really Pegasuses?" Natasha asked. "I mean—"

"I don't know," Nova replied. "But I like to believe that there were. Something bright and wonderful to balance out all the nasty werewolves."

"But will the Pegasuses come back?" Veronica asked.

"All things come in cycles, honey. All I know is the wolves have been running things for too long. It's about time some Pegasuses came back."

"So where exactly are we going?" Shane asked.

"We're going to my brother's house."

"Is he—"

"A werewolf? Indeed he is. A dangerous one. The born were-wolves are always the most dangerous."

They drove along a twisting road through the redwoods until they reached a small cottage perched over a shallow river. The cottage looked unremarkable, with its graying shingles, its peeling paint, the moss and lichen growing up its walls. They got out of the car and Veronica rang and rerang the doorbell until the door opened.

"Well . . . hello," Nova's brother said.

His face resembled Nova's, but he was taller, broader across the shoulders, and he had the same treacherous glint in his eyes as Shane LaSalle. He looked down at Veronica. "It's a woodland sprite. And you've brought guests, I see."

"Joseph, love, hi," Nova said. She kissed her brother on both cheeks. "I brought you a werewolf."

"I can smell him," Joseph Z'Rhae growled. "Tell me, young werewolf, why have you come to my lair?"

Shane LaSalle told Joseph and Nova Z'Rhae about his Barrington Equity partners, and how they had inducted him into partnershipdom, about Duane Beckman and the Lake Orange Forest, about the werewolf dinner party and how his partner had urged him to kill Natasha, and about how she had pepper-sprayed him instead. Natasha told them about her roommate, Marie, cor-roborated Shane's account of the werewolf dinner party, and, while omitting any physical description of Shane as wolf, noted how hideous and slimy he had been. Veronica drew a picture of Nova

Z'Rhae riding a Pegasus, then another picture of Nova Z'Rhae and three wolves riding in a boat: the Wolf Shane, the Wolf Joseph, and a third she referred to as the B-Wolf. Eventually, Nova and Lee took Veronica outside to wade in the river.

"Mr. LaSalle, Ms. Porter," Joseph Z'Rhae said, after Shane and Natasha had finished their stories, "I'd like to show you something. Follow me."

Joseph Z'Rhae led Shane and Natasha down a flight of stairs. At the bottom there was a heavy steel door with an electronic keypad, entirely incongruous with the woodsy cottage setting.

"What is this place?" Shane asked.

"This is my lair."

"Your lair."

"My lair, yes. Or you could call it my office, but I like lair better. I work for a . . . I guess you could call us a nonprofit organization. My grandfather was one of its founders. We track the country's most dangerous werewolves."

"Are you serious?" Natasha said. "The *most* dangerous? Like— Sorry, this is just unreal. To be standing here talking about were-wolves like they're an actual thing. I mean, I know I saw it happen, but I still can't quite believe it."

"So what do you do, then?" Shane asked. "Are you just watching them, or do you, you know . . ."

"Mostly we just keep track," Joseph Z'Rhae said. "But on occasion, we have to neutralize them."

Shane blanched. "You mean, you *kill* them."

Joseph shrugged. He entered a code on the door lock. "If we need to. But not always. I presume you're familiar with the Watergate scandal?"

"Yeah."

"That was us. I mean, not the scandal part. Nixon did that all himself. But we were responsible for it getting exposed."

"Wait . . . Wait a second," Natasha said. "Was Nixon— Are you saying that Nixon was a werewolf?"

"*Of course* Nixon was a werewolf."

The lock beeped. The door opened. The lights inside flickered on. Shane and Natasha followed Joseph into a large room outfitted with a dozen or so computers, machines sleeker and newer than any they had seen before. Nearby stood rows of cabinets housing assorted weapons: assault rifles, handguns, grenades, small gas canisters, and crossbows, all of them marked with the letters *Ag*. Clusters of photographs covered the walls. Natasha recognized some of the men in the photographs, but others she had never seen before.

"*This* is your office," said Natasha.

"I work in a dangerous profession. Hence 'lair.'"

"No shit," Natasha said. "This is, like, some sort of secret-agent hideout. This is insane."

Shane pointed to a cabinet on the wall, marked with the letters *Ag*. "Is *Ag* . . ."

"Yes. Silver."

"As in, silver bullets?" Natasha asked.

"Silver bullets. Silver arrows. Tear gas laced with silver particulate."

"So, like, in all those dumb B-movies, where the werewolves can only be killed with silver bullets—that's true?"

"Oh no, no," Joseph said with a chuckle. "We can be killed just the same as any human. We're just flesh and blood. Other than the initial healing that occurs right after the first bite, we have only a *slightly* enhanced healing capacity. So any regular bullet could conceivably kill us. But what the silver does is interfere with the transformation process. Also, it hurts like hell. Silver has the highest electrical conductivity of any metal, and this conductivity inhibits transformation from human to werewolf, or vice versa. This can be useful if you need to defend yourself against a werewolf. If the werewolf knows you've got silver bullets in your gun, it won't want to risk getting shot in its wolf form, because then, unless the silver gets out of its system, it'll stay wolf after the full moon ends. And that would be extremely inconvenient. It's not as if a werewolf can waltz down the street and check into the hospital. Most of the werewolves who get shot by silver bullets die as wolves for lack of treatment options. Thus the myth that only silver bullets can kill them."

"Hey, is that . . ." Shane pointed to a picture on the wall of a balding white-haired man with an American flag on his lapel.

"Dick Cheney," Joseph answered.

"Is he a werewolf?"

"Are you surprised?"

"No, no. It makes sense."

"And his pack," Joseph said. He pointed to the photos clustered with Cheney's. "Donald Rumsfeld, Roger Ailes, those are the ones you've probably heard of."

"So these pictures," Shane said, gesturing at the wall, "all of these are werewolf packs?"

"Most of them."

"Is that Steven Tyler?" Natasha asked.

"And his pack. Aerosmith."

"Aerosmith is a band of werewolves?"

"Indeed."

"What's with the color?" Natasha asked. Most of the photos were framed with red tape, but the Aerosmith band and several others were framed yellow.

"Not all werewolves are problematic. Many of them keep to themselves and try to lead quiet lives. The Aerosmith pack hasn't caused any real trouble, but they were a bit wild in their youth, so we still keep an eye on them. That's why they're framed in yellow. The others, the ones framed in red, those are the really troublesome ones."

Shane gazed at the wall of pictures. "But there are good werewolves too?"

"Of course. The werewolves working with my organization are . . . well, I don't know if you'd describe all of them as *good*, but they're not amoral killers."

Natasha glanced at the weapons cabinets. "Who are they? Anyone we would have heard of?"

"Yeah, like, do you work with any good werewolf senators or CEOs or rock stars or whatever?" Shane asked.

"A few you may have heard of. But I'm not going to name any names, just in case . . . Well, it would be better not to tell you any more about the organization than necessary."

"Are there any good ones who aren't part of the organization?"

"That you may have heard of? Hmmm . . . Well, there's Keanu."

"Keanu—"

"Reeves."

"Keanu Reeves is a werewolf?"

"One of the nicest damned werewolves I've ever had the pleasure of meeting."

"What about him?" Shane pointed to one of several photos not clustered with any others. "Isn't that Elon Musk? *Is he a werewolf?*"

"Oh, Musk? No."

"Okay—"

"He's a vampire."

"Vampire? *Those* exist, too? But I've seen him in the daylight. I mean, on TV."

"You've heard of Photoshop, right? Deep fakes?"

"They're all men," Natasha remarked, frowning. "All the pictures are of men. Where are the female werewolves? Or are werewolves always men?"

"Not all werewolves are men," Joseph said. He glanced at another picture, of an older woman beside his younger self, in a gold frame on his desk. "My mother was a werewolf, and one of the strongest, fiercest wolves I ever met. My aunt and her eldest daughter are werewolves as well. But you are correct, most werewolves, and all the ones pictured on this wall—well, with the exception of Liz Cheney there—are men. They're mostly men for the same reason that they're mostly white."

"White male werewolves only make white males into werewolves," Natasha said.

"Well, yes. Like Mr. LaSalle here. But . . . well, let me tell you about my great-uncle, Zachary Z'Rhae. He was also a werewolf. He lived in Denver, where he ran a small grocery. He kept to himself. He only ever hunted in the forest, mostly deer, buffalo. He would never hurt a human. He was a good man and a good wolf. In 1935, my great-uncle came across a man whom he recognized as a werewolf. That man's name was Matthew Carver."

"Carver . . ." Shane shuddered.

"Indeed, Mr. LaSalle. Carver. I believe you know his grandson, Ronald. Matthew Carver likewise recognized my great-uncle as a werewolf. You can see it in the eyes, if you know what you're looking for. You can smell it. It's like musty ozone, like a wet forest, but some mask it with cologne and cigars. Matthew Carver was a successful banker. He planned to make a bid for mayor. He did not like that my great-uncle, a mere grocer, a man of modest means, a Black man, had the same power in his blood. And so he burnt my great-uncle's grocery to the ground, and then he killed him."

"Oh God, that's terrible," Natasha said.

"It was terrible," Joseph went on. "But my great-uncle's death was only the beginning. Matthew Carver hunted down the werewolves in my family, and he killed a great many of them. The ones who survived went into hiding, including my grandfather, who hid up north in Alaska. He returned in 1948, after he learned that Matthew Carver had died in a car wreck. But Matthew Carver had many friends who shared his feelings about who should be a werewolf and who should not."

"So, wait," Natasha said, as Shane continued to examine the pictures on the wall. "Nova said that you were born as a werewolf. And your mother was a werewolf, and your aunt. So, then how does that work? Is it genetic, or—"

"I cannot profess to fully understand the science," Joseph said. "But yes, it seems that lycanthropy works the same as any genetic trait. A werewolf parent can produce a werewolf child, but it won't necessarily happen. Nova and I have the same parents, but I was born a werewolf, whereas she was not. The same is true of our cousins."

"I still don't understand," Natasha said, pointing to the wall of pictures. "I mean, it makes sense that white male werewolves turn white males into werewolves, but if it's passed genetically, then where are all the white lady werewolves?"

"Well . . ." Joseph said, "they don't make it."

Natasha froze. "What do you mean, they don't make it?"

"They don't make it," Joseph said. "SIDS. Pneumonia. Stillbirth. Cord wrapped around their neck."

"What . . . what are you . . ."

"Statistically—"

"No . . ."

"Statistically, the infant mortality rate for girls born to these werewolves is—"

"No. What are you saying? They can't be . . ." Natasha shook her head.

"They die at a much higher rate than the boys," Joseph concluded. "And from what I know about werewolves, I cannot think of any *physiological* reason why this would be the case."

Hot rage blurred Natasha's vision. She felt sicker and angrier than she had ever felt in her life. She felt like she could stab out Shane LaSalle's gorgeous gold-flecked eyes even though he was just a pretty boy who had played no part in this monstrosity. She wanted to pack a rifle with silver bullets and go on a werewolf killing spree. She screamed.

"Fuck. FUUUUUCK!" Natasha yelled. "Those evil fuckers! *Fuck! Fuck fuck fuck fuck fuck!*"

Natasha screamed again. She paced. Her hands shook. She tried to breathe deeply and calm her rage.

"This is just fucked," she fumed.

Beside her, Shane's eyes were wide with horror, but Natasha hardly noticed.

"Yeah," Joseph said. He shook his head. His eyes looked sad. "I know."

"How the fuck do they get away with it?!"

"A man can get away with a lot, if he has enough money."

"But what about their wives? The mothers?"

"I imagine some of them probably never know. Though some . . . I suspect some are complicit."

"Fuck. Fuck. Oh my God, shit. There was a woman . . . a pregnant one . . ." Natasha recalled the hushed conversation she overheard in the Olympic Club hallway, on the night she sprayed Shane LaSalle with pepper spray. She recalled the fear in the pregnant woman's voice. "Fuck."

"Misti Buxby," Joseph said. He opened a binder on his desk, labeled *Barrington Pack*, and flipped to a photo of Darren Buxby, and next to him a photo of Misti beside him, a line drawn between them. "I know of her. Married to Darren Buxby, one of your partners, Mr. LaSalle."

Natasha's mind reeled with all the Misti Buxbys out there in the world, all the Misti Buxbys who had existed through all eternity, whose choices and bodies had been stolen. Their husbands stole—or their boyfriends, their fathers, their complicit mothers, their governments.

"It's not their choice! Those assholes! We have to help her! We have to take those fuckers down!"

"Ha, well, it's not easy," Joseph said. "They're powerful. They're well-connected. They're protected by immense wealth and privilege. They're cunning; the ones who aren't cunning never last. We can't just chase after them with our silver bullets and hope for the best. It takes a lot of planning to neutralize a whole pack of werewolves. But . . . our organization has been hoping to take down the Barrington pack for quite some time. That's why we were so pleased to learn about you, Mr. LaSalle."

Shane examined the pictures of his partners clustered on the wall—Dick Barrington, Ronald Carver, Darren Buxby, Don Morgan, Stanley Rollins, Clifton James—all of them framed in red. Next to them was Shane's own photo, unframed.

"Are you sure . . . *all* of them?" Shane asked.

"Your pack, Mr. LaSalle, they have done tremendous harm," Joseph said. "You know the story. It's the same story every time. Though maybe you don't know all of it. It goes like this: Once upon a time, there was a business. Let's say, for this story, it was a certain toy store. A big-box toy store chain. The merits of its existence are debatable, as undoubtedly it put many small local toy stores out of business over its own lifetime. But nevertheless this toy store employed many thousands of people. Then it made a deal with your pack, Mr. LaSalle. Your pack loaded it up with debt and sent it off to bankruptcy. Your pack sucked it dry and got richer in the process. And when there was nothing left, the toy store closed its doors and thousands of people lost their jobs and the CEO of that toy store, the sorry sap who had convinced his board to sign on with Barrington Equity, he slit his wrists. Now perhaps you're thinking, isn't this just what venture capitalists do? They see an opportunity, right, and they pounce? But there's more to this story. The part you haven't heard. Because you see, the CEO of this company was not in his right state of mind when he made the deal with Barrington. The month before, he had lost his wife and daughter. They had gone out for a walk in the woods behind their house one evening. They never came back. But their bodies were found later. And of course there was never any investigation. They had been unfortunate victims, the official report said, of some sort of vicious animal, a mountain lion or a bear." He leaned in close and stared right into Shane's eyes. "But we know what sort of animal it was, don't we?"

It took Shane a moment before he said it. "Wolves."

"Wolves."

"Why did they die? I mean, they got attacked and it killed them, and it killed my friend Duane, but I lived. I turned. Why?"

"It could be that they wanted to kill your friend. But it may also be a matter of whether your genetics are compatible with werewolf DNA."

"Which they wouldn't have known."

"No. There's not been any research into werewolf genetics, at least as far as I know. Putin may be conducting some."

"Putin. As in—"

"Yes."

"Is a werewolf."

"Well, he's . . . something like that."

"Mr. Z'Rhae, can I ask—" Shane said.

"Please, call me Joseph."

"Joseph . . . why are you trusting me with this?"

"I'm not trusting you with much. I won't tell you any more about my organization, if you'd planned to ask. You work in a werewolf den, Mr. LaSalle. If your pack suspects something, well . . . better that you don't have too much information for them to extract."

"But . . . I mean . . ." Shane shifted nervously. "What if I'm . . . How do you know that I'm not like them?"

"Perhaps you are like them. The wolf is inside you. I know what that feels like. The bloodlust. The hunger. But as Plato said, the measure of a man is what he does with power. You could have killed Ms. Porter here. Surely the wolf wanted to. But you protected her instead. I believe you're a good man, that you'll do the right thing."

"I . . . I hope so," Shane said.

"Besides, I don't have much choice. If we want any chance at taking down the Barrington pack," Joseph said, "we need someone on the inside. We need *you*."

Natasha screamed with rage.

As Joseph spoke more to Shane of werewolves, how to spot them by the sheen of their eyes, how to sniff them out, Natasha's anger grew and grew, until she felt too furious to stand around and listen. Frantically, she had run outside. Had run past Nova and Lee and his children into the redwoods. She had run until her lungs burned, and when her legs had grown tired, she'd tried the screaming thing.

When she returned to Joseph's cabin, her legs rubbery, her throat sore from screaming, she found him in the kitchen brewing tea. Everyone else sat at the table eating cake.

"Have a seat, honey," Nova said. "Let me cut you a slice. It's chocolate raspberry. Joseph has no good food in his house. He only eats meat. Nothing but raccoons, squirrels, possums, raw birds—"

"Hey!"

"Do you really eat raw birds, mister?" Veronica asked, glancing around. There was no sign of slaughtered wildlife. The shelves were stacked with books, pictures, ceramic vases, blown glass. Potted plants and herbs grew in a box by the window.

"Only sometimes." Joseph laughed. He brought a tray filled with teacups. "But not in front of guests."

"Joseph doesn't have many guests," Nova said, distributing the cups. "I always tell him, if he spent less time here alone in the woods—"

"I like it out here."

"If he spent more time out in the real world, if he made more friends," Nova said, as she passed a generous slice of chocolate cake to Natasha, "he'd be better positioned to take down those big bad wolfies."

"I'm better positioned when I'm off their radar."

"He was irate when I gave that *FreaKountry* interview," Nova told Natasha. "The one you read—"

"You took a needless risk—"

"It's not like the wicked wolfies on your wall downstairs read *FreaKountry* magazine—"

"They don't have to," Joseph growled. "If they have bots searching the internet—"

"Besides," Nova said, "my interview brought us Shane." She patted Shane's shoulder. "And isn't he just the cutest?"

Shane beamed. "So, like, has the werewolf gene always been in your family?" he asked, as he spooned honey into his tea. "Or did it start somewhere? Like, did someone get bit?"

"The first werewolf in my family," Joseph said, "was my

great-great-great-grandfather. Efram Z'Rhae. Efram was born in New Orleans, but as a young man he traveled north, up to Cincinnati. He found a job tending animals at a rich man's estate. It was there that the werewolf attacked him. It tore him open, and then it dragged him down to the Ohio River and threw him in. The current pulled Efram downstream. But Efram was strong. He was a fighter. And as he drifted, his body changed and his injuries healed. He became a wolf. He swam to shore, then fled far away from the wolf that had bitten him. And Mr. LaSalle, I think you will find this very interesting. The rich man who owned the estate at which my great-great-great-grandfather worked was, by most accounts, one of the first of the American werewolves: a man named Bartholomew Barrington."

BARTHOLOMEW BARRINGTON

ABOMINATION

Cincinnati–1848

UPSTAIRS, ROSALINA SCREAMED and screamed.

"Is this usual?" Bartholomew Barrington asked the doctor.

"Oh yes. Quite." The doctor pressed tobacco into the bowl of his pipe. He stretched back on the divan. "Were you not here when—" He nodded at the boy who played by the fire, constructing around himself a fortress of blocks. The boy had Bit's face, but softer, not a trace of wolf in him.

"I had been away on business when he was born."

"Oh yes. A good time to go away," the doctor said with a conspiratorial chuckle.

Bartholomew Barrington nodded. His firstborn had come early, the human boy's recessive nature spurred by the rising full moon. Bit had fled into the forest. All night he ran, he hunted, he killed. He feared what he would find when he returned: his wife clawed open from the inside, his child of fang and tooth, blessed with a power he could not yet wield. But when Wolf was laid to rest and Bit returned home in the morning, he had found his wife aglow, a bundle in her arms, a dear baby boy. *Michael Barrington. Hold him, darling.* His wife placed the baby in his arms. *See what we have made!*

"How long will it take?" Bit asked the doctor.

"Hard to say. We could ask the midwife if—"

"No, no."

The midwife business made him squeamish. But also, he felt afraid. The sun was still high, but the moon already throbbed in Bit's heart, swelling, overripe. The blood moon. Same as the night Michael had arrived.

"Might be any time now. Might not happen till tomorrow. Hard to say how long these things take. Say, shall we have some supper?" The doctor glanced toward the kitchen, where the Barrington family's cook was baking pies and cakes. There was, it was rumored, always an excess of delicious foods at the Barrington estate.

The doctor helped himself to a slice of tomato pie.

Bit could not eat. He paced. His wife howled.

Michael Barrington covered his ears with his small, human hands. His eyes blinked tears. "Make her stop, Dad, make her stop!"

Such a tender child, Bit thought. Too tender.

"This is the way of things," Bit told the boy. "All things come in cycles, and sometimes they hurt. But we don't cry about it."

Bit paced more. He worried more. He chastised the boy for tearing up like a weakling girl. He watched out the window as the sun sank lower, lower. He felt the prickling on his skin.

"I must go," he told the doctor. "I have urgent business."

"Yes, well, that's very understandable," the doctor said, nodding up at the ceiling, which seemed to shake with Rosalina's screams. "Very understandable at this, uh, hour. Shall you be taking the boy along, then?"

"No. His nurse will mind him. He cannot go where I am going."

Bit ran outside, into the woods. He stripped his clothes. The winter air felt cold on his bare skin, for a moment. Then Wolf sprang forth from the body of the man, and he looked up at the great moon and howled, for in his heart he knew what was coming.

All night Bit ran. He hunted. He tore weaker creatures apart, out of hunger, or instinct, or because he was Wolf and he could. Then dawn came. Wolf rested. The man returned. He dressed himself and went inside, and though he was strong and vicious, his hands trembled as he opened the door. His heart beat too fast as he climbed the stairs. The house had fallen quiet. The doctor was gone. The midwife was gone. Bit smelled blood. He opened the door to his wife's bedroom. And there was Rosalina, with a bundle in her arms!

"Look what we have made," he said, but too soon, too soon.

His wife looked up at him, exhausted, her eyes bloodshot from pushing.

"What . . . what is it?" He could hear the baby's small, thumping heart.

Rosalina gazed down at the bundle in her arms. "The littlest Barrington," she whispered. "A full-moon baby. Like you."

"What . . . let me see—"

Bit stepped toward her. She looked up at him, expectant, but when she saw his face, she pulled the baby closer.

Her voice trembled with fear. "Bart, no."

"Let me see it!"

"No!"

"Rose—"

"She will change, Bart, I can see it—"

"Give it to me!"

"No, please—"

Bit snatched the bundle from her arms. She cried out. He pulled the blanket back. He looked down at what he had made. A girl. But not just a girl. The moon still held sway over her small body, suspending it midway between girl and wolf. Bit looked down at the patches of fur on her skin, at her wolfish face still toothless, her stub hands. He remembered Eleanor, lovely Eleanor, whose transformation he had watched, whose transformation he had caused: lovely Eleanor to hideous wolf, beauty to freak.

"An abomination . . ." he said.

"She's changing," Rosalina wept. "She was . . . when I birthed her . . . but now—"

"An abomination," Bit repeated. Although he could see the baby's fur receding, he knew it would come back. Her teeth would grow sharp. She would transform, just as he had transformed, from boy to wolf, from Bit to Barrington. He thought of this girl, his girl, transformed, hairy, repulsive, monstrous. He could not stand it.

"But you—"

"*I* am a man." He thought about the things he had done. The blood he had spilt. "But this . . . this thing . . ."

"Bart, no . . ." Rosalina tried to stand, but her body was exhausted from birthing. Her legs buckled. She collapsed back onto the bed. "She doesn't have to be . . . Please! Give her back to me—"

"This thing . . ." He recalled the hot gush of a torn throat, the taste of blood in his mouth. He recalled the milk eyes of a woman's corpse, the cloud of flies as he dragged it across a cabin floor. *Well then.*

"Sick," he muttered.

Rosalina moaned. "No, no, please! What will you . . . what will you do?"

"What I must."

Bit carried the baby away from her mother. He carried her downstairs. In the kitchen, he found a sack. He looked at the baby. Her face had flattened, her snout turned to nose. There was nothing sublime to look at in that face. He put her in the sack. He carried her outside, down to the river. He opened the sack. He looked at his daughter, one last time. *An abomination.* He added rocks to the sack, to weigh it down. He tied it up tight. He climbed into a boat and rowed out. *We ought've bundled you up and tossed you in the river, like we did those kittens.* When he had rowed far enough, he tossed the sack of his daughter overboard. He watched her sink.

He did not return home. He would let his wife sit with her pain. Let her come to her senses. He walked past the stables behind his house. The scent of him spooked the horses, as it always did the morning after, when he still reeked of Wolf. He walked along the road, all the way into the city. He went to the tavern where Rosalina once had worked. He ordered a pint, and then another. Two men came into the tavern and sat down at a table in the back, where they thought no one could overhear them. But Bit could hear them.

"They found it in the river," one of the men said, with a titter.

"You don't say."

"Just sittin' there in the water. Nuggets as big as your fist."

"And you're sure it was gold?"

Bit's ears perked.

"Absolutely. I heard it from a man who talked to Sutter himself."

"If there's nuggets just sittin' there—"

"Where anyone could find 'em—"

"Then just think what there might be under the ground."

"Oh, I've thought about it, believe me. I've thought and thought. A man could dig a million dollars right outta the ground."

A million dollars. Bit turned and looked at the two men. They took no notice. Their eyes gleamed with imagined gold.

"So do you think you'll go?"

"Now's the time, fer sure. 'Fore word gets around and ye've got a hunderd men out there diggin'. But no. Alas, no. I've got too much settled here." The man took a long drink of whiskey, draining his glass.

"I might," the other man said.

"S'long way to California. And all them mountains in between."

"I wouldn't mind that."

"But your wife and children—"

"I reckon I'd let them stay put, if I went. Don't sound like no sort of journey for a woman. Then, when I'm richer than rich, I'll come back here and buy 'er one of them big new houses uptown, and my wife'll be so happy she'll forget I ever left."

"Ha, ha, yes. That does sound like a plan."

It did sound like a plan. Bit finished his beer. He walked home. He went upstairs, into Rosalina's bedroom.

"I have learned of a new business opportunity," he told her. She stared at her empty arms. "Out West. In California. Rose—"

"Okay."

"I shall leave in the morning. You and Michael shall stay here. I will be away for at least a year, I believe, as the journey is long."

"Okay. Whatever you need to do," Rosalina said blankly. "I understand."

"When I return, if I am successful, I will be richer than we could have ever imagined." Bartholomew Barrington leaned down and kissed his wife goodbye. He either did not notice that she shrank from his touch, or he ascribed her reaction to her inherent weakness, as a woman.

SHANNON JAMES

HELLO, MOTHER

San Francisco–Now

"HELLO MUDDAH–"

"Blake—"

"—hello Faddah—"

"Put on your shoes."

"Here I am at—"

"We're already late."

"—Camp Granada—"

"No, that one goes on your right foot."

"Everyone here—"

"Blake, could you please—"

"—treats me sweetly—"

"—just stop singing and—"

"I'll have a lotta fun . . . if wolves don't eat me!"

"Jesus."

"What?" Blake leapt up. "I'm ready."

Thank the good Lord for Velcro, Shannon James thought, but asked the boy, "Where did you learn that?"

"Everyone knows this song."

"No, where did you learn that version? It's so . . . "

"Dad taught me. There's another verse with—"

"I don't want to hear it."

"Gawd. *Mawm.* Hey, did you ever think maybe, well, like, my friend River, his mom takes these pills that make her, like, happy all the time, because before she was, like, bummed out and they had to check her into the psych ward, and maybe, like, if you had some pills like that—"

"Blake—"

"—then maybe you'd be—"

"—it's time to go—"

"—happier, because you're such a downer."

"I . . . I am not a downer." Shannon James grabbed her purse from the foyer table. She glanced at the two framed pictures on the table: her two children in their school uniforms, navy and plaid, Janie and Blake. Her heart kicked her in the chest.

"Mom?"

She could not look at the two of them lately, without thinking of the third, the one who wasn't there.

"Mom? Come on. It's time to go, Mom. Janie will be like, 'Where are they?' And—"

"Okay. Yes. Let's go."

"Are you sure you don't want to hear the other verse? Because . . ."

Shannon followed Blake out the door, down the steps, to the garage. They climbed into the minivan. She glimpsed, as she backed out, the cold blue waters of San Francisco Bay, far beneath her house on the hill.

She could have had a nanny, but she ferried her own children. She picked Janie up from after-school art club. They drove to soccer practice. She watched without scrolling on her phone. After practice, she handed out low-sugar juice boxes to the whole team.

"We wanted vitamin water," her daughter said.

"I'm just gonna stop you there, J," Blake said to his sister. "Mom's in one of her funks. You better lay off."

"It's just vitamin water."

"Yeah, but look, she's doing that thing with her lip. Mom, you're doing that thing with your lip. The one where you bite the corner of your lip, but then it looks like your mouth is stuck. Did you know you did that?"

"Here." Shannon ignored him. "Have a juice box."

It was contemptible, she knew, not to appreciate what she had. If only she could feel grateful—deeply, soul-rattlingly, gloriously grateful—for every spurned juice box, every pickup/drop-off, every tenth reminder to *put on your damned shoes already*, every silly song, every hug, every night she tucked them into bed and they looked up at her with their bright eyes, all that love shining out of them.

God. What was wrong with her?

"You have mud on your cleats," she said, to her daughter, as they trekked back to the car.

"It's just a little mud."

"Take them off."

"But then what am I supposed to *wear*?" the girl whined as she kicked off her muddy cleats.

Her brother was already in the car.

"You can wear your socks. And when— Jesus, Blake, how many times have I told you not to put your feet on the back of the seat!"

"Uh, seven hundred and, um, sixty-two times! But who's counting?"

"Mom, are we going to the country club?"

"Yes."

"I am not wearing just my socks at the club." Janie slid into the back seat.

"You can wait in the car. I just need to run in and pick up—"

"Is Dad going to be there?" Blake asked.

"I don't know."

"Can we have dinner at the club? Like we use to?"

"I am not going out to dinner in my socks."

"No, we can't."

She backed out. She drove. She pulled up outside the Olympic Club. She told the kids to wait in the car. She ran inside to the hostess stand.

"Um, excuse me, miss, I'm here to pick up a basket. For a school fundraising auction. It's under the name Shannon James. If you wouldn't mind grabbing it—my kids are in the car."

The hostess stared, as if she recognized her. Then after a moment, she said, "Sure. Sure, of course." She disappeared into the office and returned with a cellophaned basket of golf-club-related paraphernalia. "Is this the one?"

"That's it. Thank you so much."

"Hey," the hostess said, as Shannon turned to leave. "You know your friend?"

"My friend—"

"The pregnant one. I worked her baby shower. Is she—did she have the baby?"

"Not yet."

"Okay, good, I—I hope it goes well."

Shannon returned to the car, to the kids. *Her two kids.*

"But will we at least get to have dinner with Dad?"

"Dad is working late."

"He's always working late. Why is he always working late?"

"Why don't you ask him?"

Blake's feet were back up on the seat.

"Is it because you guys are always fighting?"

"Blake—"

"Are you guys going to get divorced?"

"Blake—"

"I wouldn't blame myself. Just, you know, in case that factors into your decision. But maybe if you got some of those pills that—"

The driver of the car in front slammed on their brakes. Shannon did not. It happened in an instant. She hurtled forward. Her car smashed into the one in front. She heard crushed metal, shattered break lights, a scream from the back seat. And yet the instant seemed to last an infinity. Her son's words *thoooose piiiiilllllssss thaaaaaat* stretched thin, the fifteen years of her marriage pulled taut, like a bubble at capacity, on the verge of bursting.

"Mom!"

She blinked. She turned. She looked back at her children.

"Are you both—" They looked fine.

"Whoa, Mom, you need to watch—"

"I spilled juice—"

"—where you're going. You could've got—"

"—all over myself—"

"—us all killed."

The driver of the other car got out. He surveyed the damage. He knocked on Shannon's window.

"I have my insurance info. Do you want—"

"Yes, right, here, let me find a pen—"

"I'll just take a photo of your—"

"Right. Here."

"Friggin' homeless guy darted out into the street so—"

"I see."

"That's why I hit the brakes. But the damage doesn't look too bad, at least. Worse on your end."

And just like that, her window closed, the car pulled away, off she drove. And just like that, it made her think of Clifton, how quickly he had recovered, moved on, after Lucy; how tearless, how sunny, and how at the time his disposition warmed her and she thought, *He's trying to cheer me up he's strong he's being strong for both of us,* but now she knew he hadn't felt it. Hadn't felt anything. Had pretended. A strong, amiable shell with nothing good underneath.

Lucy came second, when toddling Blake still sucked the ear of his plush rabbit to sleep each night, when Janie was a starling speck in a distant dream. Lucy grew in Shannon's womb, big and strong. Nice and healthy, the nurse had said at the ultrasound. Except there's . . . something odd about the spine, she'd thought at first, but then it turned out to be nothing, and Clifton held her hand and nodded: *Good good good. A healthy girl!*

You don't think she could be . . . Shannon had asked him later that night, when they lay in bed, his palm cupped over her belly. Clifton had confessed, before they'd married. *I don't want any secrets.* He had shown himself, on the twenty-eighth night, when the moon was full. *But it's still me, my mind. My heart.* The wolf was Clifton, and she loved Clifton, and so . . . He didn't want secrets, so he took her to meet Carver's son. *He's a sharp boy*, she recalled saying. The boy was too sharp, and once a month they muzzled him and locked him in a kennel because he hadn't learned self-control. *Will he ever?* she asked Clifton. He nodded. *I did.* She loved Clifton and she loved him more when Blake arrived, a boy a boy a boy, nothing too sharp about him.

Then she had Lucy.

I'm sorry. Clifton had stared. Into. Her. Eyes. *I'm so sorry*, he'd said after it happened. Lucy came out blue. Umbilical cord wrapped around her neck, they said. They scurried the baby away before she could see. *But I want to hold her and . . .* They brought Lucy back to her in the morning, hours after the birth, her body already cold, and Shannon held her and cried, and Clifton said *she's with the Lord now* and *there's nothing we could have done* and *we can try again we can make another one.*

Not another one of those.

Not until later, when Blake was in his pig latin phase and Janie papered the fridge with crayon pictures of unicorns, when what had happened to Shannon happened again, to Darren Buxby's second wife, now ex, did Shannon begin to understand. *They said she was stillborn*, Buxby's ex had told her, *but I heard her crying. I heard it.* And then Shannon started to think that she had heard it too, Lucy's small whimper, the cry of a babe that was not quite a babe, that was also something else.

Because they don't want girls to have it, Buxby's ex had said.

Everyone said Buxby's ex was a crazy bitch.

But she wasn't wrong.

That's ridiculous, Clifton had said, when Shannon inquired. *I would never. Buxby, never.* But Buxby had before, with the wife before. SIDS, his first wife said, when Shannon had found her. She only made it three weeks. Buxby would again, with his third wife. Ditzy Misti, the other wives called her, behind her back.

But you're not ditzy, Shannon told her. *You're smart. You'll be smarter than I was. You'll be stronger.*

SHANE LaSALLE

WHAT TO DO ABOUT WEREWOLVES

San Francisco—Now

YOU ARE SHANE LaSALLE. Shane stared at his reflection in the men's-room mirror. *You are a partner. You are . . .*

He smelled Don Morgan approaching in the hallway.

Don't be afraid. Don't be afraid. Don't be afraid.

He practiced his expressions in the mirror: his pleasant golf-buddy expression, his don't-fuck-with-the-venture-capitalist expression, his what-are-you-doing-this-weekend-oh-I'm-going-parasailing!!! super-gleeful happy face. He smelled Don Morgan pass the bathroom door and continue on. He looked down at his hands. They were shaking.

"Fuck."

No, he told himself. *You will not be afraid. You will be strong and fearless. For Duane.*

Except that he had hairs creeping out of his cuffs, sprouting on the backs of his hands. He plucked them out with the tweezers he kept in his pocket. He blinked back tears. *You are not afraid. You are not afraid. You are Shane Fucking LaSalle. Rising Star. Werewolf.*

But he was afraid. Every day, when he came to the office, when he pretended to be *one of them*, he feared that they would figure him out, that they would strip off his werewolf mask and see the little gay human boy underneath. He went through the motions, the jolly hallway chats, the Boulevard dinners, the after-work golf games. He excelled at pretending. He had done it for years. He had done it so well that he had convinced himself that the straight parasailor bro Shane LaSalle was real.

He had recurring dreams of fat Stanley Rollins eating babies. The babies came on silver platters. They slept on beds of radicchio and sautéed kale. Their heads rested on Yukon Gold potatoes, pork dumplings. They wore a balsamic reduction glaze. Stanley Rollins ate them whole. His mouth opened into a monstrous chasm. He dropped one girl baby after another down his gullet. *So messy,* the dream Clifton James would declare, as he wrapped the girl baby up in a garbage sack, platter and all, and tossed her in the dumpster.

Shane LaSalle awoke each morning drenched in cold, embarrassing sweat. He trembled through breakfast. He gorged on sausage, and yet the thought of sausage made him sick to his stomach. It made him think of Duane Beckman. It made him think of Duane Beckman's last blueberry muffin, and every morning on the way to work he stopped at a coffee shop and bought all the blueberry muffins and left them sitting on a bench outside in the hopes that some poor homeless woman would pick them up and maybe feel less hungry.

He felt monstrously hungry.

He put on his face and went to work.

"Hello, Mr. LaSalle!"

"Great to see you, Mr. LaSalle!"

"You're looking well today, Mr. LaSalle!"

Only after two rounds of waxing and a last-minute pluck-fest. And yet, as soon as he plucked them, the hairs grew back.

"I'm freaking out," he told Natasha, in a clandestine coffee-break phone call.

"Is this about the hairs?"

"No. Yes! What if they get worse? I found one on my knuckle! What if my whole hands are covered in hair, like a, like some kind of—"

"Dog?"

"Yes. God! What's wrong with me! I'm surrounded by murderous werewolves and I can't stop freaking out about my hand hair!"

Clifton James teased him about the hair. Don Morgan teased him about how ugly he looked as a werewolf. Stanley Rollins invited him over for dinner. Stanley's wife was not cooking steak—she would serve it raw, but warmed, with a side of mashed potatoes. Shane graciously accepted the dinner invitation. He brought a bottle of wine, and a raw rack of lamb. He watched Stanley Rollins gnaw the meat from the bones, and he thought about the werewolf Richard Nixon, and the werewolf Dick Cheney, and the others whose pictures he regretted not having committed to memory, the werewolves who stalked the halls of the White House, the werewolves who presided in boardrooms, who devoured every bite of profitable meat from viable companies and threw the bankrupt bones aside, the werewolves who killed their babies.

"It's me again." He called Natasha late at night, when he couldn't sleep, even though the wispy moon made his eyelids heavy.

"Shane, hold on for a second." She sounded tired. Shane heard traffic in the background, street sounds. He waited. "Sorry, trying to find a spot to park for the night where I won't get towed. Did you try that hair remover?"

"It gave me a rash." Mortifying red, up the length of his hair-studded back. His spectacular apartment could not bear the sight of him. "I'm freaking out."

"You'll be okay."

"I'm terrified."

"Just keep on doing what you've been doing. How was dinner?"

"Stanley Rollins ate the heart."

"The heart—" Natasha made a retching sound.

"Of the cow. He sliced it up and wrapped the pieces in cheese. He stuck little toothpicks in them, like they were, like it was . . ."

"That's so gross."

"It was delicious," Shane admitted. "I feel so sick. My partners are terrifying."

"Um, yeah."

"What if they find me out?"

"They haven't yet."

"But what if they do? What if they find out that I'm a spy? That I'm . . . Oh . . ."

"Shane?"

"Oh God . . ."

"Shane, are you okay?"

"Yes, it's just . . . there's a new one. It's on my foot. I swear it wasn't there yesterday. I am such a freak."

"Some of the best people I've ever met are freaks."

"Natasha?"

"Yeah?"

"There's something . . ." Shane took a deep breath. "I've never told anyone this. . . ."

"Yeah?"

"I'm gay."

"Yeah, I kind of figured as much."

"You did?"

"Well, you know, when you were talking about Duane, and you started crying, I kind of assumed . . ."

"Oh."

"But . . . good for you. It's good. To say it out loud. It's a big step. You should be proud."

"What if they find out? My partners, what if they know already?"

"They don't have any reason to suspect," Natasha said. "Just—"

"No, I mean, what if they know that, um . . ."

"That you're *gay*?" Natasha laughed. "You do know where we live, right? I mean . . ."

"Yeah, but . . ."

"I know. Just . . . keep pretending, okay? Keep it up, what you're doing, for just a little while longer. Keep it up. For Duane."

They all met the next week, in Joseph Z'Rhae's underground office.

Nova brought coffee cake. Natasha brought a stack of werewolf drawings, drawn and signed by Veronica, who had lamented (loudly, tearfully, in a fit of bonelessness at the supermarket checkout) the injustice of being made to stay home with a babysitter and bathe and eat boring spaghetti for dinner while Dad and Ghost and Wolf got to visit the Glitter Lady. Shane produced a thumb drive.

"It's all I could get," he said. "I don't know if it's enough."

"Let's take a look, shall we?" Joseph plugged the drive into his computer.

"I feel like they're watching me."

"Did you follow the instructions I gave you?"

"I checked for bugs and cameras, always used my nose, everything you said."

"You're probably fine, but . . . well, let's see what's here."

Joseph opened and perused the first of the files on Shane's drive. Shane tapped his fingers.

"Quit it," Natasha said. "You're making me nervous."

"I am so nervous," Shane replied. "I'm like— Oh my God, do they sound like claws? Do my fingers sound like claws?"

"No, they don't sound like claws," Natasha said, stifling a laugh.

"Because they seem sharper, you know?" Shane examined them. "And, like, yellowish."

"They look normal to me."

"My mother keeps asking me about Thanksgiving. She wants me to come home. And I keep thinking, what if she sees? What if she can see it in my eyes? And then I think, what if the partners find out what I'm doing and I can't even make it home, because I'm dead?"

"Oh, honey," Nova said. She set a slice of coffee cake in front of Shane. "Don't fret. We'll make sure nothing happens to you."

"Mr. LaSalle, you're right to fret."

"Oh, *Joseph*—" Nova interjected.

"Your partners are dangerous," said Joseph.

Nova smiled. "And that's why we're going to take them down."

"And my sister here is overly optimistic."

"I can't help it. I see the glittery side of things."

"My mom keeps telling me," Shane said, "there's this girl she wants me to meet."

"A *woman*," Natasha corrected.

"Right. A woman. She's already bought theater tickets for us. But I . . ."

"Are you going to tell her?" Natasha asked.

"It's . . . it's not like she's prejudiced against gay people. I mean, she has gay friends, or, well, she has one gay friend. But she's always had this idea about how everything will turn out, this fantasy future. Like, *Shane LaSalle* will go to an Ivy League school and *Shane LaSalle* will have this amazing career and he'll marry some beautiful woman from Bloomfield Hills and they'll make lots of beautiful babies. And now what am I going to tell her? 'Oh, hi, Mom, guess what? I'm gay. And also, I'm a werewolf. And I just got fired! I'm an unemployed gay werewolf.'"

"Well, you might not get fired," said Lee.

"And can they even fire you, if you're a partner?"

"If the SEC investigates," Natasha said, "I think everyone might get fired. Like, that's the end of Barrington Equity."

"They'd kill you before they fired you," Joseph said. "But there's probably some good stuff on this drive that we can pass along to the SEC."

"But . . ."

"But there's no guarantee the SEC will do anything, or that they should. Just because something's unethical doesn't mean it's criminal. And if the SEC does act it might take months or even years. And then, even if any of them get charged, how many rich white men who get charged with white-collar crimes go free? If anyone gets thrown under the bus, Mr. LaSalle, it'll likely be you."

"So we have to plan for that," Natasha said, and for the next hour, through several cups of tea and more cake, with an intermission video call art-show of Veronica's latest werewolf portraits, they debated how to keep Shane from getting punished for the crimes of his partners, and how to make the partners pay, and not use their riches to buy their way out of any punishment.

"What if . . ." Natasha said at last. "What if they don't need to be convicted of anything?"

"What do you mean?"

"I mean, what if we only need to get them arrested?"

"Are you thinking—" Lee started to ask.

"Before the full moon." Joseph nodded. "If we timed it just right—"

"So somehow, they get arrested and thrown in jail, and before they have a chance to make bail—"

"They turn into werewolves." Nova smiled.

"They wouldn't be able to break out, right?" Lee asked. "I mean, like, they couldn't, like, tear down a wall or anything like that?"

"No, no," Joseph said. "That wouldn't happen."

"But what would happen to them?" asked Shane.

"They might still get out after," Joseph said. "There are werewolves in high places. They won't want any publicity about the existence of our kind. So either they'll make sure the Barrington pack never sees another full moon, or they'll try and make it look like the whole thing was a hoax."

"But maybe it'll be enough," Natasha said. "Maybe if they get arrested it'll be enough to link them, or at least one of them, to what happened to Marie."

"And Duane," said Shane.

"And Duane."

"Well," Joseph said with a sigh, "it's a long shot. But it might be worth it."

NATASHA

THE PLAN

The Redwoods—Now

THEY STAYED AT Joseph's into the evening, on his back deck, beneath the towering redwoods and the rising moon, and together they devised a plan. After they had all the pieces, Natasha laid them out: First, Shane would arrange an afternoon partnership luncheon at the Olympic Club. Natasha would spike the partners' drinks with roofies, and—

"Wait, so how is it that you're still working there?" Nova asked Natasha. "I mean, you saw the wolves, and it sounds like at least one of them got a good look at you."

"Carver," said Shane.

"So—"

"Yeah, I'd wondered whether they might try to get me fired," Natasha said. "But I guess they don't see me as a threat. I mean, what am I going to do? Out them as werewolves? Who'd believe me?"

"Just in case," Joseph said, "we should try and disguise you. I can supply you a pheromone so you'll smell different."

"Well, that makes sense, but just . . . watch your back, darling, okay?" Nova said, her eyes full of concern. "Anyway, I interrupted—" Natasha continued:

—their drinks spiked, the drugged, drunk, rowdy partners would cause a disturbance. Natasha would make sure the other staff saw. Someone would call the cops, who, upon arrival, would arrest the partners and cart them off to jail.

"But what if they don't go for the luncheon at the Olympic Club?" Nova asked.

"They will. I mean, they always go for lunch there," Shane said. "Or, well, they always go out for lunch somewhere. But it'll be easy to convince them to go there."

"And what if Natasha isn't scheduled to work?" Lee asked. "Or if she can't manage to spike the drinks?"

"I'm sure I'll be able to pick up a shift even if I'm not on the schedule," Natasha said. "But if I can get to their drinks—"

"If you can't," Shane said, "I should be able to. You can pass the roofies off to me."

Lee seemed nervous about the whole endeavor. "And you're going to spike their drinks right there at the table in the middle of lunch?"

"Well, I mean, if I don't have a good opportunity, then I'll do it later," Shane said. "I'm sure I can get them together for a drink somewhere else. There's always some sort of boozy pack gathering before the full moon. And do you know how much these guys drink? They go crazy. There's going to be a happy hour somewhere for sure. I'm more worried about what happens after. I mean, assuming we can get the cops to show up, and the cops arrest them, won't they just get out on bail? Or the cops will just bring them home—give them the rich guy Get Out of Jail Free card?"

"Look," said Joseph, "you guys just make sure the cops show up. I'll handle the rest."

"What do you mean, you'll 'handle the rest'?" Lee asked.

"I can make some things happen, with those fancy computers in my lair." Joseph grinned.

"But even if it works," Shane said, "and they do get arrested and locked up, what if there are other people locked up with them? And they—"

"Fair. But there won't be," Joseph said. "I should be able to take care of that, too. You just need to make sure the cops come. . . . But even so, this is not likely to work out."

They all knew: The wolves would smell them coming. The wolves would dump the spiked drinks, or run off before the cops arrived, or turn werewolf in the back seat of the squad car.

Joseph Z'Rhae knew that he had not survived three and a half decades as a werewolf by making hasty decisions. He brewed another pot of tea. He spoke slowly. He sniffed the breeze for the scent of wolves. He suggested caution. They should wait and see, plot and plan. Werewolves were cunning, ruthless creatures.

"And how many more people will they kill, while we sit around plotting and planning?" Natasha pounded the table. She stomped back inside. She stood for a moment, trying to calm her livid mind. She saw, in the kitchen, that one of Veronica's pictures had been stuck to the fridge: a werewolf, paws in the air, riding what looked like a roller coaster. Or the stock market. She fumed. The fucking werewolf culture. All its misogyny and bloodlust, its bullshit country clubs, all the thousand-dollar-an-hour lawyers it could hire to dodge the SEC. She wanted, more than anything, to stop them.

"You never would have made it as a werewolf," Joseph said, when she finally returned. "You're too rash and fiery."

"Yeah? Well, fuck you."

"Hey, honey," Nova said, "we're all on the same side, remember?"

"Yeah, I know. I'm just fucking pissed," Natasha said. "I get why you want to be cautious. But what about Misti Buxby? And her baby?"

"Every option has its risks," Joseph said.

"We need to save her."

Joseph nodded. He sipped his tea. "So you should go ahead with your plan, then. If you want to take the risk. I wouldn't. I'd wait and see if we can try the SEC angle. But it's your risk to take. If it doesn't work out, this will fall back on *you*. You and Shane. You might get fired, or arrested. Or worse. The Barrington pack might kill you."

"What have I got to lose?" Natasha said. "But Shane—"

She looked at Shane. His brow was furrowed. He stared out into the darkening forest. He had everything to lose.

"What about you, Shane?" Nova asked.

For a moment, he didn't respond. Then, at last, he said, "I . . . I can't keep this up. I can't keep faking. They'll find me out regardless. And I understand the risks. But . . . money is just money. I already lost the thing—the person who mattered most. I want to take them down. For Duane."

"For Duane." Natasha squeezed Shane's shoulder. "And Marie. We are gonna take those fucking werewolves down."

"Okay then," Joseph said. "But if you're going to do this, you need to be prepared. Does either of you know how to shoot?"

"Like, a gun? No."

"No."

He sighed. He got up and went inside. A moment later he returned with two small spray canisters, which he handed to Natasha and Shane. "All right, let's try these since you're fond of pepper spray."

"Is it—" Natasha asked.

"Ghost pepper spray laced with silver. It won't stop them from turning, but it'll blind them for a good two hours. I can also put together something for you to use in their drinks. Like roofies, but more . . . potent."

MARY BARRINGTON

HARD CHOICES

San Francisco–Now

THE YOUNGER ONES never understood, about hard choices. The diamonds on their fingers were born in the jewelry shop. The mink that lined their coats grew on mink trees. The handbags and high heels they spotted at Saks became theirs through the magic of a plastic card, produced by a magic husband, whose magic was best left undiscussed. But then they'd get all worked up about some sweatshop in Myanmar. *Good God, don't you know those sneakers were made by child labor? I read all about it on the internet!* As if they had never heard anything so awful. Well, they didn't know awful. Not until they had to lock awful up in a kennel each month, while he begged and pleaded *please mama please I won't bite.* Not until they had to hold their hand over awful's mouth until it stopped squirming.

The younger ones wanted bacon, but they didn't want to think about how the bacon got made, or who made it, or how if you shared your bacon it meant less bacon for you. Like Darren's wife, little Ditzy Misti, all swept up in her penthouse, raving about Darren and the Emeralds, Darren and the Weekend in Cabo, Darren and the Swiss Ski Vacation. As if Darren Buxby were a children's book where everyone learned a valuable lesson about generosity and manners. Though, Ditzy Misti had seemed more subdued of late. Maybe she had found out about Darla, or Christa, or Carla, or maybe some random drunk girl selected by Darren for the shortness of her skirt and the bazookaness of her breasts had answered Darren's office phone when his wife had called. *I'm sorry, Darren can't come to the phone right now. He's about to get his dick sucked.*

Everything had a price.

Everything was capable of being bought, sold, auctioned to the highest bidder. And if you had expensive taste, well . . .

Now, the older ones understood the sacrifice. Like Nora Rollins, whose husband ate the next-door neighbor's dog. Stanley Rollins wasn't a neat eater, either. He left a trail of entrails leading from the neighbor's yard into his own. And who had to go outside at five in the morning with the hose? Who cleaned bloody paw prints off the hardwood? Who lied when the neighbor came knocking? *Your dog? Oh gosh, I am so sorry to hear! Well, if I see him I'll be sure to bring him right over.* Or Clara Morgan, who bore twins: two little boy pups with fingernails that could slit a throat. Mary brought over the kennel they had used for their own little boy. *But they'll cry! What if they're hungry? What if—* Best to let them cry it out, Clara Morgan had learned quickly, when she'd taken one out and tried to sooth it and it ripped into her arm with its teeth. She couldn't wear sleeveless blouses anymore, but now those little pups were on their way to Harvard!

Shannon James understood, Mary had thought. Mary had felt a kinship with Shannon that she had not had with the others, not pudgy Nora Rollins, or Clara whose scars made her overly methodical, or Ron Carver's wife, with her Botox and her diet pills. Mary had taken Shannon under her wing, had introduced her to the world of charity galas and country club luncheons, had taught her where to shop and where to find the best caterer for your cocktail party and how to wash the wolf-smell from your husband's clothes when he put them on the morning after without bathing first. Shannon never complained about sweatshops in Myanmar. She never bitched about her husband's instincts or lamented a lost career.

Shannon said of her husband: *He can't help what he is, and it's my job to support him.*

She said: *I love being a mother. Why on earth would you ever want to work all day in an office when you could just stay at home with your kids?*

She said: *We will do whatever it takes to support our men.*

That was a few years back, when some money-grubbing ex-secretary had filed a spurious lawsuit against the firm, alleging discriminatory hiring practices and a workplace culture that encouraged sexual assault. *It's bogus. Bogus! We have to stand strong,* Shannon had said, and Mary did not see any reason to let her know that Darren Buxby had pushed the ex-secretary up against the conference room wall and unzipped his fly while no less than three (names redacted from the complaint) Barrington Equity partners walked past and did nothing and the only reason there hadn't been more onlookers was because some Boy Scout named Duane Beckman wandered in and saw her struggling and said, *Hey, uh, Mr. Buxby, can I borrow your secretary for a minute?* and sent her out for a coffee, which of course she never brought back. There was no reason for Shannon to know all these pesky details. Shannon knew they had to stand by their men, and that was enough.

But lately, Mary had begun to doubt whether Shannon really understood. Shannon still said the right things or, more importantly, refrained from saying the wrong things. Shannon still volunteered to chair the committee for the breast cancer fundraising gala and she still played ladies' doubles with Mary every Tuesday morning, but more often, it seemed, the ball would zip past her and only after would she swing. Mary had not gotten where she was and stayed there for so long without cultivating a finely tuned intuition. With each bungled serve, with each point scored because Shannon swung too late, Mary's doubt grew.

Her doubt had already amassed considerable size when she finished a late lunch at the Olympic Club and she saw Shannon James rush into the lobby. Shannon's shirt was untucked in the back. Her brow was creased and her lips pinched. If she kept them pinched like that, Mary thought, she'd ruin her pretty face and even Botox couldn't fix it. A year earlier, Mary would have walked right up and asked Shannon about the kids and confirmed their Friday lunch date and passed along a nice tidbit of club gossip. But now—now Mary's intuition told her to step back, to watch and listen, to not let herself be seen.

"I'm here to pick up a basket," Shannon said to the hostess. There was something distrustful about the hostess. "For a school fundraising auction. It's under the name Shannon James. If you wouldn't mind grabbing it—my kids are in the car."

So Shannon had taken to leaving her kids in the car. Mary shook her head. Shannon paced. She looked harried. The hostess returned with a basket. Then, as Shannon turned to leave, the hostess asked about her pregnant friend.

"Did she have the baby?"

"Not yet."

"Okay, good, I—I hope it goes well."

"Thank you.... Me too," Shannon said. But Mary heard in her voice notes of fear, despair, betrayal. Shannon carried her basket out to her car, where her neglected children waited. At least it wasn't hot out there, Mary thought. But still. Her mind raced bitterly. Children alone in the car. A faulty tennis swing.

And then that hostess, that uppity hostess, remarking on Ditzy Misti's baby. There was something detestable about that hostess.

Although most of the early accounts of American lycanthropy originated from the mid-Atlantic region, principally Pennsylvania and Ohio, the majority of werewolf sightings during the nineteenth century occurred in the mountainous and coastal regions of the West. The werewolves, it would seem, seized the same manifest destiny as human pioneers, charting a bloody westward course.

Either the werewolves of nineteenth-century America did not make the same efforts to conceal their wolfish form, or there were simply far more of them. Sightings were numerous, particularly in the century's middle decades. Werewolves were spotted on the streets of Denver, Topeka, Grand Junction, and Kansas City. Their appearances often coincided with incidents of looting and violence. Werewolves were seen stalking and attacking rioters during the Cincinnati riots of 1841 and reportedly instigated several outbreaks of violence in Kansas during the 1850s, during a protracted period of guerrilla warfare referred to as "Bleeding Kansas." On numerous instances, werewolves were reported to have broken into houses and business establishments to steal money and jewels. And in 1878, a werewolf reportedly exited a San Francisco bank carrying a bag of gold in its teeth. None of these reports were ever confirmed, and the werewolf assailants and robbers were never captured. Having resumed his human form by the following day, the werewolf's identity could not be established.

Perhaps the most famous of all werewolf attacks occurred in California, in 1848, when more than sixty people were killed at a mining camp near Sutter's Mill over the course of a single night. Six months earlier, gold had been found at Sutter's Mill . . .

Marcus Flick, American Myths and Monsters: The Werewolf, 2nd ed. (Denver: Birdhouse Press, 2022), 157–58

BARTHOLOMEW BARRINGTON

GOLD RUSH

California–Summer 1848

BARTHOLOMEW BARRINGTON ARRIVED at the camp with nothing but the clothes on his back, and the several hundred dollars he carried in a pouch tucked into his trousers, and his gold pocket watch, and his sack of jewels, and his team of four horses. He had started out with ten horses, but he had gotten hungry.

Bartholomew Barrington bought himself a cabin a mile from the camp, newly built, the wood so fresh he could still smell the pine needles.

"And what happened to the fellow that built it?" he asked the seller.

"I reckon he struck gold. Then he had an unfortunate accident."

"Oh?"

"He went and got himself drowned in the river."

"So how is it that you came to own this cabin?"

The seller grinned. His teeth were capped with gold. "Same way most things are come to be owned round here."

Bartholomew Barrington paid for the cabin. He hitched his horses outside. He waited for nightfall, and then he followed the scent of the man who had sold him the cabin to a saloon at the edge of the camp. The saloon was nothing but two tents with a circle of logs for sitting and a vat of moonshine.

"What's that fellow's name?" he asked the proprietor. He pointed to the seller, sprawled drunk over a log.

"That one ain't got no name."

Bit drank a mug of moonshine. He waited on a log seat for the nameless seller to awaken. He waited late into the night, as the moon was lustrous and he did not feel tired. When the nameless seller arose, near dawn, and stumbled through camp toward his own cabin, Bit followed him.

He sprang from behind.

He slammed the man's head against the earth. He reached into his mouth and, with the pliers he had pocketed earlier that day, he pulled out five nameless golden teeth.

"What fun!"

Bit looked up. He saw another man, a man dressed in fine clothes, a man with a fine face and glossy hair and eyes as cold and black as a starless sky.

"Did you pull them all out? Or has he got any left in there that I could pull?"

The man called himself William Carver. He had claimed the name as his own.

"I will not tell you the name I was born with," he said later that morning as they strolled through the camp, Bit surveying and noting the smell of things. "What is that thing you are doing with your nose? You keep scrunching it up."

"This camp has a foul smell."

"I killed a man, a few years back," Carver said. "'Cept he was an Injun, so not really a man and it warn't no crime. After I kilt him, I carved him up with a knife and fed 'im to my hogs. His name was William. Who ever heard of an Injun called William? Anyways, that's hows I got my name. William Carver. Do you get it?"

"Yes."

"'Cause I carved up William. See? *See?* William Carver! Hey, you ain't laughin'."

William Carver looked hurt by his companion's failure to laugh.

"Why'd you kill him?" Bit did not understand Carver's amusement. Bit had killed plenty, with great satisfaction, but death had never seemed funny. He took what he needed, what he felt he deserved, and if death played a part, well, all things came in cycles, and he was only speeding the cycle up.

"I dunno."

"And why are you telling me this?"

"'Cause you and me, we're the same."

"I hardly think that we're the same."

"Oh, we're the same, you and me. I can see it in your eyes. We're both killers."

Bit tried to shake this interloper. Bit wanted to continue his scheming in peace. But this William Carver always seemed to appear out of nowhere. He had, strangely, almost no smell. He followed Bit around like a dog begging to be kicked. He bragged about his sins, about the pocketbooks he had thieved, the girls whose screams he had muffled as he deflowered them, the boy he had pushed from a moving train. Carver seemed to find these accomplishments all very amusing.

"You see? You see?" he said to Bit.

"No, you and I are not the same."

"Well, we will see about that."

Bit counted the tents at the camp. He counted the men who came and went, and he listened to what they said and did when they thought no one could hear them. He listened to the paper crinkle of their precious deeds. He listened when they hid their gold. He watched the gold-seekers scoop pans of silt from the river and dig open the dusty earth. He studied the scent of gold. He counted the days. The moon grew full. He walked into the brittle woods behind his cabin. He stripped his clothes. He looked up at the sky, as the moonlight struck him, and his body transformed, Bit-to-Wolf, Bit-to-Wolf, Bit-to-Wolf. He looked at the swelling brightness in the sky, and he thought about Rosalina, about his big house along the river, his bank, his horses, his jewels, all the bounty this New World had given him.

No, not given. Bit had taken it for himself.

He looked up and smiled his sharp-toothed smile.

Hello, Moon, he said.

But the moon was silent.

William Carver was not.

"Hello, Mr. Barrington."

The man stepped from the shadows. Bit growled.

"I know that it's you. I saw it happen."

Bit growled again. He walked toward Carver.

"You are the devil," Carver said. "I knew it when I saw you. The devil takes the shape of a man so that he may walk among them. But this is your true form."

Bit walked closer. William Carver laughed.

"But I have never feared the devil."

Bit leapt. He ripped Carver's neck out from beneath Carver's smiling face. Carver fell to the ground laughing. Blood spurted from his neck and gurgled out of his mouth. He laughed and laughed.

"You see?" he said, gagging on his own blood. "You see?"

Bit saw. Bit saw what he had not seen since the night he killed the young rapist Bartholomew Barrington whose name he had stolen. Carver's eyes shifted. His body contorted. He laughed and laughed, until he couldn't laugh any more, until his laughter became a howl.

You see?

William Carver rolled over and stood on his new legs. His fur bristled. His eyes flashed. His hideous teeth glistened in the moonlight. He turned his hungry eyes toward the camp.

You see?

Bit saw. He ran ahead. Carver followed behind. Bit stopped at the edge of camp. Carver did not. Carver stalked up behind a young gold digger dining on a late supper of venison and bread. He closed his jaws around the young man's thigh. He tore the muscle from the man's leg and swallowed it down in a single gulp, while the man screamed and groped for his gun. Too late, when he secured it. Carver had already moved on.

William Carver spread terror through the camp. He moved from tent to tent, killing the old men, maiming the young. He ripped limbs from bodies. He slashed throats and split bellies. He found the nameless man whose teeth Bit had pulled and he ate the flesh from his face.

Bit crouched at the shadowed edge of the woods. He watched.

The strongest men at the camp gathered together. They argued. *It was a wolf,* some said. *That was no mere wolf,* said others. *But regardless we must kill it,* they finally agreed, though their discord had given Carver time, and with his time he killed more. He ripped through tents and knocked oil lamps onto the dry ground. He started fires.

Bit watched the fires blossom. The strongest men at the camp had to turn their attention to fighting them instead of the wolf. Carver picked them off. A leg here. A forearm there. The camp filled with thick smoke. The dry trees crackled as fire swept through them.

And Bit, cunning Bit, ruthless Bit, he crept through the camp, his snout low to the earth, and he sniffed out the gold. For days he had scouted and listened. He knew who had buried nuggets beneath their bedrolls. He knew who stashed nuggets in their boots, who carried them in pouches around their necks, who had traded them already for stacks of bills. Bit found the bills and the gold. He carried them into the forest. He ran back. He found more. He found deeds to land, land ribboned with gold, and he took those, too. He ran back. He found more. He killed seldom, only the ones who strapped their riches to their bodies, who resisted when he tried to take what he meant to be his. He left the killing to William Carver, and William Carver howled gleefully, and his howls rang like gruesome laughter through the burning camp.

Morning neared, and the strongest men, the few of them left, whose tents had burned, whose wealth Bit had plundered, extinguished the last smolders of the last fire. Carver prowled among the dead, searching for others like him, others who might turn from man to wolf. He meant to kill them if they did.

Bit-to-Wolf fled into the forest. He lay down beside his mound of riches. He laughed, and watched the sky grow light, and felt Wolf fall into his cycle of slumber.

"You see now?" William Carver appeared, stark naked, smeared with blood.

Bartholomew Barrington had already dressed in his fine clothes and begun to gather his new deeds. "You, sir, are the devil."

Carver laughed. "It is past breakfast time. I am feeling very hungry. And some indigestion. It feels as if there's a bone stuck right here, in my chest."

"You ought not to have eaten the bone."

"We make a splendid team, you and I." Carver picked up a chunk of gold. He turned it over in his bloodied palm. "Don't you see it?"

Bit looked at William Carver. Then he looked down at the treasures in his hands, more valuable treasures than he had ever collected before.

"Yes," he said. "I see it."

NOT-SO-HAPPY HOUR

San Francisco—Now

NATASHA SLEPT THROUGH the early morning in her car, scrunched in the driver's seat. Lee and Shane had both offered to let her sleep on their respective couches (*though your car might be more comfortable*, Shane had said, of his couch), but it would be dangerous to spend too much time with Shane (his partners might smell her), she didn't want to overstay her welcome with Lee, and she was too stubborn and embarrassed to ask the famed Queen of Sequin Pop for help. But she joined Lee Curtis at his house for breakfast while his wife worked and the peanut slept and Veronica mashed ketchup into her eggs until they transformed into an orange egg paste, which she then declared gross and refused to eat.

"I'm going to fuck this up," Natasha mumbled, as she dabbed her wrists with the pheromone Joseph had provided.

She had felt nervous ever since she picked up the bottle of super-roofies from Joseph. What had seemed like a brilliant plan when she had first envisioned it now seemed stupid. She was a hostess, not a bartender. So what would she say? *Excuse me, Mr. Bartender, but why don't you let me deliver those drinks, ha ha ha ha* (wicked laughter). *Or excuse me, Mr. Bartender, but can you step aside while I slip some roofies into those martinis you just poured?* And what if they didn't order drinks? What if they just wanted water? Or sparkling water, the type that came in roofie-proof opened-at-the-table bottles? Or what if they caught her and she went to jail for trying to drug the respectable businessmen?

"Dad, she said fuck," Veronica tattled.

"I'm sorry—"

"Sometimes grown-ups use words that kids should never use, honey," Lee said.

"Like *fuck*?" Veronica chirped. "Or *shit*? Or *aaaaaasshole*?"

"Do not say those words," Lee scolded.

Veronica sculpted an egg-ketchup volcano on her plate. "*Which* words?"

"You know what words."

"I'm sorry, I'm just nervous," Natasha said.

"It'll be okay," said Lee.

"He says, with the eternal forced optimism of parenthood."

"You know, you don't have to go through with it. You can wait. You can just forget the whole thing."

"I can't. You know I can't, Lee."

"Yeah. Just . . . don't be too hard on yourself. You've never done this before."

"Right. I've never taken down a pack of werewolves."

"So give it your best shot, and if doesn't work, you can try again."

"All right, *Dad*," Natasha joked.

"I mean it."

"Unless they find out, and they kill me."

"Oh no, Ghost!" Veronica squealed. "They can't kill you! You're a ghost!"

"You make a good point, Vee," Natasha said. "What have I got to lose?"

Veronica scooted over to Natasha. She whispered into Natasha's ear, "But they might fuck you up."

"*Veronica*," Lee admonished, "what did I just tell you?"

"You said not to say. But I didn't *say* the word! I whispered!"

Lee sighed.

"Well, there's only so much they can do," Natasha said. "I mean, what have I really got left to lose? I don't have a career. I don't have a house, kids. You're basically the only friend I've seen in months, unless you count Shane, and he's . . . well, he's . . ."

"A little too concerned with body hair."

"Exactly. He's got his own issues to work out. And I probably won't be able to spike their drinks in the first place. I probably won't even get close. And then— Ugh, I just hate them all so much. I think . . . I think that's the only reason this seemed like a good plan in the first place. Like, when you look at something through rage-colored glasses . . ."

Natasha finished breakfast, and then she helped Lee wash dishes and clean the orange egg paste out of Veronica's plushie tree house. (She could have sworn she overheard Veronica whisper, in the voice of the plushie squirrel who lived in the tree house, "Let's fuck this place up," as the little girl spooned egg paste through the windows.)

Then she packed up and stepped out into the bright

mid-morning sun. On the other side of the earth, the full moon rose.

Natasha drove part of the way to work. She did not feel ready for what she might be about to do. She parked near the beach. She walked the rest of the way, and as she walked she clutched the bottle of roofies in her pocket and considered the futility of fighting werewolves. She arrived at work. A manager met her at the door, the same thin-nosed manager who'd given her instructions for the werewolf dinner party.

"I'm sorry," he said, pushing his glasses up. "You're going to have to leave."

"What?"

"The premises."

"What, I . . . I don't understand."

The manager sighed. "I think you do."

"Am I being fired?"

"I'm surprised, honestly. You seemed, well . . . But you're lucky we decided not to call the cops."

"The *cops*?" Natasha's heart thudded frantically. The bottle of super-roofies in her pocket felt lava-hot. Had they figured her out? Did they know what she had planned to do? "Look, I really don't understand. Why? . . . What is it you think I did?"

"Well, there was the spitting, for starters."

"The spitting." Natasha looked at him, confused.

"Into the bread baskets. Which, really? So juvenile."

"I did not spit into the bread baskets."

"And then the silverware. One of our members saw you slipping silverware into your bag."

"What? I would never—"

"Twice."

"But I didn't! I swear! Can't I at least . . . I mean . . . there can't be any proof. How can you fire me without proof?"

The manager's glasses had slipped, and he pushed them back up again. He looked at Natasha. Maybe he believed her. But it didn't matter. "It's a private club. Look, maybe you didn't steal anything, I'm obviously not calling the cops. But it doesn't matter if you did or not. All that matters is that our members say you did. So I have to let you go."

There was nothing more to be said. Natasha turned and left. She felt bewildered. She felt cold and hot at the same time. Those fucking werewolves. In their dumb country club. Playing stupid golf. Drinking their martinis and laughing—*laughing*—about getting her fired from her lousy job. And then when they got good and drunk and hideous they'd go out killing, and what could *she* do to stop them?

As she walked through the parking lot a Mercedes-Benz pulled to a stop in front of her. The window rolled down. Natasha recognized the woman in the driver's seat from the baby shower.

"I am sooo sorry to hear that you lost your job," Mary Barrington said. "How unfortunate. But I suppose that's what happens, when you steal the club silverware."

Oh. Natasha stared at the woman, as she began to realize what had happened.

"You're not sorry," Natasha said.

"You need a lesson in minding your own business."

"You need a lesson in not being a fucking tool for the patriarchy."

"Sweetie," Mary Barrington said, as she rolled up her window, "you better watch your back."

Mary Barrington drove off. Natasha wanted to scream, so she did.

"Aghhhhhhhh!" She kicked the shiny hubcap of a parked car. "Fuuuck! Those fuckers!"

The car alarm wailed.

She took off running before someone could call the cops and they could come and arrest her and she got so mad that she tore their heads off. She wanted to call up Shane LaSalle. She wanted to say: *Shane, bite me. Turn me into a motherfucking werewolf so I can beat them, so that I can stand a chance in this fight.*

She called Shane LaSalle.

"There's a problem."

"Who is . . . ? Natasha?" Shane whispered.

"Yes, it's—"

"Shhhh. I'm in the office. Talk quiet, or they'll hear you."

"There's a problem. I just got fired."

"Oh, shit. . . ."

"I've got the stuff from Joseph in my pocket, but there's no way I'm putting it in anyone's drink."

"Shit. Okay. Okay. Everything's still okay. Just . . . come downtown. Can you meet me down here in an hour?"

"Probably."

"Okay, meet me down in Embarcadero Plaza. Just find somewhere to sit and I'll slip out and come find you."

SHANE LaSALLE

OFFICE PARTY

San Francisco—Now

ALL THINGS CAME in cycles. And so it happened that Shane LaSalle found Natasha Porter sitting on the same bench in Embarcadero Plaza where she had slept as a homeless woman, where Duane Beckman had laid the remains of the last blueberry muffin he would ever eat.

"Here," Natasha said. She gave the bottle of super-roofies to Shane. He rubbed the bottle down with hand sanitizer.

"So they don't smell you," he said.

"What will you do?"

"I don't know. We've got lunch at the club, but I think that'll be too hard. . . . Maybe after, I can probably get them all back here to the office, maybe convince them to start the happy hour here. . . . I will. I have to do something. I told Jeanie—"

"Is she the woman from Ohio, the one whose company your firm is after?"

"Yeah. I told her to just hang tight. If I don't do something they'll destroy her company. They'll destroy her."

"Why the hell did you get into this business, you know, sucking other companies dry? You seem too nice."

"I guess . . . I guess it didn't seem real. When you don't know the people who get hurt, when all you see is what's on the screen right in front of you, it's easy to forget about the real effects on real people. It's like you know what you're doing, but really you don't."

"Yeah. Yeah, I know exactly what you mean."

Good luck followed Shane through the morning, into the afternoon. None of the partners caught Natasha's scent on the roofie bottle. None of them seemed to notice the slight increase in Shane's heart rate, or the way his left eyelid twitched when he lied.

"I am so excited," he said to Clifton, as he walked into the conference room around lunchtime and saw that his affable partner had already gathered there with Don Morgan and Stanley Rollins. "The full moon . . . Last month was . . . well, it was thrilling."

"Good boy." Clifton James clapped him on the back.

"I was thinking of heading up to the Marin Headlands," Shane went on.

"That's a great place to run," Don Morgan said.

"Do you think there are any deer up there? I'd love to catch a deer."

"Not as many as in the woods down toward Santa Cruz, but I've caught one there before."

"What are you guys all doing?" Shane asked.

"Rollins has a farm scoped out," Clifton said. "He and Morgan are going to hit it up."

"I have a weakness for sheep," Rollins added.

"Carver is staying home with the wife."

"Is she . . . Does she . . ."

"You don't wanna know," Clifton said. "Buxby, Dick, and I are undecided. Maybe I'll come along with you."

"That would be great," Shane said. "But we're, uh, we're all going to have a drink together first?"

"I think so," Clifton said. "If Rollins can last that long."

"I'm barely buzzed, and I've been drinking since breakfast!"

"His full moon coffee is mostly Kahlúa."

"What if instead of going out for drinks after work," Shane said, hoping he didn't sound nervous, "we just order in more food and have a drink right in the conference room? That way we can talk and eat freely."

"I like the way you think, LaSalle," Rollins said. "You ever go to a restaurant and try to order six steaks and three plates of ribs? Ha, ha, ha."

"Ha, ha, ha, ha, ha."

The wolves all laughed, and Shane laughed with them, though he felt sickened by the image of Rollins eating six steaks and three plates of ribs, and even more sickened by the wicked peal of Carver's laughter, as Carver stepped into the room behind him.

"Ha, ha, ha, ha, ha!!!"

But Shane LaSalle was an excellent liar.

The wolves had a three-martini lunch. They hit a few balls at the driving range. They drove back downtown, to their office. Some of them worked. Rollins napped at his desk. Buxby ordered Darla to his office and closed and locked the door. Shane LaSalle pretended to look at maps of the headlands. He pretended to plan his running route. Full moon's eve was like a Friday afternoon at the Barrington Equity office, for the partners, and especially when it fell on a Friday. The associates had all been sent home early, but they would all still work late into the night, every one of them except for Duane Beckman. The light in Duane Beckman's office was still out, his door still closed, his chair empty, his untouched desk preserved under the illusion that he had gone away for vacation—a long, long vacation, from which, eventually, he would fail to return.

Happy hour struck. The steak and ribs snacks that Rollins had ordered for everyone arrived. The partners gathered in the conference room.

"I'll fix drinks," Shane volunteered, and then felt instantly self-consciously gay. He'd never seen any of the other partners fix drinks.

"Oh, we can have one of the girls do it—"

"Girls always mix them too weak," Shane said. "I can fix a better drink than any of the girls."

"Of course you can, LaSalle." Clifton James chuckled.

"You go for it, LaSalle."

"Save me some of those ribs, will ya? Otherwise Rollins'll eat them all."

"Ha, ha, ha, ha, ha!"

Shane hurried into the kitchen. He pulled a bottle of gin from the liquor cabinet, tonic and lime from the fridge. He set seven tumblers on a serving tray, mixed seven strong gin and tonics, and pulled the bottle of super-roofies from his pocket. He read the label on the bottle, handwritten by Joseph Z'Rhae. *200 lbs = ¼ teaspoon.* The super-roofies came in powder form, unpressed. *What the fuck, Joe,* Shane thought. Was he supposed to measure the drugs out with a quarter teaspoon? Because they definitely had one of those lying around in the office kitchen.

Shane unscrewed the cap. He sniffed the roofie inside. It didn't smell so super. It smelled like—

"What are you doing?" a familiar voice said.

Shane nearly dropped the bottle. He spun around. With his senses focused on the drugs, he had failed to smell Darla at the door.

"Oh, I'm just mixing some drinks."

"Yes but," Darla said, eyeing him curiously, "there's something behind your back."

"Oh, that's just—" Shane fumbled with the bottle behind his back, trying to screw the cap back on.

"What is it?"

"—bitters. It's just bitters."

"You're adding bitters to your gin and tonics."

"Yes. So?"

"You don't put bitters in a gin and tonic."

"*I* do."

"Is one of those for Mr. Buxby?"

"Yes. But what are you still doing here? The office closed early."

"Mr. Buxby asked me to stay. And he won't like your gin and tonic. And then he'll call me in and order me to make him a new one. So you might as well mix it right in the first place. I'm happy to help you, Mr. LaSalle." Darla walked toward him. "I just—"

Fast as a fox, Darla reached behind him and snatched the bottle from his hand.

"Hey!"

"This isn't bitters."

"It's none of your—"

"What is this?"

She darted for the door. Another sort of wolf would have lunged for her. Another sort of wolf would have grabbed her, held his hand over her mouth, told her what he would do if she tried to scream. Shane stood immobile, as his brain replayed the memory of Darla serving him a drink on the Barrington jet, him and Duane and *Duane Duane Duane Duane* and his instincts told him: Trust her.

"It's just—"

She closed the door. She read the label. "Flunitrazepam and . . . I know what this is."

"It's . . . it's not exactly what you think."

"And you said one of these drinks is for Mr. Buxby?"

"Yes, but—"

Darla laughed. "And you were going to . . . It always seemed like there was something different about you, Mr. LaSalle. Please, allow me the pleasure."

She did not wait for permission. She marched up to the tray of drinks and, without minding the label, poured the entire bottle of super-roofies out into six of the seven gin and tonics.

"That was . . . You were supposed to measure."

She gave a faux shrug. "Oops."

"It was supposed to be a quarter teaspoon. . . . Do you think that was—"

"More? Gosh, probably."

"Shit. Shit. I don't know what will happen. What if—"

"You could always pour them out and mix some more."

"No," Shane said. "No, I have to do this. These guys are... They're—"

"Rapey, thieving assholes."

"Worse. Way worse." Shane picked up the tray of drinks. "Look, this is all me, okay? So if anything happens, I didn't even see you here."

"Mr. LaSalle?" Darla said, as Shane carried the drinks out of the kitchen.

"Yeah?"

"The one on the right is yours."

Once in the conference room, Shane set the tray on the table and immediately grabbed the drink on the right, draining half of it in one gulp.

"Ha, ha, you're in the mood to party, aren't you, LaSalle!"

"Tonight's the night! I'm—" Shane looked at his partners, Stanley Rollins devouring his second steak, Clifton James and Don Morgan grabbing gin and tonics from the tray, Darren Buxby leering at something pornographic on his phone. But the other two were gone. "—I'm so excited! Here, Buxby, have a drink! Let's toast!"

"Tonight *is* the night!" Rollins said. "Buxby just got a call. His wife."

"She's going into labor!"

"That's great," Shane said quietly, then more loudly, "Just *great!*"

"To Buxby, and his new baby," Clifton James said.

"To Buxby!" Shane raised his glass. "Say, should we wait for Dick and Carver?"

"They just left. Dick got a call, too. Some urgent business came up."

"Oh."

"So—"

"Cheers!"

Five of the seven Barrington Equity partners toasted. Shane knocked back the rest of his gin and tonic.

"Here, have another one, LaSalle." Clifton James slid one of the tainted cocktails over to Shane.

"You know, I think one's enough for me."

"Oh, come on, LaSalle. It's the full moon!"

"Well, I mean, I only wanted one cocktail. I'm kind of in the mood for a glass of red wine. You know, to complement the steak. Does anyone else—"

"I'll take one," Rollins said, through a mouthful of steak.

"Better bring a few bottles, LaSalle. Rollins'll drink a whole bottle himself."

"Ha, ha, ha, ha, ha!"

Rollins grinned. "At least a bottle."

Shane hurried back to the kitchen: *Shit shit shit shit shit.* He had just poisoned four of his partners. He had been *so obvious.* He might have just killed them. He probably hadn't, because their werewolf bodies were grotesquely resilient, but also he almost wished he had, because then at least they couldn't kill anyone else, but of course the cops would show up and investigate and they would find out about his drink-spiking and send him to prison, and you know what they do to werewolves in prison? And if they *didn't* die, then they would know what he had done. They would tear him apart. And before they tore him apart, they would end his career. They would unleash a smear campaign to rival the worst smears the internet had known. His brain flooded with malicious false hashtags: #ShaneLaSalleJerksOffOnTheBus; #ShaneLaSalleFartsCauseGlobalWarming; #ShaneLaSalle KilledDuaneBeckman; #ShaneLaSalleIsAWerewolf.

So the last one was true. And the one before that? If he had been honest enough with himself to be honest with Duane . . . if he had taken Duane's hands in his own, had stared into Duane's eyes, had pressed his lips against Duane's lips and run the tip of his tongue across Duane's darling snaggleteeth while he had the chance, then maybe he and Duane Beckman would not have flown on a private jet to Lake Orange, where the wolves had decided their fate.

Shane called Natasha on the phone.

"Hey, we've got a problem."

"Of course. It was a stupid plan."

"I slipped the stuff to four of them. But I think I gave them way too much. And Barrington and Carver ran off before I could, like, super-roofie them, and I have no idea where they went."

"Shit."

"Yeah. This is fucked."

"Should I . . . I'll call Joseph and Nova. See if they've got any ideas. Do you want me to meet you?"

"At my apartment. If I can make it back there. If not, then . . ."

"I'll be there."

Shane hung up. Would he be there? He paced in front of the wine cooler. The Pinot or the Cab? Merlot or Shiraz? Jail or death?

"Hey, LaSalle!" Clifton James yelled, from the hallway. "Be a good boy and (hiccup) get Rollins a bottle o' (hiccup) wine, would ya? He's (hiccup) thirsty!"

Inebriated Clifton James stumbled into the kitchen. He pulled a bottle of wine from the cooler. He stood, swaying, trying to read the label. The bottle slipped from his hand and shattered on the floor.

"Iths slippery," he slurred.

"Shit," Shane said. He had not expected the drugs to work so quickly. The swift werewolf metabolism must have quickened the effect. "Okay. Okay, I'm going to clean this up and—"

"Naw, (hiccup) just leave it. The girls'll clean it up. Won't they? (hiccup) Won't you girls clean it up? Not you, LaSalle. You're a (hiccup) man."

"Okay, Cliff. Okay, why don't you go back in the conference room and have some food. Tell Rollins I'll be right in with his wine, okay?" Shane asked. Clifton swayed like a ship about to capsize. Shane reached for Clifton's arm, to steady him. "Can you make it back there?"

"Get your (hiccup) paws offa me. I'm not a (hiccup) faggot."

Clifton James staggered out of the kitchen, down the hallway. Shane picked up the broken shards of wine bottle. He soaked up the wine with a roll of paper towels. He thought: *Shit shit shit shit shit*. He thought about Clifton James, the faith Clifton had placed in him, the kindness Clifton had shown. His seeming authenticity. But then he remembered what Clifton James had said, on Shane's last human day. *I've been watching you*. Clifton had selected him.

You, LaSalle. Clifton had convinced the others. *This one, fellas. Let's tear his throat open.* Clifton had bestowed the partnership upon him with a wink and a laugh, by sleight of hand, the same way he convinced companies to open their doors to Barrington Equity. The companies thought they had caught a lucky break, that they had secured their financial future. But instead Clifton James threw them to the wolves. *These bastards deserve it,* Shane thought. Even Clifton. Whatever they had coming.

Shane grabbed two more bottles of red wine from the cooler, and some glasses from the cupboard. He walked back to the conference room. He could hear Clifton James babbling from the hallway.

"—an' that's why you're so fat! (hiccup) You fatty. You remembaber that time when, uh ... uh ... (hiccup) ... when we hunted giant ... (hiccup) ... giant pandas? And I said, (hiccup) what did I say? Oh! (hiccup) I said, Stanley, I said (hiccup) Stan Stan my man you better eat just one because they're (hiccup) en— (hiccup) endangered, and you said ... well I'm gonna take what I can ... I'm gonna (hiccup) ... You know what I like about you, Rollins? I ..."

Clifton James clapped his hand on Rollins's meaty shoulder. Stanley Rollins was passed out. His head rested in a pool of mashed potatoes and meat juice. He held a sprig of gristle in the corner of his mouth. Don Morgan and Darren Buxby had also passed out. Morgan slumped in his chair. Buxby lay spread-eagle on the conference room table, with an empty glass in his hand and the button of his pants undone.

"I like ..." Clifton James went on. "I like ... uh ... hold on a minute, Rollins ... I've (hiccup) just gotta ..." Clifton stood up. He stumbled over to the corner of the conference room. He dropped his pants and proceeded to pee on the floor.

"Shit," Shane muttered. Beneath the stench of Clifton James's piss, he caught a whiff of Darla.

"Oh my God . . ." Darla said. She walked up next to Shane.

"You should get out of here."

Clifton James teetered backward. He tipped back onto the floor, pants around his ankles, and fell asleep.

Darla walked over to Darren Buxby. "I fucking hate that creep," she said. She examined him, his pitiful unbuttoned pants, his gross mouth ajar, his lower legs dangling over the edge of the table. Her face contorted with rage. She turned away, then changed her mind, spun around, and kicked him in the shin. He snorted, but he didn't wake up. She kicked him again, harder.

"I need a new job," Darla said. "Fucking wolf."

"What?"

"That's what he makes me call him. 'The Alpha Wolf.' Which is hard to say with a dick in your mouth. What a sick fuck."

Shane wanted to kick him too, but instead he said, "Seriously, you should get out of here. I need to call the police."

"No. What? Why? Can't they just sleep it off, or—"

"They won't just sleep it off. I have to."

"And tell them what? That you—"

"No, no . . . God this was such a stupid plan. They were supposed to be drunk, and cause a disturbance, so that someone would call the police and they'd get arrested and . . . I don't know. . . . But now they're—"

"Well, they're definitely drunk."

"Yeah. But they're not exactly causing a disturbance."

"Why are you . . . I mean, why would you call the police? What did they do?"

"They . . . they killed Duane Beckman." Shane's eyes blurred with tears.

Darla looked at him. She nodded.

"I see."

"I can't prove it. But I know it was them. . . . And if I don't stop them . . . " Shane gulped back a sob.

"Well, then we've got to stop them."

Shane looked at his partners. They looked so benign, in their passed-out state. They looked so human.

He picked up the conference room phone. He dialed 9-1-1.

"Hello, I'm calling to report a dangerous situation. . . . Yes, that's the address. . . . Well, it's my partners." Shane told the first lie that popped into his mind. "They've brought wolves into our office building. . . . Yes, wolves. . . . Yes, I'm sure they're not just dogs. They're definitely wolves. They're leashed right now, but my partners have been drinking. They're, uh, very drunk, actually, and they're planning to let the wolves loose. . . . Their names? Darren Buxby, Stanley Rollins, Don Morgan, Clifton James. . . . Okay, thank you."

Shane hung up the phone.

"Wolves?" Darla snickered.

"Well, it's not entirely untrue."

"That's for sure. Are the cops coming?"

"Yeah. You should really get out of here now, before they wake up or the cops get here and start asking questions."

"Okay. Okay, I'm going. And Mr. LaSalle?"

"Yeah?"

"I'm sorry about Duane."

"Yeah. Me too."

Darla left. Shane LaSalle hurried through the Barrington Equity office halls.

"We're closing early tonight," he told the few associates still in the office on a Friday evening. They could all still work from home. They could all come in early Saturday morning in the scramble to outwork all the others, to make the senior-level cut, to achieve the transformative reward bestowed on Shane. "The partners want you all to go home right now. *Go on!* Take the night off!"

He returned to the conference room. It reeked of piss. Clifton James snored. Darren Buxby's hand had migrated into his pants. Stanley Rollins jerked up. He belched. He looked around the room, but his eyes were glazed over and disconnected from his brain. He belched again, and then he slopped back onto the table, his head splatting in the mashed potatoes.

Shane waited. He listened to the last of the Barrington associates leave. The office fell quiet. Shane waited. He watched the clock. Happy hour neared its end. Soon, Shane's own gorgeous face would morph into a monstrous snout. Misaligned rows of disgusting teeth would sprout in his mouth. Tufts of fur would mar his lovely smooth skin. Already his blood felt itchy. His heart felt luminous. He looked out the window, at the fading daylight. He wondered how much longer the police would take, because he wanted to see this through, and he did not want to be the wolf found loose in the office building.

Stanley Rollins lifted his head again. He smacked his fat lips.

"Hey," he said, "where's all the steak? Where's all the steak, LaSalle?"

"I think you ate it, buddy," Shane said. Stanley Rollins's drunk head bobbed on his fat neck.

"I'm so hungry. You know what it's like, to be so hungry? I could eat a . . . a . . . pretty little girl. I ate one once. Tasted like . . . well, it was like . . . strawberries. Ripe, red, bloody strawberries. But Clifton, Cliff here says . . . he says . . . bad form . . . don't eat the humans! Isn't that right, Cliff. Not unless they're causing you trouble! Ha, ha, ha."

"Ha, ha, ha," Don Morgan echoed. His eyes rolled opened. "Humans!"

Buxby laughed in is sleep. "Ha, ha, ha, ha."

"Ha, ha, ha, ha, ha!" Morgan laughed again.

"Ha, ha, ha— Oh, no!" Rollins exclaimed. "I've had some pee. It's—"

"Ha, ha, ha, ha, ha!" Morgan roared.

"—it's gotten on my pants—"

"Ha, ha, Rollins, you pisser!"

The laughter roused Clifton James. He pulled himself upright.

"Rollins is a pisser!"

"Ah, ha, ha, ha!"

"Ha, ha, ha, ha!"

Clifton James looked at the pants around his ankles. He reached down and pulled them up, though his fingers couldn't seem to manage the buttons.

"What's . . . what's going on here?" Clifton James asked, swaying.

Morgan laughed. "Rollins just pissed himself!"

"I did, ha, ha, ha!"

"Ha, ha, ha, ha!"

"LaSalle, what's . . ." Clifton James looked at Shane. Shane, who wasn't laughing. Shane, whose heart beat a tad too fast. Shane, whose fear he could smell. His eyes came into focus, and in them Shane saw a dawning comprehension of his own mutiny. "LaSalle . . ."

Shane heard the distant *bing* of the elevator. He heard the scuffle of boots on the marble floor.

"LaSalle, what is this?" Clifton heard it, too. Shane shook his head. "You're . . . you're one of us, LaSalle—"

Shane stared at his partners. He had wanted to be one of them, until he finally understood what that meant. He might be rich, entitled, superficial, stupidly obsessed with status. He might be hideous, in his changed state. But he would never be one of them. He was Shane LaSalle, gay boy, torn apart by wolves, and reborn to take them down. He was a motherfucking werewolf. "I am not."

Clifton's brow furrowed. His eyes sharpened. He snarled, and Shane saw the wolf inside him.

"You're done for, LaSalle," Clifton said. "I'm going to fucking kill you."

"Ha, ha, ha!" Morgan laughed.

"He's going to kill LaSalle!" Rollins howled.

"Ha, ha, ha, ha, ha!"

"Just like you killed Duane Beckman?" Shane said.

The laughter stopped, and at the same time a small phalanx of cops burst through the conference room door.

"Hands in the air!" an officer yelled. Several more officers from animal care and control filed in behind them. Shane raised his hands. Stanley Rollins burst out laughing.

"Where are the wolves?" a voice demanded from somewhere.

"I'm sorry," Shane said. "The wolves aren't here yet."

Don Morgan guffawed. Stanley Rollins laughed so hard that he puked, all over the front of his shirt.

The lead cop pointed at Rollins. "What's his name?"

"Stanley Rollins," Shane answered for him.

"Rollins pissed himself!" Don Morgan laughed.

"And the rest of you? *Names!*"

"That's Don Morgan," Shane said, gesturing with his head. "And Clifton James. And the one on the table is Darren Buxby."

Buxby, hearing his name, opened his eyes and sat up.

"And you?"

"I'm Shane LaSalle."

The cops pounced. They handcuffed Darren Buxby, who swayed drunkenly as his eyes rolled back in his head. Don Morgan fought, and it took two officers and a dog net to restrain him. Stanley Rollins laughed as they cuffed him and read him his rights. Clifton James tried to run, but they caught him in the hallway.

"This is a mistake!" Clifton yelled and thrashed as one officer held him and another snapped handcuffs on his wrists. "What's going on? Officer, you need to let us go right now! Do you know who we are?"

"Clifton James," the cop said. "Don Morgan. Darren Buxby. Stanley Rollins. We know we've got warrants to arrest the four of you."

"Warrants? This is ridiculous. Is this some kind of joke?"

"No, sir."

"What— What are the charges?"

"Mr. James, you are being charged with ten counts of sexually assaulting a minor, kidnapping, conspiracy to—"

"What? No! No!" James cried. "We didn't do anything! You have to let us go!"

"I have to follow the law, sir. I have a warrant for your arrest. Now, you have the right to remain silent. Anything you say can and will be used against you . . ."

The cops carted the four of Shane LaSalle's partners away. Two of the cops stayed behind, to question Shane about the wolves, and about what his partners had done to those girls referenced in the warrants—fictional warrants, Shane assumed, created and planted by Joseph Z'Rhae on the eve of the full moon.

However, with each passing minute, daylight dwindled. Shane's wolf scraped at his insides. It wanted out.

"Please, I need to go home," Shane begged at last. "It's . . . my dog. I need to let him out, or he'll pee on my brand-new rug. I'll come to the station first thing tomorrow and give an official statement."

Though perturbed at him, the police let him go. Shane ran outside. He ran down the sidewalk. No use hailing a cab. Cars clogged the city streets. The fog rolled through the darkening sky. Shane ran as fast as he could, hoping that the speed would pacify the wolf for just another moment, long enough for him to make it home. He turned the corner onto his block. His skin tingled. He felt a nest of hair bristle across his back. A sharp tooth punctured through the roof of his mouth, and then another, another. He yanked open the door to his building with a hand that no longer felt human.

"Mr. LaSalle, are you—" the guard called, as Shane ran past. Shane pushed the elevator call button. Fur spread across his forehead. The elevator opened. He jumped inside. His fingers retracted as he pounded on the buttons. The elevator whooshed up. The seams of his shirt split apart. His face twisted into a gnarled visage.

The elevator opened on his floor. He ran through the hallway. He turned the last corner.

Natasha Porter and Nova Z'Rhae waited at the door to his spectacularly photographable apartment. They both looked horrified to see him.

JANICE CHIN

A TRANSFORMATION

San Francisco—Now, Just Before Moonrise

"BUT MY WIFE—she's having a baby!" Darren Buxby yelled, as Corrections Officer Janice Chin shoved him into the jail cell.

"Hey!" yelled Clifton James. "Hey! You have to let us out of here!"

Corrections Officer Chin slammed the door. She ignored the pleas of the rich, wasted, piss-soaked assholes on the other side. She sat down at her desk and surfed the internet on her phone. Everything interesting happened out there, on the internet. Pigs wore jaunty vests. Bipedal cats sparred to the techno remix of your favorite movie score. Someone you knew you hated just from looking at them had made an egregious remark that confirmed just how awful you suspected them—and everyone like them—to be.

"Please!" one of them yelled. *Which one? Who cares.* "Can't I at least call my lawyer? I have rights."

Officer Chin was unmoved. Everyone had rights, sure, but these rich creeps thought they had somehow acquired more rights than everyone else. These creeps thought they had the right to kidnap teenage girls and force them to perform unspeakable acts of sexual depravity. That was what the charges said, anyhow, and Chin knew just from looking at these douchey moguls, with their Rolex watches and their Italian leather shoes and their professionally tailored trousers, flies-down, wet with piss, that the warrants had it right.

And also, Chin had a teenage daughter.

"Can I use your phone?" said the one with the most expensive watch. Don Morgan, according to the warrant. Chin had always had an excellent memory for names. "Please? I'll pay you? I'll pay you a lot of money. A thousand dollars—ten thousand! Just for one call!"

Everyone had a price, these assholes thought.

"Twenty thousand!"

. . . and it *was* tempting. But temptation strengthened Chin's resolve. They couldn't buy their way out so long as she was in charge, and *screw them* for thinking they could.

She watched a viral video of a man caught picking his nose in his car. The man's nose harbored an obscene volume of boogers. She rewatched the video. It was fascinating, really, how an ordinary nose could function as a snot factory. As the video ended, the desk phone rang.

"Chin, block D," she answered.

"Hey, Chin, this is Morales from across the hall. One of the drunks over here just vomited. Like, projectile, all over the walls. We gotta find a place to stash a few of these guys while we get this place cleaned up. Can I bring 'em down to your side?"

"No, you can't, sorry."

"It says you got one cell with only four guys in it. You got the space."

"Yeah, but these guys are dangerous. They're supposed to be locked up separately."

"Damn. Well . . . Oh, shit, it's everywhere. Come on, dude, help me out."

Chin looked at the wealthy rapists in the holding cell. They didn't look that dangerous, at least not while they were locked up. They looked doughy and entitled. Maybe they didn't deserve a whole big cell all to themselves.

Besides, what could they really do, locked up, with her there watching?

"Sure," Officer Chin said. "Fine, bring 'em down."

Morales escorted six vomit-splattered men across the hall. Chin ordered the rich assholes to stand facing the wall.

"Stand back or you're gonna get tased," she shouted at them, as she opened the door to their cell, ushered the six new detainees inside, and locked the cell door behind them.

"Hey! You can't do this!" the one named Clifton James yelled. "You can't lock us up with them! It's not safe for them!"

Chin did not have a chance to consider what he meant, because she was too distracted by the guy's associates. One of them had upped his twenty-thousand-dollar phone call offer to fifty thousand. Then one of the vomit-splattered men opened his mouth and puked all over the fattest of the richies.

"Morales!" Chin complained. "You brought the sick one? Now we gotta clean this place up too!"

Morales shrugged. Chin looked back at the fat rich man in his vomit-smeared suit coat, just in time to see him pick a chunk of something from the smear and stick it into his mouth.

And then, as if these guys could get any worse, Chin saw that the last asshole, the one called Darren Buxby, had taken off his pants.

No. Not taken off.

Busted out of.

The dude tore out of his pants. His back arched. His face contorted. Then his face wasn't his face anymore. His face became a snout—a sickening, phallic snout looming over a monstrous mouth, full of gnarled razor teeth. His wicked eyes turned yellow. Fur rippled across his chest and back. Claws sprang from his hands. He lunged forward and landed on forepaws.

That rich asshole was a wolf.

"Holy fucking shit," Morales said. "Are you seeing this? What the fuck!"

Officer Chin grabbed her phone. She turned on her phone's video camera. She pressed Record, just as the second of the four rich creeps burst out of his suit.

"Hey! You have to stop!" Clifton James yelled. "You have to let us—" But he didn't finish the sentence. His throat gurgled. His vocal cords began their wolfish transformation.

Officers Chin and Morales stood, transfixed, video filming, as the four Barrington Equity partners transformed into werewolves. The six men locked up with them started to scream.

"Let us out!"

"Fuck!"

"Oh my God, oh my God! Let us out of here!"

Officer Chin held the key in her hand. She felt awful. But she was too terrified and bewildered to move and she could not open the door. She could not let those wolves out. They were too dangerous to ever get out.

"Hey, man! Please!"

"Let us out!"

"Fuck!"

"What the fuck are those things!"

"They're going to kill us!"

And then one did. The fat one who had eaten the vomit pounced. He knocked one of the men down, slamming his head against the concrete floor. He opened his hideous mouth and bit down on the man's arm, tearing through the meat of his bicep.

The other men from the drunk tank screamed. They piled against the cell door, as if they could push their way through solid metal. The wolf who'd tried to bribe his way out now resorted to force. He attempted to scare the other men away from the cell door with a snap of his jaw, to push past and through them. He swiped at the cell door with his paws. He howled and snarled, and in his snarls Officer Chin could almost hear words, dollar amounts: *Two-hundred thousand. Half a million. Five million. I'll pay anything, just let me out.*

"Oh fuck oh fuck oh fuck!!!"

The detained men screamed.

The vomit-eater swallowed the bicep.

"Oh fuck oh fuck oh fuck!!!"

After the bicep, the fat wolf chomped down on the man's neck. He licked down a strip of flesh. Blood sprayed out of the man's artery. The wolf slurped it up.

"Oh shit holy shit fuck fuck fuck!"

The wolf who'd first busted out of his pants—the one called Buxby—had enough with all the screaming. He swiped at the loudest screamer. He knocked the man down. He flipped the man onto his chest and clamped his paw over the man's head. His claws pierced through the man's cheek and eyeball. His hind legs scraped at the man's back, tearing through his shirt and jeans. The Wolf Darren Buxby growled. He circled the man, his hairy ball-sack swinging. He mounted.

"Oh God . . ." Officer Chin gasped.

"Is it . . . ?" Morales started to ask.

It was. The charges were right. That fucker was a vicious rapist.

The briber continued to hurl itself against the door. The fat one crunched through a breastbone, ate up a heart. The last one—Clifton James, according to the warrants—stepped back into the shadowed corner of the cell, away from all the blood. Police officers flooded into the area beyond the bars, guns drawn.

Over the San Francisco Bay, the full moon rose.

THE GLITTER WOLF

San Francisco—Now

NATASHA DUG THE keys out of werewolf Shane's torn pocket. "Looks like you made it just in time," she said.

"The guard in your lobby let us up," said Nova.

"He didn't believe that Nova was really Nova."

"I'm Nova incognito, darlings. Nova sans sequins." She was dressed plainly in jeans and a T-shirt, but her eyelids were dusted with glitter. She patted Shane's head. "My, Mr. LaSalle, you really are an immensely ugly wolf."

Shane Wolf whimpered.

"It's all right, doll. Joseph is just as hideous."

"Damn," Natasha said, as they walked into Shane's open concept living space. "You *live* here?"

Shane grunted. Natasha sat down on his couch.

"Huh," she said. "Is there something wrong with this couch? It's really hard." Nova sat down next to her.

"It's not a real couch, honey," Nova said. "It's essentially a prop. It's made to be photographed, not sat on."

Shane paced. He glared at the view-blocking shell of skyscraper rising up in front of his window. He felt hungry and terrified. He wanted to sit on the rug, but he feared besmearing it with his werewolf juices. He wanted to forget all about Carver and Barrington, who were out there doing whatever business they had gone to do. He wanted to crawl into Duane Beckman's lap and rest his head on Duane Beckman's shoulder. He raised his head and howled, for the rising moon.

Hello, Shane, the moon said.

Hello, Moon, Shane growled.

Don't despair, Shane, the moon said. *You can rest soon enough. All things come in cycles.*

"Shane, when you called," Natasha said, "you said you'd drugged four of them, right?"

Shane nodded.

"Did it work?"

Shane nodded.

"So they're in jail?"

Shane nodded again.

"You're sure?"

Shane wasn't sure, but he nodded anyway.

"But the other two—you said they ran off before you could drug them, right?" Natasha shifted uncomfortably on Shane's prop sofa.

Shane nodded.

"So they're still out there. Barrington and Carver, right?"

Shane nodded fearfully.

"The most dangerous two," Nova said, as she fidgeted with a

hideous black obelisk-shaped object on Shane's coffee table that he'd paid a lot of money for because someone called it modern art. "We have to track them down."

"How? It was hours ago when Shane called. They could have gone anywhere. They could be halfway across the country by now."

"But we have to try," Nova said. "Shane just took out most of their pack. And he exposed them, which makes them even more dangerous. If they figure out that he was responsible . . . Let's just say he'll be glad when they finally kill him."

Shane whimpered.

"Okay, so . . . where do we start? Do you think your brother would be able to help?"

"I called him right after you called me. He said he'd drive into town. But at this point"—Nova gestured toward Shane by way of example—"there's no way to reach him."

"Oh, right. Werewolf. So . . ."

Natasha's phone rang. She answered. "Natasha?" Lee Curtis's voice was brimming with terror.

"Lee? Is everything—"

"It's here."

"What? What's there?" she asked. But from the look on her face, it was clear that she already knew.

"A wolf. It's outside—"

"Okay, just sit tight. We're coming, okay? Or, wait, no, you should call the cops. He should call the cops, Nova, right?"

"They'll scare it away," Nova said. "But I don't think the wolf is after Lee. I think it's after you."

"Lee, call the cops. But we're coming, too." Natasha hung up the phone.

"We can take my car," Nova said. "I'm parked right out front."

"Okay, but what about him?" Natasha nodded at Shane Wolf.

"We should take him. He can help us track the scent if it runs off. And honey, look at those claws of his. Yikes!"

"Yes, but then they'll know for sure that Shane is—"

"They may already know," Nova said. "They've gone after your friend. That wolf didn't show up at his house by accident. If they know about you, they may well already suspect Shane. For all we know, the other one is waiting for us in the lobby downstairs. . . ."

Shane shook his head.

"No? See, if it was there he'd smell it."

"Yes, but he can't just go out like that. I mean . . . look at him . . ."

They both stared at Shane: grotesque werewolf against the backdrop of city lights; narcissistic werewolf posed on alpaca rug, his sloppy jowls draped open to reveal a spread of gnarly teeth; vainglorious werewolf squinting his yellow eyes in the shameful glare of his five-figure chandelier. The beast howled, mournfully.

"He wants to help," Natasha said.

Shane wanted to help. And also, he wanted not to die. He wanted revenge, for his darling Duane. He wanted to be the only werewolf left standing on the yacht deck. #FullMoonYachtRide; #NobodyCallsWolfLikeShaneLaSalle.

"Honey, I've got a spectacular idea," Nova said. "I'll be right back."

"Where are you—"

"Just down to my car to grab something."

"Okay, but hurry."

Nova Z'Rhae ran down to her car. A minute later she returned with a zebra-print suitcase. She opened the case and took out a sequin-and-feather headdress.

"Shane, darling, you are going to look so pretty!" Nova Z'Rhae strapped the headdress onto Shane Wolf's hideous head. She tied a pink feather boa around his neck, and a glittery tulle skirt around his waist. Natasha wrapped each of his four ankles with rhinestone bands, drawing attention away from his horrible claws. She covered Shane's snout with a sparkling bird mask. Then, the final touch, Nova sprayed his exposed fur with Glitter-Spritz hair spray.

"My, look at you!" Nova Z'Rhae declared. "Gorgeous! Baby, you are ready to tear some throats!"

LAURIE CURTIS

YAY, MOM!

San Francisco–A Few Minutes Earlier

LAURIE CURTIS DROVE through the sleek city, homeward, trying as she went to shed the work thoughts. The partially finished brief. The minefield of discovery responses. The ABA presentation she had to draft for one of the partners. The other partner who'd cornered her on the way to the kitchen. *It won't be any problem for you to get this done by Tuesday, will it? Because, you know, I could always ask* . . . And she had shaken her head *no no, no problem at all* because she knew it was the right answer, the only answer. Because she heard the words behind his words, the ones he knew better than to say out loud. She hurried to the kitchen, with her indiscreet black bag of breast milk. Her breasts felt emptied out, hollow, like her heart.

I'll be home around six, she had told Lee, and in the background she heard Veronica squeal, *Yay, Mom!* But six had this way of morphing into seven, and by seven you thought maybe if you pushed through, just a few more minutes, you could leave your work in the office overnight, and then the minutes ticked by until your husband called and told you: *Bedtime. If you want to see them.* ... And you thought: *I'm a terrible mother.* And you had only the din of work to drown the thought out.

She sped through red lights (because *I'm a terrible mother*), and in the back seat her briefcase wailed, *Me me me me me! I'm the only baby for you!*

She called Lee. "I'm coming."

"Okay," he said, and she could sense his weariness.

"Please keep them up."

"You think she'll let me put her to bed before she sees you? I told her, 'Time to brush your teeth.' She squeezed the whole tube of toothpaste down the drain."

"Lee . . ."

"Laurie . . ."

"I miss you."

"I'm right here. I'll be right here waiting."

Lee was right there, but where had Laurie gone? There were no billable hours in self-reflection. She turned onto Kezar, then right on Lincoln, westward, the stucco houses of the Sunset on her left, and on the other side the creepy park. It had charmed her, initially, when they'd bought the fogbound house near the beach. On weekends, she had imagined, she would stroll through the urban forest, where the improbable buffalo roamed. She and Lee would take evening walks along the shore, as the pink-fire sun set over the Pacific. But the fog obscured the sun and she worked evenings and weekends and then they found that poor girl's body all chewed up in the park, just blocks from her house.

She pulled up in front of her house. She parked on the street. She reached into the back seat for her briefcase. Then, from outside her car, she heard a hissing noise. She felt something jostle her car. She quickly locked the doors. The hissing grew louder. It seemed to come from all around her. She had a sinking sensation.

"What the fuck . . ."

She felt, literally, as if she were sinking. But the brain could play weird tricks when you kept it bottled up in work-mode all the time. She turned her car off. She reached for the handle. But something made her stop.

Yay, Mom!

She heard her daughter's voice, clear as the rare fogless night, clear as if Veronica had cheered from the back seat. *Yay!* God, she loved that girl. *Mom!* She looked over her shoulder, at Veronica's empty car seat. Then, through the rear window, she saw the yellow glimmer of eyes.

She locked the doors again, in case she hadn't gotten it right the first time. She turned her car on. She would drive around the block, and by the time she got back . . . She tried to pull forward, but the car seemed to stick beneath her. She pressed her foot down on the gas pedal. The wheels clunked. She checked the rearview mirror for yellow eyes. She saw no eyes. *There are no eyes, Laurie,* she told herself. *You imagined them. You have no evidence that—*

Then she saw them again.

She saw the wolf. It stalked along the sidewalk next to her car. It stared at her with its ghastly yellow eyes. *It's not a wolf,* she told herself. It's just a dog. A big, ugly dog. It opened its mouth, exposing its jagged range of teeth, teeth so numerous that their existence seemed to defy the laws of physics, teeth so awful that they could not have spawned from her universe, or any proximate universe.

Laurie screamed.

The wolf tilted its teeth skyward, and from its mouth came a horrible laughter.

"Shit, shit, shit . . ."

Laurie tried to pull away from the curb. The wolf laughed. Her tires thumped. They were flat. The hissing—she understood now. It had slashed her tires. It was crazy to think that a wolf had slashed her tires. But she knew it had. She pulled into the street, fearful that the wolf would follow, that it would leap onto the hood of her car and try to smash the glass.

But that wouldn't happen until later.

The wolf laughed. It trotted over to her house. It lifted its immense paw, and, with a claw befitting a velociraptor, it pressed the buzzer.

Laurie grabbed her phone. She saw then that she had several missed calls from Lee, all from the last five minutes. She called him back.

"Don't answer the door!" she yelled, as soon as he picked up. "There's a wolf!"

"Oh shit. Shit . . . Laurie, where are you?"

"I'm in the car. I'm right outside."

"I tried to call you. Don't get out of the car."

"I'm not getting out of the car."

"Can you drive away?"

"Lee, it's at the door! It just rang the fucking buzzer!"

"Can you drive away?"

"It slashed my tires!"

The wolf laughed. It pressed the buzzer again. It rattled the downstairs gate. It paced in front of her house. It leaned against the garage door, testing it. It could break through, Laurie thought. A creature that size, its claws could splinter wood. It looked at her, and laughed, and embedded in its laughter Laurie heard a wicked voice: *Yes, I could break through. I could kill them all.*

"Okay, just try and stay put, okay?" Lee said. "Help is coming."

"Help...?"

"Laurie, I... There are some things I haven't told you."

Laurie's heart dropped. She trusted Lee. Lee loved their girls. Lee loved her. But where was she, through the long, lonely hours of his life, the hours spent folding laundry, loading the dishwasher, scrubbing the floors, baking dino-shaped chicken nuggets, tater tots, airlifting corn into a child's mouth (*here comes the helicopter!*), reading and rereading and rereading the same book about the hungry caterpillar because Veronica never got her fill of that book? Until the one time Laurie tried to read it to her, and Veronica said, *Don't you know anything, Mom? I don't like that book anymore,* and Laurie witnessed her fears confirmed. She didn't know anything.

"Lee..." Her voice trembled.

"It's not a wolf."

"What?"

"It's a werewolf."

"That's... That's crazy. There's no such thing as—as werewolves. It's—" She looked at the creature. It rang the buzzer again.

"I know that's how it sounds. But look at it."

"Yeah..." The werewolf strutted toward her car. It pressed its face right up against the glass. It snarled laughter. Laurie slid back, into the passenger seat. She wanted to close her eyes. The sight of its face made her stomach sick. But she couldn't turn away.

"Lee, how do you—"

"I've been . . . Well, you know my friend Natasha, from college?"

No. No no no no no.

"Yeah? The, um, one you've been hanging out with. Oh God . . ."

"It's not, I mean, she's just a friend."

"Okay."

"But she needed help. She met this guy and it turns out he's a werewolf, but not a bad one. But he was mixed up with these other werewolves. Really bad ones. That girl whose body they found in the park, that was Natasha's roommate. And they killed her. So we've . . . well, really Natasha and Nova and her brother—"

"Nova—"

"Nova Z'Rhae, and her brother, they're trying to take the bad werewolves down."

"Lee—"

"Yeah?"

"This is crazy. This is just crazy." The werewolf outside her car laughed. It pawed at the door handle. Then it leapt up onto the hood of her car.

"Ahhhhh!" Laurie screamed.

"Laurie—"

It threw its body against her windshield.

"Oh my God, Lee, it's on the car! It's trying to break in!" The werewolf lay on the windshield. It opened its mouth. It licked the glass. Its spit was yellowish, like sick phlegm. Laurie could see all of its teeth, an abyss of teeth. "Lee, it's going to break the glass!"

"Then drive away! Just drive—" The werewolf slammed its paw against the glass. The car shook.

"But the garage— Lee, what if it breaks through the garage door? If I try to go— Ahhhhh!" Laurie screamed again as the wolf lunged at the windshield.

"Just stay in the car. Help will come soon. Just stay there, okay?"

"Okay."

"Hold tight."

"I'll try."

"I love you, Laurie. More than anything."

"I love you too, Lee. Tell the girls—"

The werewolf snarled. It sharpened its claws on her hood. It jumped up, onto the roof of her car. Laurie saw, in her mind, the wolf's claws tear through metal, its head ram through the shredded roof of her car, its mouth open, and all of those teeth, those awful teeth. She saw all the moments missed, the subtle moments, the ones she couldn't collect in photographs. Veronica's hands still clutching Cheerios as she slumbered in her car seat. The peanut rubbing tired eyes with her tiny fists. Veronica decorating tangrams with permanent marker animal shapes. The peanut yawning, her perfect toothless mouth, the petals of her pink lips so lovely they could make you cry. *I'm a terrible mother*, she thought, to leave them like this in the end, having left them so often before. The wolf drummed its paws on the roof of her car. It laughed. It scratched at the metal. It jumped down, onto the hood. It slammed its huge, horrible head against the windshield.

Yay, Mom!

She looked up, at her house, at her older daughter watching from the window.

The glass cracked.

NATASHA

GOLF

San Francisco–Now

NOVA Z'RHAE SEEMED calm behind the wheel as they coasted down Lincoln, alongside the foreboding groves and windswept trees of Golden Gate Park. Where Marie had died. Natasha tried to steady herself, but she was terrified. She didn't want to fight a werewolf. She had never been in a fight. She had no weapons other than a canister of silver pepper spray. And now the nasty werewolves had used her friend Lee and his family as bait, to lure her here.

"I don't want to die," she said as they turned onto Lee Curtis's street.

Shane Wolf yelped in agreement. She saw him in the rearview mirror, head bowed, hideous visage concealed by a sparkly bird mask, his yellow eyes wide with fear.

"Honey," Nova Z'Rhae said, "I wish I could promise that we'll all live to dance another day. But all I know for sure is that the Barrington pack has always taken what isn't theirs to take—other people's lives, their money, their choices. And they'll keep on doing just that, as long as they exist. They deserve to be taken down. But if you don't want to fight, that's okay. I'll find someplace safe to drop you off, and then Shane and I—"

"No." Natasha didn't think before she spoke, but the answer felt true. "No. I'm with you. Yeah, I'm afraid. But I'm not about to let those wolves take any more of my friends. I— Oh, shit . . ."

A block ahead, in front of Lee Curtis's house, Natasha saw a wolf. A hulking, horrendous thing, its fur dark and matted, its claws like talons. It stood on the roof of a car. It stared straight at them, its yellow eyes phosphorescent in the headlights.

"You think it knows we're coming?" Natasha asked.

From the back seat, Shane Wolf yelped.

It knew. And Natasha knew from the shape of its jaw and the wicked glint in its eyes that this was the werewolf who had killed her friend. This was the Wolf Carver. The most unhinged, Shane had said. The wolf who had chased her across the golf course, who would have killed her too, if not for Shane.

"We should let Shane out here," Nova said. "He can circle around the block and come from the other side."

In the back seat, Shane Wolf whimpered. He shook his grotesque head, releasing a flurry of glitter.

"Okay, and what about us?" Natasha asked. And the other wolf—the one who wasn't there, but might be waiting, hidden, or already on its way.

The Wolf Carver leapt down onto the hood of another car. It turned toward them, raising its paw, as if it meant to flip them the bird.

"Holy mother, would you look at the teeth on that fucker!" Nova gasped.

Then, before they could plan anything else, the Wolf Carver jumped up and slammed its body against the windshield of the car it straddled.

"Shane, honey," Nova said. "Time to hop out."

The Wolf Carver pounded on the windshield of the other car while Shane Wolf clawed at the door handle.

"He can't get out," said Natasha. "His claws."

Nova rolled down the back window. Shane Wolf hesitated. He was scared too, Natasha could tell, from the frantic pant of his foul breath. But then he pulled back, like a cat about to pounce, and launched himself through the open window, a wolf-tempest of sequins and feathers, his tulle skirt billowing around him, his monstrous legs bedazzled by rhinestones bands, his glittered fur gleaming in the moonlight.

The Wolf Carver stopped its pounding. Its cold eyes watched the sparkling Shane Wolf, and for a moment Natasha thought it might chase after her friend. But then it cackled and resumed its attack against the windshield.

"What now?" Natasha asked.

"I don't know," Nova said. "I should have asked Joseph for one of those silver-bullet guns."

They both stared at the lunatic wolf as it snarled and clawed at the windshield. Natasha heard a muffled scream. Then she saw, for the first time, the dark shape of a person inside the car. A woman. Natasha couldn't see her clearly, but she could guess who this woman was.

Laurie Curtis.

Bait.

"Fuck. Nova?"

"Yes?"

"I think Lee's wife is inside that car."

"Shit."

"How pissed would you be about wrecking your car?"

"You want to ram it," Nova said, reading Natasha's mind.

"Yeah."

"Buckle up, darling!"

Nova hit the gas pedal. Her Blend-In-Mobile sped forward. The Wolf Carver bashed its head against the windshield of Laurie's car. The glass cracked. The wolf hammered the crack with its paw. Inside the car, Laurie Curtis screamed. She looked past the wolf, at the vehicle speeding head-on toward her. Her eyes met Natasha's.

"I'm sorry," Natasha whispered.

Nova's car slammed into Laurie's. Natasha's body hurtled forward, then slapped back against the seat. She heard shattered glass, crunched metal, the *whoosh* of airbags. She heard a scream, and a thump, the sound of a body hitting concrete. Her head felt caught in continuing acceleration, past fifty miles per hour, one hundred miles per hour, two hundred. Her mind spun with the impending crash of everything, the collision of woman and wolf.

Outside the car, she heard brutal laughter.

She heard a small voice, a voice from above, a girl's voice: *Yay, Mom!*

"Natasha—"

"Nova?"

She had just ridden shotgun while the Fantabulous Queen of Sequin Pop weaponized her Prius against a venture capitalist werewolf.

"—are you—"

"I'm okay. You?"

"I'm spectacular. Did we hit it?"

"I think so. I heard a thud. . . . But I can't see past the airbag."

"We need to get out," Nova said. "If we act fast while it's still down—"

"Right."

"Can you find your pepper spray?"

Natasha reached beneath the airbags for her purse. She dug out the silver-laced spray. "Got it."

"On three. One, two—"

They flung the doors open. Natasha ran around the car, pepper spray out. She saw a smear of blood on the sidewalk, but no other sign of the werewolf. The crash had totaled the two cars. Lee Curtis's wife was slumped over the steering wheel. Blood trickled down her forehead.

"Laurie—shit," Natasha said, panicked. What had she just done? "And the fucking wolf is gone—"

"No," Nova said. "No, it's still here. I can feel it."

Natasha turned around in a circle. Her eyes scanned the street. Her heart pounded in her ears. She could feel it, too. She could feel it watching her. Carver, that sick fuck. She heard him laugh, but she couldn't pinpoint the sound. She felt the air stir behind her. She spun around.

"Natasha! Wolf!" Nova yelled, almost melodically, but too late.

The beast slammed into her. She fell back onto the sidewalk. The can of silver pepper spray slipped out of her hand. She reached for it, but an enormous paw pushed her down. Claws pierced the skin on her chest. She stared up at a hideous face. It had gotten injured in the crash, Natasha saw. The left side of its jaw hung open, the skin torn off, the teeth exposed even with its mouth closed. It opened its mouth. Its bloody juices dripped onto her neck. It smiled wickedly.

Natasha kicked. She couldn't see the trajectory of her leg, but she aimed for the balls. Her foot hit soft flesh. The Wolf Carver recoiled in pain. Natasha kicked again, and then she rolled to the side. She scrambled back, away from the animal.

But it was already up. It snarled. It opened its mouth, and Natasha stared at the mountainous hellscape of teeth inside.

This is how it ends, she thought.

But then the Wolf Carver darted past her, toward Laurie Curtis's car, where Laurie was still slumped over the wheel, defenseless.

The Wolf Carver didn't just want to kill Natasha. It wanted to kill her friends and make her watch.

"You *fucker*," she said. She scanned the ground for her pepper spray, her only weapon against the wolves.

"There!" Nova yelled and pointed, as she opened the back hatch of her car. The pepper spray had rolled to the curb, between two parked cars. She ran for it. As she grabbed it, the Wolf Carver jumped up onto the ruined hood of Laurie's car. It slammed its gruesome paw against the cracked windshield. The safety glass shattered into a thousand chunks. And now there was nothing between the werewolf and Laurie Curtis.

Except a streak of fur and glitter.

The Wolf Carver looked up. It saw the other werewolf, decked in jewels and feathers, fur shimmering beneath the dazzling light of the full moon, pink feather boa streaming behind. Shane Wolf had lost his bird mask, or cast it aside, and his face was awful but earnest, and fierce. The Wolf Carver sneered, his eyes brimming with hatred for this other wolf, this strangely beauteous creature, his partner.

The sparkling Shane Wolf leapt. He slammed into the Wolf Carver. They tumbled off the car in a flurry of snarls and claws. And Natasha took her chance.

While the two werewolves fought, she ran to Laurie's car. She opened the driver's side door. She heard a whimper. Laurie was breathing. The woman was alive, but dazed, and bleeding. Natasha pulled her halfway out of the car. Then she felt another hand reach around her.

"Laurie—"

Lee Curtis helped Natasha pull his wife from the car. Together they carried her back to his house.

"Get her inside," Natasha said. "Call the ambulance."

"I already did," Lee said, as he unlocked and opened the front gate. They set Laurie down on the other side. Natasha stepped back out.

"Wait, Natasha—"

"I'm sorry," she said. "I'm so sorry I got you into this."

"Don't go back out there," Lee said. "You're bleeding." Spots of blood blossomed across Natasha's shirt, where the wolf's claws had pierced her chest.

"It's not bad," she said, as she pulled the gate shut behind her. "I have to help my friends."

On the street, two werewolves circled each other. Blood leaked from the Wolf Carver's jowls and head. His ear had been torn off. He had a deep gash along his side. Shane Wolf had lost his boa and his headdress, but he still sparkled. The Wolf Carver snarled. It swiped. Shane Wolf spun away. Natasha saw now that he was bleeding too, from a bite along his hind leg. She pulled the silver-laced pepper spray from her pocket. She stepped closer, hoping for a chance to use it. The wolves snarled and snapped. She stepped closer. The Wolf Carver lunged at Shane Wolf. He dodged, giving Natasha an opening.

"Close your eyes!" she yelled to her friend. She ran at the beast. She closed her own eyes and sprayed. The Wolf Carver howled. She sprayed again. She coughed, inhaling burning pepper. She turned and ran, keeping her eyes closed tight until she'd escaped the aerosol.

She opened them just in time to see Nova Z'Rhae, wielding a nine iron with a sparkly purple grip.

The Wolf Carver lay on the street, blinded, howling. Shane Wolf slashed. He dug his sharp claws into Carver's neck, drawing a spray of blood. Carver thrashed. Shane pulled back and then attacked again. He seized the torn skin of Carver's face between his teeth and ripped it off. Carver roiled in agony. Then Shane Wolf stopped. He tilted his snout slightly, as if he had caught a scent on the wind. In the distance, there came the wail of sirens. Shane looked at Natasha, and then at Nova Z'Rhae.

"Don't worry, honey," the pop star said, as she walked toward the Wolf Carver with her golf club. "I'll finish him off. I always adored golf." She looked at her weapon. "Custom-made. The head is silver. Because you know, darling, a lady's got to come prepared, *and* look good."

BATTLE OF THE WEREWOLVES

San Francisco—Now

SHANE RAN TOWARD the scent of the alpha wolf, his partner, Dick Barrington. Then the breeze shifted. For a moment, he lost the scent. He turned back. He saw, from a distance, the Fantabulous Queen of Sequin Pop, Nova Z'Rhae, swing her golf club at the nasty werewolf's head. She swung again, and again, bashing away, bits of bloody fur and brains flying forth. The sirens wailed closer. They converged around the wrecked cars and the bleeding werewolf. He could still hear the Wolf Carver, laughing until the end.

Shane looked at Natasha Porter, whose life he had saved, and who in turn meant to save him. He looked at the famous Nova Z'Rhae, her sequined soul cloaked in jeans and a T-shirt, a golf club in her hand; she looked back at him, and her dazzling eyes said: *I understand. I understand you.* And Shane felt something he had not felt before, except in the rare and fleeting moments when he and Duane Beckman had looked at each other for too long. He felt, beneath his glossy surface layers, the existence of a real self, capable of being seen and understood.

He knew in that moment that whatever happened, it would be all right.

But he still had to find the other werewolf.

The problem was that Dick Barrington had a smell like cedar and bourbon, like an antique rug on a polished floor, a cut cigar, a finely crafted shoe, Italian leather, its sole soundless. A smell like money: hard to detect, in a city where a million bucks might count as pocket change. And yet, Shane knew the smell, when it sailed past on the salt breeze. He knew it even as his glittered snout reeled from the hot stench of Carver's blood. The Wolf Dick Barrington was near.

Shane turned and sprinted down the sidewalk. Wind pummeled, damp and relentless off the great cold ocean. Barrington's smell blew away, but after a moment Shane caught it again, stronger this time. It was not late, and the streets were not empty, and so people saw Shane as he ran past. They saw a glittered flash, a blur of tulle skirt and rhinestone bands. They pointed and took pictures, and for once Shane did not care. *Let them see me*, he thought. *Let them post their pictures.* Because what would Duane Beckman have thought?

Perhaps, perhaps, Duane Beckman would have loved him.

Shane ran southward. He smelled dinner cooking inside houses, rice and sesame pork, spaghetti carbonara, tandoori chicken, microwaved mac and cheese. He smelled the perfume counters inside the Nordstrom at Stonestown, the terminally clogged freeways, the foamy waves crashing on Ocean Beach, the fresh-mowed expanse of the Olympic Club golf course. Dick Barrington's smell grew stronger.

Barrington would run to the golf course, Shane reasoned. Barrington would seek out familiar terrain. And so the Wolf Shane ran to the golf course, and again Barrington's scent grew stronger.

Then it was too strong.

Shane stopped on the golf course green. He spun around. He couldn't gauge the trail's direction. The scent seemed to converge from every direction. He ran another block. He turned west, toward the beach. The wind assaulted him with Barrington's stench. The fog swept across the sky. For a moment, the fog parted and the moon peeked through, huge and bright.

Then Shane felt teeth in his back, and the smell of Barrington was all around him. Barrington bit down. Shane howled in pain. He kicked his hind legs. He slashed with his back claws. His claws sliced through the older wolf's flesh, and Shane felt the wolf's jaw slacken. Shane jerked away, leaving a strip of his furry back behind in Barrington's mouth.

The Wolf Dick Barrington growled. He stared at Shane with his hateful eyes, and Shane felt his judgment, his revulsion toward Shane's costume and the glittery wolf inside. *Outsider*, his eyes said. *Faggot. You'll never be one of us.*

Shane didn't want to be.

Barrington pounced. Shane batted him away with some effort. His torn back throbbed. His leg hurt from the earlier blow landed by Carver. The pain made him dizzy. Barrington pounced again. His teeth came down on the back of Shane's neck. Shane snapped at the other wolf, but his jaws could not reach. Barrington bit off another chunk of Shane's flesh. He ripped off the rhinestone bands on Shane's right leg. He snarled. He was stronger than Shane. Craftier. He had lived his whole life as a man in the body of a wolf. Brutality coursed through his blood. His heart was ravenous. He lived for the kill.

Shane turned and retreated into the trees along the edge of the golf course. Barrington pursued him. Shane circled back to the green. He studied the alpha wolf for soft, susceptible spots. But the older wolf was all muscle and bone and sharpened teeth. He was swift and wiry. He attacked again. He leapt with his claws out. His claw dug into Shane's brow. He pulled down, tearing a long gash through Shane's eye.

Shane howled. The vision in his eye went black. He felt blood pooling in his socket. He howled again. Barrington yanked back, and through his good eye Shane saw the white bulb of his stolen eye stuck to Barrington's claw.

The Wolf Barrington flicked Shane's eye onto the ground. He snarled. He lunged forward. Shane tried to dodge him, but he was too slow, unsteady on his paws, racked with pain.

Barrington knocked Shane over onto his back. Then the older wolf stepped onto Shane's chest. As Shane gazed up at him, he saw the same gruesome face he had seen that night in Lake Orange. This was the wolf that had turned him. Not Clifton James. Barrington. This was the wolf who had decided for Shane who and what Shane would be, who took a choice that wasn't his to take. This, Shane knew in his heart, was the wolf who had stolen Duane.

The Wolf Barrington opened his horrific mouth. His teeth swooped down. They closed around Shane's paw. They ripped through skin, through tendons and bone. Barrington bit Shane's paw off and tossed it aside. He opened his mouth again, and Shane thought: *This is how it ends.* He thought: *But Duane. Duane Duane Duane Duane Duane.* His mind swirled with a dying man's dreams of Duane Beckman, of revenge, of the world gone on after him, the hashtagged, videotaped, captioned, memed, and posted world, and the real one beneath it. He thought: *Goodbye, Moon.*

Not so fast, Moon replied.

For out of the corner of his good eye, Shane LaSalle saw two other eyes, green eyes luminous as emeralds: the eyes of another wolf.

He smelled redwoods and pine needles; creek and cake.

He saw a streak of black fur, and teeth like knives, straight and sharp and silver.

The Wolf Joseph Z'Rhae pummeled Barrington, knocking him off Shane. Z'Rhae clawed Barrington in the gut and when he pulled back, the senior partner's blood splattered across the sidewalk. Z'Rhae attacked again, this time ripping open Barrington's jowl. Barrington yowled with rage. Z'Rhae pulled back. He circled. Barrington lunged, he failed. Z'Rhae was stronger and faster than the old wolf, and more patient.

Barrington lunged again, but Z'Rhae dodged and swiped, slicing open the old wolf's side. Shane limped into the shelter of a tree on his three paws. He had no strength left to fight. He licked his oozing stump. He watched with his one eye, as Barrington attacked, and Z'Rhae skirted out of the way, and stabbed and sliced, until the old wolf bled from a dozen places, and had spent himself.

The Wolf Joseph Z'Rhae pinned Barrington on the ground. He nodded toward Shane. With his paw, he gestured toward the Wolf Barrington's throat, offering Shane the final blow. Shane limped back. He stared down at his hateful partner. He imagined how it would feel to slice through Barrington's flesh, to watch the life pour out of Barrington's arteries, to taste revenge. But then he recalled the story that Joseph Z'Rhae had told about his great-great-great-grandfather, left for dead, turned wolf; the first Z'Rhae whose life was taken by the Barrington pack. But not the last.

Shane extended his claw. He dug it deep into Barrington's yellow eye. He tore the eye out and flung it into the grass. Then, with a nod, he stepped back and offered the Wolf Joseph Z'Rhae the last blow.

The Wolf Z'Rhae grinned. In a single swift assault, he unleashed the ferocity of his wolf self.

The Moon winked.

The Wolf Dick Barrington was dead.

ROSALINA BARRINGTON

BLOOD CAKE

San Francisco—1860

ROSALINA MEASURED FLOUR. She cracked eggs. She gazed out the window of her house on Mason Street, overlooking the bay. The day was bright and balmy. The moon would not rise until later, under cover of clouds. Who could tell when it rose full, with such relentless fog? The men her husband killed could not.

"Mama, what are you doing?" the young lady Eleanor asked.

"I am mixing batter, for a cake."

"But why is Miss Abigail not making the cake? Miss Abigail makes all the cakes."

"This is a very special cake."

"But, Mama, why does it have that red color?"

"Eleanor, you must learn not to ask so many questions. Curiosity is not befitting of a young lady of your station."

Eleanor sat in a chair. She sat with a straight back, her small hands folded neatly in her lap, her dress plumed out around her.

A lovely girl with many lovely qualities, curiosity not among them.

Eleanor persisted. "Mama, why is it not befitting?"

"Did I ever tell you about my grandmamma?" Rosalina asked her daughter. "She was a mute. That's someone who doesn't speak. She wasn't born mute. She was born with a penchant for talking too much, for asking too many questions. Like a certain young lady I happen to know. Her husband was displeased by her excessive yapping, and so he cut out her tongue and fed it to the wolves."

"I should rather not have any husband."

"You should rather not let your husband hear you express such a preference."

"I should rather bake cakes, like Miss Abigail."

"You will certainly not."

"Then I should like to work at the bank, like father. Or perhaps I shall become a doctor, so that I can cure people who are ill."

"No one has ever heard of a woman doctor."

"My friend Jane told me she had heard of a woman who became a doctor. So—"

"Your friend Jane has told you a lie. The closest you will ever get, Eleanor Barrington, is to hitch your wagon to a doctor's horse, so to speak. But I reckon we will find a much finer horse for you than that. Now, go and fetch your brothers. Tell them it is time to wash up. We are dining tonight with your father's partner, and he will arrive soon."

Rosalina Barrington poured blood-cake batter into a pan. She put the pan in the oven. She went upstairs to her chambers, where her nameless servant had readied her bath and laid out her gown. She bathed and dressed. *Mama, why is it not befitting?* She wore her emerald ring, a circlet of diamonds around her wrist, a gold pendant shaped like the head of a wolf, with rubies in its eyes. *He cut out her tongue and fed it to the wolves.* She strung pearls around her neck. She looked at her reflection in the mirror, her eyes sharp like the eyes of a fox, her age just beginning to show, her lustrous hair thick and black. Rosalina Barrington brushed it straight and coiled it into a bun on the top of her head. Rosalina who was not Rosalina. She had stolen her name, just as her husband had stolen his.

She greeted Mr. and Mrs. Carver in the parlor.

"Mr. Carver, it is always a pleasure to see you," she lied. "And Mrs. Carver, my! Please come, sit down and rest your feet."

Mrs. Carver was moon-bellied.

"The baby has dropped," she told Rosalina.

"Any day now," Rosalina replied. "Perhaps today. But I do hope it will wait until after dinner."

Rosalina had selected the cut of wood for the table, the finest silverware, linens laced with gold. She had selected the chandelier, the carpets, the window dressings. They dined on aged cheeses and bread baked fresh that morning, on bottles of wine from fledgling vineyards in Sonoma and Merced, on meat Wellington.

"And what meat is in the Wellington?" Mr. Carver asked.

"What is it? Why, it's the *best*," Bartholomew Barrington said, with a wink.

The Barrington children dined with them: placid Michael, nearly a man now; lovely Eleanor, who picked the meat of her Wellington apart with her silver fork and ate only the pastry shell; and Daniel, the wildling, who ate only the meat.

"We shall run along the coast tonight," Bartholomew Barrington said after dinner.

Rosalina cut and served three slices of cake.

"You don't eat this cake?" Carver laughed. He stared at Rosalina with his dead eyes, his lips tinged with blood.

"We shall have the chocolate cake instead. Shall you be taking Daniel with you?"

"Yes, I think," Barrington said. "He's old enough. Older than I was, when I set out on my own."

"Yes. Well then . . ."

"All things come in cycles," Bartholomew Barrington said. And for a moment his eyes glimmered with a faraway light: the light of the moon rising in a distant forest, over a clearing, where a spire of smoke rose from a chimney and a fire crackled in the hearth.

The sun slipped low into a belt of fog. Bartholomew Barrington departed, with his partner and his son.

"I shall arrange a carriage to bring you home," Rosalina told Mrs. Carver.

"It is just a short walk. I can—" Mrs. Carver cringed.

"Is it—"

Pain twisted the woman's face. Water leaked down her legs and pooled around her feet. "Oh . . . oh, oh, oh—"

"It is."

"It feels . . . ahhhh!"

"You," Rosalina ordered, pointing to a servant. "Run and fetch a doctor. And you," she said, pointing to another, "bring a tub of warm water and a stack of clean cloths. Mrs. Carver's baby is arriving tonight."

All things came in cycles. The evening fog rolled away. A full moon crested over the silvery bay. Mrs. Carver screamed, and stopped, and screamed, and stopped, as the contractions rolled through her. The doctor stood by, noting the minutes on his watch. *Perhaps I shall become a doctor.* Rosalina held Mrs. Carver's hand. She patted Mrs. Carver's forehead with a damp cloth. *No one has ever heard of a woman doctor.* Mrs. Carver's contractions came faster, faster. Over his protestations Rosalina ordered the doctor to retreat to the parlor.

"This is only for women to see," she told him. "Her husband has instructed."

The moon slunk toward the sea. Rosalina ordered Mrs. Carver to push. The laboring woman screamed.

"Push!"

No one has ever heard . . .

Mrs. Carver screamed.

"Again! Push!"

Your friend Jane has told you a lie.

Mrs. Carver's screams shook the house.

"Push! Push! You're almost there!"

The closest you will ever get . . .

"I can see the head!"

Rosalina reached her hands between Mrs. Carver's legs. She guided the baby out. She held the bloody thing in her arms. A baby girl. Except not a girl.

Matted fur covered its spindly frame. Petite claws grew where its fingers should have been. It looked up at her, with its small yellow eyes.

An abomination.

All things came in cycles.

"My baby—I want to see it."

Rosalina held her hand over the wolf girl's snout.

"Please!" shouted the panicked new mother.

Rosalina held her hand still until the wolf girl's legs stopped kicking, until her breath fell away, and her heart gave out.

"There is nothing to see," Rosalina told Mrs. Carver. "You did not birth a baby. You birthed a beast. And besides, she is gone."

SHANNON JAMES

ALL THINGS COME IN CYCLES

Oakland–Present Day

SHANNON JAMES DREW a warm bath for her pregnant friend. She stripped the white sheets from the rental house bed and remade the bed with new sheets she had packed, navy blue, to hide the bloodstains. She spread a mattress protector beneath. Outside, she heard sirens. She looked out the window. She saw a blur of red and white. An ambulance sped past, toward the hospital, two blocks away. She worried, her mind replaying the same fears Misti had expressed:

What if something goes wrong?

What if the cord is wrapped around her neck? What if she's breech?

What if we don't make it?

Shannon lit a stick of incense. She sprayed citrus-scented air freshener around the doorways, the windows, all the cracks from which their smell might leech out. The husband had been notified, but he would not attend the birthing. Mary Barrington meant to attend the birthing, but she had received the wrong address. She would arrive at the wrong rental house near the wrong hospital.

But what if she finds us?

What if she sends his partners?

The husband would be transformed, his clawed fists incapable of answering a cell phone. But still, he scared Misti. Mary Barrington scared Misti. Breech, hemorrhage, the cord coiled so tight it turned the baby's skin blue; the days and weeks after, when she would not have Shannon's hand to hold; the long years bound to the moon cycle; that she could teach her daughter not to bite, or at least not to bite too hard; all this scared her. Misti Buxby had a lot to fear.

"You're not Misti anymore. You're Megan Smith. You're from Indianapolis. You moved to Denver because you love the sunshine. Your child's dad is not in the picture. He's in jail."

(The last part was true, though Shannon James did not know it.)

"I'm Megan Smith from Indiana. Oh . . . oh God . . ."

She sat on the bed, hand on her belly, a grimace on her face. Shannon timed the contractions.

"Breathe through it. Good. Good."

"It's not the life I thought . . ."

"It never is."

"I was just remembering . . . you know the lobby, in my . . . Darren's apartment building?"

"Yeah."

"The first time I saw it. I thought . . . it was like the time I went to Disneyland, as a kid, and I saw the castle and it was like ... it was like I had been living underground my whole life and then I finally made it up to the surface, and everything was so bright, the sky, the birds. The whole thing was so fucking ... oh ... magical ..."

"You're okay. Slow, deep breath. Relax your shoulders. You got this."

"And ... Okay ..."

"You okay?"

"Yes. No ..." Misti laughed.

"What?"

"It's funny. Now I'm going back underground." Misti stood up. She paced. She rubbed her distended belly. Outside, the moon rose. Misti clutched her belly in pain. "I can feel her. I can feel something happening. Something shifting—"

"Are you—"

"I'm okay. . . . She's okay, I think. It's just her."

"Yeah." Shannon remembered. Or she thought she did. The contortions of the baby inside her, twisting, thrashing, as it changed from girl to wolf. She hadn't known at the time. But Mary Barrington had squeezed her hand and told her not to worry, not to worry her pretty little head.

"Do you ever wish you had known?" Misti asked.

"Sometimes. I think about her. About what I would have done. How I could have kept her and ..."

"Did she have a name?"

"Lucy."

"That's a good name."

"It was more complicated, though. Because I had Blake already.

And then I think, if I'd done what you're doing, if I'd found a way, I never would have had Janie. So . . ."

"Yeah . . . ahhhh . . . ahhhHHHH!"

"Just breathe through it—"

"Fuuuuuuck!"

"You'll make it."

"Ahhhhhhhhhhhhhhhh!"

"You can do this."

"I'm gonna die."

"You're not gonna die."

"I'm gonna die giving birth. I'm gonna die. Because all things come in cycles, right?!"

"No. No, that's a load of shit," Shannon said. "Some things come in cycles. But cycles can always be broken. And sometimes the things that happen—they're all new."

Misti cursed. She screamed. She drank a bottle of water and a shot of bourbon to numb the edges, because she wasn't stuck in a hospital and there wasn't anyone to tell her what she ought to do with her body, her baby, herself. There was only her, and her friend, doing what they must.

Shannon continued to time the contractions. She helped Misti in and out of the bath. She tried to remember the training she had gathered from YouTube, her unofficial course in midwifery. She told Misti: Time to push.

Misti pushed and screamed. She pushed and screamed. She demanded another shot of bourbon, but the pain was so bad that she puked it up. She cried and insisted: Death was coming.

"No," Shannon said. "Not this time. This time there's only life."

Shannon reached her hands between her friend's legs. She saw the crown of the baby's head.

"Push! Damn it! PUSH!"

The head emerged.

"Again! PUSH!"

Shannon held the baby's head in her hand. She guided the baby's body out. She wrapped the small, damp infant in a clean towel.

"My baby—"

"She's . . ."

"Let me hold her."

Shannon placed the infant in her mother's arms. Her small body was covered in clammy fur. She had four perfect paws and two bright yellow eyes, the color of sunshine. She opened her mouth and yelped.

"She's hungry."

She had no teeth in her mouth, as she was just a baby, but Misti could see the ridges where her teeth would grow.

"She's beautiful," Shannon said. Misti kissed the baby's head. She held the baby to her breast. In the morning, she would hold a human girl in her arms, but that night it was a baby wolf she nursed.

"What will you call her?"

"I'd like . . . if you wouldn't mind . . . I'd like to call her Lucy."

NATASHA

AFTER THE MOON

San Francisco—Six Weeks Later

VERONICA CURTIS UNVEILED a masterpiece of glitter glue, puff balls, and Popsicle sticks glued to a large sheet of construction paper.

"It's for you." She handed it to Natasha. The glue was still wet. Glitter snowed from the back side. "See, there's the wolveses." She pointed to three brownish puff-ball blobs with stick legs and glued-on googly eyes. "That one is the bad wolf. See how bad he looks?"

"He does look wicked," Natasha said.

"And that's Mom." Mom occupied the foreground of the picture. She held a black splotch of a briefcase in her stick-figure hand. "And that's Mom's work."

Laurie had taken three weeks off work after the werewolf attack. She had suffered a mild concussion, plus some cuts and bruises. But mostly she just needed time to recover from the shock and adapt to the reality of venture capitalist werewolves.

"She looks happy," Natasha said.

"It's because of me." Veronica pointed at a cluster of white puff balls, next to a larger sparkly puff-ball mass. "And that's you." Natasha had transformed from invisible ghost to ghost with googly eyes. "And that's the Glitter Lady. She's a badass."

"Veronica—"

"Dad, I promise I won't say *badass* at school—"

"Come eat your eggs. Don't smush them up." Lee Curtis set a plate of eggs in front of his daughter. "You're right. She is a badass."

"Will you hang this picture on your fridge, Ghost?" Veronica asked.

"I don't have a fridge."

"Well, where do you keep your waffles?"

"Look, I promise when I have a fridge, I'll hang this picture on it."

She would have a fridge soon. Shane had sold his high-rise condo and purchased a two-bedroom flat near Twin Peaks. He wanted a roommate, he said. And Veronica's picture would look great in their new kitchen.

"You swear it?"

"Cross my heart." Natasha crossed her heart. She grabbed her purse and put on her jacket. "I'll see you both tonight for dinner."

Natasha got into her car, which no longer looked like a homeless lady's car now that all the boxes and garbage bags of her stuff were stored in Lee's garage. She turned on the radio.

. . . circulating a petition to make the Glitter Dog San

Francisco's official mascot. The petition began after repeated
sightings last month of what appeared to be a giant dog
wearing sequins and a sparkling tutu running freely through
the city's streets. There is also speculation, however, that this
giant dog might be responsible for the mauling of French
exchange student Marie Babineaux. Police have reopened
the investigation of her death, after reportedly finding new
evidence, but the nature of the evidence has not been disclosed
due to the ongoing investigation. If you'd like to sign the
petition to make Glitter Dog the mascot of San Francisco, or
would like to see some of our listener photographs of Glitter
Dog, you can go to www dot . . .

Natasha drove south, past the Olympic Club. She thought about
Nova Z'Rhae wielding her nine iron with its sparkly purple grip,
and how maybe golf wasn't an elitist white male werewolf game
after all. Maybe golf could be fantabulous. She thought about Ron
Carver, who had chased her from the Olympic Club parking lot,
whose body, along with that of his partner Barrington, had been,
covertly and without any public recognition of the existence of
werewolves, donated to science. Many very wealthy, very powerful
werewolves favored scientific exploration of their genetic condition,
Joseph had explained. And so the police that found the bodies
ferried them away. They described to reporters the two largest,
most hideous wolves they had ever seen, but none suspected that
either wolf harbored an evil venture capitalist inside it. The police
officers who had posted videos of jail-cell werewolves busting out
of their Friday casuals were deemed, by the wisdom of the internet,
to have perpetrated an elaborate hoax.

"But do you know what happened to the werewolves?" Natasha

had asked Joseph Z'Rhae, when she and Shane met him and Nova for lunch a few days after.

"They've been disappeared."

"Seriously?"

"The other packs are probably fuming about the publicity," Joseph had said. "Naturally, they did what they had to do to clean everything up."

"That thing with the warrants," Shane had asked, "how'd you get them anyway?"

"A hacker never shares his secrets." Joseph laughed. "But what matters is, they got what they deserved."

"Damn straight. But, are we . . . are we still in danger?" Natasha had asked. "I mean, do you think any other wolves will come after us?"

"Wolves are pack animals, and the Barrington Pack is no longer a problem. As for the other packs, I think they'll leave you alone, unless they see you as a threat," Jospeh had replied. "So it'd probably be best to keep your mouth shut."

Natasha had never excelled at keeping her mouth shut. But she would try.

She clocked in for her lunch shift at the Sharp Park Restaurant. She ushered guests to their tables. She ferried bread baskets and trays of water. She stood at the host stand and counted the minutes, the hours. They felt less interminable now, and more like her life, sweeping her along.

After the lunch rush, Nova Z'Rhae sashayed through the door in her golfing outfit (pink polo shirtdress, glitter belt, sequined visor). "Well hello, Ms. Porter, darling!"

"Nova!" Natasha set down the tray in her hands and ran to hug her friend. "What are you doing here?"

Nova hugged her back. "I just finished a round of golf." Nova tapped her visor. "There's a lovely course. We should go sometime."

"You know I don't know shit about golf."

"Honey, that doesn't matter. The scenery is fabulous. And you get to whack balls as hard as you can. You know, I always wanted to join the Olympic Club. But there was a bad, wolfish smell. It's gone now, thank the Lord." Nova winked. "Joseph sends his smooches, by the way. He called them regards, but smooches is better, don't you think?"

SHANE

WHEREIN SHANE LaSALLE REALLY GETS THE DEAL DONE

San Francisco—Seven Weeks Later

SHANE SAT AT his desk in his modest downtown office, newly leased. With his one eye, he reread the article from the *Lake Orange Gazette*:

Victim of Mystery Animal Attack Identified

by Emma Barrett

The dead body found several months ago by two hikers in the First Bank of Lake Orange Forest has finally been identified as San Francisco resident Duane Beckman. Mr. Beckman, a thirty-four-year-old Ohio native who worked for the now-disbanded venture capitalist firm Barrington Equity LLC, had traveled to Lake Orange with the firm for a private celebratory dinner at the Century Boathouse, the scene of the tragic "Killer Bee Wedding Crash," as it has come to be known, that claimed the lives of fourteen people. Shortly before the dinner, Mr. Beckman wandered off into the woods. His absence went unnoticed, except by his colleague Mr. Shane LaSalle, who went out looking for him and got lost.

"Words cannot describe how saddened I am by what happened to Duane," Mr. LaSalle said. "He was a good man and a dear friend. He did not deserve this." Barrington Equity's other former partners were not available for comment.

Police have made no progress toward identifying the creature that killed Duane Beckman.

Shane had read the article at least a dozen times. Sometimes, he still couldn't quite believe everything that had happened. He half expected to wake up in his old Barrington Equity office, to Duane, still alive. Then he ate a whole undercooked rack of lamb with a side of slippery bacon for breakfast, and he knew his life would never be the same.

Shane heard a knock on his door. He closed his laptop. He glanced at the picture of Duane on his desk, taken during their first year together as associates.

I'll do better, he promised himself, and Duane. *I'll make it better.*

He stood. He opened the door, and Jeanie Glass stepped in, followed by Shane's office manager, Darla. They chatted for a while, then Shane produced the paperwork.

"Your lawyers have looked it over?" he asked.

"They said everything looks good."

He slid the papers across the table to Jeanie Glass.

"I flagged the pages that you need to sign," said Darla.

"Thanks," Jeanie said, with a genuine smile. "And thank you, Shane. This means so much, for the company. And for me, and my dad, to know that we'll be able to stay competitive."

"You've got a good company, Jeanie," Shane said. "It's a solid investment. So thank you, for waiting. How's your dad doing?"

"He's in remission. He claims it's because of the two months we spent in the Keys. But I spoke with his doctor, and she told me he'd gone into remission before we left."

Jeanie Glass, CEO of Alvin's Sports and Supplies, signed the paperwork.

"So, you never told me, what happened to Barrington Equity?" she asked after.

Shane told her part of the truth: "They ran into some trouble with the SEC."

"How unfortunate for them."

"The company was dissolved," Shane said, continuing with the story that he and his friends had all agreed on. "The feds seized a large portion of its assets. I was the only equity partner left, after the ordeal. So I thought, why not give it a go on my own? Though, I'm not entirely on my own. I convinced Darla to join as my office manager, and we've been poaching associates from other private equity firms."

"We don't pay as much," Darla said. "But no one works on Saturdays. And we have happy hour every Friday after work on Shane's boat."

THE END

SHANE LaSALLE

Principal, LaSalle Capital Investments LLC

Profile picture: Headshot. Debonair Shane LaSalle, the private equity pirate. He wears a velvet suit, the suit he always wanted but feared to wear, until he faced something truly terrifying. A golden paisley ascot highlights the curve of his jaw. A silver hook covers the stump of his wrist; this he wears only for the photo, because hooks are impractical in the business world. A black patch conceals the remains of his left eye, and from the patch a jagged scar extends across his face, forehead to cheek, like a bolt of lightning. His right eye is the color of fire. You do not trust him. But you like him.

Cover picture: Landscape. Blue sky, mottled clouds. Blue water, solid, sun-tipped. A boat on the water—nothing spectacular, nothing gorgeous about it, except the man on deck. He is marred, and yet disfigurement improves him. He is unadorned, and yet he glitters. Shane LaSalle raises his glass: a toast! To the sun, which warms his blemished skin; to the moon, which illuminates his darkness; to friends, who raise their glasses with him.

About me: Duke University grad. "Rising Star" on *Venture Capitalist Monthly*'s biennial list. Founder of the Beckman House, an emergency shelter and bakery supporting the LGBTQIA+ community. Loves anything meat, barefoot trail running, full-moon parties.

ACKNOWLEDGMENTS

This book scratched and clawed its way out.

Years ago, in 2018, my husband said, "You know what you should write a book about? Werewolves." I laughed, because *Wait, wait, whuuuuut? Werewolves? Really?*

Really.

The werewolves became venture capitalists (as they should be). The idea became a book. The book taught me how treacherous the publishing world can be. A book's fate is shaped by the decisions of others—often financial, rarely predictable. As an author, a reader, a human, you want to chart your own course. But often, the choice gets taken from you, as it does with the characters in this book. They find themselves in a world not of their making, the circumstances of their lives shaped by wolves.

This book also taught me perseverance, and hope.

I finished writing it in early 2019. My agent sent it out to publishers, and for a hot minute I thought all the dreams I had for it might come true. Then the world changed, and the book didn't sell, and I shelved it, and wept. Dark times.

But I kept writing. I kept trying.

I don't think I would have, if not for that same amazing dude who planted the werewolf idea in my head, my husband, Steve. He always believed in me and my work. He read every word. He helped me keep going through the darkest of times. He supports me, encourages me, inspires me, makes me laugh, and just generally makes everything better.

Sometimes, admittedly, I resent his faith in me. It feels misplaced. Rejection—an inherent part of the process for all but the most fortunate of writers—sucks. Publishing is painful. Sometimes I get sick of it, and I just want to give up. But mostly, I'm grateful that because of his faith, I can share my stories with you. I hope they entertain you, that they bring you joy, that they strengthen your resolve to fight against the wolves.

I'm grateful too for the other members of my pack. In particular, the brilliant and insightful Ella Jane, who is wise beyond her years and has loved this book from the beginning; ferocious Sammie, who could eviscerate those wicked wolves if she had the chance; Nymeria, our own little house-wolf; Taylor, who graciously gave design input and made my website gorgeous; and my whole Pleasant Ridge crew, who I know will throw the most amazing werewolf party when this book comes out.

This book would still be collecting dust on my shelf if not for my agent, Holly Root, who persisted, despite all the rejections and setbacks, and kept me going. Holly, I can't ever thank you enough.

Thank you also to my fantastic editor, Adam Wilson, who helped me polish and refine this book, and who took a chance in publishing my weird books in the first instance. I'm so glad we get to work on more books together. I'm grateful also for the team at Hyperion Avenue—Tonya Agurto, Jennifer Levesque, Monique Diman, Vicki Korlishin, Crystal McCoy, Kaitie Leary, Sara Liebling, and Guy Cunningham—not only for their wonderful work on this book, but for their long-term vision and efforts to bring my multiverse to life. And a very big thank-you to Amanda Hudson at Faceout Studio for my last three gorgeous covers.

Finally, thank you to my readers. I'm thrilled and humbled by your support. It's such an honor to share my stories with all of you.

I hope you'll join me on more adventures in the future!

MR. YAY

BRADFORD AND THE DOG

Maybe *This Random Dog* was why he dreamed of the dog. Him and the dog on a boat, waves sloshing all around them, water the color of a blue-raspberry slushy. A pod of dolphins swam alongside the boat, except the dolphins were also dogs. Dogphins. A man rode one of the dogphins. He wore a denim jumpsuit and a fat gold chain. He waved and said, *We're making it stronger!* The Dream Dog gave a thumbs-up, even though he didn't have thumbs. The Dream Dog wore a captain's hat. Bradford had seen this dog before. This dog got to captain his own ship. The dog decided when to set sail. Which port. What they ate next. No one said *C'mere, boy. Roll over.* No one said he had to be a Good Dog.

Maybe he was a good dog, but that was beside the point.

This Random Dog had a cold wet nose. It used the nose to wake him up.

Not a good-dog move.

Bradford opened his eyes. The dog's eyes stared back. The dog's eyes were glossy brown, and way too fucking close.

"What . . . the . . . fuck," Bradford managed to say, before his brain caught up with his eyes and mouth. He scrambled back, into the corner of his bed, up against the peeling wallpaper.

"What the *fuck.*"

The dog's tongue slopped out. The dog's bright pink tongue had two black spots, and later he named these spots Zoey and Ernestina. But right now, the spots were both called: *What the fuck.*

The dog was a pit bull type. A full-bred pit bull? He didn't know. He hadn't majored in dogs at Canine Academy. It had the stocky bod of a pit. The *I-will-crush-you* jaw. Floppy triangle ears. Its fur was sleek, dark brown with a white tuxedo.

The thing was, Bradford Pierson didn't have a dog.

The thing was, Bradford Pierson lived in a studio apartment on the third floor of an old building on the boarded-windows-and-graffiti side of downtown, with a big sign in the lobby that said NO SMOKING – NO PETS.

In case the sign wasn't clear enough, the month-to-month lease that Bradford had signed in exchange for a key to that craptacular apartment said NO PETS, and then specified all the animals a pet might be. He couldn't even own a fish or a hamster.

Ironic, given the rats in the basement and the cockroaches in the walls.

But Rules were Rules. Just like his dad always said. *Son, the Rules are the Rules. You can't just pick up your golf ball and drop it in the hole.*

Bradford had tried to tune out the Dad Platitudes and get on with his life, and yeah, maybe in his heart he'd always wanted a dog, but he didn't have the cash to feed a dog or de-flea a dog or get the bones and treats that a dog deserved.

He didn't own a dog.

This Random Dog seemed to disagree. It stared at him like, *You know you want to feed me now. Let's take a walk. I know I'm a good dog, so you don't need to say it.*

It stared at him like it knew him well, and why was he getting so weird about their morning routine?

Technically, it was afternoon.

Bradford inched around the side of the bed. He slipped out. He walked over to the sink. The dog trotted after him, tongue out, goofy smile.

"Dude. Dude, stop. You're freaking me out."

He turned on the faucet. It gurgled out some brown water, but after a minute the water turned clear. He filled a glass, drank. The dog sat. It stared up at him.

"What, you want water?" The dog didn't answer. "Fine. But I'm warning you—I know it tastes bad, but you better not spit it out. This isn't a resort. Dogs don't get bottled water."

He opened the cupboard. On the shelf, next to the bowls, was a bag of dog food.

"What . . . the . . . fuckity fuck . . ."

Bradford reached for the bag. Value-Kibbles. Lamb flavor.

"Really? That's what you like? Lamb flavor?"

The dog barked once.

"Shhhh! Shut up! You can't bark in here! You tryin' to get me kicked out?"

The dog gave a pathetic whimper. Oh, woe is hungry dog. Bradford filled one bowl with food and another with water. He set them on the floor. The dog scarfed down the kibble. It slurped up the water. It got water all over the floor.

Bradford shook his head.

This dog.

It followed him around the apartment, even though there wasn't much apartment to follow him through. Just a box with two dirty windows, a kitchenette, a tiny bathroom tiled in pastel pink and blue. There was one dresser that Bradford had found discarded on the street, a couch abandoned by the prior tenant, and an air mattress that a dog's claws could easily pop.

"Hey, you!" He turned to the dog. "Yeah, you. You better not get on my bed. That's *my* bed. Capisce?"

Bradford had moved to the apartment from a dorm. He had moved to the dorm from his parents' house. He had taken nothing from his parents' house, because he was doing this himself. Whatever *this* happened to be. He didn't want their strings. Their guilt. Their disdain.

He had, as a child, wanted a dog. He drew a picture of said dog on the front of his letter to Santa. He was nine. He had, he thought, been good enough at least, despite what anyone said. He had good grades and washed his dishes and made his bed. He didn't set fire to ants with a magnifying glass or pour salt on the garden slugs for fun.

He had found the letter to Santa in the trash, crumpled up, beneath a sprinkle of coffee grounds. He dug it out, brushed it off, and stuck it in the mailbox. But he forgot about postage, and no dog ever came. Until now.

"What? Why do you keep staring? Why are you following me around? Bozo."

On his heels. Would not leave him be. That damned tongue with its two black spots.

Then it occurred to him that, of course, the dog wanted to go out. And if he took it out, it would be out instead of in here, threatening his lease.

He didn't own a leash because he didn't own a dog. But whoever this shitty apartment belonged to—*not him*—had dog food, so maybe they had a leash too.

Oh, damn. They did.

Right there, hanging from a nail by the front door.

"This is fucked up," he told the dog. "You get that, right? You and me, we're not a thing."

The dog had a collar, plain blue, nondescript, no name or address tag. Bradford clipped the leash to the collar. But he couldn't just march out the door, down the stairs, past the No Pets sign in the lobby. He and the dog would have to sneak out.

In his closet, he found an old hiking backpack that looked big enough to fit a pit bull–type dog. He picked up the dog. He slid the dog, hind legs first, into the backpack. The dog didn't struggle. It hung limp, like it knew how this worked. Like it rode in this backpack *all the time*.

Bradford buckled the top, leaving a gap for the dog's eyes and snout to peek out. He put the backpack on.

"Damn. You weigh like a thousand pounds. You need to chill on the dog food."

He opened the window. Cold air plowed through. He had forgotten his coat. He took off the backpack and set it on the couch. The dog didn't try to escape.

He put on his coat, shoes, and hat. He checked his pants pockets. His phone and wallet were both still there, where he had left them. He checked his phone. The screen said 2:19 p.m., December 21.

He had not jumped forward in time to a magic, dog-filled future. As far as he knew.

He strapped on the dog-backpack. He stepped out the window onto the fire escape. He climbed down the ladder, one floor, two floors, ready for each rusty step to crack beneath his weight, which was, his dad said, *not appropriate for a man his size*. This was a generous translation of Helena Pierson's words. *Grotesque,* she said. Not to his face, but in earshot. *Disgustingly fat.*

Yeah, but no. He was not. He straddled the line between standard-fat and chubby. Big-boned. *Impressively boned,* Tommy said. He tried to embrace it. His parents had named him Bradford Pierson III. But screw them, he was Fatty Bratty.

Bradford—or Bratty—hopped down from the last ladder rung. He shoved his frozen hands in his pockets. He walked around the building, to the street. The sky was drizzle gray. The ground was damp and littered with cigarette butts and broken bottles. Cold wind whistled through the boards that covered the windows of the building across the street.

"Festive as fuck," Bratty said, remembering the date. December twenty-first. The winter solstice.

"He has to go," Bratty told the receptionist at Happy Paws Veterinary Clinic. "I mean, he's all right. But I have no idea where he came from. He just showed up. And I can't have pets. So can I just like, leave him here?"

"Um, no," the receptionist said. "Sorry. We're just a vet. We don't take strays."

"Oh. You know where I can take him? 'Cause like I said, I can't keep him."

"Hmm." The receptionist looked at the dog head poking out of Bratty's backpack. "Yeah. So. The thing is . . . he's a pit bull."

"Yeah. So? I mean, is he?"

"Looks like a pit bull to me," the receptionist said. "And most of the shelters don't take pit bulls."

"Oh. That's, what, they're like, anti–pit bull?"

"That's just their policy."

"So they're prejudiced against pit bulls."

"Yeah, I guess so."

"So what, they just turn them away? Or—"

"Um, not exactly. . . ."

The receptionist didn't want to say it. But Bratty knew exactly what she meant.

"That's fucked," he said.

"Yeah. Yeah it is. Pit bulls get a bad rap. But they can be really nice. Unfortunately, there's only one shelter around here that takes them, and they're full right now."

"Oh. So, um . . . you want a dog?"

The receptionist laughed. "I'd take all the dogs if I could. But I already have two at home."

"What am I supposed to do with him?" Bratty asked.

"You said he just showed up?"

"Yeah."

"But he looks healthy. Maybe he's not a stray. Maybe he's lost. Let's see if he has a chip and we can scan him."

Bratty took off the backpack. He let This Random Dog out. The receptionist scanned the dog with some scanner. Bratty shuddered at the thought of under-skin microchips, body scanners, registries of numbers embedded under the skin. The dystopia toward which they were all headed, dogs first.

"Yep," the receptionist said. "He's got a chip. Let's look him up. I bet someone'll be glad to have this nice boy home for Christmas."

Bratty rubbed the nice boy's head. The receptionist looked

him up in Big Brother's National Doggie Database, or whatever it was called.

"Yep," she said. "There he is. Looks like he lives less than a mile from here. It says his owner is Bradford Pierson. Should I—"

"Stop."

Bratty froze. He looked over his shoulder, down at the dog, up at the receptionist. This was the moment he wondered whether he had somehow accidentally ingested an entire sheet of acid and hallucinated this new reality.

"What?"

"You said— What was the name. Say it again. Please."

"Bradford Pierson," she said, slowly.

"Bradford Pierson."

"Yeah. What, do you know him?"

MATH

Imagine that you are an astrophysicist.

Imagine that your name is Robert Kai. That you are renowned. That there are three moons in orbit around a distant planet named after you: Kai 1. Kai 2. Kai 3. On these moons, there may be life.

This is a cocktail-party fact. A triviality, here on Earth. What matters, here and now, is the hydroponic lettuce you are growing in your basement. Your vinyl collection. Your corgi. His name is Samwise, and he sleeps on your bed. He sits on your lap, at the window, as you gaze through your personal telescope at the elusive stars. The telescope was a birthday gift from your parents. You were ten. An infinitesimal fraction of the age of those billion-year-old stars.

The stars are just orbs of fiery gas, or sky volcanoes, or disco balls adrift in empty space, or math.

It's all math.

Math is the only thing that always makes sense.

Imagine that you are the boy Robert Kai and you have just turned ten. You are home. You are safe. Your mom is safe and your dad is safe and you just ate pizza and cake and now you are outside, in the yard, setting up your telescope, staring up at the night sky, and then at something much closer. Something moving fast. So fast you don't even see it. You only see a streak of flame. And then it hits. And everything explodes. The ground shakes. The air burns. Wood and shingles and bricks rain down. There is smoke and dust and screaming. You are screaming. Your mom is screaming and your dad is screaming and they convene around you. They squeeze you between them like a boy sandwich. Their faces are covered in ash and blood, and they hold you and weep, and you do not yet fully comprehend how lucky and unlucky you are.

The meteor destroyed your house and everything inside it.

But because it is your birthday, because you got that telescope, you were not inside it. You were outside, contemplating the odds that your telescope would reveal extraterrestrial spacecraft or eldritch horrors or vast planetary cities teeming with alien life. Your parents were outside, watching you, their marvel. Their creation.

If the meteor fell on any day other than your birthday, you and your mom and your dad would all be dead, but instead you spend seven months living in a hotel while your house gets rebuilt. Your new house is better than your old one. The odds that a meteor will hit your house now are exactly the same as they were before the first meteor hit, even though it doesn't feel that way. You feel safe.

You feel unsettled by the disconnect between perception and math. You want certainty. You want answers. You go to college. You apply for a PhD. You must make a choice: physics or astrophysics. You graduate. You are offered a high-paying job for a nanotech corporation in Raleigh, but you choose academia instead. You buy a house. You adopt a dog. There are so many to choose from. Can you explain why you picked the corgi?

Math could explain.

If you knew every variable. If you plugged them in to the correct equation. All the numbers would add up to corgi, or pit bull, or retriever, or mutt. A slight variation could produce a different dog, or a cat, or an astrophysicist with a bearded dragon.

But this math made you and your corgi. You go together to the Green Creek Observatory. You evaluate the data collected by the telescope array. You fall asleep to the background hum of a distant star. You and Samwise corgi watch the desert sunrise, and then you attempt to unravel the mismatch in measured rates of universal expansion. Dark energy is math, which means that you can understand it, theoretically. Sometimes, in the vacant hours of a star-studded night, you almost feel like you do understand it. The numbers flicker in the corner of your eye. The equation is almost tangible. A thing you can hold, in defiance of all that empty space.

You are almost there, when Samwise corgi barks. At nothing. There is nothing, and yet there is something. You can feel it. But what, or how, or why, you don't know. It is faint as a bristle, soft as a breeze. It is nothing and everything and when you turn back to the numbers they make no sense.

"What? What the hell?"

Samwise barks again.

The numbers howl.

The numbers that had shown a rate of cosmic expansion of 73.3 kilometers per second per megaparsec now say 67.1 then 58.9 then 52.7 then 49.8. They are falling, falling, falling and nothing has ever made less sense in your life than this math.

"No, no, no, this is impossible. . . ."

You check and recheck, and the numbers return to their prior normal rate, but you are still bothered. For days you haunt the banks of supercomputers. You pace and mutter. You calculate and recalculate. You make frantic phone calls to the math-wraiths of other telescope arrays. Some of them noticed something odd, but no one else recorded this exact data. *It must be an error,* they say.

But it wasn't. You have the record. Math doesn't lie.

Still, you check and recheck and recheck, and you try to reenvision the universe. The grand equation. You forget to eat. Your sleep is broken by phantom math. Your dog eventually insists: time to go home. And there is nothing now to do but let it settle in your mind, and hope that big brain of yours can make sense of the nonsensical. Brains are great for that. They gather random data, stray numbers, strange events, and weave a story to explain, or to comfort.

There is nothing now for you to do but let go. To *hang low like a hermit crab*, like they used to say on that old kids' TV show you loved so much. To listen to your dog, get into your car, and drive and drive.

LOOKING FOR MORE
GENRE-BENDING STORIES FROM
EMILY JANE?

A romance author takes a trip to her childhood beach home, but her summer is upended by the startling return of a deceased childhood friend, newfound love, and . . . sea monsters?

In Emily Jane's rollicking debut, when spaceships arrive and then depart suddenly without a word, the certainty that we are not alone in the universe turns to intense uncertainty as to our place within it.

AVAILABLE WHEREVER BOOKS ARE SOLD

HYPERION AVENUE